NEAR CANAAN

NEAR CANAAN

Liese O'Halloran Schwarz

Carroll & Graf Publishers, Inc.
New York

This is a work of fiction. Any resemblance to actual
persons, living or dead, is purely coincidental.

Copyright © 1990 by Liese O'Halloran Schwarz

For permission to reprint from William Somerset Maugham's *Of Human Bondage*, grateful acknowledgement is made to Bantam-Doubleday-Dell.

First Carroll & Graf edition 1990

Carroll & Graf Publishers, Inc
260 Fifth Avenue
New York, NY 10001

Library of Congress Cataloging-in-Publication Data

Schwarz, Liese O'Halloran.
    Near Canaan / Liese O'Halloran Schwarz.
    — 1st Carroll & Graf ed.
        p.   cm.
    ISBN 0-88184-627-9 : $18.95
    I. Title.
PS3569.C56785N4   1990
813'.54—dc20   90-2329
                                                   CIP

Manufactured in the United States of America

for Wright

Chapter One

The Journey

There might have been a faster way to get there, but he didn't know it. He had asked no one's advice before starting off; only three people in the world knew he was going at all, and had one of them proposed a shorter route to him, he probably would not have taken it. He was a person made uncomfortable by complexity; and shortcuts, side roads, bypasses, all of those inventions of an impatient civilization, held no attraction for him. Not that he was not impatient—he was—but his impatience was far outweighed by his fear. He did not himself know this; and he could not call many of the things that he feared by name; but they were diverse and numerous, and the immense capillary network of the country's road system was among them. With its twists and turns and long lightless stretches of tarmac, it stayed at the back of his mind in some preconscious category of evils. He stuck to the main roads; and it took him nearly all day.

He was nervous even at the beginning; to the last minute, he hadn't been sure if he was really going to go at all. He had first had the idea while drunk, after all, and nearly asleep. Throughout the week following, he had enjoyed dwelling upon the thought of it, his own private adventure; it had seemed exciting then, and probable. Two days ago, he had gone about borrowing a car from a fellow in the dormitory who was notoriously openhanded with his possessions. Yesterday, he had procured a colored road atlas. Yet none of this had truly convinced him; none of it had warned him for this moment, this sudden and stark intrusion of reality into his fond daydreams. The early morning light, the bag in his hand, the car he had finally located, standing forlorn-looking in a No Parking zone on a side street, waste paper blown up against its front tires. He considered it, mustard colored and rusty, peering at it as though it might tell him something.

"Hey, man, your car?" A voice at his elbow; when he turned, it was a stranger, one of the millions of people in this city who were strangers to him. He had learned to classify them by dress, by mannerisms, by speech. Whom to ignore, whom to answer, whom it was safest to placate. He turned away from this one.

"Somebody did some shit to it, that's for sure," said the stranger. "But if it's been here more than a day, you're lucky. This your car?" he asked, edging closer. Getting no answer, the stranger reached out and actually touched the paint of the car, watching him the while. "I need to know is this your car, man," he said, losing patience. "I mean, it's still got some good stuff on it."

The car did look like junk: rusty, dusty, one sidelight smashed in and repaired clumsily with orange tape. He hoped it ran better than it looked.

"See that tailpipe," said the stranger.

He nodded.

"Muffler could be shot," said the stranger, bending down to peer under the car, and straightening again. "Looks okay," he reported.

Without knowing what he was doing, still nodding, he brought out the unfamiliar ring of keys from his pocket.

"Shit," said the stranger, hearing the jingle, looking up. "Fuck you, man," he said, moving away.

He poked the key into the lock; a twist, a pull, and all the gathered breath of the car was upon him, stinking vinyl and mentholated cigarettes. He tossed his light duffel onto the backseat, and lifted the two heavier cases after it, setting them down more carefully. Then he slid into the driver's seat. That was that, then; he was ready to go.

He studied the road atlas carefully, following with his index finger the route he must take, memorizing lefts and rights. He creased the atlas fiercely at the proper page, and left it open on the passenger seat, glancing frequently at it as he drove. Seeing nothing but a tangle of blue and red lines against a cream yellow background; but still, it reassured him. He peered through the windshield, listening nervously to a rattling from the engine, shifting gears tentatively, chanting to himself. *Bleecker to Broadway, Broadway to Canal.* This first part was to be a simple effort, in distance less than a dozen city blocks, and all of it tolerably well marked with dirty but legible road signs. Nevertheless, he didn't trust the city not to rearrange itself while his attention was diverted; and when Broadway indeed led him to Canal Street, he idled at the stop light, pleased and self-congratulatory.

There it was, Canal Street, broad and decrepit, lined on either side with tall crumbling buildings. He peered upward at the stone against the sky, and then, his eyes insulted by the early sun, he brought them down again and studied the sidewalks below, their confusion of vendors and pedestrians, the sun glinting off rows and rows of sunglasses, batteries, cassette tapes. He fumbled in his shirt pocket for his own sunglasses, watching a worried-looking man fuss behind his stall of flimsy carnival toys. Suspended from a crenelated steel overhang above the man's left shoulder, a cellophane fish turned in the wind.

The light changed, and the rush began again. The line of cars all surged desperately forward together, only to decelerate suddenly, less than one hundred yards ahead, for a line of stopped traffic which had been well within view from the previous intersection. He was dismayed by the weaving, the horn blowing, the intrusion into his lane from either side by cars at high speed, cars whose drivers seemed to understand intuitively that he was unused to this, a novice, an easy mark. A taxicab swelled suddenly into his lane to avoid a delivery truck, missing his right front fender by millimeters. He pushed hard on the horn, but no sound came forth. He punched it again, and was rewarded with a short, nasal bark. The taxicab was long gone; the protest was useless; and the effort of making it had taken his attention from the road, so that he nearly rear-ended a Toyota, which had stopped at the next intersection and was idling, primly.

A few jolting blocks later, he was at the mouth of a tunnel, obscurely frightened by the pulsing darkness within, the thought of the rushing water overhead. He inched and stalled his way into and through, his sunglasses now off, his eyes pale and weak looking without them. Progress was slow, but at least here the cars obeyed the Stay in Lane signs: they fell into two orderly lines, and sudden peace reigned. It was much as though these drivers had never driven any other way and had never subscribed to any method of transportation other than this one, this uniform stream of polite traffic; there was no horn honking, no weaving, no hurry-and-stop. Just the twin lanes, the cars flowing along slowly under the arch of the tunnel, their headlights making long light streaks on the tiled sides, their taillights winking back red through the collecting fumes. There was a putrid twenty minutes or so at a complete standstill, dozens of cars wheezing and vibrating in place; and the young man's eyes began to water from the exuberant gases of the road: he had come to his senses only belatedly, rolling up the car windows full minutes after entering the tunnel. At long last, traffic began to move again, in jerks, and then the road began to rise ahead of him, and they were all being lifted toward the far opening.

Then the tunnel was past, and there was just the open sky above and a chaotic jumble of cars below. Previously constrained, so well-behaved just moments past, they were now set free to resume their dangerous business of rearranging. They went about it with a happy vengeance, straddling lanes, interweaving recklessly, swerving inches from one another's fenders, the drivers leaning hard upon their horns and making angry faces from their windows.

He found signs to the road which would take him much of the way, and when he had achieved entrance to it, he noticed an immediate difference: cars were not so ill-behaved here. There was more space, for one thing, and the possibility of travelling at ninety miles per hour; but also, it seemed that travelling was a more serious venture for the turnpike driver, who was not so concerned as before with the transgressions or progress of his neighbor, and was not so apt to blow his horn. The turnpike was not a Manhattan thoroughfare, littered with heedless pedestrians and intrepid taxicabs; it was no Broadway, and it was no simple unchallenging tunnel: it was a wide straight ugly slash through the countryside, meant only for drivers of the long haul. The spirit of grim purpose penetrated even to him, where he slouched in his borrowed car, and he sat up a little straighter behind the wheel.

He stopped once while still in New Jersey, pursuing the blue signs off to the right, stalking past the groups of windblown travellers clotted in the lobby of the rest stop. He lumped them all together in his mind—all the mothers, daughters, uncles, and brothers, all the sweethearts and secretaries, all the toddlers and truants, all the grandfathers—*all* of the people standing here on their way from one place to another. Taking in their garish cheap jerseys and tight blue jeans with one contemptuous glance, he summed them up, collected them all into one oppressive whole: the Talkers, the Gigglers, the Unthinking. Passing through them, though hating them, he felt less real than they were, less solid; and in the men's room, combless at the mirror, he winced at the nearly transparent pallor of his skin. He ran wet fingers through his hair; the face hanging before him was resolute, with a fluorescent light bone-lessness to its features. He frowned at himself; and his image looked hungrily back at him.

Back in the car, there seemed no end to the sameness and flatness of the road. The weak spring sun moved across the sky, and he followed, his mind strangely emptied. Imagining nothing; driving. Coming out of the chemical plains of New Jersey, plunging into another tunnel and emerging again, into the steaming downtown heart of Baltimore. The sky here was nearly white, pencilled with smokestacks, patterned with drifting factory smoke. He took the tight cement curve around Washington, eyeing the cars strung out across the lanes. They had an air of fellowship about them now, all part of a loose army, marching toward the capital.

The Beltway was nestled in a flashing gem bed of glassed-in high rises. He passed between these, examining them at high speed, appreciatively. Some were modest, only twenty shining stories of amber glass; while some were more grand, fifty or more levels of smoky mirror, the clouds of the Maryland sky seeming honored to pass across their faces, while on the top of each building rode one or another intensely modern portmanteau symbol, COMSYSDYNE writ in enormous letters, identifying for all passing pilgrims the patron of this remarkable structure: *Look upon my works, ye mighty, and despair.* He, thinking none of this, admired the reflection of one in the surface of another, and drove on by.

He could tell when he entered Virginia. The roadside shrubbery was suddenly gigantic, greener and more lush than the scrubby, halfhearted foliage which had lined the Northern roads. Gone were the images of the morning; gone, the shabby crowds in the city, the painful stop and go of the traffic channeling along between the high buildings, each one separately and peculiarly demolished-looking, eaten away by the difficulties of the city. Gone, the company of other vehicles; his path had peeled off from theirs long ago, their brake lights and glittering edges of metal flashing past the turnoff, away and out of sight. Now he was marching alone, down the thin asphalt carpet unrolling between clumps of trees and occasional filling stations.

He stopped at one of these and bought a candy bar from a vending machine near the men's room. A hand-lettered sign taped next to the coin slot read, "Please Drop Quarters Real

Slow." Outside again, he waited while the attendant hooked the hose back onto the pump.

"Seven forty," he said. The first human voice of the day, apart from the caught drifts of conversation at the New Jersey rest stop. Those voices had been high, stretched thin; this one was low and substantial. *Fo'ty,* the young man repeated mentally, with deep pleasure. So this *was* the South, not forty minutes outside of Washington.

The attendant accepted his money without hurry, straightening the bills carefully, digging out a warm assortment of change.

"Looks like storm weather maybe," he commented, dropping the dime into the young man's palm. *Sto'm.*

The young man squinted up at the sky, as if seeking a password.

"Could be," he said at last, his breath coming short at his own daring.

"Come a long way?" the attendant asked.

"Yes," he said.

"You look it, son," the attendant returned, startling the other, who was no younger than he was. "Car looks worse than you do," he added.

"It's not my car," he said, automatically.

"Well, someone needs to take care of her," said the attendant. "She's seen a lot of road time. She could use a wash. How'd you like to travel all day without a bath at the end of it?"

The young man, listening, began to feel a glimmering of cynical understanding. He looked around for a car wash sign, but didn't see one.

"In New York, it's good to have your car look like this," he told the man, who narrowed his eyes suspiciously. "No, really. The worse it looks, the less likely it is to get smashed up or stolen." *But not junked,* he told himself, recalling the stranger of the morning.

"That right," said the attendant, neutrally.

"It's kind of like a car alarm," explained the young man, and instantly realized he was going too far. He gave a short, false laugh.

"Well," said the attendant, easily. "You just turn that alarm off now, if you want." He slapped the car as he passed it. "You get where you're going, you take a hose to her."

"Maybe I'll let the rain do it," said the young man, in a last attempt at camaraderie.

"That you could," said the attendant, with a smile. "Well, you sure could," he repeated, nodding, smiling larger now, and moving away. "Take care now," he said over his shoulder, leaving the young man to his car, that private interior world of cracked vinyl and AM radio. He slid stiffly into the front seat, pulling the atlas across to him. He consulted it briefly, then slammed the door and started the engine. He was nearly there.

He had to confess his surprise, reviewing the interaction he'd had with the gas station attendant. He hadn't been hillbilly, exactly, or even *Hee-Haw;* but he hadn't been what the young man had expected, not an hour from the Capitol building. Of course, he knew that Washington, D.C., was Southern by location, but he considered it a neutral place, a *normal* place was how he thought it to himself. He'd been to Washington once on a school field trip, and it hadn't seemed odd to him then, not foreign or Southern or slow. And later, looking at maps, he'd always seen the capital as a kind of buffer state or even a sort of oasis, like divided Berlin nestled deep within East German territory, the Western democrats going about their business in the tiny half city allotted to them, as though on all sides they were not breathed upon by the enemy. At least the West Berliners had a wall to protect them.

When he thought of the South, he thought of Mississippi, and no matter what his mother had said, he couldn't take Virginia all that seriously as a Southern state. Tennessee, yes; and Alabama, and Kentucky. But Virginia? Virginia was too close to the capital, right up against Northern culture; some of it must have rubbed off, over the years.

But that fellow had been Southern, in a way that even he recognized; more than that, the whole place had been Southern, as though somehow, without knowing it, he had driven across an invisible dividing line. But maybe the gas station attendant had been from somewhere else, somewhere in the deep South; that would explain his voice, and his manner, his *Southern*ness. But who would come so far to work in a gas station?

Wrestling with the matter, glad of something to occupy his mind in these last miles of the drive, the young man leaned back in his seat, and fussed with the radio, finally snapping it off altogether.

He had been driving for hours, and for hours the sound of

the buffeting wind had been rough in his ears; abruptly, it was less obnoxious, and the immediate world peaceful, almost shockingly still. The highway narrowed and grew friendlier; businesses crowded up to its edges, dozens of frame houses with signs painted on their roofs: ANTIQUES. He poked an elbow out of the car and grasped the side view mirror, letting the wind make free with his arm. It travelled up his shirt sleeve and rippled the thin fabric there.

He passed signs advertising fresh fruit and hand-woven baskets. The frame houses and farm-equipment dealerships had given way now to pastureland, great rolling swaths of grass, cut here and there by streams, zigzagged by split-rail fences. To the east, mountains, blue giants, heavy and presiding, the green rushing up to their feet like a tide of wilderness. To the west, more distant peaks, hung about with mist. Now flat farmland stretched out on either side of the highway, draped with power lines strung from tall poles standing at the verges. Stiff, aluminum grey, they were motionless but graceful, resembling great flat-headed birds caught in a moment of astonishment. On a hill against the sky, the black shape of a cow; further on, clusters of them, their white faces looking amused, grazing just beyond the chain-link fences separating them from the shoulder of the road.

It was not just that the greens here were deeper; it was also that they seemed to have all colors in them, so that if he looked hard enough, he could detect a fleeting rainbow. Yellow to violet to black, they were all in there, diffracted into that green, that silence, nothing but the onrushing wind and the hum of the engine. Making a hall for him, a safe-conduct.

And for the rest of the journey, there was almost nothing else: just the sound of the car and the wind, and the green, the everycolor, bursting up from the earth, and him passing swiftly between. Little brooks glittered in the uncut brush alongside the road, which now curved more extremely, swinging back and forth along property lines, delivering him smoothly south at the rate of one mile a minute.

He entered the town at a little past five o'clock. At first it was frightening to be off the highway, bumping along through quiet intersections, stopping for red lights. He drove numbly, running his eye over unfamiliar storefronts and the darkened windows of a modest church. Spotting a bar to his left, its sign unlit but obvious, he turned into the lot behind the building.

Outside the car, he stretched, and tucked his striped cotton shirt into his jeans. Walking, he was loose jointed, his body reacting to its abrupt freedom with an excessive limberness.

It was dark inside the bar, and cool, and musty, as though all of the dampness of the weather had collected and intensified in the one large room. The door swung closed behind him; after his eyes had adjusted, he could pick out the groups of men. Several together at a table near the counter, carrying on a low-pitched conversation. A pair of men at a table further back near the pinball machines; they sat unspeaking, their large hands curled around the necks of beer bottles, so that the glinting brown glass seemed to rise from their fists like stilled columns of blood or tobacco juice. One man by himself, at a table near the window, smoking.

The young man went up to the counter and ordered a beer, which the bartender provided without comment. Leaning up against the wooden counter, smoothed to slickness by the intermittent pressure of a thousand elbows, the young man tipped the bottle up, swallowed, lowered it. He looked around: at the linoleum floor worn through in patches, at a dismal oil painting mounted on one wall of a ship listing badly in a storm, at a decrepit poster advertising a country-music duo appearing Thursday nights, at the poster next to it, offering half-priced drinks to ladies during Tuesday happy hour. The place was clean, but reeked with the passage of generations, the sweat and grime and worry of a town. Pushed tidily into corners, smeared between the wide cracks in the floor, it was hidden but powerful; and the young man's nostrils flared, as though he could smell it.

He looked around the room again, and then seemed to come to a decision, pushing himself away from the bar counter with the fingertips of one hand. He walked past the table of men, who fell silent as he passed them, and made his way to the solitary man by the window. After he'd gone by, the table of men began their soft muttering again, a slow, deep rumbling without inflection.

He stood by the table for a minute, talking, and then was offered a seat. He sat, and went on talking, his face earnest and pinched, setting his beer bottle on the table, leaning forward. The older man said little, listening, sitting with his legs wide apart, resting his beer in a hand dropped against a thigh. If his face seemed to change while the other spoke, it might have been a trick of the waning light, which filtered in over the red half-curtains stretched across the windows, and changed things.

After a while, the older man got up, the young man trailing him, and went over to the table of men near the bar.

"This here's Buddy Gates," said the older man to the group, who lifted their heads to look up at him. "He's come home."

Chapter Two

The Stranger

He went to Jack first, I'm not sure why. I suppose there were a dozen reasons for approaching Jack; I didn't know any of them then. Jack introduced him as Buddy, and we all called him that. Some of us didn't even understand that the boy's real name wasn't Buddy or anything like it, nor that he'd never been called that before he came to Naples, but I suspected it. I figured that Jack had given him that name; knowing Jack, it's what he'd do; and from looking at the boy, you could see that he'd take it, that casual nicknaming, without a murmur. He probably even felt it was a sign of acceptance, a friendly nickname, although it was hardly that. Jack-style, it was the antithesis of friendliness, a tip-off that this boy was not our buddy, and would never be.

Jack called for two beers; Wallace, the owner, delivered them; and we all kept silent, drinking.

"This is Buddy," said Jack again. "Treat him right, you all, he's making a movie about Naples. Tell them what you told me," said Jack, around the mouth of his beer bottle.

Buddy cleared his throat and began, in a high, nervous voice that went with the baby-fine hair and clean, though wrinkled, clothes. His voice was flat and lifeless, Northern; but not unpleasant.

He'd grown up in Connecticut, said Buddy, but his mother had been born in Naples. He was here on his spring vacation to do a project for school.

"What school's that?" asked Sam Lucas, finally.

"In New York," began Buddy, timidly.

"We-ell," drawled Sam, interrupting. "Stands to reason they got a school up there."

"Now they got everything up there, don't they?" put in Ned, Sam's brother, who acted sometimes as his sparring partner, sometimes as a kind of Greek chorus.

"I'm taking a film class," Buddy broke in, explaining. "I want to make movies."

At his first syllable, the men, who had been talking to one another, turned back to him and left off speaking. Buddy stood self-consciously finishing out his statement, his voice too loud now in the sudden silence. It was a palpable thing, that silence. Not a weapon, exactly; a tool. A kind of trap to make the pale embarrassed boy more aware of his own intrusiveness and to hold him there before us while we looked him over.

"And he's starting right here," said Jack, covering up the general quiet with his mocking ringmaster voice. "Line up, boys; he'll make you famous."

Jack's statement had an immediate effect; the men relaxed, even went to rustling and moving around a little, where before they'd been keeping still, so as to maximize the silence. I looked on, amazed at the force of Jack's charisma. It had been a long while since Jack had been friendly with the men I was sitting with now; he'd heard what they'd said about him around that time, and he had withdrawn a little then and still kept himself apart. For twenty years, my brother and I had taken our liquor at opposite sides of the same room; now, in a simple five minutes, Jack had destroyed the veil between our two groups. Now, frustrated, I could see that it had been flimsy all along, and that he'd always had the power to destroy it. People just liked Jack; they couldn't help themselves.

He had given the signal, the way he used to do when he was the hub of this group of men; he'd sent the message to them: *relax,* and they had obeyed. Buddy, with some kind of animal sense, perceived the lessening of tension and began to speak again.

"My mother talked a lot about her hometown," said Buddy. "I wanted to see it for myself." No one said anything; inwardly I rejoiced. Jack might be able to call off the dogs, but he couldn't make them friendly. His power was not absolute, after all; the men had some will of their own. The boy was uncomfortable again, still speaking.

". . . she left here a long time ago." He forced the words out against the silence and then stopped.

"What's your mama's name?" asked Steve Grissom, blandly, but meaning to be kind.

"Beth Gates," said Buddy, gratefully, turning to Steve. "I mean, Crawford," he corrected himself. "Her name was Crawford when she lived here."

That changed things. We'd had only a passing interest in the unnamed stranger who might have lived in Naples at one time in her life; with the name, he invoked her presence, and we all sat up a little and looked at the boy with greater attention.

Buddy looked back at us; he seemed to be waiting for something, and no one about to provide it.

"You mean Miller," I said, finally. "Miller was her maiden name."

"That's right," said Buddy, looking at me.

"My brother," said Jack, introducing us. "Gil Corbin."

"You knew her, then," said Buddy, smiling. I stood up, and he moved closer, to shake my hand.

"From the time she was a—" I said, grasping his hand and stopped. Buddy looked confused, but everyone else simply waited, without seeming to, as though time had stopped. "Girl," I said, releasing his grip. Buddy nodded, looking expectant, but I said nothing more.

"This is Ned Lucas, Sam Lucas, Steve Grissom, Andy Swann," said Jack. Buddy shook hands all round. "Our cheerful host there, that's Wally Stokes."

Wallace, behind the counter again, nodded to Buddy.

"Beth Miller," mused Sam. "She was something around here for a while. Tobacco queen back in forty-eight."

"Forty-seven," said Ned.

"I heard she went to New York," said Andy.

"That's where I was born," Buddy told him.

"I guess she left here in sixty-four, sixty-five maybe," said Sam.

"Sixty-three," said Ned. "There was all that trouble downtown, right afterward."

"Nope, it was sixty-six," said Sam, as though Ned hadn't spoken. "She had a sixty-six Ford Mustang," he told Buddy. "Candyapple, a beauty. I remember that car. Our daddy tried to buy it off her once, but she wouldn't sell."

"He never did," said Ned, but it was heatless, compelled by a lifetime habit of arguing.

"If I recall," responded Sam, as mildly, "you weren't seeing too much more than that Baker girl, around then."

"Pah," said Ned, a sound somewhere between agreement and dismissal.

"What trouble downtown?" asked Buddy, who had been following the conversation between the two with his head, like a table tennis spectator.

"Well, now, people always fussing about something or other," said Wallace, who was wiping a glass behind the bar, listening.

"It's the blacks," said Ned.

"Not just the blacks," said Sam. "Whites, too. But they was all poor, and angrier than hell."

"Riots," said Buddy, comprehendingly. "You had riots down here?"

"Riots makes it sound like more than it was," said Steve. There was a little pause while he considered his beer. "Some folks get to thinking they deserve more than they got." He looked at Jack. "It only takes some little thing to remind them."

Sam took up the story.

"Some fellow got hisself killed somewhere, and some of them here rose up and went crazy for a while. Stopped traffic on Main Street, heaved a few bricks through a few windows, then it was all over."

"Lots of trouble right around then," said Steve.

"Strange times," agreed Sam and seemed about to elaborate, but I interrupted, turning to Buddy.

"How is—" I said. The group went silent, waiting. "Beth?" I finished. "New York treating her all right?"

"Connecticut," said Buddy, flushing. My stutter embarrassed him more than it did me. "She, um, died about two years ago."

There was another silence.

"I'm real sorry to hear that, son," said Sam.

"Sad thing," agreed Andy.

"She was a looker," said Ned, shaking his head.

I looked over at Jack, to see how he was taking it. I myself hadn't heard from Beth in many years, and this was the first I'd been told of her death. Jack showed nothing; obviously, he had already had the news from the boy when they were alone at the table by the window. He'd had time to cover over any initial shock.

"She died young," I said, to Buddy, who lowered his eyes. "She—" and I paused, while the other men fell silent, "was only a little older than me."

"She'd be fifty-six this spring," mumbled the boy, sounding a little choked, his eyes still on the floor.

"Sorry to hear it, son," I said, turning away, making my way to the bar. The conversation continued at my back.

"I can see her now, clear as day," said Sam. "A real knockout."

There were murmurs of agreement.

"Kind of a hellcat," said Andy, with a smile on his face, then darted a look at Jack, then at Buddy. "Sorry," he said.

"She talk some about this place?" Wallace asked Buddy.

"About her childhood here," said Buddy. "School dances. A place she used to go to, to swim—a lake."

"The quarry," said Ned, with satisfaction.

"What else she tell you?" asked Jack. I turned around and leaned up against the bar.

Buddy gestured vaguely. "A lot about the town," he said. "I even thought I might know my way around, just from the way she described it. But I guess it's changed since she left."

"Yes sir," said Jack.

"She didn't talk too much about people," said Buddy, almost apologetically. "Names, sometimes. Someone she called G.I."

Smiles broke out now, spreading across leathery, deadpan faces, twitching at colorless lips.

"No one," I said, and hesitated, "calls me that anymore." I smiled.

"Not to his face, anyhow," said Jack.

Jack, anyway, never said anything much to my face. The two of us hadn't spoken directly to one another for many years. If one had anything to tell the other, he enclosed it in a comment of a general nature and addressed a room. It was a quiet sort of feud, and no one had remarked upon it, not in all of this time. It was just something they respected, like the way Sam and Ned bickered all the time; it was something to do with brothers, and they let us alone.

"She marry again up there?" asked Wallace, who was gathering up empties.

"My father. Bill Gates," said Buddy.

"Youda thought she'd had enough of those," commented Andy, and there was an indulgent round of smiles.

"Your mother's first husband," I told Buddy, who was looking bewildered, "was also named Bill."

"And he never paid none," said Andy, happy with his pun.

"He left town a step ahead of the law," said Ned, dramatically. "Went to Texas."

"On his way to California," said Sam. "But old Billy Crawford only had him just about enough get-go to take him to Dallas. I guess he's still there."

"I thought he was in Houston," said Ned.

"Naw," said Sam.

Buddy, looking impatient, cut in.

"What I want to do—" he began.

"You want to start with Tess DeWitt," Jack interrupted; and the others nodded their heads. "She's lived here all her life, and a long one, too. There ain't much she don't know about Naples. She's a little deaf, but sharp as ever. What she don't find out for herself, Gus tells her."

"Gus," snorted Andy. "He ain't no servant, now," he said, in a high voice, mock stern.

"No sir," said Jack, gracing Andy's remark with a smile.

Buddy looked puzzled; no one offered to explain.

"What I want—" he began again.

"What you want is a good meal, and a night's sleep, and see Miss Tess in the morning."

"But—" said Buddy.

"Tess is where you want to start," said Jack, firmly. "And you want to start tomorrow. You just got out of a car, boy, and a long drive behind you. It can wait until tomorrow."

"Well," said Buddy, giving in. "Thanks. Where can I find— what's her name again?" he asked, taking a small spiral notebook out of his front shirt pocket.

"Where she's always lived," said Sam, looking curiously at the notebook. "In her father's house, over on the hill."

"Her grandfather's," corrected Ned. "Her family ran to girls."

"It's in the old village," said Jack. Buddy looked blank. "I can take you there tomorrow." Buddy nodded. "You look half dead, boy," said Jack. "You got a place to stay?"

"I was looking for a motel," said Buddy. "It doesn't have to be too fancy," he added. "Just a place to sleep."

"Plenty of room at my place," said Jack.

"I couldn't," said Buddy, but it was unconvincing.

"We'll stop by Susie's on the way," said Jack. "You hungry?"

"Boy, at your age, I was hungrier than I was horny," said Sam.

"Still are," said Ned.

"You better eat, son, before what you got falls off your bones," said Steve.

"Susie'll fix him up," said Jack.

"Is she your girlfriend?" asked Buddy, shyly.

"Might as well be," said Steve, smiling.

"She cooks for him every night," said Sam.

"She's four hundred pounds and ugly," said Jack. "But she makes a mean gravy."

Buddy looked from one to another, uncertain.

"Susie runs a diner on the south side of town," said Wallace, passing by.

"Marry her, save yourself some money," said Sam.

"I been married," said Jack, shaking his head slowly, side to side. "Cash is cheaper, in the long run." He turned to Buddy. "We'll get on over there, sooner or later."

It was sooner rather than later, I suppose; I left Stokes' a few minutes after that, dribbling out of the bar with the rest of the men, separate from them, and yet all of us furtive in the same way, scraping back our chairs and mumbling our good-byes, leaving Jack and the boy alone to finish their beer. We didn't stop to talk amongst ourselves the way we'd usually do, either, when we were alone together outside the door. We didn't comment on the boy or even look at one another, just went silently to our cars and trucks and drove off, taking our memories with us, as though we were jealous of them and wanted to hold them to ourselves a while longer before giving them up to the scrutiny of the stranger.

Naples blood or not, Buddy Gates wasn't quite welcome.

I went home to the house across town. It was dark when I drove in, but no lights shone in the windows. I found my wife, Joan, in the room that used to be my father's, reading by the light of a single lamp. She was in the old rose-patterned chair, absorbed, with her feet curled up under her, and she looked up when I came in.

I smiled, not yet certain what kind of day it was for her.

"Hello," I said, and bent down to kiss her. She drew away a little at first and then relented, accepting my lips against her cheek. As though we had not been married these thirty years. "What are you reading?" I asked her, pulling up a footstool.

"Josephine Tey," she answered, in a voice light as leaves and without expression.

"The one about the king?" I asked. I had never read any of the books, but Joan had, again and again, and had repeated their plots to me so often that I felt as familiar with them as if I had read them myself. Early in our marriage, she had even read one or two of them aloud to me, in a fine, expressive voice. It was an evening ritual, once; we had abandoned it long ago.

"The one about the boy who comes back," she said.

I reached out to take one of her hands; she let the book fall closed upon the other, keeping her place. I traced the veins running over the fine bones, the slight white knobs of knuckle, the short fingernails, and then looked up into her face. At fifty-two, she was still beautiful, as beautiful as when I'd married her, although in a different way. She'd been fey then, with a transparent, distracted look. Age had robbed her of that youthful blitheness; it had pulled away the air of vulnerability which in our early marriage had shrouded a surprisingly steely will. Then, she was an ultimately practical woman with a fairy look; now, ironically, her appearance was far more ordinary. She looked capable and determined. It was an impression she sought to reinforce beyond the barriers of the house; but within it, she often left off that veneer of competence and skill, and drifted through the rooms like an uncertain ghost.

"I'll make supper," I said.

Joan shrugged.

"Did you see the doctor today?" I asked, gently.

She nodded.

"Bad?" I asked.

She looked away, toward the shuttered windows. "It was hard," she said, at last.

"But it's helping," I said.

"I guess so," said Joan.

"Good," I told her, pressing her hand.

"How can you live with me?" she cried suddenly, dropping her face forward, so that a dark eclipse of hair fell across it. I reached out and smoothed the hair back, behind her ears.

"Everything's all right now," I said.

She looked at me, as an animal might examine its captor; searchingly, as though estimating my power to harm.

"You stay here, read some more," I said. "I'll make that chicken thing."

"No," said Joan, pulling her hand from mine, putting the book aside, and straightening her legs, preparatory to rising. "I'll make soup," she said.

"Fine," I said.

"If you can wait a while," she said. "I got some things at the market."

"I can wait," I said.

"Before we were married," she said, looking into my eyes, "I promised your father I'd cook for you. He said you'd been in the kitchen too long." She stood up, and I stood with her, marveling. So sudden, her changes; released now from her mood by some private alchemy, Joan stood solid and strong. She lifted her hands and ran her fingers through her hair, which fell around her face in the old style, girlishly simple, now streaked with grey. She smiled, tipping up her chin, so that I might kiss her. I did, hardly bending at all to accomplish it. She was a tall woman, coming up past my shoulder, although she gave the impression of being much smaller, and she made no noise when she walked.

"A nice cream soup," she said. "And biscuits and salad." She might have been completely normal, her eyes blank and calm, fitting with her expression, as though she were thinking of nothing, nothing at all besides the evening menu. That's how she does it, I thought, that's how she goes into the world and fools everybody.

"Sounds good," I said, giving an ordinary response, to fit into that highly ordinary conversation. Sanity resides in such small exchanges as these. I followed her into the kitchen.

Joan herself had told me once that I worried too much over her. "You needn't be so careful with your every word," she said. "And that doting expression." She made a moue. "It makes me feel like an invalid auntie."

That had been one of her good days. She labelled them herself: good and bad. "On good days," she'd told me, "I feel hopeful." I didn't ask her what she hoped for then. On good days she confided in me and recovered her sense of humor from that lost dark place where she wandered during the other times. On bad days, she trembled at every sound and hardly spoke at all, carrying herself cautiously across the floor, as though it might shift and open up at her feet. Twenty years, a deep tunnel and hardly any sight of light at its end. But lately, so many more of her days had been good than bad; we were seeing the far light now.

Going behind her, turning on lights, I wondered how to tell her. I knew I ought to; otherwise, she would certainly hear about it elsewhere, somewhere harborless and cold, outside of the house, where she would be defenseless. Better that I be the one to tell her, and better it be here, where she could react. I watched her silently, as she moved around the kitchen.

"There was a stranger in Stokes' tonight," I said at last, rattling ice cubes into a squat heavy glass. Joan was half listening, flipping through her box of recipe cards.

"Oh?" she said.

"He says he's Beth Miller's son," I said carefully, measuring out the whisky.

"Who?" said Joan, and then, "Oh." She looked at me. "You mean Crawford."

"Gates, actually," I said, conversationally. "She married again, in New York."

"Beth's son," said Joan.

"He says so," I said. "He's just a boy, maybe nineteen."

"What's he like?" she asked, surprising me.

"Skinny. Shy." I hesitated. "Nothing like her."

"What does he want?" she asked.

"I don't know yet," I said. "He says he's making a movie."

"Did Beth come with him?" asked Joan, standing very still, looking down at the index card she had chosen.

"Beth is dead now." I said it as gently as I could.

"Oh," said Joan. "Oh," she said again, turning, going toward the stove, then turning again and going toward the refrigerator, blind, half-completed movements. Finally, she stood still in the middle of the floor with her hands at her sides.

"Thank God," she said, hissing into the air between us.

"Joan," I said, moving slightly toward her. She flinched at my approach and moved away. "Joan." She said nothing; she stood with her fingers tensed up on the counter like thin white-legged spiders, her back to me.

"We can talk about it later," I said.

I retreated to the living room, where my own book lay, abandoned since the night before, split and flattened, facedown on the coffee table. I picked it up; a history of the Reconstruction, it had been a birthday present from Joan nearly six months before. I was a fast reader, but the book was dense, and I had gotten only to the seventh chapter in that time.

A clatter of pots began from the kitchen, signalling that Joan had left her frozen stance by the stove and was now engaged in the fragrant mysteries of soup making. She had a large repertoire of soups, nearly all of them gleaned from her Hungarian grandmother's collection, copied carefully by Joan onto those tidy index cards. She made *gulyás,* fat chunks of meat and clear limp onions floating in liquid scummed livid with paprika. She made thick white soups from cauliflower, and thin beef stocks with soft slices of carrot, the beef falling into slivers under the fork. She fed me well, as she always had, but always now with some reservation, with a kind of pinched goodwill, as though she were feeding the enemy, a Yankee soldier quartered in her Southern home. Though it was she who was the foreigner, the Yankee, and it was my father's house we lived in, built deep into the Virginia soil, and my mother's saucepan that Joan was now filling with water and carrying over to the stove.

It would be some time until supper; some time until Joan spoke again. But I had known she would take the news badly, and I could wait. She often took herself off like this, in order to recover from a blow; somewhere in the chopping and simmering, she would mend whatever injury my news had caused her. She would call to me to help her, some simple task like slicing bread or dressing salad. By then, she would have set the stage for intimacy, and we would find ourselves cheek by jowl in the kitchen. Conniving together, so that even in that large space, there would not be room enough to keep us distant. I would put my hand over hers accidentally, reaching for a cloth, and she would brush by me on her way to the sink. Eating, we would be restored again, newly allied, no longer sheared by doubt.

I settled to the waiting, opening my book. Drawing comfort from the definite: the dark clear letters against the white paper; the words they made up; the facts and names and dates. From the real: the lamp glowing above my chair; the textured binding of the book I held; the faint cacophony of cookware in the background. I fastened to these details. Better not to think; better to grasp what could be grasped than to look back into darkness past or to look ahead to disasters that might not come. Better to revel in the good things, the things that could be counted upon: the rich story in my lap, the rich soup to come. The sounds of healing, the promise of mercy.

Chapter Three

The Belle of Naples

C C Talk about yourself," *says the young man, Buddy, from across the room. He's fiddling with black, shiny equipment as he speaks. He keeps saying he wants me to be comfortable, but I am not; I am very hot in this chair; he's gathered all of the lights in the parlor around me, plugging and re-plugging them until the wall sockets bristle with electrical cords.*

"Say anything," *he says, looking up from where he is struggling.* "Tell me anything at all."

Jack Corbin, now, he's a slick one, and no mistake. I knew him when he was small, and he was always the same, always up to something. Those kind that don't say much, they're the ones to watch, they know more than they're telling.

Fancy, schoolwork meaning all of this truck; all we got to do was parse sentences and memorize arithmetic tables. Here you are telling me that you've got to make a moving picture. Times move on. You wouldn't understand, though, you've lived all in one time, haven't you? You'll understand by and by, I expect, unless they manage to do away with old age entirely by the time it's your turn.

That sounds nasty, doesn't it? *Your turn.* Don't mistake my meaning; I'm not one of those bitter old ladies, those Faulkner Emilies, locked away into their houses, mourning their withered youth. I never valued youth all that much when I had it; it would be pure hypocrisy to start weeping over it now.

Can you tell, from looking at me, that I used to be known as the Belle of Naples? A ridiculously romantic appellation, but then it was a romantic era. To tell the truth, I was no prettier than the average pretty girl, but there weren't all that many girls here then, at least not of my class, and so I stood out. I was quite sought after, can you believe it now? Don't be embarrassed; I know what the years have done to me. I've made peace with it now; I'm no miserable aging belle with all of the mirrors shrouded and the curtains pulled. And I don't lie about my age. I'm eighty-four next month, born with the new century. Eighty-four; that's old. Yes, old. Practically nothing is euphemised so much as age. You're said to be 'getting on,' as though you hadn't gotten there already. You're deferred to by people with rigid, polite faces, while it's obvious they don't care a hoot what you say or think, they just can't wait to get somewhere and talk about the things that truly interest them. I've been called 'wise' so many times you wouldn't believe it, and by the most unlikely people. What do they know about wisdom? What do they care? It's a cheap commodity; by the time you've gathered some, no one wants to hear about it.

You're not here because I'm wise, now are you? No; you're here because I'm old. No need to look apologetic. You're not the first. When the Historical Committee, as they call themselves, that bunch of hens and milksops, were looking around to gather up facts about Naples, they came running straight up here with their tape recorders. By now, I'm quite accustomed to my role as a font of local history; but I must confess that the camera's new to me.

Being old isn't so bad. I'm old, I ought to know. And I daresay I'm wise, too, although the one has little to do with the other, in my opinion. Age doesn't engender wisdom as surely as it engenders boredom; unfortunately, the world prepares one for the wrinkles, but not for the ennui.

There *are* consolations. When one is young, one is forever sneaking about trying to learn things—at least I did as a girl, the world wasn't anything like as liberal then as it is now—but now I'm old, people often simply talk in front of me, as though I were a piece of furniture and incapable of understanding. They assume that I'm hard of hearing, you see, and although I never have been afflicted that way, I let them go right on thinking it. It's amazing what I learn. Sometime I do have to strain a little, to hear whispers. Even if they think me deaf as a post, they still go and whisper sometimes. Seems that when the subject is delicate, people instinctively lower their voices. As if they'd shock me. Strange, that I am treated more carefully at eighty than I was at eighteen. As though living made one more fragile, instead of harder.

Of course, it's not so nice, is it, eavesdropping all the time, instead of being told things straight out. But if I adhered to the niceties of etiquette, I'd never hear anything interesting at all. It's terrible that I have missed all this—freedom, would you call it?—by an accident of birth. Timing plays a greater role in things than people imagine. I wouldn't want to be growing up nowadays, however. No, if I could, I'd go right back to the time when I was young and be young all over again. Decrepitude is mighty dull, but this time has no magic in it. Everything laid wide open, nothing mysterious anymore.

But I am not a good judge of what the world is like now; Gaston reads the paper to me, but it has been a good while since I saw anything for myself, or had the desire to. It is all much of a muchness to me now. It didn't used to be that way. When I was a child, there were ordinary days and holidays; and then school came along and divided up the days quite nicely. As a young wife, my days were tagged for baking, washing, marketing, paying calls; and when I had a child, his needs got crammed in, too, so that the time just flew by. How I longed for Sundays! Now, the days are much the same, and time is endless, with an abhorrent divisionless quality to it. I mourn my crested and variegated weeks. Now they are marked only by Sunday; church, of course, in the morning, and afterward I sometimes receive visitors. Every day before and after Sunday falls away from it, like pitted fruit falling away from the stone. I try to keep track, for appearances' sake. Today is Tuesday, but it might as well be Thursday or Monday for all it signifies. All I am certain of is that it is not yet Sunday.

But listen to me, going on about getting old, so like the people I despise who are obsessed with it, as though it were not nature but some private injustice, something that happens only to them. I'll tell you a secret: *everybody gets old.* It's not a secret, of course, but the way people act it might as well be. And I'll tell you something else: I wouldn't really want to be young again. For the most part, I have seen and done what I wanted to see and do; I went to Europe twice, and how many people in Naples today can say that? And it's not such a small town anymore, upwards of twelve thousand where there used to be four, and they're talking about *another* shopping center, as if we hadn't enough of those already. Or so I understand from Gaston. He keeps me abreast of local developments, and he's not one to exaggerate.

Gaston; that's his name, though you'll hear him called Gus around town. It *is* a silly sort of a name for him, I don't know how his mother came up with it. I'm sure there's not a drop of French blood in the family. You may have assumed that Gaston is my servant; a common mistake, fostered by those insipid tales of the South. I never had an eighteen-inch waist, and my family may have owned a few slaves at one time, but just a *very* few, and I am quite sure they were never whipped. Television stories; people believe what they see; just so many cattle. I actually see it that way—all across America, horned beasts tossing their heads and lowing, the silver antennae poking up, and all the time that irritating whine from the box itself. Mercy, *this* isn't going to be on television, is it? Well, good.

As I was saying. Gaston is not of the servant class. And my family never owned his, or anything like that. The Taylors were free even before the War. I suppose they really were tailors at one point in their history, but in Naples they run a sort of general store, down near the railroad. Gaston still works there sometimes; he took it over from his father, and his son has it now; Donny's expanded it and put in a lunch counter. They've done well, the Taylors; some of them have risen far from the humbler trades, and travelled far from Naples. Gaston's nephew is an attorney in Maryland. The family had to struggle some, certainly, but that wasn't unusual; the whole town fell on hard times in the teens and twenties. The Taylors weren't as poor as some, but even if they'd been starving, none of them would have gone into service. Gaston's father wouldn't have stood for it. Not even for the girls; they became typists and clerks and later housewives. Somehow, they all got by without ever cleaning a white person's home, not even so much as polishing a doorknob. The Taylors were not of the servant class; it was a point of pride with old Joseph, and it passed on into his children.

Gaston and I were playmates when we were little. My grandfather did something nice for his grandfather once upon a time, and the habit of friendship persisted between our two families through the generations. He was slightly younger than I, and I bossed him dreadfully. I didn't go too far; he had a special look he'd wear when I'd hurt his feelings; and that look would be followed by silence. He'd ignore me, never flickering an eyelid, even when I shouted. I'd been brought up with all the fuss and flurry that surrounds an only girl; I'd been teased and petted and punished and spoiled, but I'd never been ignored; and I couldn't stand it. And no one could ignore a person so thoroughly as Gaston could when he wanted to make a point. It kept me walking a line.

Looking back on it, I guess Gaston and I suited a well-worn stereotype, Missy and her black playmate. So typical of pre-War times. But I didn't see it that way. Does any child ever see any of its life as typical of anything else? Its life is its life, and that's all. To a child, everything is exactly as it should be, as it *must* be, in fact.

School separated us, of course, but outside school hours we were always together, always up to some mischief or other. We spread newspapers over Minnie Tolliver's back doorstep once, just before a big rain; she was *furious*. Of course, the wet paper stuck to the stone like it had been glued there, and it dried like that. It was the devil's own work to get it off. A whole afternoon of scraping, and still you could make out the backward letters of the headline, ever so faint, for months afterward.

Now, my father was a mild man, and my high jinks made him laugh; but my mother scolded. She was worried about me, loping around the countryside like a boy in the company of Gaston and my older brother Harrison. How I adored Harry! I would have done anything he told me to do; once, I jumped into the river with all of my clothes on because he dared me I wouldn't do it. 'You're as good as a boy, Tessie,' he said, after that. His praise rang in my head and made the subsequent scolding easier to bear. I often took all the blame for our escapades, and all the punishments, too; I didn't mind. It was pure common sense: my father had a soft place for what he called 'spirit' in a girl; in Harry, it would have been called irresponsibility, and he would have gotten a whipping for it. So I confessed alone, and scraped off the Tolliver doorstep alone, and went by myself to apologize to Russ Winter for stealing peaches from his orchard. If Mother was really displeased, I went to bed straight from the supper table without having my dessert. Sometimes, she'd forget, but still I missed a regular three or four desserts a week; it seems to me I'm still owing a few. All this, while the boys went scot-free.

The arrangement had been Harry's idea in the first place, but after a while it started to bothering him. He was getting older, you see, and was beginning to develop what he called 'a sense of honor.'

"Would you rather get a whipping?" I asked him, reasonably.

"Maybe," said Harry. "I should take my punishment like a man."

"She takes it like a man," said Gaston, and I smiled at him.

"She's a girl," said Harry. "I'm supposed to protect her. It's not right, that's all."

"I don't mind," I said. "And Gaston doesn't mind. Do you?" I asked him.

"Well, he wouldn't, would he," said Harry, keeping his eyes on me. "I don't expect him to understand. It's not the same."

Gaston went quiet when Harry said this, and I looked from one to the other.

"Don't be stupid," I said, finally, and the matter was dropped there, although I could see it lingering in their faces the rest of that afternoon: the half mentioned, the evil, imprinted on their features like bedsheet wrinkles on skin after a long, hot sleep.

There was that little unpleasantness, and a few other episodes like it, but for the most part, those were unsullied years, comradely and smooth. I withstood the seminary in the morning, with its idiotic backboards and foolish young ladies, my fellow pupils. In the mid-afternoon I was rewarded with release. Release, to the freedom of the countryside and the company of the boys. It was a perpetual childhood, such as children don't have now. Children today are expected to be responsible, but are given no responsibility. Harry and I would not have dreamed of shirking the light duties our parents demanded of us, and I don't like to think about what might have been the consequences of such carelessness. But at the same time, most of our pranks were indulged as entirely natural, as examples of youthful exuberance, and we were not seriously upbraided for them. Even at fifteen and sixteen, we were considered to have only just left the throes of infancy behind us; we were free.

When I was seventeen, everything changed. Harry went to war, and Gaston went to work for his father. The house seemed very empty without my brother's clattering footsteps. At school, all the talk was of cotillions and betrothals. I felt abandoned. Gaston and I did manage to meet some afternoons down by the river, but we had little time for mischief anymore. We mostly giggled and talked, and parted before supper. Without Harry, the friendship began to change. The three of us had had a reckless camaraderie, a Musketeerlike partnership, and Harry had been the dominating figure. With all of the privilege of seniority, he had suffered our presence, and we had followed his lead gratefully. Gaston's and mine was a gentler alliance. In Harry's absence, the two of us moved a little closer to one another, and told each other everything, things we might not have revealed if Harry had been there to scoff at us.

But now my mother, who had always permitted my father the upper hand in these matters, began to remonstrate against my wild ways. She wanted me to devote more of my energies to the arts of womanhood and to stop getting the edges of my skirts muddy. I resisted her, and I had a will of iron, forged by years of getting my own way. Mother was easy to get around, too, distracted as she was by worry about Harry, who was fighting in France. When he was killed, Mother went sort of limp; and she sagged a little forever after.

There's a portrait of me in the hall, done when I was eighteen. You can see how I was, how spirited I was. Remarkable, isn't it? how that painted arm, ivory and firm, was once this arm, which is now lax and freckled. I had no lack of suitors, but the local swains who were considered suitable seemed soggy to me, brainless, with no ambition. They had too much money; it made them soft. The ones who weren't soldiers were defectives or cowards; the soldiers weren't much to speak of, either, but they were better. Still, I wouldn't look at them. I knew that being a soldier's wife was just courting sorrow.

Down by the river, Gaston and I made fun of the hopeful young men; I ridiculed every detail of their various characters, and he endowed them with witty nicknames. Together we thought up ways in which I could discourage them. When a young man showed too much interest, I'd be cool to him; and when he asked me for another date, I'd tell him that 'I didn't know, I'd have to check my appointment schedule.' Gaston invented that baffling phrase; we found it hilarious; and I used it again and again.

At the same time, I was conscious of my mother's feelings; she was grieving deeply for Harry, and she poured all of her hopes into a good match for me. I too was grieving, and would have liked to mourn with her, but she kept me at a distance, shutting herself into her bedroom every afternoon and evening, taking her meals in private. If I mentioned Harry to her, it was as though she had not heard me; she spoke only of my "prospects," or to reprimand me upon my behavior with one suitor or other. "You'll end up alone," she warned me. "Unmarriageable, thirty." She meant well, but to me then thirty was a world away, impossible that I should ever reach it. I knew that my obstinacy vexed her, and sometimes, seeing the new weakness to her chin, hearing the new tremor in her voice, I softened toward her. But when I considered a lifetime with any of the men who courted me, I made my heart cold again.

Franklin DeWitt was an older man, nearly forty. He owned a lot of property in West Virginia. I found him attractive, and his quiet manner intrigued me, but by that time I was in the habit of nastiness, and I behaved as callously to him as to any of the others. But unlike the others, Franklin's interests were not spurred on by coldness; once, when I had been terribly, deliberately rude to him at a dance, he carried me across the floor and deposited me summarily with my parents, bowing to my mother, and leaving without a word. It was a public disgrace, and I deserved it, but I was angry. I reported the matter to Gaston.

"Looks like you found a live one," he said, shaking his head.

"Nothing of the sort!" I told him. "He was badly brought up, is all. Carrying me across the floor in the middle of a waltz. I never heard of anything like it."

"What'd you say, made him so angry?" inquired Gaston.

"Oh my," I said, and, giggling, began to tell him. But then I caught sight of his expression, innocent and mocking, and I shut right up. "Just never mind what I said," I told him. "It's what I'll say when I see him next that matters."

I waited for him to call again, all the time preparing the words I should use to spurn him. I went to dances on the arms of other men, and moved slowly around the floor with them, all the time craning my neck for the sight of those ridiculous side-whiskers he affected. I even scraped a conversation with Sylvia Tolliver, thinking she would have news of him, if anyone did. But although I listened through a tide of gossip, I never heard any mention of his name. He seemed to have vanished. Weeks went by, and winter began to turn, and still he had not reappeared. I grew more and more anxious: surely he was not to have the last word, so to speak. Was I never to be given a chance to use the reproof I had rehearsed so exhaustively, even watching myself in the mirror, so as to achieve the perfect disdainful lift to my lip? I was irritable with Gaston, and snapped at him.

"Why you waiting on him so, you hate him so much?" he enquired.

"I don't hate him," I retorted. "I feel nothing for him at all. Well, no. I feel contempt, is what I feel."

"Contempt," repeated Gaston.

"Yes," I said. "And pity. It must be awful to be so ill-bred.

Imagine, humiliating a lady that way, and then just skulking away, never giving her a chance to say a word."

"Seems that's what started it," said Gaston. "You saying a word."

"Oh, be quiet," I said. "You don't understand."

"Oh, I *understand*," said Gaston.

"I said be quiet," I said. "And I never want to hear—*that man's*—name again. Never."

"I won't say it again," agreed Gaston.

"Well, all right," I said.

"Not even if I hear that somebody is coming back to Naples," he said.

"Somebody?" I said.

"Not even if I know from somebody's housekeeper that she's opening his house somebody just bought, sweeping out all the cobwebs cause he's coming here to live," said Gaston, ignoring me. "No sir, not even then."

"What are you talking about?" I asked, pulling at his arm.

"Somebody's coming to live in Naples," said Gaston. "And no doubt looking for a bride to put in that big old house just the other side of Doc Williams' place." He swung his head from side to side. "And even was a person to *shake* me like you're doing, they couldn't get me to tell that somebody's name. No, sir." He cut his eyes at me.

"Gaston, tell me," I said. "Is it true?"

He wouldn't tell that day, but it was certainly true that Franklin DeWitt had bought old Kerry McGee's place, the one his widow'd been trying to sell for years. I heard he was having it painted; I heard what color he had chosen for the trim; but I saw nothing of the man himself until one evening in early spring, at Missy Booth's birthday dance. I spotted him across the room, and when at long last he did come up to me, I felt literally dizzy, watching him approach. While he bowed to my mother, I scratched another fellow's name off my dance card. Dancing, I tried to recall the words I had prepared, words intended to shrivel him, finally and absolutely, but they didn't come.

"How's somebody?" asked Gaston, when we were by the river a few days later.

"How would I know," I snapped.

"No reason," said Gaston. "But your mama's looking mighty pleased. Been a long time since she looked so happy."

After we parted, I cried, knowing it was the end of something.

And it was. As a married woman, I had to take my place in society; I had duties to my husband and to my family name. It's something young women now don't understand about the way things used to be. If I'd wanted something else, I'd have gone after it. But I loved Franklin, and I wanted to keep his home and bear his children. These days, that kind of feeling is scoffed at, and only the woman who goes out working is treated with respect. The way I see it, both desires have been there all along, portioned out, so that every person gets some of both. I hear it all the time, about the freedom of the modern woman, but she's not free if she can't choose. Well, it took long enough for word to get out that women might be interested in the workings of the world; it'll take some time for people to understand that it's not *what* she wants, but *that* she wants it what matters. And I don't agree with the fools who say that fulfillment has to come from anywhere in particular, whether inside or outside the home. The Working Woman. Work! I had more work than I could do. It's fine that some need other things, and put them before home and family, but I was content, keeping house.

And so I was a wife, and shortly after, a mother, and Gaston worked in town for his father; we saw one another very little during the next twenty years.

I was married during wartime, and widowed toward the end of another war, and my husband never once a soldier. I had given my son, Harry, to the effort; he fell in a foreign land, like his namesake, and was buried there. Two weeks after we'd gotten the news, Franklin, coming home from the mill, died in a railway crash.

It was tragic, in keeping with those tragic times, but I didn't manage the double mourning gracefully. I fled to my mother's house, which had been standing locked and empty since my parents had moved to the Cummins house in Tennessee, years before. I stayed there with only two servants and saw no one. I wanted nothing more than to be left alone; but of course I had gone about it absolutely the wrong way; a hermit is always a curiosity; and so the bell was going all day long, with one lady or another calling to pay her respects. I didn't feel like making conversation or being stared at; I had the girl send everyone away, and got so that I hardly got out of bed.

Gaston rescued me then, you might say. He came knocking

at the door one afternoon with a basket of vegetables, which he gave to the cook. I refused to see him that time, but the next day he was back, and the day after. By the end of that first week, I was at the window watching for him, and by the end of the next, I had let myself be washed and dressed, and told the downstairs girl that I would be receiving in the parlor that afternoon, and to lay out tea.

We talked of nothing in particular, at first.

"Real meat," said Gaston, pulling the sandwich flaps apart, and bringing his face close to inspect the contents. "I can't say when it was last I saw any."

"Wartime," I said, and stopped, the words cut off.

"Hard times," said Gaston, putting the sandwich down and looking at me. I nodded, with my head bowed; I couldn't speak. He must have gotten up, for a minute later I felt his hand on my shoulder, a light pressure, there and gone. I began then, slowly at first, and then faster, my words borne on a great tide of misery. I told him of my son and husband, idiotic things, things I had never told anyone, things Gaston already knew, every thought unconnected to the one before it, every sentence forgotten as soon as it was spoken. It was not the sense of it, but the telling, that mattered; I was the only one left of a family; I had to tell someone. I laughed, talking; and I cried, something I hadn't done yet, and when I was done, I was hoarse and darkness was at the windows. Gaston, who had been silent and gently attentive whilst I talked, stood up to light the lamp.

"Leave it," I said.

"There's enough darkness," he said, and when he brought up the flame I could see how dark it had been before.

"What you want to stay in here all the time for?" asked Gaston, bluntly.

"It's safe in here," I said.

"Jes as safe on the porch," said Gaston. "And there's a breeze."

I shook my head.

"I don't want to see anyone," I said. "You can't possibly understand." Now here, I was being cruel, for Gaston had lost his mother not long before and was in mourning himself; but I was selfish, you understand, and didn't care if my words hurt him.

"All right," he said. "If you don't mind what people are

saying about you." And he plucked a sandwich from the tray, its edges curling up now, and bit into it.

"What are they saying?" I asked.

"Jes gossip," he said. "I know how you hate gossip."

"Well," I said.

"Is there any more tea?" he asked, looking into the pot.

"Of course," I said impatiently, and lifted the bell. "More sandwiches?"

"Well, now," said Gaston. "Seems that something sweet would be just right, about now."

"Bring the rum cake," I told the girl, who had entered the room while Gaston was talking. She nodded, her eyes wide, and retreated.

"Ain't seen sugar in a long time, neither," said Gaston. "Whatever we get in the store gets bought up right away. Dad lets it go, doesn't save out any for our own sugar bowl. Dad's got him a soft heart, all right." He smiled. "But I got me a sweet tooth."

"I remember," I said. "You were always begging sweets." I beckoned to the girl, who was peeking around the doorjamb, the silly creature. "Come in." She laid the tray down, and I lifted the knife, and placed its edge against the springy surface of the cake. "You were talking about gossip," I said.

"Not me," said Gaston, watching the knife. "Well, I can't deny it," he said, weakening. "I've heard some talk. But hearing's not the same as telling."

"No indeed," I said, placing the knife for the second cut. "Who's talking about me?"

"Now you know I can't tell you that," said Gaston, recoiling.

"Well, all right then, no names," I said, drawing the knife through and slipping the slice onto a plate. "Just tell me what they're saying."

"You know how people will talk," said Gaston, accepting the plate I held out to him. "It don't mean anything."

"Of course not," I said.

"Now," said Gaston. "Now that is *cake.*" I waited. "They're saying you're ugly now and afraid to show your face," he said, finally.

"That's ridiculous," I said. "I'm in mourning, that's all."

"Lots of people in mourning these days," said Gaston, around a mouthful. "They go out of their houses."

"I don't care what other people do," I said. "Or say," I added.

"Good," he said. "Cause they're saying that you've gotten fat."

"I have not," I cried.

"Hard to tell, in the dark," he said, cocking an eyebrow at me.

"You're making fun of me," I said. "You're heartless, coming here carrying gossip."

"Not me," said Gaston. "Not gossip, either. Information. I guess you won't be surprised now, you hear some of it yourself."

"Well, now I know," I said. "And I don't care."

"Acourse, you ain't heard the worst," he said, thoughtfully. "That might give you a turn, now."

"The worst?" I said. "What—never mind. I don't want to know."

"Uh huh," said Gaston, holding out his plate for another slice of cake.

"I don't care what they say about me," I said, giving it to him.

"It's a good thing," said Gaston. "Because they keep on saying it."

We ended that day at a stalemate, but the next day, at teatime, he returned.

"You said something yesterday," I began, when he was into his second sandwich. "Something about the worst thing they're saying about me."

"Oh, yes," said Gaston. "I couldn't forget *that.*"

"What is it?" I asked, casually. "What are they saying?"

"Uh *uh,*" said Gaston. "I don't carry tales."

"Nonsense," I said. "You told me some yesterday."

"Well, that's true," he said, consideringly.

"And it's helpful for me to know," I wheedled. "As you explained yesterday."

"Maybe helpful about the fat and ugly," said Gaston. "But you don't want to know about this."

"What?" I asked, whispering in my urgency.

"It's terrible, what people will say when you ain't there to prove them different," he said, shaking his head. I said nothing, and he lifted his eyes to mine. "They say you're bald, and your skin gone all dark, like you was colored."

"Bald," I cried. "That's ridiculous." I gave a little shudder and looked down, along my arm. "Does that look colored to you?" I asked.

He inspected the hand I held out.

"No, ma'am," said Gaston. "White as ever."

There was a pause.

"How can they tell such lies?" I asked, finally, putting my hand down. "Bald, indeed. Whoever heard of such a thing."

"Ladies go bald sometimes," said Gaston wisely, stirring sugar into his tea. "Dora Mae Jessup's balder than an egg."

"Dora Mae—?" I breathed.

"Like an egg," he assured me. He sipped at his tea. "How're they to know you ain't the same way?"

"I'm not," I said.

"*I* know it," he said, as though to an idiot child. "But *they* don't. Now if you was to go into town—"

"I don't believe they're saying anything about me at all," I said. "I believe you're just trying to get me to go out of the house."

"Well, now," said Gaston. "If you think that—" and on his face was the look I'd known since childhood.

"No," I said, quickly. "I'm sorry, Gaston." His face went back to normal, and I relaxed. "It's just that I don't want to go downtown. I refuse to be gawked at."

"They could come here," said Gaston.

"Visitors?" I cried. "I'm in mourning."

"So's everybody else," he said. "These days. Everybody's grieving, and sick of it. A little bit of society would be welcome to them." He added, persuasively, "Jes the ladies, acourse. A ladies' day."

"A ladies' day," I repeated. "And at home. So they can see me for themselves."

"Maybe some tea," said Gaston, helpfully. "And sandwiches."

Thus the Wednesday teas came about. As I have just told you, they were Gaston's idea originally, and he helped me with them. We banished the cook for the day and made the sandwiches ourselves, watercress and salmon and other delicacies almost unheard-of during the wartime deprivation. This was just at the end of the war, the time I'm talking about now, and the town was starved for luxury. The first tea was a great success, and after that Gaston and I flung ourselves into the business headlong.

We planned and planned, so that hearing us, you might

think us mad. We debated the merits of China versus India, (Gaston even promoted flavored teas, until I pronounced them vulgar); we schemed elaborately about ingredients for pastry. The next Wednesday, we gave another tea, and they became a sort of tradition. They occupied our weeks: we haggled over the invitation list from Thursday to Sunday; Monday, I wrote out the invitations, and Tuesday Gaston delivered them by hand to the ladies. He did last-minute marketing then, too, and all Wednesday morning the downstairs girl and I prepared the parlor and arranged the tea things.

I was in a delicate position then, feeling all of the guilty freedom of the not-so-fresh widow, after the first period of mourning has passed. My first wild sorrow had been for Harry; I hadn't even seen his body, and I couldn't believe he was dead. I used to think I'd caught a glimpse of him, just the back of his head, and then I'd hurry to catch up to him, and it would be someone else entirely. It was that sort of thing that drove me into seclusion. But after the initial madness, there came a kind of calm, and I began to grieve for my husband, less urgently, but sadder and deeper, like a bell tolling. And finally there was just the ache, and the world fresher around it, as though it had been raining for months, and everything clean again. I began to come alive. I felt hollow and brittle and light, and terrifyingly free. There is nothing like taking care of a man for years to make you feel unfettered when it suddenly stops. It brings tremendous sadness, at first—you remember all of his favorite things, his little peculiar tastes, the unscented soap and the particular grind of coffee, and how he hated, simply loathed, raisins. And when he's gone, you find yourself near tears over the grocery list, thinking: *What do I buy?* I hadn't chosen for myself in so very long. Nearly forty, and I didn't know I had any preferences. But I did, and I do, and it was, after a little interval, a pleasure to discover them, albeit a guilty one.

Gaston made it easier for me to circumnavigate my guilt; he had a way of convincing me of things, without letting me admit to myself that I was being convinced until it was done. The teas were my return to society, from the place where I had gone to hide myself. And so, I was able to make the transition from the dark world of my grief back to the light, without too much self-punishment.

You might not be talking to me now, if it weren't for those

teas. They were the height of sociability in Naples; we saw to that. Of course, I knew full well the principal reason for their initial popularity: people were curious to see me, to see how the Belle had disintegrated, alone in her old house. I didn't care why they came; they all came; no one ever refused an invitation; all of the important people in Naples passed through this parlor during that time, nearly a dozen years. Of course, I am speaking only of the women.

Your mother was among them; she came during the later years. Not every week, of course; the invitation lists varied; but she came here two or three times, certainly. She was just a young bride when she first came, and the last time must have been before all the trouble, so maybe she was twenty-five, and Amanda just a baby.

"You look surprised; did you think I hadn't heard about it, what happened to your mother, her divorce, and Amanda? On the contrary; that was more than twenty years ago, and I was still getting about quite well then. I heard everything there was to hear, everything that people talked about, and there was plenty of talk about your mother. It was a good thing, perhaps, for her, that I stopped giving the teas before any of it happened; the ladies were quite conservative and didn't approve of divorce. And then the rest of it—no, your mother would not have been invited back, could not have been, although I personally found her very charming and didn't blame her for any of it.

The last tea—Gaston and I had been fussing over it for days. It was summer, I recall, and terribly hot; and both of us were out of temper. We fought about the kinds of cakes to serve—I insisted upon napoleons, which was foolish, because of course they melted, and most of them had to be thrown away after the ladies left. We argued about which silver service to use; Gaston wanted to bring out my mother's, as it didn't need to be polished, but I wanted to use my wedding silver. We argued because the day was hot, and because a whole quart of mayonnaise had gone bad, and for a thousand other reasons. I won about the cakes, but Gaston won about the silver; we used my mother's.

If I close my eyes I can see it. Your mother wore a blue dress; she was so vivid beside the older, faded women. She was a lovely girl, but she looked a little pale that day, with dark rings under her eyes. I remember wondering if she was getting

enough sleep. Enid Bascomb was there, in something hideous
and yellow about which we all tried desperately to be polite.
Even Sylvia Tolliver, who is not overblessed with tact. Enid
never had any taste; whatever was newest would do for her, no
matter what it looked like. She suffered a lot in Naples for her
fashion-conscious ways. She's dead now, of course, buried in
the cemetary next to her husband. Julia Eldridge was here as
well that day, and dead now, too. The four of us had our
comings out in the same year; and now only Sylvia and I
remain. Sylvia is very much alive; that kind don't die, they just
stop talking. She came to the teas fairly often, although I
didn't like her at all. Better to hear gossip than to be it, I
always said.

It was a dreadful afternoon; I was still cross from arguing
with Gaston and irritated by a suspicion that he had been right
about the napoleons. And it was *very* hot, and Julia Eldridge
had insisted on bringing Tracey with her, although I had made
it very clear that children were not welcome. No one to watch
them, you see, and too many precious things about; if I looked
away for a moment, Tracey would have put his face, all
smeary with custard, right into the silk sofa cushions. It was
really too much.

Your mother seemed a little nervous; her hands were shaking, and she dropped a napoleon, I remember, onto Papa's
Persian rug. There, right there where that end table is now. It
wasn't her fault; the pastries were that limp in the heat that
they'd fall apart in one's hand. But Beth was very flustered,
and during the fuss of cleaning it up, she got down on the rug,
actually *on her knees,* and Sylvia, who had been in the middle
of telling a story when the incident occurred, said irritably,
'Leave it, for heaven's sake, Gaston will take care of it.'

I fixed her with a cold eye.

"Gaston is not a servant," I said. "He helps me with these
teas out of kindness, that is all."

"Oh," said Sylvia, taken aback by my ferocity, but recover-
ing quickly. "Well, how nice," she said. "Then you won't be
worrying about losing his service, when he marries."

"Gaston marry?" I said, foolishly letting her see that I was
surprised.

"Oh, Sylvia, that's just gossip," said Enid, quickly.

"Not at all," Sylvia told her, pleasantly. "He's been walking
out with Annie for months. The engagement was announced

last week. My Jessie attends the same church." Turning to me, she said, "I thought surely you knew."

This was patently untrue; from the expressions around the room, I could see that everyone else had known, but had taken pains not to mention it to me.

"No," I said. "He would have told me."

"I assure you—" said Sylvia, but I cut her off.

"He would have told me," I said.

There was a little silence, and then someone spoke. It was your mother, and I remember how she looked—she had an expression of pain, almost, as though it were she who'd been done an injury. She looked that way, but her voice was quite gay. All the ladies seized on the new topic immediately, and the conversation went off on that tangent, and the subject of Gaston and his fiancée was dropped.

After the ladies had left, I went into the kitchen, where Ellen was washing up the tea things. She was new, and had to be taught how to handle good china, and not to leave any spots of water to discolor the silver. I happened to notice then that a teaspoon was missing. Eleven instead of twelve; what would my mother have said? It had been her mother's wedding silver. Because of Sylvia Tolliver, and the heat, and Tracey Eldridge, I was immediately, coldly furious.

I brooded about it all that night, my anger swelling to unmanageable proportions, and when Gaston came to visit the next day, I spoke to him about it as though it were his fault. In a sense, I really believed that it was: the old silver wouldn't have come out at all if he hadn't insisted, and if it hadn't come out, one of the spoons wouldn't have been lost. Or stolen; I was not above mentioning that possibility, although I did not exactly accuse Gaston. But I think both of us had the same image when I said the word—how would she have managed it, one of those stiff, respectable ladies? Had she walked out of here with it stuffed into her purse or slipped into her sleeve or the pocket of her skirt? Ridiculous. And why would she have done it? Most of those ladies, their father's old fortunes newly inflated by shrewd investment, could have bought and sold me twice over. It was impossible that any of them should have taken the spoon. Still, I didn't suspect Gaston, not really; I suppose I just wanted him to apologize, as though he'd done something wrong, and then I could have forgiven him, and it would have been over. But I was angry, and I wasn't careful what I said, and we had words, and those words led to more, and—I was really in a vile humor that day—it ended with him stalking out of my house and down the path, while I called after him from the hall, terrible things, things he couldn't even hear, being too far away.

Harsh words, difficult to smooth over. Especially as the spoon turned up the next afternoon. Julia Eldridge brought it to my door, apologizing. She had found Tracey digging with it in the yard. Evidently, the child had taken it while no one was watching.

I swallowed my pride, and went to Gaston, who was still living in his father's house. He let me in without a word, and would not look at me while I explained.

"It was a misunderstanding," I told him. "Nobody's fault, really."

He slid his eyes around to me.

"Nobody's fault," he said.

"That's right," I said.

"That right," he said.

"All right," I said, after the silence had grown too long to bear. "The unpleasantness was my fault. I am so dreadfully sorry, Gaston, I do apologize."

"Accepted," said he, after a moment.

"Then you'll come back?" I asked, humble enough for anything now.

"Well," he said, slowly. "I'll check my appointment schedule." And he laughed, as if the very phrase, used in that insulting way, was not bad enough. I suppose, looking back, that I deserved it, but then I was shocked, and backed away from him. Maybe he just wanted to twit me, and after a moment all would have been forgiven, but I didn't give him a chance: I fled that place, with him still laughing behind me.

He married soon after that, and he and his bride eventually moved into the house he lives in now, one of those ramshackle sorts of houses which used to be fine; you can distinguish them easily from the ones that were built in the old style but recently, meant to mimic a house like my own, which started out however long ago as a truly fine house, and stayed that way. The newer ones have thicker columns holding up their porch roofs, while the old have thinner columns, and they're generally set about with trees. Walnut trees, particularly: they are last to lose their leaves in autumn, and first to gain them back, so that they provide shade more dependably, and longer, than

other trees. An important consideration, for those house build-
ers who planned without benefit of air-conditioning.

Gaston lived down there, and I up here, and we hardly saw
one another at all during the next few years. We passed one
another on the street from time to time, and we'd nod, or
speak very briefly; and I sent a basket over to his wife when
she had Donny. We fell into a habit of distance, as though we
had never been friends; and I gave up all thought of reconcilia-
tion, so that even when the news reached me that Annie had
died with their second child, not even then could I rouse myself to overcome my pride. It was not just pride; it had been
years at that point, you see, years and years; and I didn't know
how to change things. And the Wednesday teas were long finished; I hadn't the heart for them anymore.

And then I had my stroke, and Gaston came back. Of
course I had a nurse, but he guessed that I would prefer his
company. He knew that I'd find helplessness humiliating, and
that it would be easier to bear in the context of friendship. He
got me through the worst of it, and he stopped working so
much down at the store, and we fell back into being together.
Nostalgia, I suppose; no one else that we'd grown up with had
survived so long. He comes here nearly every day, and we keep
each other company.

At first, we expended an awful lot of energy trying to behave
as though nothing had ever happened between us. We were
remarkably awkward with one another, considering that ours
had been a lifelong friendship, and the argument we'd had had
lasted only a few minutes. But we couldn't seem to fall back
into that old comfortable manner; there was always that little
distance between us that wasn't there before. And finally we
gave up trying to recover what we had lost, and accepted the
new way; we learned to live around it, in that way people do
when a new baby has come to disrupt the household, and after
a while it's like it's always been there.

Amazing, that we could be divided, after so much time and
trust, by a little piece of silver. Bent past its original curvature
by a child's ill-use, changed forever by its short flight out of
this house.

But it wasn't about a little piece of silver, twisted and covered with earth when Julia brought it back, as though she had
wanted to bring proof with her. It wasn't about anything you
can hold in your hand or drop on the pavement or forget. It
was about larger things, about the friendship of years dis-

carded in a few moments of temper; it was about a man who had been reared to a higher station than servitude, and about a woman pushing him right down there again, the one woman he might have trusted never to do such a thing. It was about becoming conscious all over again of his blackness, my whiteness, and about being afraid and ashamed. He couldn't forgive me. One afternoon, to change us forever.

I'm tired. I didn't know your mother all that well; there's nothing more that I can tell you. Gaston will see you out.

Chapter Four

Buddy Downtown

What am I doing here? he thought. Listening to an old woman's life story. Sure, it makes for great footage, all that corn-pone stuff, but it's not what I came for.

Maybe he should have asked questions, directed her a little, instead of just letting her talk. But the assignment was pure documentary. And Mr. Szilardi always said, *The best documentary comes out of unexpected places.* Still. All he'd learned from Tess was that his mother went to a couple of tea parties in the fifties and got divorced. And something about a child, Amanda.

Of course, that wasn't all he knew about his mother. He knew where she'd been born (Episcopal Hospital, Naples, Virginia), and where she died (her own living room, Darien, Connecticut), and the real color of her hair, which was a medium honey blonde. She lightened it with a package bleach to the hair color she'd had as a child. She called it "doing my roots," and the two of them had played backgammon while the stuff was on, thirty-five minutes by the kitchen timer, her head wrapped in an old towel, ammonia fumes escaping, her eyes squinting up while she watched the board.

He'd known she was from the South; her voice gave that away. "All of them back home would say I sound like a Yankee now," she told him, when he imitated her. But she didn't say much more about her home, apart from the occasional stories about childhood birthday parties and teenage beauty contests. "I won them all," she'd said, simply, and he'd believed her.

Hard to understand now, why he'd never asked her about herself, why she'd left Virginia, or anything about her first husband, whom she referred to as Old Beerbelly. She'd never volunteered anything about their marriage or divorce. Like most children, Buddy had been self-involved, dimly convinced that his mother had had no other life before his arrival. He'd never thought to press her for information: when he'd asked about grandparents, his mother had said, merely, "They're dead, honey," and he'd accepted it, childish, trusting.

But I'm not a child anymore.

He had been walking, muttering to himself, down the long path which led away from Tess' house, carrying the last load of equipment. He dumped it rather recklessly into the trunk of the car and sat for a minute in the driver's seat, his fingers on the ignition.

He had a theory about secrets: they could do no good. Concealment permitted things to fester, things that would be neutral and sterilized by the open air. Something in his mother had festered, enough to make her insides bubble and churn, enough to make her shoot herself through the forehead, one afternoon not long after Christmas.

She'd left a note. *I love you.* He assumed it was written to him, since his father had been out of town. But he couldn't be sure.

There had been the questions, then, from the female police detective, and Buddy's creeping sense of shame when he knew none of the answers.

"Was she depressed?"

Shrug. Who wasn't, sometimes?

"Did she have—excuse me for this—a boyfriend?"

Not that he knew about. But he was away at college, and his father away a lot on business. She could have filled this house with admirers, and neither of them the wiser.

"I ask these questions," the policewoman had said, putting a gentle hand on Buddy's shoulder, "because we need to be very clear about what happened."

"She shot herself," said Buddy, his first words, strangled sounding.

"How old are you?" the woman had asked then.

"Old enough," Buddy had said, surly.

"I'd guess seventeen," she'd said.

"Eighteen," he corrected.

"Well then," she'd said, and made a place for herself on the step next to him. "We have to be very sure how this happened," she said.

"She pulled the trigger," said Buddy. The detective threw him a sharp look.

"You say yourself that she didn't seem overly depressed," she said in a soft voice. "And—well, it just isn't usual for a woman to do it this way."

"I don't understand." His voice was flat.

The detective sighed. "The gun," she said. "Women usually . . . use . . . pills or poison. Softer methods, which don't always succeed. Your mother's death was . . . unusually violent."

"You're saying she must have really wanted to be dead," he said, raising his eyes to the detective's.

"Son," she said, looking back at him, dead on. "That's exactly what I'm saying."

Violence. What did Buddy know of it, apart from television and the newspapers? When he was eight, the tabby cat had had kittens, six of them in a miracle afternoon, on a pile of old coats in his bedroom closet. He and his mother had counted aloud: three tabbies, two orange, one pure black. "That clinches it," his mother had said, when the first orange one appeared. "Marmalade must have paid us a visit." When the last tabby emerged wetly, his mother looked at it closely. "Honey," she'd said. "This one's sick." He'd looked, and had seen the intestines hanging out like little worms, gathered behind a tough cloudy membrane. "It's going to die," said his mother, softly. "It's crying," said Buddy, horrified. "It's hurting," said his mother. "We can help." He'd looked at her, not sure he understood. "You don't have to watch," she'd said, and waited. "Stop it crying," said Buddy, finally. He'd watched the little jaw opening and closing, the chest heaving, while his mother went away and came back with a bucket of water. "It's warm," she said. "Like a bath."

At the last minute, Buddy had looked away, but then he made himself look back again, in time to see his mother's strong hand in the dimpled water. The kitten was tinier in death.

"I know you're sad," his mother had said, hugging him. "But it's better this way."

"It's not crying anymore," said Buddy.

They buried the kitten in the backyard of that house, and ten years later and many miles away, they buried Buddy's mother. The ceremonies were remarkably similar—simple and sad, only a few mourners, his father and he standing close together, his father weeping as Buddy had done that time before, Buddy propping him up as his mother had done for him when he was eight.

The two of them stayed in the house, rotten now with mourning, while the police crawled over everything and reluctantly pronounced the death a suicide. Buddy hadn't gone back to school for the spring term; he got a job and hung around with his father, until the fall. Then his father had decided to sell the house. "There's a good job in California," he'd said. "I need to get away from here. I'd like you to come with me—you can transfer your credits to a school there, if you like."

California was too far away; Buddy decided to return to college in New York, although he really didn't want to go to school at all. In September, he was in classrooms hating everything. All those heads looking forward at the lecturer, all those hands taking notes, nobody seeming to think about anything. He bumped dismally along in his courses, putting off choosing a major; the only class that interested him at all was the introduction to film, which he'd taken largely because it fit into his schedule. It was different from his other classes: most of the homework was watching movies, and most of the class meetings took place in the screening room, with the chairs in a long row in front of a large blank wall.

After the first screening, Professor Szilardi had snapped on the lights and put a question to his blinking students.

"What did you think of the filmmaker?" he asked.

No response. The students huddled down into their chairs, shy and confused. They were afraid to speak, afraid to be wrong. Buddy huddled down with them, made as blank-minded as they by the most fearsome kind of question—the one with no clear-cut answer.

"I'll tell you what I think," said the professor. "I think he's an asshole."

Asshole. Magic, magic word, spoken by a professor in a college classroom. Buddy, along with some of the other students, sat up a little straighter and looked more closely at Mr. Szilardi, who stood smiling before them. The word had demystified him, and at the same time contributed to his deification. Buddy was entranced, and took out his notebook as the professor began his lecture.

After that, Buddy never skipped Szilardi's class, as he did so many others. He liked everything about it—the mote-ridden darkness, and the way Mr. Szilardi's hands cut through the beams from the projector. He liked the vocabulary of film— *wild sound, focus, candela.* But most of all, he liked its magical property of arranging things, the power it gave to intervene, to splice and resplice until a scene was flawless. Film was about control.

But that's not where you started. According to Szilardi, you started with documentaries, editing scriptless potluck footage into a meaningful whole. "Reality first," he said. "You have to earn your fantasy."

So here he was, filming reality. He had followed Jack up here to Tess's this morning, and now it was past noon, and he had nowhere in mind to go. Still unsure, but feeling restless, he started up the car and pulled away from the curb.

It was a lucky break, wandering into that bar that first night; he'd hit upon a nest of good old boys, drowsing over their beers. They had warmed up to him after a few minutes, and had seemed friendly enough and willing to talk. At first. When he'd tried to pin any of them down to interviews, they'd melted away like spring snow. Shy, he thought. Or maybe stubborn. They didn't hold with all this newfangled equipment. Weird, that one guy with the stutter, how they all acted like they didn't hear it. And he was Jack's brother!

Buddy by now was developing a slight hero-worship of Jack; he found it impossible to believe that Jack and that skinny, stuttering man were brothers. They hardly even looked alike. Well, maybe half brothers, or maybe one adopted.

He had turned from the shady quiet of Tess's street onto another winding avenue; at a stoplight, he turned right, and found himself downtown. The ground was level here, and the streets were white, dazzling; everything looked old but terribly clean. He spotted a sign affixed to the side of a building. NA-PLES HISTORIC PRESERVATION SOCIETY. Buddy had seen the same kind of sign before, during summer vacations in various "rustic" locations in New England. It was a cinch that the committee was nothing more than a dozen serious old ladies and a handful of draggled husbands. They'd come in here and scrubbed and repaired and painted everything, and slapped these signs up so that no one might threaten their hard work with a neon sign or parking lot. Of course, the ladies had done the planning, and the men had gotten up on the ladders and done the work.

He crawled up and down the streets of downtown, which turned out to be four parallel roads, all equally pristine. Buddy, seeing a Village Barbershop and a Village Florist, guessed that this must be what was called "the old village." These folks should see the real Village, he thought to himself, meaning New York. They'd rush back here and call it something else.

He drove in widening circles. As one left the old village, there was an abrupt degeneration, a sudden neglected quality to the buildings. Not historic enough for their troubles, thought Buddy. He had noticed a smallish house with a plaque on its edifice proclaiming it the headquarters of the Historic Committee. He turned back in that direction, and parked.

I like this, he thought, slamming the car door. Park anywhere. What a town.

Inside, the building was cool and institutional. A row of pamphlets poked out from a wooden rack on the wall, just inside the door.

"May I help you?"

He turned. One of the old ladies.

"Yes, please, I want to know more about Naples."

"Well, now, that's what we're here for. Or at least part of why we're here." She wasn't that old, maybe sixty; she had white hair but a curiously unlined face. A giant brooch pinned under her chin bobbed as she talked. "Where are you from?" she asked.

"New York," said Buddy, uncomfortably, feeling like he was lying. Well, he wasn't lying; that was where he lived now; but there was no easy answer to that most common of questions; there never had been.

"If you'd just sign our register here," said the woman, pushing a book toward him. He bent over it, taking up a pen from the desk. "We like to keep track of our visitors," she said, cheerily. She peered at his handwriting. "New York City, well," she said. "I guess that's New York, all right."

Buddy smiled, not sure how to respond.

"I'm Millicent Grass," said the woman, flipping up a small brass name tag attached to the front of her dress. "We have a brand-new pamphlet here," she said, proudly, indicating a glossy stack to the right of the visitors' book. She lowered her voice. "The old one wasn't as good, it left out all kinds of things. I was on the committee that designed this one." She pulled one of the pamphlets toward her, and flipped it open upside down, so that Buddy could read it. "The other one had all the *important* facts, you know, but not all of the *interesting* ones." She set a pink fingernail against a column of text. "For instance, did you know that Naples was completely spared during the War?" She nodded, as though he had expressed disbelief. "It was next in line to be burned," she said, "when the Yankee general was suddenly called to Washington. So a lot of the houses around here are original. You won't see anything like them anywhere else in this part of Virginia. See here, for instance," she said, tapping her nail against a photograph in the pamphlet.

"Uh huh," said Buddy politely. All houses looked much the same to him. True, he'd been impressed with Tess's old house; he hadn't seen anything like it before except in movies. Now, while Mrs. Grass talked on, he compared the mansion of the morning to the brick house in Connecticut, and both of those to his father's ranch-style house in California. He had a glimmer of understanding; but still, he wasn't much interested in the subject.

Mrs. Grass finished her little speech about local architecture, giving a light laugh.

"I *will* go on about Naples," she said. "I haven't even asked you if there's anything specific you need to know." She put her head on one side.

"Well," said Buddy, not sure how to explain. "My mother was born here."

"How nice," she said. "You wouldn't be that young man staying with Jack Corbin, would you?"

Buddy nodded.

"Well, how convenient," she said, beaming. "I'm vice president of the Historic Committee. We were going to send you a letter, but seeing as you're here . . ." Her face dissolved alarmingly from smiling welcome into severity. "We have some pretty strict rules about movie-making in Naples."

"But I'm just—" began Buddy. She ignored him, ticking off on her fingers as she spoke.

"One," she said. "The committee must screen and approve all footage. Two. The committee reserves the right to confiscate and destroy all footage which it deems offensive or inappropriate. Three. The committee may, at any time, withdraw its previous approval. Four. Any revenues—"

"There won't be any revenues," said Buddy.

Mrs. Grass frowned slightly.

"Four," she said.

Buddy capitulated and listened through all of the seven rules. When the woman had finished, she folded her hands on the desk and smiled.

"But this is an independent film," said Buddy. "I'm a student. It's a project for school."

"Oh," said Mrs. Grass, and frowned again. "Well. We don't have any rules about that." Then she brightened. "But maybe we'd like to see it when you're done."

"Of course," said Buddy.

"What else can we do for you?" she asked. "Let's see, you got one of the new pamphlets; would you like to take a look around the museum? It's free of charge. Tours of the historic district are during the week, at eleven and two—"

"I'm interested in talking to people who knew my mother," said Buddy, desperately. "Beth Miller, later Crawford."

"Oh, *yes,*" said Mrs. Grass. "She was Tobacco Queen in forty-seven, wasn't she? My husband remembered her right away. He went to school with her. A few years ahead, of course."

"Maybe I could talk to him," said Buddy.

"Well, now, I don't know how much he could help you," she said.

"But you said he remembered her."

"From the newspaper, of course," said Mrs. Grass. "His family sent him clippings when he was in the war, and even after. They kept him up to date on everything going on in Naples. He's got whole scrapbooks filled with articles about— oh, just everything—swimming contests, the big rain in forty-six, the new mayor who's dead now. Books and books of it. I can't get him to part with them for anything." She mock frowned.

"Did he know her during the fifties?" asked Buddy.

"Who?" she asked.

"My mother."

"Oh, no," said Mrs. Grass. "He went to Norfolk after the war, stayed there for years and years."

"Well, what about you?" asked Buddy. "Would you be willing to give me an interview?"

"Oh, my," said Mrs. Grass, smiling. "Oh, dear." The novelty of the suggestion appeared to occupy her for several moments. "I'd love to help you," she said. "But I'm not a *true* Neapolitan. I only came here twenty years ago. I didn't know your mother at all."

"Oh," said Buddy.

"You know what, though," said Mrs. Grass. "You ought to try Eugene Stubbs, over to the *Chronicle.* He's the one wrote all those articles about your mother. Every time she threw a baton in the air, Gene got out a column about it." She sighed and added, "and Ed pasted it into his scrapbook."

"Where can I find him?" asked Buddy.

"He'll be over there in the *Chronicle* building, I guess," she said, pulling a Xeroxed map from a desk drawer. She made a star on it in ballpoint. "Here we are," she said. "And here's the *Chronicle,* right where Beverley and Vine meet. Gene's office is on the second floor, right at the back."

"Thank you," said Buddy. "I appreciate your help."

"That's what we're here for," she said, reverting to the collective again. She was smiling as he shut the door behind him.

Chapter Five

The Indians

Wednesday was clear but cold, a shiny blue sky with sterile-looking clouds whipped up against it. Joan got up before I did; I lay in bed and listened to her shower noises. When they stopped, I swung my legs out of bed and sat there with my head bowed, my hands on my knees. When Joan had passed by, trailing a whiff of shampoo, I went to take my turn in the bathroom.

I showered quickly and then wiped the steam from the mirror and shaved. Combed my hair, and went into the bedroom to dress.

As I descended the stairs I could hear the characteristic grunting of the percolator. Joan was in the kitchen, setting the breakfast table. I leaned against the pantry door and watched the coffeepot. It whined and groaned and finally rattled silent. I poured out two mugs and set them on the table.

"How's your day look?" I asked Joan.

She seemed surprised at the sound of my voice, as if she had had it on good authority that I was mute.

"Medium," she said. "One or two troublemakers. One college-bound. A parent conference in the afternoon."

"Mmm," I said, into the coffee, turning away. "Do you want to go to the movies tonight?"

She didn't answer. I turned back; she was standing by the stove, looking at me, one hand balancing a wooden spoon against the rim of the skillet.

"Careful," I said. "They're burning."

She turned her attention to the eggs.

"Are you going to talk to him?" she asked.

"Who?" I asked. "Oh. No," I said. "Not if I can help it."

"He's been all over town," she said. "I heard it at school."

"That doesn't mean anything," I said.

"How long is he going to be here?" she asked.

"I don't know," I said. "He's on his spring vacation. Maybe two or three weeks."

"That's a long time," said Joan, slipping toast onto my plate.

"Don't worry," I said. "I'll keep him away."

She nodded, and took her place across from me. Her face was very taut.

"Don't worry," I repeated, reaching across to her, seeking her hand. After a minute, she touched her fingers to mine. "I'll protect us," I told her.

"I know," she said, looking away.

I grew up, for all intents and purposes, in a world of women, a manicured, sweetened, neatened version of the world, all its corners and sharp edges and harshnesses taken away, everything smoothed out, a linen napkin of a childhood. So clean and featureless was it, that when I look back I remember almost nothing in particular, just a general haziness of impressions, the days blurring into one another, until one day I stood nearly full grown at eleven, a man-boy at my mother's graveside, with a wristwatch buckled onto my left wrist and a tie knotted at my neck.

The coffin had been carried by two uncles and some of my father's friends. They walked carefully and slowly, in step like sorrowful soldiers, while my father and Jack and I trailed after, behind us Ellen and her husband, and far behind, the full complement of my mother's friends, plentiful and snuffling. Jack and I walked on either side of our father, who limped from an injury he had gotten in the Great War. The day was wet, and the grass slick, and my father sometimes fell behind, so that Jack and I walked a few steps together, ahead of him. I panicked when this happened, and slowed so that my father would catch up, and come between us again.

Ahead of us lay the grave; and for a moment I stopped breathing, overwhelmed by the depth of it, imagining lying in there myself, and the black earth thrown down on top of me. I worried for my mother, who would lie in there alone, and for myself, for what Jack might do to me if he had the chance, and no one were looking.

Jack and I were separated by four years, a veritable chasm between boys. As children we rarely played together; but on rainy days, confined to the house (meaning Jack hadn't been able to slip outside unnoticed), he went down to the cellar to play, and permitted me to toddle after him. The cellar of our house was unused and damp, a fascinating place with an old-library smell. In generations past, the house kitchen had been located there, but now it held nothing of value. We ventured together into the blackness under the house, and I watched while he played at excavation. He buried bird bones, the remains of the victims of Sammy, the tomcat, in a pile of ash, and then found them again with a flourish. He moved on to other investigations, venturing into the least lit corners to retrieve the damp artifacts of civilizations which had gone before ours, lifting ancient lidless jelly jars from the dust, examining them with scholarly gravity.

I must have been nearly five on the day Jack found the empty barrel, evil and rotting. Somehow he cajoled me into crawling into it, and when I had drawn my legs in, he tipped it back upright. He hung over me, laughing, for a few minutes, and then his face disappeared, and the cellar light went off.

At first, I was not too frightened; the darkness was warm and friendly; I may even have been laughing as he went up the steps. Soon enough, however, I discovered that I was alone, and began to cry. The splintery walls of the barrel rose high above my head; I made vain attempts to climb out, but could not manage it. The monster stories Jack had so obligingly related to me whenever we were alone came rushing back, and I hallucinated fangs, foam, hairy werewolves, all in the barrel with me or approaching the barrel across the cool stone floor, step by step. I whimpered and moaned, my own voice distorting eerily in my little prison, and frightening me the more. Finally, I fell asleep.

I don't know how long I was abandoned there; it may have been less than an hour, but it was certainly more than a few minutes, as my sister and mother had had time to miss me and grow worried. They made a search of the house, and Ellen found me, and lifted me into her arms. I must have been a repellent sight, all mucus and ancient mildew, but she clasped me tightly and kissed me, and took me upstairs to my mother. "Here he is," she said, and my mother's face, which was tightened and strange with anxiety, fell into its soft familiar lines again. "Naughty baby," said my mother. "Worrying us like that." The two of them fussed over me gently. They imagined, I suppose, that I had climbed into the barrel for fun, and had somehow turned it up on end with my weight. I was too young to articulate an indictment of Jack, and so they never knew the truth. They carried me off for a wash; and over my mother's shoulder I spied him, playing with some lead soldiers on the floor. He didn't even look up.

The incident was promptly forgotten within the family, for

when I asked Ellen about it much later, she had no recollection of it. Only I remembered it, and I considered it a watershed experience—it endowed me with the beginnings of a lifelong mistrust, and it introduced me to the concept of mystery. Not whodunit, in this case, but why?

Perhaps it was merely a prank, a feat of nine-year-old irresponsibility; or perhaps Jack was seeking to punish me, for some plaything of his I had destroyed. Perhaps he was jealous of me, something I might have understood better had I ever been an older brother. Or maybe, and this is what I suspect, Jack's motives were truly murderous, and he had hidden me with diabolical purpose, intending that I should never be found.

Jack had no doubt been surprised by my arrival in the first place; and at first, I was clearly useless, a sailor-suited blob who made messes and drooled on himself. But instead of condemning me straight away, he was patient, and held himself off through my infancy, watching with the best of optimistic goodwill to see what I might turn into. When five years—an eternity—had passed, Jack took stock of things. I was still no more than an irritation, worse now than before, because now I was fairly mobile and talkative. The way I see it, Jack, looking me over, said *Right, that's enough,* and went about getting rid of me. Perhaps the barrel incident was his Pilatean crisis, a washing of hands intended to be final.

Jack, for his part, probably gave the matter very little thought. From his point of view, it must have been simple: he had waited on the sidelines for me to reach an interesting age, and when it became clear that I was a failing investment, he did the logical thing and shut me up in a barrel to take my chances. When I reappeared scant hours later, whimpering in the arms of my sister, he accepted my survival with a philosophical shrug. Having done his bit to help the situation, he was well out of it.

Because we shared a bedroom, and could not escape one another entirely, he took it upon himself to be my tormentor. Knowing my tendency to nervousness in the darkness after bedtime, he told me grisly stories (gleaned largely from forbidden comic books), or more usually (which was more cruel), he lay silent in the dark and ignored me when I whispered to him. I listened to his evil tales, rapt and terrified, and suffered from his silences.

Jack, who moved silently through the house and the town,

whose eyes and ears were everywhere, was privy to all kinds of information. He overheard a remark to the effect that I was an unplanned baby, and he gleefully passed the information on to me.

"You know what that means," he said, and paused significantly.

"What?" I breathed.

"They got you from the Indians," said Jack, with all the authority of ignorance. "So you better act right, or they'll give you back."

I was thrilled by the information, and in the way that children will do, I worried over it, embroidering the bare facts Jack had given me with tidbits of my own. I was a resourceful child, working in scraps of *National Geographic* articles melded with Wild West tales; and, piecemeal, the story emerged. Jack's nasty fiction might have been wasted on another child, but I was gullible and literate, with a wide streak of self-pity. At bedtime, forbidden a reading lamp, I told myself about the Indians, and thoroughly frightened myself.

I had been gotten from the Indians in trade, usually for six fine Arabian horses, although when I was sad and feeling diminished, my price was a lone bushel of wheat. I conjured up a sleek-headed, ruddy squaw, my natural mother, who wept as she handed me over. My tribe (bloodthirsty but honorable) rode away into the sunset, leaving me behind. Years later (my imagination supplied a variety of reasons here), having lost patience with the white man, the tribe plotted its revenge, which included a bloody ambush and of course a kidnaping.

I dreamt of their arrival, in soft moccasins and long feathered headdresses, creeping up behind me. Alone in the front yard, I expected at any moment to feel that heavy hand descend upon my shoulder. Turning around, I would look into the face of the chief. He had sharp black eyes in a weathered face; his hair was plaited; he spoke not at all. Or he spoke in chopped imperatives: "Come. Hurry."

I worried about the fearsome manhood rituals which I would be compelled to undergo in order to become a full-fledged member of the tribe. I knew, with heartsick objectivity, that I would not make a good brave: I could not ride bareback or use a bow and arrow or track a deer. Moreover, I was something of a sissy.

From birth, I had been vastly spoilt by my mother and Ellen. If I dropped something, it was instantly gathered up and folded into my fat little fist; if I whined, the women hearkened immediately, my mother stopping her sewing and my sister her reading, to placate me. "What is it, baby?" "What do you want?" They surrounded me, in a fluffy feminine mass, and cooed and coddled. Beyond the tight cluster of my mother and sister, I glimpsed my father's face, longing, almost sorrowful. He couldn't get at me. "Walk to Daddy," they told me. Stumbling, I was whisked away before he reached me, taken up into the loving arms of mother or Ellen. "Don't cry, baby, there's a good boy." Through the mist of their hair, over the soft shapes of their shoulders, I saw my father's long and sun-browned face, distant and unreachable as a mountain peak. Once, at a picnic when I was four, I cried when he held me. My mother scooped me away, scolding. "It's your beard, Jacky," she said. "You swing him too high," reproached Ellen. But, sniffling, back in familiar arms, I knew the truth, which was neither of these but something deeper, far more injurious: I was afraid of my father, who was a stranger to me.

Daily more fearful of the Indians' scorn, I sharpened compensatory skills—I studied the patterns of the stars and learned how to make fire without matches. I developed a hefty self-consciousness, fancying that the Indians were spying on me, secretly appraising my development. I feigned stoicism, performing for them. I was afraid of the Indians, and logically it might have served my ends better if I had tried to appeared so unappetizing that they lost all interest in me, but I knew what Jack hadn't told me: that it didn't matter how I behaved, the Indians would come. They would set terrible trials for me, and if I failed, they would deem me useless and send me off into the plains to die.

The Indians dominated my nightmares and formed my dichotomous self-image (half mama's boy, half tough Indian brave), until I was eight or nine. Then, like all childhood horrors, they faded into the mists, along with other delusions in which I had once firmly believed, like the watermelon that would grow in my stomach if I ate the seeds.

Ellen married when I was nine; and Jack took up residence in her old room on the third floor, while I stayed in the bedroom we had shared, just down the hall from our parents. The new distance was a relief, helping us to avoid one another; and on the infrequent occasions when we were alone together, I was wary. He had tipped his hand, all those years ago, when I was five. He had shown himself to be, at heart, my enemy.

Thenceforward, my life was different from his, as different as though we were growing up in separate families altogether. And so it was that I was spared the normal boy's youth in Naples, a muddy, irreverent life-style, in which Jack indulged heartily, roaming the town in the company of other boys, or with a scruffy, redolent dog, through the farms just outside of town. I was afraid of Henry, Jack's dog (Jack, in an idle moment, had explained that Henry's saliva was highly corrosive), and I didn't get along easily with other boys, tending to want my own way and to cry when I was tackled in a game. Consequently, while Jack took himself off on his boy errands around the neighborhood, wandering far afield and coming in late for supper, sleepy and thickly grimed, I stayed at home, whiling away my time in solitary, tidy play. I occupied myself with any one of dozens of games I had invented to amuse myself, or trailed my mother around the house. Not for me the spitting contests or the fat pink worms harvested from the banks of the flood-swollen river, carried in coffee cans lined with dark river mud. Worms with their moist blind ends nauseated me; I found fishing repugnant; at ten, I could not throw a baseball any distance or intercept one in mid flight without dropping it.

I spent summer days in our front yard, reading, always reading. I had a favorite spot, in the crotch of an apple tree. I took my lunch high into the leaves and lay there from breakfast to supper. Sherlock Holmes was an early favorite; the tales absorbed me, so that, looking up when my mother called, I'd be surprised to see nineteen-thirties Virginia and not, as I'd expected, nineteenth century London. Climbing down, my eyes aching and my head thick, as though stuffed with cotton batting, I'd spy Jack coming in from his forays, river damp and whistling. During wintertime, I watched from the porch while Jack and his comrades stockpiled snowballs, packing them tightly, building a neat pyramid of them, ammunition against the afternoon skirmish. Later, I watched the battle, also from the porch, until a stray snowball caught me on the cheek and chin, drawing blood. I removed myself promptly indoors, where I could observe in safety.

My father remained a dim figure throughout that time, a greying, smoky giant with callused hands, who hardly spoke to me. When he glanced my way, it was always with an expression of bafflement, as if he hadn't any idea what agent had dropped me there, into his living room. He was horrified by the slightest show of affection: at Christmas, he retreated to the furthest corner of the room while presents were being opened, as though in our joy we children might forget ourselves and run to embrace him.

Nonetheless, my father was an important part of Christmas. He made presents for each of us in the privacy of his workshop, and he wrapped them in dull brown paper which contrasted strangely with the gay greens and golds and reds of the wrapping paper both my mother and Santa used. The workshop presents were all the more intriguing for their odd shapes, their brownness. Our other presents were desired but unsurprising, answers to the lists we'd all painstakingly written out at the end of November, but my father never paid attention to these lists, and might have made anything, anything at all. They were slipped under the tree on Christmas Eve, and we were forbidden to touch them. Even though I caught Jack more than once in a trespass—shaking the brown lump with his name pencilled on it vigorously to and fro beside his ear like a maraca—even he never guessed ahead of time what lay within.

One year, my father fashioned for me an ingenious game, comprised of a series of hinged wooden chutes and a little bag of marbles. A marble dropped into a cylinder at the top emerged from a little doorway, and commenced rolling along the first chute, making a slight clicking noise, until at a certain point its weight caused the chute to swing sideways, delivering the marble to the next conduit. There were seven chutes in all, and at the end the marble fell neatly into a little carved cup. It made a terrific noise when it was really going, all seven marbles dropping, all seven chutes swinging out and springing back into place. My father must have worked especially hard at making the toy, for he actually left the room as I was opening it. He slunk back to his chair a few minutes later, while my sister was pulling the wrapping paper away from a new blouse. I was engrossed with the toy, and could hardly be coaxed to attend to the rest of my presents; I lay on my belly playing with it, and as I did so, I thought I saw my father peeking at me from the corners of his eyes.

When I was eleven, my mother died, and the Indians came to get me. Wearing shoes, not moccasins, and normal hats instead of feathers, and in place of the chiseled cruel faces I had expected, their features were familiar. Despite their disguises, I knew them; the hand from my dreams fell upon my shoulder as I stood at the gravesite while the mourners drifted away. I knew before I turned: it was the Indians. It was logical, after all, that they should come now. I steeled myself and turned around, and looked into my father's face. I peered at him, and at my brother Jack behind him, and the delusion which I had carried through my childhood, vague and buried, took its shape. My father and Jack were the Indians, and I would have to go home with them, and live with them forever. Ellen would not protect me; she was going back with her husband to the town they lived in, a hundred miles away. I was beyond her reach now; I was lost, in a foreign wild land, the property of my tribe, who had come to reclaim me after all.

I went with them, to the house which a few hours had changed to a strange place, and we all sat down, all men now, and helpless in the kitchen.

My father, stiff and unrecognizable in his jacket and tie, sat opposite me at the kitchen table and said nothing. He felt around in his pockets for the pipe that wasn't there: I had watched him take it out and leave it by the sugar canister that morning. Finally, he gave up the search and folded his hands together on the bare wood of the table.

"Well, boys," he said.

And that was all he said; he began the reflexive searching once more, then stopped himself again. Jack glided across the room and took down my father's pipe from the shelf where he had tucked it. My father accepted it, but didn't light it right away; he turned it over in his hands, examining it as though he'd never seen it before.

"Well," he said again, and picked up the nail-shaped tool which Jack had placed, along with the pouch of tobacco, on the table before him. He set to cleaning the bowl of the pipe, short, industrious scrapings to loosen the dead tobacco, which he then knocked into the callused cup of his hand and fastidiously transferred to a saucer at his elbow. He packed the pipe anew, tamping down the oily brown shreds with the other end of the reaming tool. He drew out a match and prepared to strike it. But then he didn't; he removed the pipe from his mouth, and cleared his throat. Using the pipe stem as a pointer, he poked it toward the plates and covered dishes ranged along the long table.

"How about supper," he said.

I took this as my cue to unwrap and investigate the various dishes which the womenfolk of the town had left for us.

"Here's stew," I reported. "And yams. And pie. Peach pie, Dad," I said eagerly, "with two crusts, the way—"

Snap. The pipe my father was clutching broke, at the narrowest part of the stem. He held the two pieces for a moment, looking chagrined.

There was a short silence.

"That oughta fix easy," said Jack, edging closer to our father, who looked up at him with a vague, surprised look. Then he looked more closely at the broken pipe in his hand, and gave a little meditative grunt. He set the pieces down on the table and poked them with an index finger, shedding little strands of tobacco across the surface. Then he gathered them up again. Getting up, he seemed to notice us anew.

"I'll just," he explained, and went toward the back door, which led onto the yard. "A minute," he said, opening the screen door, which flapped to behind him.

"He ought to change his clothes," I said. "He'll get glue all over them, or whatever."

"Never mind," said Jack. He looked toward the table. "Near suppertime," he said, and his mouth worked into a tight smile. "I guess it's on you," he said. "Heat something up. If Dad or I tried, like as not we'd burn the house down."

He went toward the door that led into the hallway.

"Gonna get some real clothes on and go out there with him," he said. "Give a holler when it's ready."

"You know you can't hear from way down there," I said. The wood shop was located at the very edge of the property.

"Well, come get us, then."

"No," I said, thinking of my new funeral shoes and the long, slippery walk to the workshop. "Just be back by six."

"Fine," said Jack, but he hesitated in the doorway. "Not the yams," he instructed.

I twitched the cover off an earthenware dish. "Here's some potatoes."

"Good."

"Stew okay?" I asked, like a new wife, greedy for approval.

"That'll be fine," said Jack magnanimously, and swept away, leaving me to my new province. I didn't mind; I was grateful for something to do; there had been too many idle days recently, days spent sitting and waiting, feeling clumsy and distended with grief. I got to work.

I cooked for the three of us for three years, until Jack left for the war, and then I cooked for my father and myself. The first meals were haphazard, poor approximations of my mother's solid Southern fare. The meats were overcooked and the grits gluey, and beneath the credible layer of golden breading, the chicken meat was cold and raw, all of its fascial planes intact, glistening like a traitor under Jack's scornful fork. But I got better with practice, and my first Thanksgiving table was properly laden, a simulacrum of my mother's traditional feast, faithful even to the choice of serving bowls. I had toiled for two days, and had a moment of crisis just at the end, frozen in the kitchen. Had our mother used the wheat-speckled crock? Or maybe it was the one with the blue ring. I narrowed my eyes, trying to remember.

"What's the holdup?" said Jack, coming in.

"Did Mama use that bowl for the potatoes?" I asked.

"Who cares?" he said. "We're starving."

"I can't remember," I said, and to my great shame the tears forced themselves to the very edges of my eyelids and hung against the lashes. I opened my eyes wide, to keep them from spilling down.

"It doesn't matter," Jack said, looking at me closely. He seemed about to say something more, but he didn't; he went over to the table and laid his hand on a bowl. "I think it was this one," he said. "Yep, I'm sure of it."

I nodded, and we stood silent for a moment. I looked at Jack's hand, where it rested on the serving dish.

"Now get those damned potatoes in there and let's eat," he said, taking his hand away.

After Jack went to the war, my father and I took our meals alone, and largely silently, my father out of habit and I because I had developed a stutter, which caused me much humiliation. It came on gradually: at first, my mouth merely lingered overlong on certain sounds. By the time I was thirteen, I had a full-blown speech impediment. Hard consonants gave me the most trouble—*g*'s and *b*'s and *k*'s, and for some reason, also *w*'s. The classroom was particularly embarrassing, so I shut my mouth and studied hard. My father, seeing my struggle, was alarmed into speech.

"Slow down, son," he'd say. "Let your mouth catch up."

Sometimes it helped to slow down, but mostly it didn't. And so I became a silent teenager, given to nods and frowns and gestures, and I spoke very slowly when I spoke at all, and I avoided strangers altogether.

With Jack away, I was left alone with the chief, my father;

we fell into monkish habits, sometimes meeting only twice a day, at breakfast and supper, which I cooked using the ways I had learned from my mother's recipe books. I went to school, and studied, and thought hard about what I might become, and about what I wasn't and about Jack, who was learning to fly an airplane. I read *All Quiet on the Western Front,* and I worried, and I wrote long, informative letters overseas, which Jack answered very infrequently, short narratives so heavily censored as to be meaningless.

Those were quiet years. I kept to myself, having no close male friend and certainly no girlfriend. The only girl I saw regularly, in fact, was Beth Miller, who sometimes took Sunday dinner with us.

Beth was Jack's girlfriend; during wartime, the status of soldiers' girlfriends was elevated somewhat to the realm of quasi-wife, and once a month Beth came to Sunday dinner, and once a year our families exchanged Christmas presents. I hated going over to the Millers' on Christmas afternoon, partly because I sensed Mrs. Miller's dislike of my father and me, and partly because I shrank from large gatherings of any kind. I hung back, away from the holiday chatter, filling my mouth with punch in order to have an excuse not to talk.

My father liked going to the Millers'. He liked the jolly decorations and the noise, and he thought the house grand, even while he detested the furniture. I couldn't understand how he could fail to interpret Lucy Miller's disdainful glances at his hard, scarred hands, and I gritted my teeth when she spoke to him, raising her voice just slightly and enunciating every syllable, as though he were feeble minded. The Millers had no real right to scoff at us: both families had been working class for generations, constituting part of the good, solid Naples stock that had introduced industry to the town during the last century. But Beth's father wore a tie to work, and Lucy Miller had a cook *and* a maid, and hobnobbed with members of the country club. The Millers were nouveau riche, a relative rarity in a town that didn't offer too much in the way of social mobility. Lucy Miller had done it, though: she had moved up, initially through circumstance and subsequently by design.

Daughter of a highway worker, she had done the usual thing and got engaged at seventeen to an eminently passive man with a steady income. She had her bridal shower and her church wedding, and then settled down to boss her husband the rest of her life. Dale Miller surprised us all, though, show-

ing a real aptitude for his work, rising swiftly through the
ranks of his company, until one morning Lucy Miller née Stur-
gill, twenty-eight, awoke to find herself a vice-president's wife
and a candidate for membership at the country club. In short,
a Somebody.

Lucy, whatever she was, was not stupid. From her new
perch in the airy regions of Naples she took a hard look at her
husband's colleagues, realizing quickly that there was a tendency for able men to rise only so high in the hierarchy, but no
higher; clearly, ability was not enough for advancement. More
was needed, it seemed, to carry a man beyond that invisible
ceiling. With a canny eye, Lucy Miller reckoned the possibilities, and determined not to languish in executive limbo, she set
out to be the perfect company wife. She began by scrutinizing
the other wives, dissecting their characters ruthlessly, adopting
what she admired, discarding the rest.

At first, they say, she was a snob only by association, still
unpretentious and close to her old friends. But around the
time that her daughter turned five, Lucy Miller began to
change. Perhaps it was too much for her: one day making her
last year's coat do for another season, the next dining off country club china. Perhaps it was overwhelming maternal instinct,
to provide her child with all that she herself had never had.
Perhaps the temptation was simply too great: seeing elegance
so near, she strained at it and lost her balance. Whatever the
reason, Lucy Miller became irrational in her ambition. In a
town where memories are long, she tried to deny her background, delicately pruning her family tree, sanitizing its history, to remove all traces of sweat. She broadened her *A*s and
dropped her *R*s, until she sounded strange, like the women in
the movies. Worst of all, she snubbed her old friends, who
would have withstood almost any amount of highfalutin behavior but who wouldn't tolerate being cut dead on the street.
They abandoned her; and she found few friends to replace
them. The country-club set wasn't stupid, either; they'd seen a
few Lucy Millers over the years; they bore her presence, and
that was all. And so she bounced friendless between the two
strata, all through Beth's childhood.

She set goals for herself, like the athlete who divides up his
long-distance run, so that he might triumph all along the
course. Most of her campaigns concerned Beth, and one of the
earliest involved the female seminary. Lucy was determined to
have her daughter admitted there, and for a time she devoted

every ounce of her energy to the cause. When finally she succeeded—after scraping acquaintance with one of the more approachable society matrons, after countless prim teas, after leaving her calling card at one esteemed lady's home *six times* before receiving a return call—after all that, Beth pursed her miniature lips and said no.

Everyone heard the story: how Lucy went into her daughter's room on the first day of school, all a-twitter; how she found nine-year-old Beth neatly combed and dressed, seated on the edge of her bed, surrounded by the remains of the navy uniform she had calmly cut to pieces minutes before. (She had gotten up early to do it, Beth told me years later.) A forty-dollar pinafore, ruined; and all of Beth's chances at an exclusive private education ruined with it. It is said that, seeing her dreams reduced to an armful of scratchy serge strips strewn across a counterpane, Lucy Miller bowed her head and wept. It is said that an hour later, she was still clutching some of the scraps in white fists. It is known that she lost her temper and that her voice rose harshly, a fishwife's harangue ringing out in the neighborhood of the hill. She raved for thirty solid minutes, while her daughter sat immovable on the edge of the bed, the storm raging around her. It was an event not soon forgotten, the topic on everyone's lips for a week. Some said Lucy Miller deserved her comeuppance, and maybe it'd teach her not to scoff at her own family. Some clucked their tongues at the little girl's insolence and the waste of good cloth. Everyone had an opinion; and the outcome of it all was that Beth put on one of her regular dresses and came to public school with the rest of us.

Beth Miller, whose reputation was thus ensured before she was ten, grew into something of a town sensation. A popular girl, and an intelligent one; the two don't always coincide. Early, the boys began to follow her around, hoping to gain her favor; and the girls strained after her, copying her hairstyle, her dress, her gestures. She was a beautiful, airy thing, descending from the white stone porch of her mother's house each morning and floating ahead of me on the walk to school. She was unreal, and she was Something, and that was all I ever knew about her, until she started dating Jack.

The liaison made perfect sense: Jack was the football star, and Beth his natural partner. They seemed intended for each other; a haze of excellence surrounded them as they walked through the shabby corridors of the school building. Even the most devoted of Beth's suitors gave up the chase after a while, seeing how the two belonged together.

Lucy Miller, who had sacrificed a great deal so that her daughter might shun families like ours, was furious. She expressed her anger through gossip, and the unholy alliance lifted the Corbins out of the swell of untouchables. Soon it was my own name about which I heard sly mutterings at the butcher's, and it was about my father that dark rumors began to pass, concerning my mother's death and what *really* went on in that secluded little workshop where Jacky Corbin spent so much of his time. My father was, of course, oblivious; but each Saturday at the market, handing my usual list across to Dean Purdy and waiting in silence for him to fill it, I suffered the tide of whispers. *Can't even talk—idiot—poor Angela, you know, the grief of it killed her.*

It lasted only a little while: then Lucy Miller seemed to appreciate the misdirection of her efforts, and she took the campaign home. She lectured Beth at length; there was no effect. She forbade Beth from dating Jack, and beamed upon the dull acceptable boy who came to call that night at eight o'clock. After they had gone, Lucy Miller looked out of her upstairs window in time to see Beth, now joined by a shadow sauntering down the middle of the street, part from the acceptable boy and bid him good night. She then forbade her daughter from dating at all, and to reinforce her words, she locked Beth in her bedroom at night. Soon, tales were flying around Naples about Beth Miller, past midnight, climbing up the trellis outside her bedroom window and making so much noise that Lucy Miller thought it was a burglar and had Dale up and actually loading his rifle before the truth was discovered. She grounded Beth for a week; and almost immediately we heard how Beth was found swimming in the moonlit quarry, clad only in her slip, and more: how two days later Lucy Miller's front doorbell rang at 3 A.M., and when she opened it there was Beth, plucked from who knew where, grinning, and an apologetic Luther Coggswell, Chief of Police. No doubt about it, it was a mother-daughter war, and gossip the spoils. The girl's trespasses grew more flagrant, and the mother's punishments more severe, until at last she threatened to pull Beth out of school entirely. News of this reached the ears of the vice principal, a most conscientious man, who took it upon himself to visit the Millers one evening.

Dale Miller, who had been a neutral participant in the con-

flict, hearing words he didn't understand—*minor child* and
endangerment—merely gaped at the vice principal, who sighed
and explained it all over again from the beginning. Finally
comprehending something *(jail time)* Dale Miller came to life.
Under his wife's astonished eye, he got to his feet, still holding
his *Chronicle*. "I don't see what's so bad about that boy," he
said to his wife, and held up his hand as she began to speak.
He turned to Beth. "He's quarterback, isn't he?" he said. She
nodded. "Well, then," said Dale firmly, sitting down again, in
a rush of newsprint. The vice principal went away; the matter
was settled.

Her hands tied, Lucy Miller turned to her country-club
friends for advice. They, deeply immune to the glamour of
athletes, pooh-poohed the romance.

"They all do it," they yawned. "You ought to have seen
what Teddy brought home to dinner when *he* was sixteen.
Don't worry, dear."

Coming back to her house after these conversations, Lucy
Miller was soothed, her equilibrium restored. She would call
for some iced tea and settle into a chair with the interesting
bits of the newspaper, and read about engagements and weddings with a new, more hopeful eye. How it must have
tweaked her then, in her hour of fragile optimism, to hear
Beth's voice at the front door, in concert with Jack's. *He* had
walked her home from school again. Reality came back to
Lucy Miller in a tumbling rush; she threw aside the society
page, and for the rest of the day she was short with the maid
and snappish with the cook.

The war must have seemed like salvation to Lucy Miller. No
doubt she prayed daily for Jack's untimely death. Instead of
obliging, however, Jack got himself wounded; and after the
telegram came, transforming Jack to a hero, Lucy Miller
found herself in a hard place. President of the War Woollens
Ladies' Association, Treasurer of the Shirts for Soldiers Committee, personal holder of three war bonds, Lucy Miller found
her patriotism challenged. It wasn't fair; she hated Hitler as
much as the next person—but probably she hated Jack more.
Lucy Miller set her teeth in an American smile and suffered
the alliance with our family. She sent us a gold star for our
front window and began nodding to me on the street.

I learned all this about her only years after the fact; most of
it Beth told me, some of it I reconstructed for myself. It is easy
now to feel some sympathy for Lucy Miller, bound so tightly

by the fetters she had woven for herself; but at fourteen I hated her, with her yellow teeth and yellowed hair, her false light voice curling out of her mouth like an adder's tongue. I hated her house, built of prosperous brick in the Greek Revival style, set at the foot of the hilltop where the old homes were, as though it was trying to nudge its way closer to greatness. I hated her tiny glass punch cups, and the bad eggnog she served, measly with the bourbon; I hated the intricate, unidentifiable hors d'oeuvres and the cleverly molded pâtés. I hated her, and I felt guilty, because her husband seemed like a nice man, and Beth was another thing altogether.

I'd met Beth only twice in all the time she'd been dating Jack, and neither time had I spoken a word. I saw them mostly from afar, from crowded football stands or across the schoolyard. They were always surrounded, but always a little apart from the others, two golden people, the rest standing aside to give them room. Then Jack was called up, and got wounded, and Beth began eating one in four Sunday dinners with us, and I got to know her better.

At first, the afternoons she spent with my father and me were silent ones. I prepared the meals in mounting anxiety, and served them out with a kind of fatalism. While we ate, I sneaked glances at her from time to time; once, she caught me looking, and smiled. She seemed entirely at ease; and she didn't batter us with conversation right away. It wasn't until the third Sunday that she began working on us, beginning with my father. Somehow, she inveigled him into showing her his workshop. It was a tremendous achievement: no woman had set foot in that hallowed space for many years. But she managed it, with short careful comments and a flattering display of interest, and suddenly we were all trooping out the back door, past the tangled weeds which had grown up to choke my mother's vegetable garden. Down the path of smooth stones, now slippery with moss; past the rose bushes and the old outhouse. Here were real tangles, an honest wilderness, the weeds growing so high and thick that they were no longer weeds but vines and trees, weaving together into a dense, moist jungle. My father and I knew our way in the dark, but I had condescended to bring a flashlight for Beth. The round beam bobbed from leaf to bramble as we trudged on the rest of the way, right down to the bottom of the hill, a good half mile from the house.

The land out back had been a source of mild but constant

struggle within my family for generations. In my great-grand-parents' day, it had been part of a self-sufficient farm; but their only son, my grandfather, was a reluctant earth worker. He finally sold off some of the land and invested the profits; with the regular dividend and the remaining crops, he lived out his life in ease. My father, for his part, resisted farming altogether, taking a job with the railroad and telling the land to go to hell, which it did, quickly and completely. He settled into his ways, working long hours and going in the evenings to the workshop where he spent his leisure time. He married late, a sweet young bride, my mother; I am sure he expected no opposition from her on any subject. But in her first spring-clean she came across an old map of the property and realized for the first time just how large it was. She dusted off the map, and con-fronted my father with it, setting forth her opinions. She wanted to clear the land, and right away; she had visions of an English-style garden, with winding paths and maybe a box-wood maze.

My father listened to her proposal; he was agreeable, or at least not disagreeable, until she pointed to a spot on the map, saying, "And here's where we'll put the fountain."

"That's my workshop," protested my father.

"It'll be perfect for a fountain," said my mother. "Move your old woodshop."

This he would not do; and so they came to an impasse, at which they remained for the next fifteen years. My sister, El-len, remembers them arguing about it constantly, particularly over breakfast. By that time, it was part of their daily routine, and there was little animosity to it. It took up most of the mealtime conversation, Ellen says, our mother cheerily threat-ening to knock the workshop down herself while my father was at work, and my father saying nothing, clearing his throat from time to time and nodding when he wanted more coffee.

It was Jack who stopped it. As the story goes, he was five or six and had been in disgrace from the day before, after hitting Tommy Simmons on the head as he was reaching for the last oatmeal cookie. My mother had, quite properly, given Jack a stern lecture on sharing and had confined him to his room until he offered to apologize. When he refused, she let him come to supper, but sent him from the table without dessert. On the famous morning, she greeted him with a kiss and a reminder that he was to apologize to Tommy today, and no more nonsense. Then my father came to the table, and after

some minor preliminaries, they settled down to it. After a few
minutes Jack looked up from his plate, and fixing his eyes on
my mother, intoned piously: "Isn't it more blessed to give than
to receive?" He had it word perfect from my mother's lecture
of the evening before, and she, her hypocrisy exposed, fell silent. Then, Ellen says, they all began to laugh. All except Jack,
who reached for another piece of toast. "Out of the mouth of
babes," said my father. So you might say Jack shamed them
into it.

My mother's half lay right behind the house. She tended it
carefully, putting in a large vegetable patch and a flower border. We ate tomatoes and corn, green peppers and snap beans,
all from her neat fenced-off rows. She had not given up entirely on her morsel of English countryside: down at the bottom of the gentle slope which began just beyond the vegetables, she put in a row of rosebushes and a white stone birdbath.

Just the other side of the roses, my father's half began; he
strolled right past my mother, pruning and weeding, and never
cut back so much as a tendril on his side. In the summer, while
my mother's crops grew tamely taller and her bushes flared
red with heavy blossoms, my father's half of the property sim-
mered and seethed with growth. While the bees buzzed drunk-
enly among the roses, while the birds played sedately in their
bath, just yards away all manner of creatures jostled for niches
in the ecology. My father did nothing to disturb them; he
walked the long walk daily from the house down to the workshop. It was a small cabin really, perhaps part of a slave quarters left from a long-ago plantation; it had rough floors and a
fireplace at one end, and my father had had power lines run
out there, so that he could plug in his electrical saws. He spent
all of his leisure time there, merely passing through the rest of
the property on the way. In a few years, his half of the land
was sheer rainforest, and my mother worried aloud that something unusual might emerge from it and strike us all down.

Even when walking straight toward the workshop, it was
difficult to see it. It was backed by a sluggish stream which
separated the border of our land from a neighboring farm.
From our neighbor's side, not even the outline of the cabin
showed; and there was no approach to it other than the thin
path my father took each day, overgrown with slapping
branches.

In the darkness, the journey was indescribable, a kind of
descent into Hades, and I watched Beth for signs of nervous-

ness as we went along. But she seemed quite unperturbed, parting branches and waving away the clouds of gnats which hung at eye level. She stepped along gamely, and when a snake slithered across her path she didn't shrink, but simply placed her foot neatly to the right of it, and moved on.

We reached the workshop, my father leading. He fiddled with the lock on the door (near Christmas or Jack's birthday, the padlock which was usually left hanging was snapped into place. It was inappropriate now; Jack would soon be having a birthday, but not here).

"Well," said my father, stepping across the threshhold, and turning on the light.

Beth looked a little dazed by the coziness and cleanliness of the place, always so much more impressive after that wild trek. I sat on a bench to one side of the room, and Beth stood where she was, suddenly shy, waiting to be offered a seat. My father rooted through odds and ends on the shelves lining the walls. After a few minutes, he found what he was after.

"Close your eyes," he said, gruffly, intending to be playful. He set the thing he had found, which looked to be a kind of complicated box, down before her. "Okay, open," he said.

For a moment she just stood looking in silence.

"It's beautiful," she said at last, and he recognized the sincerity in her voice and smiled.

"This joint here give me a pack of trouble," he said, taking the object and beckoning her closer.

They were there for hours; I watched for a while in amazement as my father, ordinarily so secretive about his projects, outlined his works in progress, speaking in paragraphs, he who had hardly spoken more than two sentences together in the time I'd known him. They ignored me; and after a while I crept away, leaving them there, past their fit of shyness, Beth perched on a high stool with a bulb swinging over her head, looking on as my father riffled through a sheaf of drawings, looking for "that tricky carving job, wood so soft I used a toothpick in places." She had done the impossible: she had drawn him out. And now she set her sights on me.

She arrived without warning one early summer afternoon, and wheedled me down from my apple tree, to walk with her. I was startled at first, absorbed in my book, but I closed it and slid down, pretending reluctance. It was a fair day, with something of a breeze; we walked east through the high summer pastureland, toward the mountains. She talked and I listened, pulling up a weed here and there as we went along, and shredding it into bits with my hands. I was shy, and filled with nervousness, but also with an intense pride: she was Beth Miller, after all, the prettiest girl in town, and she was dating my brother, Jack, who had been the high-school football star and who was now a pilot and a war hero, everything I was not, and could never be. I sighed, walking alongside her; and if she heard me, she didn't let on.

We spent many afternoons together after that—I could never resist her summons from the foot of my apple tree—and eventually she tamed me, as she had tamed my father before me. I watched her do it, with a kind of helpless fascination; and I even participated a little, breaking tentatively through my insulation, like a chick giving the first taps on the inside of its egg. I was a most painful fourteen, and she at sixteen seemed much older; I was charmed and baffled by her, who certainly had no lack of company and yet incredibly sought mine. But familiarity wore her glamour through, and after a time, I was more comfortable with her than I'd ever been with anyone.

We talked mostly about random things, the books I was reading, and people from school, and the parties she was going to. Only occasionally did we mention the war, and then only in a general way. I would have talked about it endlessly, my head being filled with it, but Beth frowned when I mentioned battles or weapons. And we rarely talked about Jack; when she spoke his name I felt assaulted, as though a stranger had slipped into our company and put a coldness between us.

"Look at that," said Beth, one day in August. I looked where she pointed, but saw only a bird. "Imagine being so free," she said. "You could go anywhere you want."

"Who," I said, "wants to go anywhere?"

She looked surprised. "It's natural to wander," she said.

"No, it isn't, either," I told her. "Birds build themselves a nest, and stay to it."

"They go south every year," she argued.

"But they," I said, "come back."

"I'd like to try that," said Beth, watching another bird. "Maybe I'll get me an airplane, paint it yellow."

"You can't," I said, shocked.

"Why not?" she asked. "But I'll bet it isn't as pretty as being a bird, though. I bet once you get up in one of them things, there's just a whole lot of rattling and shaking and wind flying in your face. I bet it's not pretty at all."

"Huh," I said, derisively, but I had an uneasy feeling that she might be right.

"I'd still like to try it, though," she said. "I'd fly right over this little town. I wouldn't even wave."

"Shows," I said, "what you know. You don't," I said, "wave. You dip the," I took up a blade of grass, bent it back and forth. "Wings."

"Whatever," she said, carelessly. "I'd dip my wings, and go right on by." She thought for a minute. "I bet everything is different from up there. I bet I wouldn't even recognize Naples from up there."

I said nothing.

"Hell, I bet you wouldn't even know there's a town here," she said. "Especially in the dark." She stopped, struck by something. "How *do* people fly in the dark?" she asked me.

"Same," I paused, and watched the birds, "way they drive in the dark," I said finally.

"But there's no streetlights up there, or anything."

I thought about what I'd heard about pilots sitting in a dark room for half an hour before flying, to get their eyes accustomed to dim light; I thought about the simulated horizon on the control panel of an airplane; I thought these things, with a kind of despair; I didn't say them.

"Training," was what I said.

We walked along for a while, and I knew that in a minute she'd be talking again of parties or telling me some gossip about people I didn't even know. She had given me an opening, with all her talk about flying. It was August tenth, the day after Nagasaki; so far we had carefully avoided the subject, but I could hold back no longer.

"You," I said. "Watch. It won't be long now."

"I wonder what it would be like," said Beth, turning her clear light eyes upon me, "to live in Nagasaki?"

"Nobody lives there now," I said.

"I mean, before," she said. "I bet it was a place just like here, and then they dropped a bomb on it, and now it's gone."

"We dropped the bomb," I reminded her.

"I didn't," she said.

"*We* did," I insisted. "America. We dropped it, and I bet," I said. "We win the war."

"Sneaky way to win," said Beth. "Dropping bombs on little towns."

"They'da done the same thing," I said.

"That's a good reason," she said, scornfully.

I said nothing, frustrated.

"I wonder what the plane looked like?" she mused, and seeing my exasperated expression, added, "I mean, they might have thought it was one of theirs. I saw Mrs. Jenkins hanging out washing one day, and she waved when a plane went over."

"Her Ralph's over there," I said.

"Imagine, hanging out washing, and looking up and waving, and then the bomb falling."

"They don't hang out washing in Japan," I said.

"How do you know?" she returned.

I didn't, and so abandoned this point and seized upon the other. "Well, they wouldn't have," I said, "waved. Don't you know anything? The planes are different." I knew that Beth had been in the school auditorium last year when the fellow came to lecture us on civil defense. He'd shone a lantern at the ceiling and projected the silhouettes of American planes, pointing out their distinguishing characteristics, contrasting them with the shapes of the enemy. Beth often seemed to forget such things, conveniently. "They have different markings, even," I told her. "Different colors."

"So if I saw a plane, I could tell it was Jack, and not the Japanese?" asked Beth, seeming interested.

"Of course," I said. I explained how she'd be able to tell them apart. Encouraged by her attention, I elaborated, describing the body style of Jack's plane, and the markings on its wings, for all the world as though I were preparing her for a crucial and certain event.

Beth was looking at me strangely.

"What?" I said.

"Nothing," she said, beginning to smile. "Only, you said all that real clearly. You've been talking regular, all this time."

I blushed. I didn't like my stutter to be referred to in any way.

"Don't be embarrassed," she said, very kindly. "It's wonderful. Did you hear yourself?"

Oddly enough, I hadn't; the stutter had slipped from my tongue as easily as a loop of thread; I had lost it somehow.

"Peter piper," said Beth.

"How much wood can a wood chuck chuck," I said, flushed now with exultation. "She sells sea swells."

"I can't do that one either," said Beth, laughing.

Those months stand out in my memory, a time of clarity and release. I felt like a debutante must, being presented entire to the world; I, too, had my "season."

The news came: first a telegram, and then a telephone call. Jack was coming home. I made a special supper, but of course he came earlier than expected, walking into the kitchen while Beth and I were bickering over the cornbread. One minute, we were there alone, and she was grabbing the wooden spoon from me, and the next he was there behind her, shorter than I remembered. I shook his hand while Beth hung laughing first on one of us and then the other. Later, I had my first grown-up drink; and when I got up the next morning, my tongue felt thick in a head pounding from whisky, and my fluency was gone. I stuttered again: not so badly as before, and mostly with strangers, but it was a disappointment.

I fell back on my old tricks, the circuitous replacement phrases, the hand gestures, the facial expressions. Some days, the handicap remitted again miraculously, and I allowed myself to fantasize that it was gone forever; but it always returned, with a kind of maddening suddenness. I would withdraw abruptly and try not to speak at all, while Jack and my father filled the house with their own wordlessness. The three of us had that one thing in common; we became known in Naples as "still folk."

We who had been left behind had spent the years like clams in a stream, greedily filtering from the newspapers all we could of the great events abroad. We had deprived ourselves gladly for the Cause; we had clapped our neighbors on the back, and sent them away to die. It had seemed that it would never end, but it ended, and we emerged on the other side thinner, newly cynical. War had changed us. But Jack, who had been at its very center, who had been *there,* had changed very little. His injury had healed completely, not even gracing him with a limp. He seemed exactly the same age, even, as when he had left. He took a job working for Pollard's garage, and he settled into his old bedroom on the third floor. His uniform he hung at the back of his closet; he hadn't brought back any souvenirs. Was it possible, I wondered, not to have changed at all? and I watched him. I detected only slight differences. The old mocking light which had burned steadily at the backs of his eyes was gone, replaced by a new wariness. He rarely joked now, and he rarely laughed at the jokes of others. He seemed at once more careless and more serious, shrugging off things others agonized over, yet grave at times when the rest of us were laughing. His most extreme expression was a sardonic smile, which whispered weakly at his lips, while his eyes remained cold and measuring, as though he were thinking: *I could tell you all a thing or two.*

This was the postwar Jack: only slightly less cocky, slightly more tolerant, than before. War had taken his sense of humor, but then it had been rudimentary to start with. War, I concluded, was nothing much.

He and Beth took up where they left off, and there were no more afternoon walks. I had a close friend at school now, a weedy soft boy with the unlikely name of Montgomery Twipp, whose twin interests were poetry and chess. He taught me the game, and together we brooded over the wooden board, my moves halting and half thought out, his sure and brilliant. He defeated me again and again, but I wasn't bothered by the losses, having no deep interest in the game. The poetry appealed to me more. I went to the library in the morning before my first class, darting down the poetry aisle and making my selections hastily. Checking them out, I scanned the room, shifting from one foot to the other impatiently. I hid the thin volumes among the thicker, legitimate school texts I carried, and secretly I brooded over them, thrilling to the language of the dead romantics, and committing great stretches to memory.

Autumn found me back in the now-blazing arms of the apple tree, drowsing over books, or furrow browed over the chessboard, across from Monty. Sometimes, in the distance, I saw them, walking slowly down the lane that ran behind Worth Street. She wore sweaters lightly tossed over her shoulders, wonderful misty things in powder blue or yellow; he wore his old football jacket, his hands shoved into the pockets. He slouched along, while she gestured and chattered, filling up the space between them.

Wartime, the summer just past, my briefly loosened tongue, all seemed far away. Beth in the company of Jack was a different person; and when I looked at them together, the poetry died on my lips, the chessmen stood frozen and inglorious. This was the real thing, then, the two of them. It was the

Warrior Returned, and all that went with it: love and the passion of victory, and in its presence, all of my hapless pursuits turned wooden, the stuff of boyhood.

They dawdled along, while I watched them. Beth took my brother's arm and held it, looking up at him with a new shining expression. I saw it, and felt the first stabbing emotion I would ever feel about a woman. It was ridiculous, and I tried to deny it to myself, but it was too powerful. It hunted me down, followed me into bed at night, and whispered at me. I lay, temples throbbing, and confessed it. I was jealous.

Chapter Six

The Ladies' Page

Sure, I remember your mama. Even mooned around her the way all the boys did. I was older than her by some years, but I acted as much of an idiot as anyone else. It was hopeless, acourse—she only had eyes for Jack Corbin then, and him a fighter pilot in the war, and put the rest of us to shame. I was 4-F, something about my heart, although I never had any trouble with it, not before or since. You could have knocked me over with a feather when the doc stood up from listening to my chest and shook his head. He said I had a murmur, and if that's so, I'd like to tell you now I never heard it. I made him listen again, but I still went down 4-F, and sat the war out, feeling sorry for myself.

"I'd got married right out of school, with never a thought of how I was going to support us. I thought I was going to war, you see. And though *she* was tickled when it came out I wasn't going, I felt kind of stranded—married, no job, and sidelined to boot. I didn't even have an idea what I might want to do with myself. My dad, he worked over to the State Correctional Center, as a guard. All I knew was I didn't want to do *that*. So when my cousin Ernie suggested I come down here, I sort of drifted on over, not thinking too much about it. I had a kind of inflated idea of what reporters did, I guess from reading the funny pages and looking at movies. You know that old one, *His Girl Friday*? I figured everybody was Cary Grant and all the girls looked like Rosalind Russell. I didn't know damn-all.

I didn't think I'd get the job; I hadn't done any too well in school. But I could read and write, and I guess that's all they were asking. There were jobs going begging then, every American boy off defending his country. I talked to the old editor himself, that's John D., retired fifteen years ago, dead a year later. Story goes he died of boredom; they say retirement'll do that to you. I'm nearly there myself, but I keep a hand in. I'm not ready to go yet.

I presented myself to old John dressed in the only suit I owned, the same one I got married in.

"It so happens," he told me, "we got a place open." I knew

he meant that someone had gone off to fight and left a space. I felt a little like a grave robber, lying down in someone else's bed while it was still warm. 'Can you type?' he asked.

"Nossir," I said.

"Take shorthand?"

"Nossir," I said. I wasn't even sure what that was.

"Make coffee?"

"Yessir," I said.

I was hired, then and there.

At first, it wasn't much; I kind of filled in wherever there was a gap, running copy back and forth, general office-boy stuff. I was waiting for the Big Break. Sure enough, one day it came.

Fred Wiggins, second cousin to me by marriage, worked in the features department. What we used to call the Ladies' Page. I brought him some coffee one morning; he was looking fierce, and I made to leave, real quiet, so he wouldn't take my head off, the way he did.

"Wait," he said, when I had my hand on the doorknob. "Who're you?"

"Gene Stubbs," I told him. I didn't think it was the right time to point out that I'd been bringing him his coffee for two months.

"Essie's boy?" he said, kinda raring back in his chair to look me over.

"Yessir," I said.

"You ever done any reporting?" he asked.

"Nossir," I said, and then took a chance. "But I'd like to try."

"Oh, you'd like to try, would you?" Real sarcastic. He took a piece of paper and scribbled on it. "Here," he said, giving it to me.

I took it; he'd written a street address, over on the hilltop. I stood there, waiting for more instructions, but he'd put his head down again and had set to slamming some papers around on his desk.

Finally, he looked up.

"What the bleeding hell are you still doing here?" he asked. I remember his words exactly; they kind of impressed me, at the time. Before I could say anything, he said, impatient-like, "You want to do some reporting, so report. Go."

"Sir," I said. "What's it about, sir?" He really scared me, kin or no. And he scared me even more when he smiled; it was kind of a tense smile, like his face was being stretched without his permission.

"It's a hot news tip," he said. "Take a pad and pencil."

What it was was a flower show. My first story. I didn't know tube roses from begonias then, boy, but I sure did after that day. I saw enough flowers to fill a funeral home, and then some. The stink of them got together and clogged up my nose; I was sneezing the whole time I typed the mess up, and that was a time, let me tell you, with two fingers. I handed the story over to Fred, eight whole pages of crap about daffodils, and made to leave. Again, he stopped me, before I could go.

"Stubbs," he said. "How was it?" He seemed friendlier this time; hard to tell, but I took a chance.

"It was sure as hell fragrant," I said. "Sir."

"Fragrant," he repeated. "Damn, I'll bet it was." Then he said, serious, "You still want to be a reporter?"

"Yessir," I said, although I really wasn't sure anymore.

"Wal," said he, leaning back in his chair. "I know you probably have a lot of ideas about what reporting is like. But this is the Ladies' Page, Stubbs. Don't get me wrong," he said, bringing his chair back down with a thump. "We have our share of events. We cover a lot of ground. This town and two others besides. And you'd be amazed what the ladies get up to." He laid his skinny forearms across the desk. "It's more complicated than you think," he said. "Sometimes, we have to dress things up a little. Gloss over some things. This ain't a scandal sheet." He looked at me like I might disagree. "We do a real service here," he said, tapping my copy. "More ladies read the *Chronicle* than men. Bet you didn't know that," he said.

"Nossir," I said.

"Well, it's true," he said. "And we owe them something. They don't want to read about the war. War—they hear enough about that. They don't want to read about the president, and they sure as hell don't want to read about Hitler. They want the bright stuff, what's happening right here, what their neighbors have been up to, who's having a baby. *That's* their news, son, and by God we give it to them." He was breathing hard now. "We even got a few ladies right here on staff," he said, "and what do I see them reading on their coffee break?" I shook my head. "Not the *news*," he said, with a sneer. "Not the baseball scores. They're reading our page, our page before any other. If they are, so're the other women out there. Times are changing," he said, sitting up straight again. "Times are changing," he repeated, "and the *Chronicle* will change with them. Soon this department will be a real action spot." He looked at me real sharp, like maybe he thought I was laughing. "Not that it ain't already," he said. "We have rough times in here, yessir. Yes, we do," and then he seemed to kinda tail off. He looked at the copy I'd given him, and then he started in to reading it, and slashing at it with his pencil, and after a while it was pretty clear that he'd forgotten I was there. I sidled out, and this time he didn't stop me.

I thought it was strange, all that talk about the Ladies' Page, until I talked to the other reporters. They called it 'Granny News,' and I guess Fred was a little sensitive about it, having worked his whole life at the *Chronicle,* and never doing any real reporting. The boys ribbed me, too, but I could stand it pretty well; I told myself I'd be out of Granny News soon. I wasn't planning to spend *my* life drooling out copy about chrysanthemums and weddings.

Now, what does it say on my desk? That's right, this little thing here. Says, Eugene Stubbs, Editor. Editor of what? Now, that's on my door. That's right, the Ladies' Page. Only we call it Features, now, and it's a sight more interesting than it used to be. But I ain't apologizing for it, not like old Fred. I guess God never meant me to be a real reporter, son, because He saw fit to put me here, and the Ladies' Page has been just fine by me. I had other opportunities, could've changed horses long ago, but I saw where the sunny side was. By then I was married, and two kids, and I saw the other reporters dragging in here some mornings looking like a mule had kicked 'em. Not me. I was always fresh as a daisy, and I got to play with my kids, too, and supper every night bang at six o'clock. My wife and I were happy every day we had together. And why was that? Hell, son, it's just a simple fact—there ain't no emergency news in the Ladies' Page. What am I going to be called out of my bed for? Aphid attack? Sudden hemline change? Nossir, I know a good thing, and I kept on at Granny News, and let the other fellows do the dog work.

I became editor on account of Fred's retirement. I'd only been there four years; John D. passed over a couple of other fellows to promote me. Fred must have put in a good word about me; I think he kind of liked me. I was used to his moods, and didn't act so frightened of them. Also, I think it pleased him how I seemed so happy working in the department, not like all the other reporters he'd had, always scrambling over each other to get over to News or Sports.

My duties didn't change much, except I got a little more money and could sit on my butt a little more. Fred briefed me before the changeover, and it sounded fine to me: copyediting, some reporting here and there, when reporters were in short supply. Besides all that, Fred said, there was the summer fair.

By tradition, judges for the summer fair are always taken from the staff of the *Chronicle.* I guess we're seen as literate folk and unbiased.

"I won't lie to you," said Fred, seriously. "It's a pain in the ass." He sucked at his coffee cup. "I seen more flower bushes and ate more pie these last fifteen years—" He sighed. "It's on you, now," he said. He looked at me for a minute or so, reckoning something. Then he scooched forward in his chair and put on a kind of confiding expression. "You listening?" he asked.

I nodded.

"What I'm going to tell you will save you a lot of time and trouble," said Fred. "It took me a while to hit on a system, but I found it, and stuck to it, and I never had any trouble after that." He breathed in once, deep. "You ready?" he asked.

"Sure," I told him.

"Okay." He leaned forward. "This is the key: *Don't pay any attention.* Nobody's happy if you do." He let that sink in. "Just remember," holding up a thick finger. "First prize goes to the audience favorite. The one they clap loudest for. You got the majority on your side that way. *Or* the one who's won every year for the last nine years. They understand that, it's kind of like tradition." He poked up another finger. "Second goes to a pretty girl." He wiggled his eyebrows. "Nuff said." Third finger. "Third place goes to a kid. Look for freckles, missing teeth. You know. Oh, and if you get the pet show, go by the owners." He folded his fist together again, brought it down softly on the desk. "That's it," he said. "Follow Fred's rules, and it's easy. Don't say I never did anything for you."

I nodded. The summer fair was half a year away; it didn't seem anything to worry about.

Well, summer came around, like it does, and with it the judges' lottery. We had a list of the different contests, and they were drawn from a hat, just to keep things fair. Otherwise, there might be somebody crying afterward about favoritism. These contests can get pretty heated. Of course, the lottery wasn't a perfect system; there was a lot of swapping around afterward—'I'll take your Sunday graveyard if you take my pet show'—that kind of thing. Everyone wanted the beauty pageant, of course. It was a real slick job, just sitting in the sun for a couple of days over the fair weekend, and looking at pretty girls in different costumes, and asking them a couple of questions. The last two years, the same fellow had gotten it, and when he reached into the hat this year, he was smiling like he knew he'd be lucky again. Well, to make it short, he drew the quilting table, and I got the beauty pageant. Everyone crowded around me and slapped me on the back. Nobody liked this other fellow, you see, and they were glad to see him disappointed. Well, I thought I was going to pop, I was so pleased. What did I know?

It started with my wife. I told her the news, and she got a little huffy. Not right away; I told her right before supper, and it took until dessert before she started sulling up. Seemed funny that she'd be so upset about a beauty pageant. Remember, I was a lot younger then, and I didn't guess that maybe she was feeling like a dog-eared wife; I just supposed she was jealous.

What I should have done, soon as she started taking on, was to say something smart, like 'Baby, you'll always be my beauty queen,' or 'I'd give first place to you, but they wouldn't let you enter—wouldn't be fair to those other poor girls.' Something like that. But that kind of smarts takes years to learn, and I hadn't learned it yet. So when she was huffing over the pie, I said something dumb instead, like 'Can't a guy have any fun?' It's important, when you're twenty-odd and married, to act like you want to look at other women. You haven't let yourself admit that you're not much interested anymore. So things went from bad to worse, and I spent that night on the couch. And a few nights more, before the thing was over. Hell, I spent so much time on that damned couch that I wouldn't sit on it anymore. Right after the contest was over, I went out and got myself an armchair.

The beauty pageant was a three-day event, kind of a stretched-out Miss America, lasting through the whole fair. I got there early on Friday and watched them setting up the stage. Right about noon all the girls started showing up, and their mothers. I have never seen so many outfits in all of my life. They were only supposed to wear three—bathing suit, casual, and formal—but they each brought dozens, jammed into their cars and pickup trucks, and what have you. Then the squabbling started, over who was going to sit where in the tent they'd set up for a dressing room. It all looked pretty much the same to me, but they seemed to think one place was better than another, and there was a lot of ugliness. Name calling, tears. The mothers were worse than the daughters. They actually threw things.

I was just standing there, taking it all in, when one of the mothers spotted my judge's ribbon. 'Hey,' she called out to the others. One woman froze where she stood, hefting a box of powder, about to let fly. 'Here's a judge. Let him decide.'

And they all looked at me, all those wide women's eyes, quiet now, and expectant.

"I ain't the senior judge," I said. That spot was reserved for the mayor. I looked around for him or Floyd, but they weren't in sight.

"Don't matter," said the same woman. "We'll stand by what you say."

"All right, then," I said, playing for time. "All right." And I racked my brain. "Alphabetical," I decided. " 'Yall are listed alphabetically, I've got a list somewhere." I found it in a pocket. "When I read your name, go to the next empty spot, starting front to back."

Everything was just fine until I got to the *M*'s. One of the mothers started whooping "Unfair."

"Cecily's right in the sun," she said. "See how fair she is. She'll be red as a lobster by Sunday."

They set to fussing again. I held my hands up and said "Hush," but it didn't help.

"Yall said you'd stand by what I decided," I said, in a very strict voice, but no one was listening.

I left them there to fight it out; I didn't have to be back for a couple of hours, and so I spent that time wandering over the fairgrounds and drinking a share of bad lemonade. When I got back, everything was orderly; the girls were getting into their costumes and painting their faces. The tent flaps were closed, and it must have been mighty hot in there, but all was peaceful. I listened for a while to the buzz of girls getting ready. It was kind of interesting, something I never heard before. Like being there before a date and hearing what goes on in that bedroom they stay in for fifteen minutes while you talk to their father.

The first day, the girls had to do a walk, in casual clothes,

and answer two questions. That went off fine; there were fifteen girls in all, and Floyd Beeman, the fire chief, who got to
do the asking, picked easy questions. The girls were anywhere
from fifteen to eighteen, although most were around sixteen.
They walked out and turned around, and posed while their
mothers took pictures, and then they walked back again. They
came out one by one later for the questions. That was all so we
could get a good look, and start figuring out who we favored.

That was easy. I like brunettes, and your mother was a
blonde, but there was nothing to touch her on that stage. Some
of the girls walked too fast, like they were nervous; and some
were awkward. Not Beth. She swayed out there like a lily, real
cool, and gave just a little smile when she posed at the end of
the runway. The other girls were smiling their faces off—you
couldn't see for the glare off their teeth—but Beth had a real
sweet little smile, made you wonder what she was thinking.

There was only one other girl come close to her for just
natural beauty; although in my opinion, she didn't. The other
judges kind of liked her though, and it may have had something to do with her being the police chief's daughter. She was
very good-looking and had some class. She moved like she was
dancing, and she got some applause. But when your mother
come out, that girl looked like a wallflower. I could see Tom
and Floyd smiling and nodding. Beth had won the first look
over.

The question and answer helped us weed out some girls. The
questions were dumb, like, "What do you admire most about
your mother?" but some of the girls couldn't handle even that;
they stammered and blushed, and one poor thing even started
to cry. Beth handled that category well, but so did the police
chief's daughter. In fact, she started all the mothers in the
audience to sniffling a little, with her speech. The score was
getting closer.

Saturday was the bathing-suit category, and that day's
crowd was bigger and rowdier, mostly high-school boys come
to see the only part of the fair that interested them. They
whistled and carried on, and part of the difficulty of the thing
was how the girls held up under it, whether they kept their
poise. We were all surprised that afternoon, when a little thing
from the far western part of the county came out in her bathing suit. In a dress, she hadn't looked like much, and she'd
been real shy during the questioning, but in her swimsuit she
was a knockout, and she caused quite a fuss. Now it looked

like there was more competition for Beth, but I still had my money on her.

Sunday was the longest part of the contest; the girls came out in formal wear, and paraded up and down one more time, and then each one had to give a little speech. The topic had been given to them beforehand: 'America's Part in the War Effort.' By now, I was getting tired of looking at the stream of girls going by. I know you can't believe that, young as you are, but if you ever spent three afternoons in a row looking at a lot of girls who look a lot alike, you'd understand. It's not like they did much except smile and prance around, and that's entertaining, but not exactly riveting, especially when you're the judge and you have to sit up straight and pay attention or catch hell from some girl's mother about how you were looking the other way when *her* daughter came out.

All the speeches were pretty much the same, a lot of guff about Democracy and Our Brave Boys. Don't get me wrong; I'm as patriotic as the next fellow, but it's the same thing again. Once you listen to twelve speeches all alike you begin to get a little cynical.

Beth was next to last, and she came out front like the other girls had, and she gave her little smile, and she started speaking from memory. Right away, it was clear that this speech was going to be different. I don't remember what all she said or how she said it, but there was nothing about Our Brave Boys in it. It was all about war being wrong, and how when countries disagree it doesn't mean the people in 'em have to kill each other.

Well, I don't know if I've ever seen such a fuss, before or since. First people got real quiet, and then the crowd started stirring and waving like a cornfield with the wind on it, and then someone stood up and started booing. They all took it up, then: booing and hissing, and some boy threw an ice cream at the stage. It hit Beth on the chest, and sort of slithered downward, and landed on her shoe, but all the time she kept speaking, although no one was listening now. I was getting a sinking feeling, because I knew she couldn't win anymore, and I guess I wasn't as unbiased as I should have been. I was torn; I sympathized with the crowd some, because a lot of women had lost their sons and boys their brothers, and they needed to believe in the Cause. Beth's getting up there and tearing down the war was like breaking their hearts even more than they were broke already. She was ripping the flag off their loved ones' caskets, and it was a cruel thing to do.

But it was brave, too. There was real passion in that speech, before the booing got so loud you couldn't hear her anymore. She obviously meant what she was saying, and hard as it was for me to listen to it, there's something admirable in saying what you believe, when you know it's not what people want to hear. A few years later, a whole generation would take on like she did, but they would have a bunch of people like themselves, all agreeing with them, and this was one girl, alone.

The uproar went on for a while after she'd finished; the poor girl that followed her gave a sweet, predictable speech in front of an angry mob. Nobody listened; she ended by running off the stage.

There was a half hour or so for deliberation, during which the girls filed on stage again, so we could use them for a reference, I guess. When Beth came on, there was some more angry noise, but it had settled down some. People were turning their attention to the next thing—the judging.

We muttered and whispered amongst ourselves, but we couldn't come to a decision. Floyd was all for putting three girls down, and none of them Beth; and Tom, the mayor, wanted to give her third. The choice wasn't any more about who was going to come in first on the list, but only where to put Beth on it. No matter what Floyd said, she couldn't be left out entirely; it was a *beauty* contest, after all. But at the same time, there weren't two girls prettier than she was, and none of us wanted to get the mob going by giving her first.

I told them about Fred's system, and to do them credit, they heard me out. But when I was done, Floyd said, "Big help," sarcastically.

"It won't work, Gene," said the mayor. "Beth would usually be the favorite. She *always* wins these things. And we got no lack of pretty girls up there, but not one kid among them. Old Fred's rules just ain't no good this time. We got to figure it out ourselves."

So we fussed some more, and hissed back and forth, and wrote our votes down, and argued about them. It took us most of an hour to come to a decision, and by that time, the crowd was hot *and* mad.

When Tom got up to announce the vote, there was a hush. The crowd had swelled: some nincompoop had made an announcement a few minutes ago over the loudspeaker; that brought a good number of fairgoers over. A bigger number had shown up before the announcement, hearing the ruckus, and being naturally curious. Tom cleared his throat. I didn't envy him. No matter what he said, someone was going to be mad. Beth had upset a lot of people, but she still had a lot of admirers in the town, who hadn't been here before, and who wouldn't have cared if she'd gotten up and spouted Bolshevism.

"Ladies and gentlemen," said Tom. And he read the list, into a dead silence. Beth was given second place. The police chief's daughter got third, and the dark horse in the bathing suit took first, which was enough of a surprise to distract the crowd a little. The mother of the winner started to sobbing, and the chief's wife got indignant, and the boys were hooting and hollering for no particular reason. During the confusion, I slipped off and went to stand by my car. My wife hadn't spoken to me for two days, and I was feeling a little raggedy.

"Hey," said Beth, coming by, carrying her pumps hooked onto two fingers, walking barefoot.

"I thought you'd be having your picture taken," I said, surprised.

"My mother's furious with me," said Beth, and giggled. "It's the first time I haven't won."

"You would have—" I began.

"I know," she said, and her face got serious again. "I always win," she said, with a far-off look. Then she came back from wherever she'd gone and turned to me. "Don't feel bad," she said, patting my shoulder, as if I was the one who needed comforting. "It was the only thing you could do."

And she walked away. I watched her go, and almost went after her, to ask her why she'd done it, why she'd given that speech when she knew it would lose the contest for her. I've thought about it some since, and I've always wondered why I didn't ask her. I guess it had to do with the way she looked and the way she sounded. She didn't look like a kid in a beauty pageant; she was like a grown woman with that secret smile, and I respected her enough to let her keep her secrets.

Besides. I have the feeling she thought she won. Not the contest, acourse, but something.

Chapter Seven

The Confessor

The doctor had asked her once about her goals; she had been surprised at first and then blank. She knew she'd once had them, but so long ago—a pony, a husband, a house like her grandmother's—that they no longer made sense. She'd been ashamed to confess them, but the doctor hadn't scoffed. *Well?* he'd said. *Do you have what you want?* No pony, Joan had answered, smiling. Then more slowly: I do have a husband. *And what about the house?* Yes, and a house, bigger even than my grandmother's. She'd wrinkled up her face. I have other things too, she'd said. Things I never even wanted. A career. Two careers, really. *You're even a little bit famous,* said the doctor, and she'd nodded. But . . . *It's not enough,* said the doctor, putting a little twist of a question onto it. No, Joan had answered, with the relief of confession; no, it isn't enough.

Did all of it show on her face, like a television program or a computer display? She pulled out the desk drawer which had the mirror in it, and stared down. Her face, oddly framed by sloping reflections of the wood panels, looked back at her, calm. Looking down like this gave her a double chin.

She shut the drawer hurriedly when the knock came at the door.

"Your eleven o'clock," said Miss Hastings, in her tinny voice. She managed to inject disapproval into every sentence, reminding Joan of a teacher she'd once had as a girl. Miss Lamont, of Maryland; appalled by her pupils' Pittsburgh accents, she'd dedicated herself to correcting them. She'd sat on the edge of her desk, taking class time away from *Huckleberry Finn,* swinging one foot like a pendulum. "House; say it," and the students chorusing after: "Hass."

"Milk," she'd said, the short *i* hissing between her drab, unpainted lips, and "melk," the children had bleated helplessly. Looking back, Joan couldn't believe how polite they'd all been, how obedient. Even the day that Miss Lamont's swinging foot had caught the metal wastebasket in front of her desk. The thing had gone clanging across the room, skittering under desks, sending out a shower of pencil shavings and balled-up pieces of paper. They hadn't laughed, not even then. Instead, an awed silence had fallen, a curtain of privacy, leaving the teacher alone at the front of the room, opening and shutting her mouth. Joan remembered her own laughter, never released, how it had hurt to hold it in. Sometimes she felt a tightness there, as if it had lost its way inside her all that time ago and was still trapped, looking for escape.

She looked down at the file on her desk. *Sally Sloane.*

"Send her in, thanks," she told Miss Hastings.

The girl slunk in through the doorway. Joan was astonished: where had she come from? Surely she would have noticed this student before. The girl was perhaps five two, carrying at least a hundred and seventy pounds. Fat as she was, she moved delicately, settling into the armless chair in front of Joan's desk with hardly a sound.

"I'm Mrs. Corbin," Joan told her. "And you're Sally?"

The girl nodded.

"We haven't met before, have we?" asked Joan, tapping the girl's file, wishing she'd looked at it before. But she didn't like to read the file now. The first few minutes with a student were crucial, and eye contact an important part of rapport.

"I'm new," said Sally.

That explained it.

"You're in the tenth grade?" asked Joan, estimating.

"Ninth," said Sally, and added grudgingly, "but I shoulda been in tenth."

"Why is that?"

"Huh?"

"You should have been in tenth?"

"Yeah. I had trouble with math last year."

"Where was that?"

"Huh?"

"What school did you attend last year?" clarified Joan, hiding her irritation at the repetition of the ugly monosyllable.

"In Harrisburg," said Sally, shortly.

"What a coincidence," said Joan. "I'm from Pittsburgh."

Sally looked only slightly interested.

"Well, how do you like Naples?" asked Joan.

Sally shrugged. *I'm losing her.*

"Not as nice as Harrisburg?"

Sally shrugged again, and then burst out: "We had a big yard back home, now we don't have any."

"You miss that," Joan said.

"Uh huh," said Sally, falling silent again.

"Being new can be hard," said Joan. "That's what I'm here for. Did you have a guidance counselor at your school in Harrisburg?"

"I think so," said Sally.

"Then you know what I do," said Joan, brightly. "I'm not a teacher; I'm not connected with the principal's office. I'm just here to talk to the students." She waited, but Sally said nothing, looking down at her shoes. "If you have a problem, you talk to me. It can be anything," she said. "It doesn't even have to be about school." She paused. "How is school, by the way?"

"S'okay," said Sally, evasive, biting viciously at the cuticle of her left index finger.

"How's math?" asked Joan.

"S'okay," around the cuticle.

"Well, Mr. Wells seemed to think you might want to talk to me. Do you have any idea why he might have suggested that?"

"Isn't it in there somewhere?" asked Sally, gesturing with her free hand toward the file, not fooled by Joan's casual manner.

"Well, probably," said Joan. "But I'll tell you something, if you promise not to tell anyone: I haven't read this yet." Sally chewed on, but a little less avidly. "I should apologize to you," Joan went on. "I'm not really prepared this morning." The girl looked up: a *teacher* apologizing to *her?* "I'm supposed to read all the new students' files right away," said Joan. "And I'm usually very good about it. But this morning I was just too worried about other things, and I didn't get to it." Sally was looking directly at her now, her hand stopped halfway to her mouth. "I'm sorry, Sally."

"S'okay," said Sally, earnestly. After a pause, she added, "I'm not always prepared either."

"Thank you for being understanding," said Joan. "Well," she said. "How do you like your classes?"

"They're okay," said the girl, remote again.

"How about the other kids?"

"They talk funny," said Sally. "They make fun of me."

"When I came here, they made fun of me, too," said Joan. The girl looked sceptical.

"They called me a Yankee," said Joan, improvising. "They told me I should go back where I came from."

Sally said nothing, picking at her cuticles again.

"They made me feel pretty bad about myself," Joan said quietly.

"They call me Fatty in gym," Sally whispered.

"Gym's the worst," said Joan, leaning forward. Now they were off and running.

Ordinarily, she took her lunch to the cafeteria, where she could observe her charges; but today, she opened a cup of yogurt at her desk, shutting the office door, running the soles of her feet over the pebbly institutional carpet. She ate slowly, but still was finished in less than half an hour. She needed to run errands, but something within her shrank from going outside. *He's out there.* The thought came unbidden. *And with him, all the rest of it.* All the rest of what? She shook her head with irritation, slipped her feet into her shoes, and unhooked her purse from the back of the door.

Coming out of the drugstore, she spotted Gil. He was across the street, in front of the old Paramount Theatre which had been turned into a restaurant. He was occupied with something, frowning down at his hands. Joan looked harder, and saw that he was stripping a packet of chewing gum.

She liked spying on him like this. What luxury, to see her husband as others saw him, casual, unaware of her attention. She appraised him coolly: he looked like any middle-aged man, in his plaid shirt and work boots. His pants didn't go with the outfit: they were navy and shiny, and he'd worn them with a jacket and tie in the morning. He must have changed at the office before lunch, planning to spend the afternoon outdoors.

When she first met him, he was enormously awkward and shy. Thin as a reed, given to blushing. She'd had other suitors; what had made her choose him? He'd been frail and looked inexperienced, with the appealing candor of a reckless child. Not the most charming man she had ever met. But there had been something about him, a lostness, a confusion, that had made her want to rescue him. She remembered the urgency of that emotion accurately but without force, as one recalls the chill of January in July. It *had* been so; he'd depended on her then, and she'd taken charge.

He'd confided in her right away. On their first date, he'd

explained his feeling of being miscast. She hadn't understood then; and when he'd brought it up again early in their marriage, she'd challenged him.

"We all feel like that sometimes," she'd said. "Out of place." She'd looked out of the window at the Virginia landscape. "It's normal."

"Tell me Jack feels that way," he'd retorted.

"Well, maybe not Jack," she'd conceded. "But everyone else I know."

From the way he described it, his confusion reminded her of the feeling she'd had at fifteen, wearing her first pair of heels. She'd felt like a different person, with the increased height and the accompanying unsteadiness. And when she'd worn cosmetics for the first time, and when she'd begun to menstruate. She'd been horribly embarrassed by each change, and certain that she was *the only one* who'd ever experienced any of those things. She'd been ashamed, adjusting the belt in the girls' bathroom at school, thinking everyone could hear. That was it, she recalled it perfectly—it was as though she'd had a dark secret, but so ordinary that anyone could look at her and know it, know it right away. It was a feeling of exposure, of not feeling at home with herself.

"You're not happy being a man?" she'd guessed and immediately saw that she'd hit a nerve. Later she learned that when someone most wanted you to understand them, they often least wanted to hear that you had.

"You're not listening," he'd said, flushed. "You don't get it." So she'd told him what she'd been thinking. "Close," he admitted. "But it's not the same."

"It sounds—" she'd begun.

"Who showed you about your period?" he interrupted. "And taught you about lipstick, that stuff?"

"My mother," she'd admitted. "Girlfriends."

"That's just it," he'd said, bitterly.

He hadn't spoken much about it after that, but she could tell that he was still suffering. She even suspected him of enjoying a kind of martyrdom, taking himself to that old-boy bar every afternoon, signing up for the softball team at work. He played his discomfort out for years, stretching it until it was thin as paper, perhaps hoping for it to break under the tension. He was so thin then, as though he were being stretched along with his burden, trying to break himself.

And he was still thin, although the impression of coltishness

had disappeared these twenty years ago. Time had settled
some flesh on him, and permitted some fine hairs to spring up
on the backs of his hands. How the situation had reversed: her
lost lamb had become her saviour, and that attitude he'd had
of incompetence and discomfort, of waging battle on alien
ground, had given way long since to a clear appearance of
belonging. Now he seemed part and parcel of his surround-
ings. No different from the man who hailed him, coming out of
the Real Thing diner, accepting a stick of chewing gum.

Joan watched them talk together. The other man was black
and muscular, younger than Gil, someone she didn't know. He
rocked back and forth on the balls of his feet, laughing at
something Gil had said. Laughing, he brought his arm up and
then across, to slap Gil lightly on the shoulder. The universal
symbol of acceptance between men. *You hug,* Jack had told her
once, when she'd commented on it. *We hit.*

How odd it had looked, the first time she'd seen it bestowed
on Gil; and how odd he had looked, accepting it. Now it was
completely natural; she watched Gil chewing his gum, holding
his mouth slightly open. She felt the old push-pull, looking at
him. He'd changed, and she'd let him, even helped him along.
Sometimes she wondered if she ought just to go away, to leave
the scene of her undoing, but always the thought of Gil
stopped her. He was no longer the weak, searching boy he'd
been, but he needed her. And no matter what chased her, what
threatened from murky memory to overwhelm her, she could
not leave him. *Would* not. Naturally objective, she wondered
sometimes if she was merely offering up a blind repentance,
but really what she felt was love.

She watched as the younger man, still laughing, strode away
from Gil, who turned into the sun and saw her. He put his
hand up to his eyes to shade them, and smiled. Then he was
jogging across the wide pavement toward her.

"Hello there," he said.

"Hello," she replied, suddenly shy.

"On your lunch hour?" he asked. She nodded. "Walk you
back," he said.

They walked back toward the school. Joan was very conscious of the way her arm swung out from her shoulder, and
she kept a little distance from her husband, so that his arm,
swinging too, should not brush hers. He reached across the
gap and took her hand. Immediately, she felt light, as though
she might float right up and away.

"Getting hot," said Gil.

"Yes," she said. "Early in the year, too."

"Gonna be one hell of a summer."

What they said to one another didn't matter; it was the feeling that sustained her, his hand holding hers, and having seen him before he saw her. He'd seemed a stranger then, a dozen or so feet away, laughing with another stranger. Running across the street, he'd turned into her husband. Joan didn't understand why the transformation made her so giddy.

"You looked just like anybody, from across the street," she confided.

"Well," he said. "I am just like anybody."

"I guess that's true," she said.

After lunch, she had a parent conference.

"Hello, Mr. Gorman, Mrs. Gorman," she said. The father was a burly man, with an alcoholic ruddiness; the woman with him was a hard, wispy thing.

"Parker," said the woman.

"We're Danny and Edith Parker," she said.

"I'm sorry," said Joan. She looked down at the file on her desk. "I must be confused. This is the file for Charlene Gorman."

"Charlene's ours," said Edith. "Her daddy died. Danny's her stepfather."

"I see," said Joan.

"What's she done?" grunted Danny.

"It's not really that she's done anything," said Joan. "I mean, she's not skipping school or anything like that."

"We had a son, Charlene's older brother, did those things," said Edith. "I guess we're worried she's turning out like him."

"I think I remember him," said Joan. "Michael?"

"That's right. He was real smart at school, till he started getting wild like that."

"He ran away, didn't he?" asked Joan.

The woman's face pinched up, and she nodded, once.

"Sometimes kids do that," said Joan. "No matter how hard you try."

"I hear from him sometimes," said the woman, warming a little.

"What's Charlene done?" repeated Danny.

"She hasn't done anything," said Joan, a little shortly, and then softened her voice. "But we're worried about her. She seems unhappy."

"Girls," said Edith. "I was unhappy at her age."

"So was I," said Joan, and the two women shared a glance. "But Charlene's unhappiness seems to me to be more than natural teenage confusion. She's a smart girl, but she's not listening in class, and she's falling behind in her schoolwork."

"I've *told* that girl," said Danny.

"I try to make her study," said Edith. "But I can't stand over her, not like I could when she was small."

"When she was small, she had small problems," said Joan. "And she shared them with you."

Edith nodded. "She told me everything."

"Now it's a fight to get a civil word outta her," Danny said.

"It happens," Joan told Edith. "Even in the happiest of families." Not that this family is happy, she thought, darting a glance at Danny. "I think something is bothering Charlene, something deeper. I thought you might have some ideas on what it might be."

"Whyncha ask her?" said Danny.

"Well, Mr. Parker, I've tried that," said Joan. "But sometimes kids can't explain things very well. Sometimes they don't even know exactly what it is that's bothering them. I was hoping you or your wife might have noticed something."

"She seems all right to me," said Danny. "Sulky, that's all."

Joan looked at Edith, who looked like she might have something to say. But the woman put her lips tightly together and said nothing.

Thirty minutes later, the Parkers got up to leave. Joan shook hands again, with a feeling of defeat.

"I could sign those papers now," said Edith. "While Danny gets the car."

"Papers?" said Joan.

"Those permission papers," said Edith.

"What kinda permission?" asked Danny.

"For gym," said Joan, and Edith nodded. "I nearly forgot. Thank you for reminding me."

"You go ahead, Dan, get the car," said Edith.

When he had gone, Joan turned to her expectantly.

"I didn't like to say nothing while he was here," she said.

"What is it?" asked Joan.

"You asked if we noticed anything different about Charlene," she said. "Well, there is something." She lowered her voice. "She asks a lot of questions about her daddy, now. She never used to." She paused. "He died when she was real little. Her and Mike got real close; I never seen anything like it, the way they stood up for each other. When he run off—" Edith's eyes, which had been fixed on the door, came sharply back to Joan. "Dan was kinda hard on him," she said, shortly. Her eyes moved away again. "Danny's a good man, Miz Corbin. He treats Charlene all right, but," she said, and her brow wrinkled, "he's not real patient. I try, but I can't be everything to her." She brought her eyes to Joan's again, and then looked down at her own hands, which were holding her purse. "I'm not what you'd call," she said, "affectionate. Not like Jimmy. Jimmy was a loving man," she finished, simply.

"I see," said Joan. "Thank you very much for telling me this."

"I know you're trying to help Charlene," said Edith.

She left, her sad story staying behind her, fashioned of things she had told and things she hadn't, and of things she didn't even know. Edith's words, her darting, intelligent eyes, mingled with Sally's morning confessions. Joan felt them weaving together, into a winding-sheet, a thick fabric of sorrow. Why had she chosen this job, this life filled with other people's misery, with the self-pity of teenagers, the blunt agony of parents? She knew that it calmed something inside her to run her fingers daily through the pain of others. Seeing them, hearing their dread confessions without judgment, she felt herself more at peace. She *had* to love them: love Edith, love fat Sally. "I love so I will be loved," said Joan, aloud. "I love, to salvage myself."

Something that she'd been told years ago during her training floated back to her now. *Sometimes, you'll get frustrated. You'll think you can't change anything. And that nothing you do matters. You'll want to give up. Well, it's true, you can't change much. It's love and hate with us, like any addiction. And it is just that, an addiction; you get used to the role; you can't just give it up.*

Chapter Eight

Controversies

By the weekend, everyone had heard about Buddy Gates and his camera. There was mild speculation about him, but no more than mild: newcomers to Naples are largely ignored until they prove interesting. Since the early part of the century, with its dramatic boom then decline, Naples has continued to teeter on the edge of prosperity. People are drawn here from other places, but not in too great a number. They come here for the women's college or to work in one of the state institutions which have tended to collect here or for the sheer prettiness of it. There is a half-metropolitan air to the town: we are close enough to the center of things to permit us to feel a connection with the larger world, yet at the same time not quite near enough to the state university for any kind of bohemian element to integrate itself into the community. There is, in short, no thorough mixing, and the result is a divided, hybrid place, a nucleus of long-time residents surrounded by immigrants. Literally surrounded: the strangers tend to inhabit the fringes of town in hastily built developments which ring the core of old houses standing in the hilly heart of Naples, in the area known as the Village. Between the two there lies a kind of no-man's-land of businesses, some old, some new. From the time I was a young man, that was the character of Naples—a wheel within a wheel, almost no fraternization, the old preserved, the new tolerated. The people who migrated here either found their niches and settled in or more often left again, as quietly as they had come, no one having paid them much attention. There is a kind of appeal in anonymity, I suppose, and one could find that here: rarely was a stranger absorbed into Naples. A person could live here, as Joan did before I met her, in a rental apartment in one of the slap-up dwellings near the bypass, working in the business district, grocery shopping with the rest of the strangers at one of the fancy new markets at the side of the highway. One could shuttle between those points quietly for years, never approaching the nugget of Naples, not even brushing up against the rim of the inner wheel.

Attracting notice to oneself, if that was what one wanted, was a trick; for that, one had to do something rash, like running for mayor or marrying into one of the resident families. Townspeople were hardly anonymous—most were nicknamed early on—but transients went labelless, escaping categorization, it being too much bother to fix your attention on someone who might well be gone in ten years. And so there might be five doctors in town, but to most of us there was only Dr. Greene, on Cedar Street. A new barber might set up shop, but we ignored him. Harley Sweet was the only cutter we trusted; he had given most of us our very first haircuts, and held a kind of tenure in the town. Strangers tended to mix with strangers, and so new businesses always had plenty of custom, but it was never of a steady kind.

Buddy, by his association with Jack, had unwittingly found his "in." Had he not had Jack to introduce him, to smooth the way for him and his camera, he might have found the doors of Naples shutting politely in his face. Buddy was raw—he'd been brought up graceless, and he rubbed people the wrong way. He addressed them by their first names before proper introductions had been made; he seemed unacquainted with the mysteries of conversation. His speech was unmusical, all the words running together without emphasis. There was no richness to him. But doors opened to him because of Jack: everyone knew Jack, if not everyone approved of him; and they permitted the gawky unskilled boy to clamber around their living rooms with his heavy equipment. They talked to him, while hot lights shone in their eyes; afterward, he barely thanked them, just packed together his equipment and left. Buddy was a charmless rapist, taking Naples for all he could, trading on its hospitality and on the unaccountable friendship he had forged with Jack.

I didn't understand why Jack tolerated him, but I supposed that Jack was amused by him, and Jack liked to be amused. There was something in his attitude as he squired Buddy around that put me in mind of the man who has a favorite joke, one he will always tell, one he never tires of telling; one that grows longer and more complicated, and, incredibly, funnier with each repetition. Buddy was Jack's favorite joke, and we his audience.

I avoided them, for the most part, although Buddy seemed keen on me and flopped up to me in Stokes' with his arrogant pedigree-pup style, hoping to pin me down for a session in front of his camera.

"I'd really like to get you on film," was the way he put it, and there was something predatory in his manner, something eager that made me queasy. I imagined myself pressed onto celluloid and threaded onto a reel in Buddy's projector. I demurred.

"Wal now," was what I said. "It's a little late to be starting a career in the movies." Some old-boy nonsense that went over well. To Buddy, it was one and the same if you worked in the mines or tuned pianos for a living; the world for him was split into two masses: the college educated and the ignorant poor. He didn't see the texture in the rest of the world, and he bought my down-home obtuseness whole, with that air of suppressed impatience with which he treated all of us at times, even Jack.

Buddy's expression dimmed at my refusal.

"If it's your—you know, well, your—*impediment,*" he said, "you don't have to worry. The editing process—"

"Folks are lining up for you," I said. "Don't waste your," and I swallowed the last of my beer. "Time with me." Cutting him off without seeming to, giving a good-natured laugh, ordering another beer, turning away.

I was getting as good at pretending as Joan, I realized; it wasn't as difficult as I had thought.

I met Joan when I was eighteen, fresh on leave from the army, my scalp showing through my regulation haircut, feeling thoroughly ashamed of myself. I had joined up in direct defiance of my father, who wanted me to go to college. I had been offered a scholarship, but I told myself that academics bored me; that I couldn't face another four years of book learning; that I had always lived in Naples, had always been smart and weak, with my nose in a book. I longed for the change which I thought was due me. The propaganda of my youth had been funded by war, and naturally my thoughts turned to the military as an alternative to higher education. I craved the uniform, the respect, the soldier's physique, his fearlessness. I went to a recruitment center to investigate.

"Make a man out of you," the sergeant behind the desk said, when I walked in. Shrewdly, he had seen to the very soul of my weakness. "I bet your dad was a military man."

"Yessir," I said. "He was in the"—I coughed—"Great War."

"Bet he told you *all* kinds of stories," said the sergeant, his brow wrinkling up. Had my coughing fit fooled him? I merely nodded, not about to risk another slip.

"Sure he did," said the sergeant. "And let me tell you, son: *every one of them is true.*"

Actually, my father had made only one mention of his wartime experience in my hearing; a most casual remark, it was delivered to me one winter evening as we sat in front of the fire.

"You find out who your friends are, in the trenches," he'd said. "By God, that's the only time you ever know."

He never mentioned the war again and seldom referred to his wound, although I knew it bothered him during the change of seasons. For him, as for Jack, war seemed to be an essentially private experience, not to be traded on or displayed.

When my father found out I'd enlisted, he was furious. I had never seen him angry, and was perplexed at first by the changes in him: the cords standing out in his neck, the vessel beating at his temple. His face went slowly dark; and the intensity of his emotion made him uncommonly vocal.

"You belong in school," he said.

"You joined up," I argued.

"That was different," he said, with effort. "It was a crisis then. There's no war on; no need."

"Peacetime defense is as important as war," I said.

Beyond speech, he said nothing and slashed at the pork chop on his plate. I glanced at him during the rest of the meal, uneasy with my victory.

That weekend, Ellen arrived for a visit, leaving the new baby with the housekeeper and making the two-hour journey by train. She arrived mid-morning on Saturday, and that day's dinner was filled with her gentle chatter, all about the baby and Marshall, her husband, and the prices of things in the city. It was all very natural; there were no sly glances my way; no hint of conspiracy. Still, I wasn't fooled. After dinner, we all gathered in the living room.

Ellen had brought needlework; she spread the fabric across her lap and fussed with her wicker sewing basket. Her head down, her fingers on a spool, she said, "You wouldn't believe how much thread costs in the city." Without looking up, she continued, "But I expect you'll soon be finding out for yourself what it's like, Gillie."

"No, I won't," I said abruptly, irritated by the baby nickname.

"What do you mean?" she asked, looking at me now, eyes wide.

"Stop pretending," I said, rudely. "Dad told you everything, didn't he?"

"Told me—" she began, when our father interrupted her.

"It's all right, Ellen," he said. To me, he said, "Thought you might listen to her."

"He did mention it," said Ellen, still sewing. Then she dropped her hands into her lap. "Oh, let's just be honest with each other. What's this about the army?"

"I signed up," I said.

"You actually signed?" she asked, as if holding out some hope.

I nodded. "In ink," I said.

They began then, their gentle harassing, Ellen wheedling me from one side and my father bullying me from the other, until I felt myself confused, and their faces spinning into a pale anxious blur.

"Oh, Gil," cried Ellen. "You could be anything. A doctor, even. You have so many opportunities."

"Be grateful for what God gave you," my father admonished.

"He gave me," I said. "Brains." I cleared my throat. "What's the good of giving them to me if I can't choose for myself?"

"Don't talk against Him," said my father, severely.

"Do you really think He's listening?" I said, insolently. "I'm not sure I even believe He's there at all."

"You listen to me," said my father, apoplectic.

"Gil," said Ellen at the same time, deeply shocked.

"You're not too old for a whipping," said my father.

I laughed. My father had never raised his hand against any of us.

"Hush, Dad, that just makes it worse," said Ellen, who understood me better. She turned to me. "Have you thought about this, Gil? I mean, have you really and truly thought about it?"

All this time, Jack said nothing, a slight lift to his lips as he listened, but no change of expression.

I told them I'd thought about it; that I knew what I wanted, that I was adult enough to choose for myself. With rare ease, I lectured them all: my father on his hypocrisy, my sister on her treachery, my brother on his superior attitude. I expanded, berating my family for its unwillingness to make a real contribution to the defense of its country. I parroted the recruitment officer, whose resounding cliches did not appear to move my audience as they had me.

"I made my contribution," said my father. He patted his leg. "I made mine, and Jack, too, so you wouldn't have to."

"You mean so you can keep me out of it," I said. "And keep your secrets."

"Jesus Christ," said Jack, provoked out of his silence. "You don't know nothing about nothing."

"Jack," said Ellen.

"You ain't going to learn nothing you can use," Jack continued, heedless. "You think you're going to learn all kinds of things, all kinds of big secrets. There ain't no secrets, and there ain't no learning. Just stupid shit dogfaces, and stupid shit officers thumping a big fat rulebook. It's just rules," he said. "It's crap."

"Be quiet," said Ellen, in a rare display of temper.

"No," said my father. "He's right." He turned to me. "There ain't nothing in it for you, son."

His tenderness, so unexpected, made me want to weep.

"I've already signed up," I said, stubborn. Airily, I added, "I won't be a dogface for long. And as for rules, they serve a purpose. They establish discipline."

Jack whistled, low. My father looked down and said nothing.

"What do you think of that?" I asked Jack.

"I think," he said. "We got us a regular G.I. in the family."

"Oh, dear," sighed Ellen, but her lips twitched. It was the way Jack had, of playing on people, of making them smile. It got even to her, who took life so very seriously.

And that was that. They gave up their arguing and let me go about my business.

By the time I left for basic training, the town had heard all about it—how I had refused the scholarship, and the fight with my father, and Jack's closing remark. They found nothing inherently ridiculous about the military, but they enjoyed a good joke, and Jack's nickname caught on. I was hailed on the street as "G.I." Some of the wags at the barbershop offered to shave my head in advance, "real cheap," Harley said, while the others fell about laughing. Sam and Ned Lucas stiffened to attention when I passed them, and threw me exaggerated salutes. Humiliated, I counted the days until my departure and the rigors of boot camp.

After a few days in Georgia, I knew that I had made a great mistake. I had envisioned great man-making experiences, a quick rise to authority. Very quickly, I discovered the bald truth: that a rise in the army must be paid for in advance, with years of subservience and toil. I had anticipated leadership, but I was an average soldier, hardly the stuff of command. Not so inept as other recruits, not so brilliant as the best, I was treated fairly and with only random cruelty, not singled out in any way for praise or punishment. I was one of a horde of young men, a drop in a river of khaki, and my days consisted of a series of orders, everything always performed in a group, a hundred men eating, shaving, pissing at once. I had sought enlightenment, but I learned nothing about myself beyond that I detested rising early, detested marching in step, detested being an indistinguishable, insignificant portion of a greenish wave of rookie soldierdom. In short, I detested everything about the army, and I wanted out.

Pride kept me from revealing my feelings to my family. I had left Naples so cocky, so certain of success; I couldn't even admit to myself that Jack had been entirely correct. My weekly phone calls were brief, full of false cheer. Making them required all of my excess energy; I feared I would have none left to continue the pretense during my first home leave.

It was not just facing my family; it was also facing the townspeople, whose ridicule had been irritating when I had the strength of my convictions. Now, with my greater knowledge, it would be excruciating. I lay awake the night before I was to go home, concocting anecdotes to feed to the lions awaiting me in Naples.

The effort, as it turned out, was unnecessary: no one asked me anything about my experiences. Ellen and her husband came for the weekend, bringing the baby; they talked about his new position in an insurance firm, and there was much made of my nephew. My father had fallen back into his customary silence. Even Jack refrained from needling me. They called me "G.I." still, but it was pronounced with affection. Baffled by the directionless supper table chitchat, I took advantage of a silence to launch into one of my prepared stories unprompted.

The silence that followed my lies was hideous for its kindness: it humiliated and enraged me. I retreated into myself after that, and for the rest of my week in Naples I crept around the house and through the streets, avoiding confrontations. I arose late in the day to an empty house, and I prowled the streets late at night, going to unfamiliar bars, attempting to hide myself among people who didn't know me, taking revenge on my family who had tried to protect me, blaming them.

I had been slinking around Naples for three days, visiting dark, vile bars, the kinds of seedy places that spring up all in one area, in even the best of towns, when I met Beth Miller again.

I hadn't seen her for a year, not since she'd broken with Jack, suddenly, over a weekend. Naples had assumed long since that the romance would end in marriage, and had turned its eye away from the couple. When they quarreled, we all yawned: it was commonplace for courting couples to pull apart in fury just before engagement. When Beth took up with another young man, there was clucking of tongues, but no surprise: that, too, was an old trick. Hadn't many of the wives of Naples done it themselves, to force their fellow's hand? It was tiresome, but certainly not immoral.

But when, after only two months, Beth *married* the fellow, the town was wild. They felt cheated, all the more because the couple had eloped. No society wedding, no three-page spread in the *Chronicle.* From the time Beth was small, we'd been assured of a splendid wedding someday in the future. Like dedicated Royalists deprived of their event, like baseball fans who've been told there will be no World Series, we mourned. The news spread across town; and there was an ominous two-day calm, a kind of gossip cease-fire. Then the first wave of talk opened the floodgates; and after the shock came the countershock, and on the fourth day the quarreling began in earnest.

Everyone had a side. There were two main factions, pro-Billy and pro-Jack. Billy Crawford, until the weekend of his elopement, was little in the public eye. He was a dedicated hell-raiser, but his antics sparked little interest, being unoriginal; he was a stereotype, a black sheep, and not even much good at that. The Crawfords were a Village family, with a house near the top of the hill; they had three other sons and a daughter in Billy's generation; all of his brothers had univer-

sity degrees, and his sister was married to a banker in Richmond. Not Billy. Youngest of the five, he was a drinker, a
weak-mouthed and stupid-looking fellow, prone to pointless
rebellion; he was expelled from the Boys' Academy just six
weeks shy of graduation. Since that time, he'd done nothing of
any consequence, and his prodigal habits had worn his
family's patience. A few months before Beth married him,
they had severed their financial support.

The pro-Billy group was legalistic in their arguments. They
said that Billy might be a no'count, but that did not make him
malicious. Furthermore, they said, he had been within his
rights; Beth and Jack had been broken publicly for two weeks
before Billy even dated Beth; as far as anyone knew, Beth and
Jack hadn't even seen one another in months. Now here the
pro-Billy members always stopped, and carefully outlined a
tricky ethical point. If, they said, Jack had shown that he was
distraught over the separation, if he had advertised his intent
to reclaim Beth, then Billy might have been guilty of infringe-
ment. But Jack had shown nothing, had complained of nothing. He'd been in fine form two days before the elopement,
beating his buddies at dollar pool, drinking whisky all night.
So reported Steve Grissom, who'd been one of the beaten and
who was a staunch Billyite.

The pro-Jack faction used a dual argument, the first passionate. *Look* at them, they said, look at how they were together. They were made for each other; Billy Crawford had no
reason to go sticking his nose in. Yes, Beth and Jack had broken up, but it was likely that they'd have found their way back
to one another again: after all, they weren't like other couples,
who break and re-ally a dozen times in a month. They had
dated almost *four years* before having any trouble. This led the
Jack supporters neatly into their next point, which revolved
around the concept of tenure. Here, the style of argument varied; but it didn't much matter. They talked a good show, but
what their words came down to in the end was: Jack saw her
first.

There was a third, splinter faction, of people sympathetic to
Lucy Miller. This group was not as vocal as the other two, not
from lack of conviction, but because they weren't sure right
away which way they should jump. Was Lucy happy to be rid
of Jack? Furious to have been deprived of a gala wedding?
Happy that Beth, one way or another, had ended up married
into the Village? Or unhappy that she'd married Billy Craw-

ford, if anything a less impressive son-in-law than Jack would ever have been? She had equal reason to feel any of these things, or all of them, at any time; and so the Lucyites vacillated between support and condemnation of the marriage.

The Crawfords were thrilled to have Beth as their daughter-in-law; they immediately took Billy back into the family, and presented the couple with a house near their own as a wedding present. They put the title in Beth's name. "Not that we don't trust Billy," said Billy's mother anxiously to Beth.

"Don't be silly, Marian," said Joseph, scowling at Billy. "We'd be fools to trust him at this point," he said, beaming upon Beth. "Don't you worry," he added ambiguously, patting her hand.

Lucy and Dale Miller of course could have annulled the marriage; but although the town half expected it, they did nothing. Perhaps looking at the gabled house on the hill made Lucy able to smile upon her son-in-law. Billy Crawford was not a *monster,* after all; he was just weak. Beth would manage him; they would be just fine.

In the yellow house on Worth Street, the matter wasn't openly discussed. Our father had trusted Beth, and he missed her. After the elopement, he was saddened and vaguely bowed. "Too bad about that little girl," he said more than once, his eyes wandering to Beth's chair at the supper table.

No one dared ask Jack what he thought about all of it, and he did not offer his opinion. I heard him refer to Beth only once after her marriage, during a late whisky night with some buddies. I was on the edge of the group and heard it all.

"Old Beth," he said. "She was always pulling the rug out." He shook his head heavily, like a bull with sweat in its eyes. "Always surprising the hell out of me. She asked me right out did I love her. Other girls'll wait to see if you'll say it, but not old Beth." He drank. "It was right before a big game, too, and it kind of threw me off. I spent the whole game looking out to the bleachers, and hell if she wasn't looking the other way every time, yakking to her girlfriends. I lost that game all by myself." There was no rancor in the telling, but no humor either. "She sure could pull the rug out."

Apart from that single slip, Jack went about his business. He didn't get drunk and spill his sorrows to the whole town, the way Billy Crawford would do years later, after Beth threw him out. Public opinion of Jack actually rose a little after he was jilted; he got a reputation as an ironjaw.

The fuss lasted a good two weeks, and there was still hissing back and forth, tag ends of opinion, for a good month after that; but once it was done we got used to it. Beth Miller was now Mrs. Crawford, and went to live on the hill; and after a while Jack took up with another girl, a waitress from the south part of town.

I spent the afternoon with Beth on the day before she was married. She arrived at our house and stood under the apple tree, the way she used to do during that wartime summer.

"Anybody home?" she called up into the branches.

"Just me," I said, surprised: everyone knew she'd broken with Jack.

"Just the anybody I was looking for," she said. "Take a walk with me?"

I slid down out of the tree, dropping the book onto the lawn. Beth bent to retrieve it.

"Of Human Bondage," she said, handing it to me. "Is it good?"

I nodded. "I've read it before," I said. "It's one of my favorites."

"Imagine reading a book twice," said Beth. "It's not like you can run out of books to read. Have you read everything, now you have to go back and start again?"

"Some works b-benefit from a second reading," I said pompously, and then was silent, not a little disconcerted by my hesitation over the *b*. I hadn't stuttered in Beth's company for years.

"You hate to be teased, don't you," said Beth, thoughtfully. It wasn't a question, and I didn't answer it. "It's a big thick book," she said. "The thick ones are always boring."

"This one isn't," I said.

We walked through the south part of town—past the prison, where the men hanging against the screen of the open-air west tower hooted at the sight of Beth; along the railroad tracks which connected Naples to the West Virginia mines; through narrow, unkempt streets which made me nervous but which didn't seem to affect Beth at all—and then turned west, and left the city limits. As we went, I told her the story of club-footed Philip Carey, orphaned in childhood and brought up by his parsimonious uncle; how he went to London to study medicine, and then to Paris to study painting, and then back to London again.

"Sounds like he couldn't make up his mind," commented Beth.

"He couldn't," I said. "He was looking for the meaning of life."

"Did he find it?" she asked, interested.

"Yes," I said. "But it took him a long time to understand it."

"Well?" she said, impatiently. "What was it?"

"A piece of carpet," I said, enjoying myself. "A poet gave it to him just before he died. He said it held the clue to all meaning."

"A piece of carpet?" said Beth, when I wouldn't go on. "I don't get it," she said.

"Neither did he," said I. "Not until near the end of the book."

"You're not going to tell me, are you?" she exclaimed, stopping.

"Read the book," I said, primly.

"I hate you," said Beth, and we walked on.

"He's a bastard, your brother," said Beth suddenly, surprising me. "Oh, God." We were at a rough wooden fence, and she leaned against it, and absentmindedly began to pick at the grey splintery rails.

"What's he done?" I asked.

"That's just it," said Beth. "He hasn't *done* anything." There were tears in her voice, but her eyes were dry and bewildered looking. "He's just as—pleasant—as can be. It's not that," she said. "He's too pleasant," she said. "He's dead inside."

"Dead?" I had never heard anything like this before, never had a girl this near me, this near tears, confiding in me. "He's always been kind of quiet," I said.

"I don't mind quiet," spat Beth. "This is different. It's like talking to a stone. You know," she says. "You must know. I say, 'Jack, what do you think?' and he said, 'Sounds fine.' No excitement. No *life.*" She breathed in, and then out, and then said quietly, "It wasn't like that before."

"Before?" I asked, although I knew what she meant.

"He was gentle then," said Beth. "Not that he's not gentle now," she said, confused, confusing herself. "He's very gentle. He's fine. But he's not fine. I can't say it any better."

"He's a lot more agreeable now," I said.

"That's it, agreeable. What's that word they use for cows?

Docile. He's docile, like an old cow." Her face was sharp now, as though she were arguing. "And I don't care what anyone says, I don't want a docile man." I guessed "anyone" meant Lucy Miller. "That's why I liked him to begin with."

"Because he wasn't docile?"

"Because he was different," she said, leaning back from the gate now, looking upward. "He was wild, and going places. And kind of scary, like if he got mad he might do something crazy. Kill someone or something." She looked at me. "Not that I want him to kill anybody. But I liked thinking he was— dangerous."

"He's not dangerous anymore," I said, reflectively.

"No," she agreed.

We shook our heads sadly at this new, tame brother of mine.

"I don't know what to do," said Beth.

"Do about what?" I asked.

"I thought maybe I'd marry Jack, and we'd go somewhere else. Go travelling, you know, see the world."

"See the world?" I asked. To me the world was just one enormous place to stutter in.

"You just don't understand, do you?" cried Beth, seeing my puzzlement.

"What's wrong with Naples?" I asked. "I know it's small," I said.

"Small," said Beth. "Small-minded. But that's not it. I can't explain it." She thought for a moment. "There's something called a wildebeest," she said.

"Yes?" I said, surprised.

"I thought at first it was a joke name, you know, 'wild beast'? It just seemed so silly. And then I started thinking about it. There are places, Gil, where the wildebeest is normal, just like a dog or a horse. They don't look funny. And there's a different language, too; that same wildebeest has a different name. Every language probably has a different name for that wildebeest. Gil," she said, tightening her jaw and looking directly at me, *"I only know one."*

She sighed, and for a minute we didn't say anything.

"Have you talked to Jack about this?" I said.

"Have I," she said, giving a short, unattractive laugh. "He looked at me like I was crazy. Kind of like you're doing now."

"Sorry," I mumbled.

"I thought I could make him go back the way he was," she said, not listening to me. "I'd talk and talk. And the whole time he'd be looking out the window, or at me, like it didn't make any difference which. Then I'd say, 'Jack, *look* at me,' and he would, he'd just turn his face right around and look at me, listening to me like you'd listen to a crazy old woman. I'd talk to him, *at* him, and then when I couldn't say any more because I heard myself babbling . . ." and she stopped.

"Yes?" I prompted. "What did he do?"

"Nothing," she said, bitterly. "He did nothing. He said nothing. He just *breathed*. I wasn't even sure if he'd heard me."

"He heard you," I said, suddenly sure of myself.

"Maybe I am crazy," she said.

"No," I said boldly. "You know what you want, is all."

"Yes," she said, after a minute. "But what if I did something bad to get it?"

"Like what?" I asked.

"Nothing much," she said, suddenly gay. "Would you still like me?"

"Depends how bad it is," I said, in a matching, teasing voice.

"Oh, terrible," she said, still flippant, but with an edge of gravity around her eyes and mouth.

"Of course I would," I said. "I'll always like you."

"Forever and ever?" she asked, like a little girl.

"Oh yes," I told her, with all the force of honesty, and she smiled.

That was a Friday, and the next Monday Beth returned from the little town she and Billy had gone to, to elope. I heard the news, and felt the shock deep inside, like my organs were moving; then I felt a little pang of guilt. Had I helped her along? It seemed to me that Beth had abandoned one dangerous boy for another, choosing Billy out of reaction to the now-passive Jack. *You know what you want,* I'd told her.

I'd seen Beth in passing since then, but we hadn't spoken at any length, and when I spotted her in the Trough I wasn't positive that it was she. It didn't seem the sort of place she'd be, of an evening. I myself had squeezed in only with misgivings, hesitating on the inside step. The room was crowded and smoke-filled, thick with aggression and the odor of spilt beer. I'd turned to leave; as I did so, I caught a glimpse of her— *Beth?*—and I pushed my way toward her for a better look.

The girl I thought was Beth was better dressed than the

other patrons and more sophisticated looking. She didn't quite belong, although she was surrounded by people who did, and there was something hard and sharp about her face which resembled their hardness and sharpness. I looked more closely: she had Beth's hair, maybe a little darker but just as straight, and reaching to her shoulders the way I remembered. She had the same level brows, and the same little chin. Still, she seemed alien, like a clever imitation of that softer girl I'd known. While I watched, she ducked her head in laughing and threw it back again, so that I was looking at her little, flared nostrils; the movement was a particular habit of Beth's, and I was convinced. I caught her eye and waved; she looked straight at me and raised her eyebrows without acknowledging the greeting. Feeling foolish, I looked away quickly, as though our eyes had met by chance. I waved my arm at the bartender, who moved toward me with irritation. A few minutes later, I felt a tap on my arm.

"Little G.I.," she said, smiling up at me.

"Not you, too," I said, but grinning with relief. "I hate being called that."

"Buy me a beer?" she asked.

By some miracle which only women are capable of, a booth near the back of the room came free just as she turned toward it.

"Where's Billy?" I asked, looking around.

"Who knows," she said.

Our eyes met.

"It's like that, is it?" I said.

"Oh, it's not too bad," she said, taking a mighty swallow of beer and setting the glass down. "I swear they piss in the beer here."

"You look different," I said, before I could stop myself.

"Gilbert Grahame Corbin, you *know* better than to tell a girl something about herself without putting a compliment in. When you say I look different, you could mean that I look like a hag. I just hate it when men *do* that."

"What was I supposed to say?" I asked, smiling.

"Well," she said. "I'll demonstrate." Her face went cold and hard, and she looked me up and down, appraising me as a breeder looks at livestock. "You got a haircut," she said, finally, flatly. My face burned with embarrassment.

"I see what you mean," I said.

"Good," she said, smiling, becoming Beth again. "Have you

got yourself a girlfriend yet?" she asked, teasing, reaching forward to run her hand over my bristly scalp.

"Girls don't seem to like the look," I said, ducking away.

"The haircut's fine," said Beth. "It's that pity-me face you need to get rid of."

"I'll work on it," I said, irritably.

"Don't get mad," said Beth.

I said nothing.

"Okay, I can see you don't want to be teased," she said. "I'll stop. Will you be nice now?"

"Of course," I said, but coldly.

"You hold such grudges," she said. "I haven't seen you in so long, and now you won't even talk to me."

There was a silence.

"How's the army treating you?" she asked.

"Fine," I said.

She leaned forward across the table, brushing a strand of hair out of her eyes.

"I'm not convinced," she said.

I looked away.

"I thought so," she said. "It didn't seem like the right thing for you. All that group stuff."

I nodded, surprised at her perception.

"Forgive me," said Beth. "But—don't they care about your stutter?"

"They don't know about it," I said.

"How—?" she breathed.

"I've been careful," I said, shortly.

"Jesus," she said. "A double, no, a triple life. How hard it must be, Gil." She put her hand briefly over mine, where it rested on the table. Pulling it away, she asked, "What if they find out?"

"I don't know," I said. "Maybe they won't care."

"Not likely," she said, tipping up her beer. "It's not wartime. They can pick and choose." She stopped herself. "Oh God, I didn't mean that the way it sounded. It's those people I run with. They say all kinds of terrible things," she said. "It gets to be kind of a habit."

"It's okay," I said.

"I should go," she said. "Or they'll start talking about me." She laughed, unconvincingly, sending a glance toward the group across the room, sliding out of the booth, straightening her skirt. "Look, come to a party tomorrow night, if you can. My place. I mean, mine and Bill's."

"Well," I said, cautiously, but intrigued: I was not often invited to parties.

"Horrible people, but the liquor will flow," she said, false and coaxing, with her eyes darting between them and me. "There's a girl you should meet," she said. "You know what I mean?" and she wiggled her eyebrows. I looked away, embarrassed by her coarseness. Bringing her eyes back to me, dropping her shoulders, she said, "Please come. Come and keep me company."

"Okay," I said.

"Good," said Beth. She half turned, and then turned back, laying a hand on my shoulder. "How's Jack?" she asked, into my ear.

"He's fine," I said. "Doesn't say much about much. You know."

"Yeah." She sighed, looking down. I looked too; both of us stared at her hand, where it flexed on my shoulder. When I looked up at her again, she was smiling. "Don't forget," she said. "Tomorrow. Ten o'clock,"—moving away—"till dawn."

I found myself standing alone on the fringes of the party, wedged in between small groups of people, some dancing, some talking vivaciously, all drinking. The girl Beth had earmarked for me was in another room or possibly on the porch, where the liquor was; she had turned out to be a garish type, loud and gum cracking and pointy-breasted. In truth, she frightened me, and I had spent much of the evening dodging her, which made me feel churlish at first. But it became clear that she hardly minded, being less taken with me, if possible, than I was with her, and so my conscience was eased. I clutched my whisky and soda tightly, and looked around the living room. The faces were nearly all unfamiliar; I hadn't seen Beth since she had first opened the door to me, and I hadn't seen Billy anywhere at all. The room was getting very crowded, and everywhere I looked something highly amusing was going on, judging from the hilarity rising from the dense knots of people jostling for space. They all seemed false to me, and frightening, in the way that my erstwhile date had been frightening. Stuffed into their garments, they laughed as though something terrible might happen to them if they didn't. To my slightly drunken eye, they looked afraid, and their fear

infected me. I stood very rigid in the crush, as though frozen
at attention; elbows poked me in the back, and a high female
laugh shrilled in my ear.

Then, as if a mist had rolled away, I saw her. Demure,
dressed in pale green, seated primly on a sofa in the middle of
the room, she had a surprised look on her face, an air of apartness, as though she and the sofa had dropped together through
the ceiling into the maelstrom. I worked my way toward her,
through a group of raucous dancers, dodging tossing heads
and flying limbs. When I stood in front of her at last, I was
struck dumb and merely stared.

Suddenly, Beth was at my side.

"My best friend," she bawled at me, above the music, waving a hand toward the girl. She leaned over to the sofa. "Jack's
brother," she shouted. The girl considered me coolly; Beth
straightened up and pulled me aside.

"I should have known," she said. "Sheila scared you away.
Well, good luck," she said, and got on tiptoe to whisper into
my ear. "Does she or doesn't she?" she murmured warmly. "I
happen to know this one doesn't," and she pulled away and
winked significantly. I blushed.

Fortunately, someone tugged on her arm at that moment.

"Shitfire," said Beth, turning back to the girl and me.
"Something's exploded in the kitchen. These *people,*" she said,
and was gone.

The girl and I looked at one another.

"Hello, best friend," I said.

"Hello, brother," said she.

She was very serious looking, very pretty, all of her features
cleanly drawn: nice straight nose, not too small; high cheek-
bones; round brown eyes; and a lightness to it all that made me
want to anchor her, as though she might rise up and lift away
from me. But when a few moments into the conversation she
smiled, it was as though she had been ugly before, the contrast
was that great. I found myself straining to be humorous, no
amount of foolishness too great in order to gain that reward,
that smile.

"Let's go," I said boldly, after the girl's drink had been
jogged out of her hand by some passing funster. I plucked her
glass away and held out my hand.

"Where?" she asked composedly, dabbing a handkerchief at
the liquid on her knees.

"Anywhere," I said, "but here."

She gave me her hand. How many times after that did we enact that same small gesture, my hand put out, hers slipped calmly into it, resting there like a small unafraid bird? But that time was the first. I drew her out of Beth's house and into the street. Once there, I came to a stop.

"I don't have a," and I blushed. "Car."

"I do," said Joan.

We drove to the Real Thing and ate plain doughnuts and drank coffee. Joan told me about herself—born in Pittsburgh, she had come to Naples to attend the women's college. "It's a long way from home," she said, wrinkling her nose, "but I wasn't accepted anywhere else. I'm afraid I didn't do much studying in high school."

I wondered what she *had* done—dated, of course, and I felt the swift fire of jealousy.

She was studying psychology, with courses in education, and wanted to be a teacher. She'd met Beth in the doctor's office where Joan was working part time as a typist.

"She called you her best friend," I said.

"She's being nice," said Joan. "I guess she took pity on me, being new here. I don't make friends easily."

"You don't?" I said, surprised.

She shook her head. "Beth sort of took me in. But I don't know how I like that crowd she runs with. She seems different when she's with them." She thought a moment. "Beth is a nice person," she said. "But so unhappy."

"Unhappy?" I repeated.

"She hides it well," said Joan. "Under all that—shininess."

Unhappy: I had never thought to apply this adjective to Beth. I recalled her face at the bar, its new hard, protected look; I remembered her brittle gaiety at the party. I nodded, slowly. "She didn't used to be," I said.

We stayed at the diner until one in the morning. Joan drove me home; it was not until I was getting into my pyjamas, humming, that I realized I had spent an evening with a girl—a pretty girl—and I had not stuttered. Not after the first half hour. And that I felt wonderful—light, free, all of those things that you feel when you've been up late drinking bad coffee with a pretty girl. I liked this feeling; it felt like my life was finally beginning. Whatever happened, I told myself, I couldn't let this feeling pass.

Date led to date; by the time I left again for the army, I was thickly snared. I wrote the first letter to Joan on the bus, fifteen minutes after my last glimpse of her. She answered my letters, in a ratio of about one to three, and when I was stationed close to home, we rejoiced. I made the trip to Naples whenever I could: the journeys had new meaning to them now; they had something for me at their ends, not just a collection of clapboard houses and familiar faces.

In July of 1950, I rushed home on short leave. I went straight from the station to the doctor's office where Joan worked.

"What is it?" she cried, seeing me, jumping up.

"I'm—" I said.

"Sit down," she said, taking me into the waiting room. "I'll get you some water."

I shook my head. "Being transferred," I said.

"What?" she said. "Oh no."

"No," I told her. "Not there. Washington."

"Thank God," she said, the color coming back into her face.

"They're giving me a desk job," I said. "But I might see combat before it's over."

I was lying. Of course, I *had* been slated for combat; just twenty and fully trained, I would normally have been among the first to be sent to the latest arena of conflict—a little country called Korea, unimaginably far away, whose politics I didn't even understand. But the staff sergeant, who had found out about my stutter, marked me down as unfit. He was not an unkind man; he took me aside, to give me the news in private.

"They'll need good men in Washington," he said. "And you're smart, as smart as if you went to college. They can use you there."

"What does it—" I said, and blushed. "Matter?"

"About the stutter?" he said, uncompromisingly. "Come on, Corbin. You'd be giving orders, sooner or later. Men would depend on you. And you'd be standing there saying 'f-f-f-fire'?" He put a hand on my shoulder. "No offense," he said. "But I don't think so."

I lied now to save face with Joan; and it appeared that she believed me. Shaken, she put her head against my shoulder.

"How long are you here for?" she asked, pulling away, looking into my face.

"Not long," I said.

She had never looked so fragile as at that moment: all her normal good humor drained away, and the lovely bones of her face stood out starkly. The perfect picture of a soldier's girl.

And that was how I came to propose: in a tawdry doctor's office, among the violently patterned chairs of the waiting room. No train pulling away, Joan running along beside it; no roses, no moonlight, no romantic fog. Just the water cooler gurgling beside me as I knelt on the hard rug, and a middle-aged woman coughing tubercularly in my ear.

Washington wasn't so bad; foreign, of course, in a way that I hadn't expected. I had been led to believe that the capital was a Southern city. But I could find no trace of home in the heavy white buildings, no nostalgic river glitter in the Potomac. I was quartered in an apartment house near the Capitol, two rooms to myself. I hadn't had so much privacy in all of my young life; the quiet made me restless, and at night I strolled the streets, alone.

During those years, Washington was a world of bureaucrats and soldiers; but seldom did I hear the word *war,* and nowhere found the feeling of war the way it had been in the forties. Korea, it seemed, was a *police action,* a distant thought, save to those whose boys were dying there. The streets of Washington bustled, pedestrians moving along with a purpose, but I suspected that it might be the normal state of things in the capital.

Thinking to escape the downtown hubbub, I rode a streetcar out to the suburbs one weekend afternoon. I walked the sidewalks, looking intently at the houses, alert for the traces of war. The houses were familiar, much more so than the government buildings. But there were no stars in the windows, and when darkness came, no blackout. I was involved, it seemed, in a highly contained effort. Blood spilled in Korea, but on the streets of America there was only opulence; opulence, and progress.

In time, I detected a strange undercurrent to the goings-on in Washington. The newspapers began to be filled with accusations and hearings, vicious denunciations, treason. The man with the Pumpkin papers was jostled out of the headlines; a Jewish couple from New York took his place. And then the lists. It seemed the entire population was being reduced to a series of lists—long enumerations of public figures, their friends, their friends' friends. The newspaper accounts grew more explicit; downtown, daily, the hearings continued; and the streets of the city grew quieter, the atmosphere tense. A new element threatened the nation's well-being; it had nothing to do with the Asian war; it was tragically American, a fearsome kind of tyranny.

I stayed in Washington until the end of the war; Naples was only a few hours away, and I travelled there frequently on weekend leave. Now that Joan and I were engaged to be married, our comings together edged a little further away from their chaste beginnings, but as Beth had told me so long before, Joan "didn't." It didn't matter. To tell the truth, sex frightened me not a little; I was happy to be with Joan, to kiss her, to hear her say my name. She was the focus of my life, my weeks; heading south, I closed my eyes to see her, cool and perfect, radiating welcome. Her image blotted out the others— the fearful faces of the city I was leaving, the friendly-contemptuous faces I had known since birth. Her voice sang pure and loud in my ears, rising above the other sounds, the office chatter of the weekdays, the warning tones of the radio news announcers. Rising above the chorus of "G.I.," which bleated out from other, mocking mouths. I let the wheels of the train carry me; I was riding toward her, riding away from my isolation; going home.

Chapter Nine

The Gun Collector

A ll the good stories I know are telling on someone. I could tell you about baseball, I guess, or quail hunting, or women. Women. I could tell you a lot about them. Don't shake your head at me; it's distracting.

You'd think I'd want to talk about my wife. You'd be wrong; she was a good woman, and good to me, but almost since she walked out the front door, I began forgetting her. We slept in the same bed for five years, and I can't hardly remember anything about her. Think of that. No, I'll tell you about Miriam.

Miriam strayed in here like a leaf come through an open door. She didn't stay all that long, but she made her impression. She wasn't the prettiest, or the smartest, or even the one I loved the most; but she had a way about her. Like she had secrets, and like she even knew some of mine. She carried no great burden of love for me, either, if it came to that, and she didn't bear me any children. But I remember her.

She was best when things got bad. She could handle trouble, she stopped her bitching and made herself real useful. Sometimes I felt like when things were going good, she got frightened, and wanted to mess them up a little. Like she felt more comfortable with rough times; like rough times was what she was used to.

I remember one miserable run of days in summer; a bad stretch of weather, the air so hot and damp it was like breathing out of a teakettle. I had a boss then, Jed Pollard, a lazy sonofabitch. He'd bought his way into the business; he didn't know nothing about it except counting the money. There was only one other guy and me to take care of all the repair work at the garage, while old Jed lay back in his office and fanned himself with the green. I was beginning to feel a little desperate then; it was that kind of summer. The kind when time seems to stop and you realize for the first time since you were a young man expecting glory that you might be in the same job forever, and never get anywhere at all.

I hated Pollard; me and the other guy, Rupe, eventually bought the place off him. We paid a fair price, but he moaned like he was getting raped; he was that fond of money. He collected guns; used to hang around while we were working, standing right in the fan blast, telling us about the new rifle he'd just bought, how he had an eye on someone's old Winchester. We heard all about those guns, and the racks he had custom built to hold them. Rupe was a hunting man, and he asked old Jed if he ever got out after deer. Pollard said No. Just like that, No. Rupe said Turkey? And Pollard said—and I'm not kidding—'I don't *shoot* my guns. It damages them." After that, Rupe hated him as much as I did. "Can't understand a man having thirty-seven guns and never shot one of them," he said, and that was that.

The days were pretty much all the same, paddling along through that slow summer, until one day Pollard called me into the back office.

"Jack, I got a proposition for you," he said.

The way he was real casual, I could tell he was in a spot, and needed me to say Yes to what he was going to offer. So I kinda took advantage, and pulled a chair up to the window where the fan was, and let it blow on my back. He didn't even frown. That's when I knew he needed me bad. So I leaned back, put my boots up on the desk. He didn't say nothing about it, just started right in to explaining.

He'd been having a security system installed, bars on the windows of the gun room, so's no one could get in and steal his collection. But the carpenter he'd hired had taken him for a good piece of money, and then skedaddled with the job half finished.

And I thought, all of a sudden, *Jack.* I kinda shook my head, like I didn't understand, but acourse I did. "You're sumpin of a handyman, am I right?" he said. I kinda shrugged, real modest. "You sure can tinker with an engine." It was the first time he'd ever praised my work. "Thought you might be innerested in finishing the job."

"Huh," I said.

"What about it?" he asked.

"Cars ain't wood," I said.

"What's the difference?" he said. "Fixing's fixing."

Shows how much *he* knew.

Well, it didn't appeal to me too much at first; carpentry's my hobby, not my calling. And there's something about being paid for doing what you love that makes you stop loving it. But the way he described the job, it sounded like it ought to take no more than a Saturday morning, and old Pollard he waved a bunch of money in my face.

"A hundred for the job," he said. "Flat fee."

That sounded good to me; the fix-it jobs I picked up here and there generally paid worse than the garage. This one looked just like cream, one hundred dollars for the whole deal, no matter how short a time it took. Like a goat, I said I'd do it.

Rupe thought I was crazy.

"Five days a week, you gotta listen to his bullshit," he said. "Now you're gonna spend your Saturday over there?"

"He won't be there," I said. "He's going fishing."

"Fishing," said Rupe, with a face like he'd been spat on. "That's for fat ninnies who can't do nothing else."

"He's paying me a C note," I said.

"Take a thousand for me to go over there," said Rupe.

"Nobody's asking you," I told him.

I showed up early Saturday morning with my toolbox. Mrs. Pollard let me in, with a frightened look on her face, like I was gonna jump her. Then when I didn't pay hardly no attention to her, stepping carefully through the door without brushing up against her, she looked disappointed. She showed me to the gun room, and left me there.

The room was all guns and windows. Five long racks on the walls, with eight windows spaced between. A coupla deep chairs, a big old desk, not much else. The iron bars Pollard had had specially made were piled on the floor, up against the near wall. I knew they'd been milled to thirty-seven inches, so they'd fit eight to a window, in the frames the man who'd gone before me had already installed.

Even from across the room, it was real clear that that fellow wasn't much of a carpenter. The frames were scrap wood, probably left over from another job, cost him nothing. They were dirty and gouged in places. But I figured that much didn't matter; he'd done the hard part, making the windows all the same size by putting the frames in, and drilled most of the holes too, for the bars to fit in. My part was gonna be easy.

When I measured the first frame, it was a little off—about a quarter of an inch. No problem; I just had to drill the holes a little deeper, so the bars would go in snug. The first one went in fine, but the second one wobbled; I'd drilled too far. I looked the frame over again and realized that the guy hadn't only screwed up the measurements on the frames, he'd also drilled the holes just any old way, so there was no telling how much I'd have to drill to make up for it. I began to sweat. I shoulda known that a man who'd treat wood like he done couldn't be trusted with a tape measure. I did what I should've done to begin with, and measured all the window frames and all the holes. They were all different.

What should have been a couple hours' easy work suddenly looked like hard labor. But I'd started the job, and I set to it, measuring each frame again before I started, grinding anywhere from an eighth to three-quarters of an inch off each bar. Sinking it into place, starting all over again with the next one.

There was no real floor space in the gun room, so I'd put some sheets down in the living room. About four hours into the job, Mrs. Pollard came in.

"Oh," she said. "I thought you'd be in the other room."

"I needed space to work, ma'am," I said.

"I was about to have lunch," she said, looking kinda leery at the mess all over the drop cloths. "Would you like to join me?"

I was pretty hungry by then; I hadn't thought to bring any food from home, thinking I wouldn't be there that long.

"Thank you," I said, and laid down my tools. I washed up in the little john on the first floor, what she called a 'powder room.' I expected a sandwich in the kitchen, but she took me on into the dining room, and the girl waited on us. We had some kind of thick soup with little leaves in it. Hot soup, when the mercury's reading ninety-four. I sweated through that, and about a pitcher of iced tea to chase it down, while she chattered away across the table, all about her charity work and the cardigan sweater she was knitting for old Jed.

When I was done, I thanked her again and got up.

"Oh, Jack," she said, and made a fluttery sort of noise in her throat, like a bird. "You don't mind if I call you Jack?"

"No ma'am," I said, wondering what the hell else would she call me. "Jack's fine."

"Well, then, Jack," she said. I was beginning to hate my own name, hearing it said over and over. "I usually play the piano on Saturdays after lunch. Will you be done soon?"

"Well, ma'am, I'm afraid it's going to take a while," I told her. "But you go right ahead, it won't bother me none."

"I wouldn't want to disturb you," she said. And the way that word *disturb* came out kind of turned my stomach. She was probably good-looking in her day, but I wasn't thirty then, and she was looking back from the far side of fifty. She batted her eyes, setting the soup I'd just swallowed to moving around inside me like maybe it wanted to come up for air.

She came along into the living room and tinkled away half-heartedly on the piano by the bay window. I got back to work. The music wasn't so bad, but she took to making little comments to me, like 'Did you like that?' and 'I played that rather badly, didn't I?' And I'd have to stop what I was doing and tell her, Yes, I liked it, and No, she'd played it very well, and on and on. She'd ask me to listen to something, and it seemed rude to turn on the drill while she was playing. So things kind of slowed down after lunch.

By four-thirty there was about another half-day's worth of work ahead of me. There was no way around it: I'd have to come back the next day to finish. I told Mrs. Pollard, who didn't seem at all bothered by the news. Then I left, and went home and growled at Miriam.

She was mean right back at first, but when she could tell I was really bad off she got quiet, and then she started being really sweet, the way she could be. It didn't help much, though; and when we went to bed all I could think about was going over to Pollard's again the next morning. I believe I dreamed about those goddamn windows that night, and Mrs. Pollard and that soup, and her fussing at the piano.

The next day was worse. Old Jed was still fishing, and his wife was real friendly now, popping in and out of the living room all morning, asking me did I want a cold drink, what did I want for lunch. I tried to be polite, but there I was hunched down on the floor like a dog, breathing up fibers of wood and iron, running sweat, with Mrs. Pollard at my elbow, giggling into my face.

"Now maybe you can explain it to me," she said.

"What's that, ma'am," I said, kinda dull and discouraging. But she wasn't discouraged a bit.

"Why would a grown man want to go off and sit in an old leaky boat on a lake and get bitten all to pieces by mosquitoes, just so he can come back and tell me about the big one he nearly got?"

"I'm not one for fishing, ma'am," I said, patient. "But some like it."

"Well now, I just don't *understand* that," she said. "Leaving your house and your bride to go off with a bunch of boys and jiggle a worm around in the water."

Bride my ass.

"Well, ma'am," I said, from down there on the floor. She bent down toward me a little, with her head on one side like a canary, waiting. "Fish are mighty quiet," I said.

She didn't understand at first; then she got a look on her face, and hemmed a little, and got up from the sofa and left the room.

After a while, the maid came in to tell me lunch was ready. I washed up in the powder room again, and went into the kitchen this time, where there was a place laid on, a cold sandwich and a glass of tea. That suited me just fine; the maid got me more tea when I asked, and the rest of the time I just ate, enjoying the silence. I swallowed the last bit, and finished the tea; I was beginning to feel better. Then she came into the kitchen, all hoity-toity, and a chill in her voice to frostbite you.

"I hope you'll be done soon," she said. "I'm having guests at six."

"Coupla hours," I said.

"Fine," she said, and went away.

I went back to work. It was still hot as blazes, and the work was as tedious as ever, but I was on the seventh window now; the end was in sight. I started whistling; after a few minutes, Mrs. Pollard came in.

"Could you please," she said, "try to be a little quieter? I have a terrible headache."

She wasn't hardly out of the room again when it all came back. All those things I'd been able to put aside for a little while—the pain in my back from bending over on the floor; the blisters that had opened on my hands; the whole goddamn rotten experience of being in that house and doing that prissy work that wouldn't have needed doing if the first guy had done his job right to begin with. I was covered with iron filings, and I'd run two long splinters into my hands from the junk wood on the window frames. It hadn't been interesting work even, fixing up fussy little iron gates for my boss's guns he never shot, and I'd spent more effort on it than it deserved, each window a custom job where it oughta been a simple repeating pattern. And all the time I'm down there on the floor or hauling bars around, old lady Pollard is chattering into my ear complaining about the heat, pulling at her blouse so I can see the flat freckly skin of her chest. That hundred dollars was looking a hell of a lot smaller now.

It kept right on shrinking over the next coupla hours, till I was finally done. I collected my tools together and wrapped up the dropcloths, and behind me Mrs. Pollard went past to look at the gunroom windows.

"Oh, my," she said. "It looks like a jail in here."

"Jails are to keep people in," I said. "This here's to keep 'em out."

"I wish it weren't so—obvious," she said.

"Can't figure a way to make iron bars you can't see," I said.

That shut her up for a minute, but she came back quick.

"I'm afraid we'll have a terrible time getting the sawdust up off the carpets," she said pointedly. "And those wood chips won't go in the sweeper." She sighed. "I guess we'll be down on our hands and knees picking them up."

I doubted she'd be on her hands and knees doing anything; sure as shit that poor maid would do all of it, while Mrs. Pollard twittered at her from the couch. It had been the worst weekend of my life, and I was mad enough to chew glass, but I held my tongue. Just said good-bye, and got out of there.

I dragged myself home, feeling like something was broken in me, and beyond fixing. Never mind what my dad used to say, that work done with your hands is honest work. I felt low. I pulled into the house, and on into the kitchen, with nothing but nasty words and a nasty look for Miriam, who listened for a minute, and then left the room.

I followed her into the bathroom, my anger even bigger without an audience, and saw she was twisting the taps in the tub.

"I don't want a goddamn bath," I said.

"Food first," she said, calm, and went back to the kitchen. I followed her again. She fed me while the bath was filling, and then she took me by the hand and led me to the tub.

"Get in," she said.

The water was hotter than hell. "Jesus!" I said. "You trying to boil me?"

"You'll get used to it," she said.

It took a minute till I could sit down, but when I did, the water closed over me like a healing hand. I laid my head back and shut my eyes. The nastiness in me was beginning to be crowded out by the food and pure exhaustion.

I heard a kinda suspicious rustling, and when I opened my eyes, sure enough Miriam was pulling off her dress, and rolling down her panties.

"Hell," I said. "Not now."

"Shut up," she said, stepping into the water. It rippled

around her and up my chest, and lapped at the undersides of
my arms, which were lying along the cool sides of the tub.
Ignoring me, exactly like you would a fractious child, she took
up the cake of soap and began to wash me.

First my chest, where a froth came right up. Then sending
her little hands up my neck, under my unshaven jaw. Along
my arms, rolling the muscles in her hands like dough. She
rinsed me off with water, using a Tupperware bowl she'd
brought in with her from the kitchen.

She cleaned my legs, yes, and my feet, giving each one its
turn between her breasts, holding it there to soap it, working
her white fingers between my toes, tickling me. I can't do
justice to that sight—Miriam, squatting in the water between
my legs, rolling the soap in her hands. I had recovered enough
by then to play with her, sliding my foot back and forth
against her breasts, stretching out two toes to pinch the nipple.
She looked up at that, and frowned, and then smiled a little.

"Better?" she said, and I nodded.

You pick the strangest damn times to pay attention. You
perked right up when I got to Miriam's breasts. You like that
stuff about the feet, huh? Well, this ain't a story about feet.

After she'd rinsed off my legs, I thought she was done, but
she got the soap again, and reached for one of my hands which
dangled, bitten and scarred and stained, under the water. She
put the soap between our three hands, two of hers and one of
mine, and rolled it over and over, working up a foam. Then
she put the soap aside and started on my hand, rubbing with
her palms and fingers my fingers and palm, scraping her fingernails over the stubborn places, avoiding the blisters. She
rooted out the dirt from my fingerprints, picking her way
through the terrain of my right hand, and then she took up a
nail brush and scrubbed at my fingernails, which were lined
dark with grime and wood stain.

She worked until the hand was pink, and clean as it ever
would be, and while she worked I closed my eyes and lay
quiet. In all my young life I had never experienced anything to
come close to what I'm telling you about now. And I'd had my
share of women by then, and some of them like fire in bed. But
always with sex there's a certain pressure, an expectation, and
it distracts a little even when everything else is very good.
With this there was no distraction—I lay back, purely selfish,
while Miriam washed my hands.

When she'd finished with the right hand she dipped it under

the water, and began all over again on the other, just as careful
and slow, like she wasn't tired at all. I lay there lazy, being
ministered to.

When she was done, she kind of pushed my legs aside and
made room for herself. We just lay there like that, her on top
of me, her hair spreading out across my chest and her arms
tight around my back. We stayed there for an hour, maybe,
without moving. When we got up the water was cold, and my
temper was gone.

Before we went to sleep, she turned over on her side and
whispered to me.

"Be sure you get the whole hundred," was what she said.

Acourse old Jed tried to knock me down to seventy-five, but
I wasn't having any, and he finally forked over the whole
thing. So there was that. And Rupe was tickled by what I told
him about Mrs. Pollard and her piano; I didn't fill out the
story, but I let him draw his own conclusions. So there was
that.

The hundred went on a hundred different things, and Rupe
pulled that story every which way until it was thin as a thread.
My blisters healed, and Miriam left me. So the only thing that
lasted was the memory of that bath. I probably woulda remembered her anyway, but because of it I think of her kindly,
wherever she is, in spite of all the bitterness that came along
between us later. She was an unusual woman, gifted with the
understanding that sometimes a man wants to be less than he's
commonly supposed to be, that sometimes he wants to lie back
in the water and be bathed. And she understood about my
hands. When I lifted them out of the water they looked new,
and I was new too, and peaceful.

There ain't nothing like the gentleness of a gentle woman in
dire circumstances. Maybe you meet a woman like that yourself someday, Buddy. Maybe then you won't be fooling around
here, pointing that camera at people and shooting your questions off in a New York voice like you got no time to waste.
Life ain't in urgency, Buddy. I hope you figure that out.

Chapter Ten

Ladies' Man

All that talk about girls. Sometimes he couldn't tell if Jack was deliberately taunting him, or what. Maybe not; maybe at his age, every man around here had gotten laid a hundred times, and they just didn't suspect that Buddy had never had a girl.

Or had once had a girl. Just once, but it didn't really count. He hadn't even felt that way about her. She was short, with a solid build and huge Bambi-lashed blue eyes, and they'd been alone in her dorm room, looking at records. He'd been on the floor, flipping through the stack, while she sat on the bed, looking over his shoulder. That's a good one, she'd said, pointing, and out of the corner of his eye he'd seen her boot. It was a pull-on type, skintight, with a little suede fringe dangling at the top, where her jeans tucked in. The sight had charged him, and he'd stood up halfway, quickly enough to startle her, and without thinking further he'd twisted and fallen across her, by some luck catching her mouth with his.

She'd let him, never saying a word, just helping him pull her jeans down, and later reaching a hand up and ruffling it through his hair, as though he were an animal. They hadn't even taken all of their clothes off. Part of him regretted that; maybe if they'd taken that bit of extra time, she would have been more present, more involved. The other part of him knew that if he'd hesitated at all, it wouldn't have happened. He couldn't have forced her; if she'd said anything like "Stop" or "No," he'd have stopped, and maybe they would have discussed it, and then it wouldn't have happened at all.

Still, it was too bad that it stood as his only sexual experience. If there had been others after her, the first time might have become softened by successive glories, laughable. As it was, its memory was merely void, as though nothing had been gained or learned, just everything thrown into question, by the act. There hadn't even been a sense of novelty or release to it; he'd felt, slipping in, as though he'd done it before; all those movies and TV, he guessed, teaching familiarity with things you didn't really know about. He had the same feeling about skiing, or firing a gun, although he'd never done those before either; but he'd seen it done in living color so many times, he felt as though he had.

They weren't even friends after that; he passed her on campus many times, and they said Hi, but never stopped to talk. He worried for a while that she'd told her roommates about his ineptitude—*He just jumped on top of me, actually fell on top of me, it was pathetic*—but, reflecting, he knew that she hadn't; she hadn't known what to make of it any more than he had. And he worried for a while that she'd get pregnant; he evaluated her figure every time he saw her, but she never seemed any fatter, so he didn't think about it anymore. By then, he was preoccupied with something else, another girl.

Tate. What a stupid name for a girl, and how beautiful and right it was for her. With her short straight black hair and snapping black eyes, her deep voice that was like a man's, but unmistakably female. He'd joined the Glee Club to be close to her, and worked his way to stand behind her, losing his place in the Mahler they were learning, leaning forward to breathe in the fragrance of her hair. He couldn't figure out her clothes—they looked like a man's, but they fit her. She was tallish, so maybe they were her brother's. She wore loads of bracelets around her wrists, but no earrings, and she never did anything with her hair, just let it hang, glossy and smooth, to just below her ears, the forehead banged like Prince Valiant's.

He'd tried to get her to be the subject of his first short film. "It's a portrait," he'd said. "Non-synch sound." She'd looked quizzical, and her friends had jostled each other while they'd waited for her.

"A movie about me?" she'd said.

"A portrait," he repeated. "The professor said to do anybody. I figure it's more interesting if you don't know the person."

"But you know me," she said.

"Not really," he'd said, blushing. "I mean, we're not friends, or anything."

Or anything, her buddies had chortled, behind her.

"Well," Tate had said, putting her hands in her pockets. "Um. I don't think so. I mean, I haven't got much time this semester."

"But it won't take long. It's only five minutes."

"Five minutes?" she asked, like that was incredible. "What can you do in five minutes?"

"A lot," he said. "Think about it. Five minutes is a long time. We've only been talking about two. Less than that, even."

"Huh," she said.

"What would I have to do?"

Strip, said the peanut gallery.

"Anything you like," he'd said, ignoring them. "Talk, or sing, or whatever."

"Well," she said again, and the way she hesitated made it clear to him that she wasn't sure of his name, "I don't think so. But thanks."

"Okay," he'd replied, not sure what he meant. "Okay."

"Good luck," she'd called after him as he'd walked away.

He'd ended up doing a four-minute segment on the girl who lived next door to him in the dorm—someone he studied with occasionally, and who sometimes displayed signals of having a crush on him. He'd filmed her dancing in her room—she was a ballet student—using strange camera angles. Getting down on the floor while she leapt over the camera, or crouching on the top of her hastily cleared bureau. He'd used an unrelated soundtrack, taped from a study session, her explaining the significance of a passage in *Twelfth Night.*

Szilardi had liked the film, although he told Buddy that he'd have to "tone it down."

"All those weird camera angles, they're fine," he said. *"If* they have a purpose." He came closer to where Buddy sat, and shook his head slowly, to emphasize his meaning. "But not just for the hell of it." He'd walked away again, circling the room as he talked. "You show a natural ability," he'd said. "But you must avoid self-indulgence."

A natural ability. He had hugged those words to himself after class, and repeated them to his father, during their Sunday morning telephone conversation.

"He says I have a natural ability."

"Well, fine, son. That's great. How are your other classes?"

"Boring."

"Uh-oh. That means you're not doing so well."

"I'm doing okay," he had protested.

"You never were the type to try hard at anything that bores you."

What do you know about it? he wanted to say.

"Really, Dad, I'm doing fine."

"Well, good. Do you need money?"

"Of course."

They'd shared a laugh at that.

"Where does it go, son? On a girl?"

"No."

"If I'd saved all the money I spent on girls in my youth, I'd be a rich man now," said his father. "Promise me one thing."

"What?"

"Find yourself one that doesn't eat."

His father wasn't thinking of the skeletal girls in multiple layers of sweaters and huge baggy pants who hung out in the dining hall like hostile ghosts, eyeing the food on your tray, one hand cradled around their Styrofoam cup of black coffee. In many ways, William Gates' ideas about women were outdated. Girls nowadays, the ones that ate, paid their own way; they sometimes even paid the whole thing, if they were the one who'd asked you out. The rules of the game were a lot slipperier than they'd been in his father's day, but the ambiguity of the dating process was unimportant to Buddy. To him, those girls were irrelevant, except perhaps as practice for the real thing. Tate. He'd seen her in the cafeteria, eating like a starving boy, eating more than he did, flashing her teeth in laughter, swallowing voluptuously.

He'd contrived to run into her on campus the day before he'd left, and they'd had the usual pre-vacation exchange.

"Where are you heading for break?" she'd asked.

"South," he said. "I'm going to do a film."

"How'd that other one go?"

He winced. "Fine. But that was just beginning stuff. This one's going to be longer."

"Ten minutes this time?" she teased.

"Regular length," he said. "A feature." He was lying; Szilardi expected no more than half an hour.

"Anybody famous in it?" she asked.

"It's a documentary," he said.

"Like the news?" she said.

"Sort of," he said. "Regular movies are fiction, you know, made up, with scripts and actors. Documentary is real stuff, no script or anything."

"Oh," she said. "Well." She smiled. "I can't wait to get out of here. This semester's been a *drag.*" She waited. "I'm going South, too," she said, and he realized that he ought to have asked her where she was going for the break. "Florida."

"Fort Lauderdale?" He thought of her frolicking, swim-suited and tan, with the golden boys crowding around her, spraying her with beer. He saw her dozing, sun dazed and sand encrusted, on a large towel near the water, while a muscular hand rubbed oil into her back.

"Nothing like that," she said, frowning. "I hate that kind of fraternity shit. I'm going to Boca, to see my grandparents."

"Sounds great," he'd said, feeling lamed by the pallor of the conversation.

"Well, I gotta go," she'd said, walking backwards, away from him. "Good luck with the movie. See you."

"See you," he'd said, automatically, watching her stumble infinitesimally in reverse, then turn and go forward, dwindling to doll size and mingling with the other dolls. When he lost sight of her, he gave an involuntary cry, and two girls walking by had giggled, and looked at each other.

"Geek," said one.

He ignored them, lurching a few steps after Tate. She thinks I'm an idiot, he thought. A fool who talks about making movies. He heard himself, in playback, lecturing her about the difference between fiction and documentary film, and he cringed. Why hadn't they had a normal conversation? He was always talking about stupid stuff like that. The trouble was he didn't know how to have a normal conversation. Why couldn't he talk like everyone else? He'd seen them from afar, laughing and gesturing, using that secret college slang, the nuances of which escaped him. They never said *yes,* they said *really.* And nothing was *great* or *cool,* anymore. Now it was *intense, heavy duty, radical.*

"Radical," he said to himself. Sure enough, it sounded stupid in his voice. He had to face it—he wasn't made for small talk. He wanted to communicate bigger, more crucial things than small talk encompassed. Why, then, were his conversations with Tate nothing more than the smallest of small talk?

He began to walk. How could she like him? She didn't know anything real about him. What was there to tell her—*I lived in six different houses before I was five, I sunburn easily, my mother shot herself?*

Hard to believe, even now, that she wasn't somewhere waiting for him. In Connecticut, making a batch of runny brownies, her only concession to motherly behavior. Or anywhere else—the Bahamas, Hawaii. He'd always had the sense somehow that she'd leave someday, just take off somewhere. She gave that impression of impermanence, like she was listening to something far-off. But he'd thought more along the lines of a vacation, not a permanent checkout. He felt the old, the usual spring of hope that came whenever he let himself think like this. It was a few weeks after the funeral when he first realized he was thinking them, thinking them without even knowing it. All day long in his head there ran a little monologue. *It's okay, it's good that you got away. I bet you're getting a great tan. I'm not angry but I miss you. Just call me sometimes.*

Even after he'd confronted it, the madness had persisted, stretching itself out and winding into things, becoming more devious. When the first quarter grades had come out, he'd been excited by his A from Szilardi, and had found himself dialling the old number. He hadn't understood what he was doing until the jangling off-key notes came into his ear, shocking him into sanity. "The number you have dialled," the taped voice had said, and he'd put the phone down, not waiting for the rest, knowing what it would be.

He heard it now, breathing the dusty air of spring in Naples, and it seemed to fit with everything. He heard it in the operator's voice, in his mother's voice, in his own. It made a rhythm with his walking, like a sergeant calling out to his troops. *Not. Not in order. Not.*

Chapter Eleven

The World of Men

J oan was cracking, I could see it. The way she'd looked the other day when we met in town—like a ghost, flickering on the pavement in front of the drugstore. She hadn't been so bad for years, not since the day I found her sitting in the backyard and knew I had to take charge of things. Even at the worst of times she'd managed to keep up outward appearances. It was hard to believe, but sometimes it seemed like she'd forgotten it all; with the advent of Buddy, it was moving back toward her, a gigantic shadow pulsing its awful message of memory.

Thank God for the house. Within it, we were safe. It was Joan's safe haven, and now she nestled into it like a wounded animal settling in for mending. Time alone there was all we'd ever needed to put things right again. She didn't mind entertaining there—small bridge parties and larger fêtes, stringing lanterns in the yard and twining streamers through the branches of the apple tree. Joan planned these events herself, and afterward was exhausted. She went to sleep while I crept around and tidied. Pulling the decorations down, emptying the ashtrays. Dismantling the evidence of interlopers, so that the next day when she awoke, the house would be clean again, and ours.

One April evening in 1953, my father called me into his darkened room. By then, he was sleeping in the old front room, ostensibly because it was cooler there, but really because he could no longer cope with the long flight of stairs to the bedroom he had shared with my mother. An odd effect of his illness was an intolerance to light, and to spare him discomfort the house was kept perpetually dark, the curtains drawn even at night, so that no stray beams from a passing headlamp could spill in at the windows.

I had been in the army for four and a half years now, visiting Naples when I could, staying in the house on Worth Street. I hadn't been back since Jack's wedding two months before; in my absence, Joan checked in on my father, who had been largely confined to bed for the past half year. She had tried to warn me on the telephone, but nothing could have prepared me for the decline that had taken place in that short interval. He was there alone when I arrived, and I muddled my way toward his voice, passing through rooms that hadn't been so dark during the war, when we'd used the blackout. I found him in bed, coughing; the nature of his cough was light and dry sounding, not the kind one expects from lung disease. Occasionally, however, there came a deep, rasping cough, seeming to start at the bottoms of his feet, and from which he never quite caught his breath.

I had intended to see much of Joan during this visit; my next planned leave was set for the day before our wedding. Instead I stationed myself at the house, to look after my father. The woman who came in during the day was friendly enough, and seemed impervious to gloom, but the long hours told on her, and she agreed readily when I offered to take over for a week. Joan, occupied with wedding details, was understanding. "You wouldn't want to fuss with this stuff anyway," she said. "I'm sure you won't notice half of it."

Jack and his wife, Marie, lived in a small house a little over a mile away. I'd gotten an overnight pass, and made it just in time for their wedding, dashing into the church moments before the ceremony began. Fidgeting, still anxious from the split-second timing of my journey, I let my mind detach, inspecting the groomsmen, construing from their nauseated expressions that the bachelor party had gone well. Allowing my gaze to drift to the altar, and over the bridesmaids, and only briefly over my brother's profile, all the while figuring return routes after the reception was over.

The organist stopped fiddling around at the front of the church and slammed his fingers down. The organ blast; it said: *Here comes the bride.* I turned along with everyone else to see Marie, head to toe in sheer white, floating down the aisle. I was surprised at the upwelling of emotion I felt, seeing her draw closer, kiss her father, and then take her place beside Jack. The day was cloudy, but when the minister said the final words, a ray of light came through the stained-glass panel overhead, throwing the couple at the altar into a profusion of color. Jack kissed the bride; and then it was done.

I suppose I had too much to drink at the reception; or perhaps it was the proximity of my own wedding day. Whatever the reason, I quickly lost all sense of balance and wandered around being maudlin, congratulating everyone I recognized, pumping hands and slapping shoulders in a highly emotional fashion. I told sentimental stories to the minister, and risque stories to Stan the organist; only I got them confused, although I'd known both of them all of my life. I sniffled, watching Jack and Marie dance together, the only couple on the floor, Jack barely moving, looking down at Marie, who smiled up at him with her veil lifted away from her face and her train trailing from one arm. They say that in the hush I burst into song—what song it was no one could tell—and that when Joan tried to hush me, I began quoting the Bible. *I set thee as a seal upon my heart.* When the couple drove away, I tossed rice with the best of them, hurling the hard little grains toward the bride so viciously that she shielded her face with her purse.

"I was drunk," I said in the train station, a few hours later.

"You didn't have that much to drink," said Joan.

"I must have," I said.

"I've seen you drink five times that," she said. "Is it so terrible to admit that you got emotional at a wedding? He's your brother, after all."

"We're not that close," I objected. "We don't even like each other."

"I don't believe that," said Joan.

"You've never had a brother," I told her, shortly.

"I wish I did," she said. "I've always wanted one."

I let the matter lie there; but I knew it was not feeling for Jack which had moved me so, but rather the whisky on top of the anxiety.

That had been the last visit. Now I rattled around the big house all day, seeing no one, pulling dusty volumes from my old bookshelves, taking them to the window seat in my parents' old room, dropping them there when I was finished. For hours I was plunged into adventure stories, revisiting the literature of my boyhood, reading by the light of the only open window in the house, listening the while for my father's bell.

He rarely rang for me; and he seemed annoyed when I checked on him spontaneously; often I read on undisturbed until evening, when the failing light reminded me of where I was, and why. I roused myself and laid my book aside, descending the stairs to see to supper. Four days went by this way, and then one night, I heard the bell.

"You get the house," he said, without preamble. He paused, breathing harshly, putting up a hand to indicate that I should be quiet. "You—were—never my favorite," he said, at last. "You knew?"

I nodded. He nodded, too, neither pleased nor displeased, as though the statement had been merely punctuation.

"Jack—my favorite. Ellen—your mother's. You knew that, too." This time he didn't look to me for confirmation but just paused, catching his breath. "Figure we owe you something," he finished.

I could barely see my father across the lightless room; he was breathing harder now, and coughing. I hesitated; was it not now the moment for a tender exchange, some batch of conversation which could stand in my memory as a testament to the misunderstood depths of our relationship? Shouldn't I say something to connect us, father and son, in these final hours? Could I really let the moment go by?

I could. After a few wordless minutes, I stood up.

"Um, thanks," I said.

He opened his mouth to speak, but instead began another battle with the atmosphere, trying to draw his fair portion of it into his lungs. I waited by the bed.

"Don't mention it," he said, finally.

Light from the kitchen was filtering down the hall as I closed my father's door behind me. I went toward the light; but once in the kitchen I felt aimless. I went to stand on the back porch in the twilight.

The sounds of nighttime were starting: the crickets and the gentle echoes of other people's porch conversations, which crossed great distances when there was no wind. There was a smell of rain to come, and in the profusion which had once been my mother's vegetable patch there was a rustling, as though some night creature, in the habit of pillaging, had come hoping for new growth, some tasty product of human industry. Far away, at the foot of the land, hidden, lay my father's windowless workshop.

I ambled off the porch and through the weeds. I hadn't been this way for years; it was a blind journey I was making, by feel and by memory; and when at last I stood in the tall grass outside the shed, it was with a kind of surprise.

My memories of the workshop were of a silent, male place, a region golden with sawdust and filled with curious instruments which I was forbidden to touch. At four, banished to the steps just inside the door, I watched eight-year-old Jack constructing a wavery bookshelf. Across the room, my father bent his head over something much more complicated—a set of filigree boxes for my mother's birthday, or a fancy bird feeder to replace the weather-rotted store-bought one hanging outside the kitchen window.

At seven, Jack had been allowed off the steps, into an informal apprenticeship, handing Dad tools. He did this proudly, hour after hour, scrabbling nails out of their boxes and holding them at the ready. Our father never indicated what he wanted but just stretched his hand out silently and handed back each tool he didn't want until Jack got him the right one. Jack learned this way; soon he was selecting the tools before my father requested them, eager as an OR nurse slapping instruments into the palm of the surgeon. When he was eight, having lasted out a year at our father's elbow, a workbench was cleared for him, and he was given his own hammer and a small supply of nails and glue and scrap wood.

They worked in silence, my father offering only the most meager of instruction. When Jack drove a chisel into the ball of his thumb, Dad lay down his own tools without speaking and went over to inspect the damage. If it was bad enough, he doctored it out of the first-aid kit kept on the middle shelf, against the wall. When Jack, hammering, missed a nail head, my father's head lifted, as though he had heard someone calling to him. Later, he might pass by Jack's workbench, and reach out to finger the place with a grim small smile; Jack would flush and squirm.

Jack learned from watching our father, standing near him for an hour while he used a tool, then later going over and lifting the same tool down from its place. By twelve, he was expert with all but the very dangerous equipment, and it was time for my own apprenticeship.

I lasted the year, happy to be so near my father, who seemed a different person in the workshop. We were all different there: my father was knowable, and Jack and I were brothers, with an unspoken truce. I received my own hammer, and set about my own clumsy bookshelf. It was clear right away that I didn't have Jack's natural gifts or patience. He had learned merely by observation, and had rarely made mistakes; even with his instruction, I was hopeless.

"You're choking up too much," he would say, taking the hammer from me. "Like this," swinging it gracefully, bringing it to *tap* against the nail head. He gave the hammer back, stood back and watched me, shaking his head. "No," he said, taking my hand and refolding around the hammer. "It has to feel like the nail is *waiting* for it," he said. "Confidence." We swung together. *Tap.*

"I can do it," I said, pulling away, swinging, *thwacking* the nail a little distance into the wood. Stubborn as I was, I could see that there was a difference between my technique and Jack's.

"It takes practice," he said. "You'll get it."

But I never did; and before too long I gave up and relinquished the workshop to its rightful owners. The tools which scorned me, twisting and leaping in my hands, I gave back to their masters, with whom they were obedient and meek. I never even graduated to the power tools; at ten years old, I took to the steps again. I began taking my schoolbooks out to the workshop in the evenings, seating myself on the steps and reading while the others worked.

"How can you hear yourself think?" my mother asked me.

"It's quiet there," I told her, genuinely surprised. Apart from the hum of the power tools, the occasional screech of a dull sawblade, the workshop was the quietest place I knew. And even though I was not a carpenter, I loved it: it was a kingdom unto itself, of sawdust and varnish, settled into the overgrowth like a pearl dropped into a forest. It was the realm of peace; there I had a father and a brother. It was my window, tiny and smeared though it might be, onto the world of men. I could not totally abandon it.

After my mother died, my father spent even more time in the workshop. Out of habit he made things for the house, things he would normally have presented to her. It was as though he forgot everything while working, and learned anew each evening of her death. Bewildered, he'd leave the objects on the dining room table, where I'd find them, and put them to use. For a while, his work proceeded apace; then it began to change. He had always worked steadily, finishing one thing before going on to the next. Now his pace was ragged, and his attention began to scatter; he'd begin several projects at once, turning his hand from one to the other, and never finishing any of them. Like Penelope, he ripped apart a project near completion, having decided late on a crucial change in the design. After he fell ill, he went out to the shed less and less, and finally quit altogether. It was now Jack's kingdom alone, he its undisputed ruler.

Jack still arrived at the house on Worth Street one night in three, stopping in to sit with our father for a few minutes before heading out to the workshop. He worked there until six-thirty, when Marie telephoned him to come home for dinner.

Standing before the shed now, I could hear sounds from within, rhythmic scrapings beyond the planking; I pulled open the door and peered inside. The place smelled as it always had, that good clean wood fragrance. Dad's unfinished projects had been pushed onto shelves, and Jack was bent over the bench which my father had customarily used, planing a length of wood. I stood on the inside steps and watched the curls of wood lifting up like brittle wings. Jack stopped planing, and ran his hand over the grain.

"How's it coming?" I asked.

"Not bad," he said, straightening up. "Some trouble with this junk, though." He patted the wood under his hand.

I walked over, and ran my hand over it.

"Feels good to me," I said.

"Junk," said Jack. "Won't smooth down right. I should have known better. It was cheap as hell, though." He smiled. "I'll use a dark stain."

"What are you making?" I asked.

"Stereo cabinet for Marie's birthday," he said. "Gonna put in some of those smoked-glass doors."

"She'll love it," I said.

"She better," he said, without heat, turning back to his work. All the time we'd been speaking, he'd not taken his hand from the wood. "Dad give you the house?" he asked, over his shoulder.

"Yes," I said, surprised. "Did he tell you he was going to?"

"Naw," Jack said, smoothing the wood with his palm. "I just figured."

"Does it bother you?" I asked.

"Naw," he said again. "Makes sense to me."

"You can still use the workshop," I said.

"Your bride won't like that much," said Jack. "Me tromping through her backyard every day. Likely she'll be wanting to tame some of this wildness back here. Nope; figure I'll move operations to my basement."

"You can take all this stuff," I said, waving a hand to indicate the benches, the lights, the equipment; and then blushing at my own arrogance. Obviously, it was all Jack's already.

"Thanks," he said, without irony.

I watched him for a while longer.

"Well, good night," I said to his back.

Back in the kitchen, I worked under the dim light, making supper for my father. Soft things, things he could eat, although he complained that nothing tasted right. I skinned some carrots, put water on to boil. The pots and pans I had known all of my life glowed with new meaning tonight. *Yours,* they said. *Someday, all this will be yours.* The cliche made me laugh a little, and then choke on the laughter. I stood over the sink with a potato in my hand, the water running cold over my fingers, choking and spluttering, the sound making a kind of rhythm with my father's tormented coughing down the hall.

And so it came to be that the house I occupied as a married man was the same house I grew up in. The workshop was emptied, one afternoon about a week after the funeral, Jack and Rupe and Andy Swann arriving to carry it all away in Jack's pickup. I sat on the porch to watch.

"Sonabitch didn't tell about this," grunted Rupe, passing by with Andy, moving a bandsaw. They stopped near the porch to rest. "Shit," said Rupe.

"Looks heavy," I said, sympathetically.

"Son," said Rupe, looking me over, "twenty of you couldn't carry this mother." He nodded to Andy, and on the count of three they lifted again, and resumed their slow progress through the weeds.

Joan stopped by that afternoon, and joined me on the porch. There we had our first argument.

"I want to talk to you about something," she said.

There they were, the words I had been waiting to hear in some form all of this time. I hadn't trusted the luck that had made Joan love me. Our courtship had been too smooth, too trouble free; it was with something like relief that I received her statement.

"About the wedding?" I asked, stiffly.

She nodded. "I think we should wait," she said.

"For what?" I asked.

"Well," she said. *You're ugly. You stutter. I hate you.* "It just doesn't seem right, so soon," she said.

I couldn't speak for a moment, the panic and anger spreading in cold prickling waves from my lips, across my jaw, up to my ears.

"Gil," said Joan.

"We're getting married in two weeks," I said. "That's final."

"No," she protested. "It's not decent."

"Two weeks," I repeated.

"What would people say?"

"I don't care."

"Well, I do," she said.

We argued like this for a quarter of an hour; I was surprised at the depth of resistance in my beloved. I had never had to struggle against her will before. Looks deceived: Joan's weightless beauty disguised an awesome rigidity.

"You've changed your mind, haven't you," I said, numbjawed. "This is just a way to get out of it."

"Silly," said Joan, squeezing my arm.

"Then why?"

"It doesn't look good, that's all," she said, stubbornly.

"Shit," said Jack, from behind us. "Who cares how it looks?"

He was standing just behind the glider, holding a beer; it was impossible to tell how long he'd been there.

"Please, Jack," I said. "This is private."

"I don't care if y'all get married tomorrow," said Jack. "And take it from me, Jack senior wouldn't have minded none. He used to tell me, G.I. better marry that girl quick, cause he'll never find another one can stand him."

"Jack," I said. The words didn't sound like my father's; likely Jack had invented them himself.

"Hope you can cook, Joanie girl," Jack went on.

"Some," she said, giving me a sidelong glance.

"Cause with what G.I. brings out of the kitchen, it's amazing Dad and I weren't laid into our graves long ago." He tipped up the bottle and brought it down again. "I say go to it," he said, and whistling, went on down the steps.

"Damn him," I said.

"He didn't mean anything by it," said Joan. I peeked at her; she was looking intensely amused. "It's just his way," she said.

"How come you know so much about my brother?" I asked her.

"I know everything," said Joan, taking my hand.

We were married two weeks later, in a small ceremony with a weekend honeymoon following. I met Joan's parents for the first time two days before the wedding; her father was thickset and irascible-looking. He shook my hand grimly.

"She loves you, son," he said. "And do you know why?"

"No," I said, startled.

"You're not supposed to," he said, and whooped with laughter, while a baffled answering smile spread itself across my face. "We never know why our women love us," he said, with a fond glance at his wife, a pleasant, obese woman who bore little resemblance to Joan. "They don't know why either. God keeps that little secret to himself."

Jack stood up for me at the altar, and Beth stood next to Joan. We had worried that having them both in the wedding party might cause awkwardness, but there wasn't any. At the reception afterward, they danced together smoothly and politely, like people who have taken a liking to one another at first meeting.

The relatives cleared out that night, and Joan and I drove west, to a little town by a lake. In the hotel room, we unpacked our things nervously, getting in each other's way, apologizing like strangers. We had a swim, and then dinner, and then another swim. In the lake, we relaxed a bit, and I touched the water which dropped from Joan's skin as though it were a part of her, and as desirable.

Back in the hotel room, anxiety again descended, and we made foolish small talk.

"Beth and Jack seemed fine," said Joan from the bathroom, where she was undressing.

"Yes," I said, from the bed where I was lying, hands linked over my stomach.

"I mean, all that speculation beforehand, about how Jack might punch Billy, or how Jack and Beth might have a fight at the altar," said Joan.

"Uh huh," I said.

"The music was nice," she said. "I didn't know Eva could play so well."

"Neither did I," I said.

She came out of the bathroom.

"For Christ's sake," I said. "You've got all your clothes on. What have you been doing in there?"

"Don't *swear* at me," said Joan, dissolving.

"I'm sorry," I said. I wanted to get up and go to her, to offer her comfort, but my nakedness now seemed ridiculous. I felt like a fleshy sacrifice, and I pulled the sheet up to my chest. With the movement, the irony struck me—wasn't this the woman's role, to cower under the bedclothes? But I could not move.

Joan went over to the radio and turned it on, fiddling until she got ballroom music.

"Honey," I said, my voice breaking over the syllables. She kept her head down. I saw her trembling, and was suddenly unfrozen. I got up from the bed and went toward her, to where she was looking down at the radio. I turned her gently toward me and folded her hand over my shoulder, putting my arm around her waist.

"What are you doing," she said.

"Dancing," I told her.

"But you're—" she said, and bit her lip.

"I know. Don't look. Put your head here," and I pressed it to my shoulder. She slipped her arm around my back. "Listen," I said, as the music changed. "A waltz."

"You're such a charmer," said my wife, her words buzzing into my skin.

We returned to Naples the following Monday, and on Tuesday morning I watched my wife dressing for work.

Armed with her college degree, she had found herself a part-time position as a guidance counselor, over at the junior high school. She was nervous, fussing over what to wear until I had to laugh at her.

"It's not like typing, Gil," she said. "I have to look responsible, capable, ready for anything."

"You talk like those kids are going to ambush you," I said.

"It's not the kids I'm worried about," she said. "It's the administration."

"To hell with them," I said.

"Easy for you to say," she said, frowning down at her stockings.

"Let the little bastards cope without you for a day," I said. She shook her head.

"Call in sick," I said. "Call in dead."

"Not funny," said Joan, whisking neatly out of my grasp as she passed by the bed.

"It's inhuman," I said. "It's only been two days."

"I'm sorry, Gil," she said.

"Then stay."

"We need this job," she said quietly.

I winced. It was a sore point. I hadn't found a job yet, and Joan's was the only paycheck. I lay back in bed, passive now, and watched her pinning up her hair. She saw my expression, and correctly interpreted it.

"You'll find something," she said.

I pulled the blanket over my head.

"Maybe you'll find something today."

I rolled over.

"See you at two," she said, cheerily.

"Bye," I said, through the tufted chenille.

I waited for the front-door slam before getting out of bed. I went to the window, and watched her walk down the path, thinking she might turn around, but she didn't. She got into her car and drove away. I regarded myself in the window glass.

"Hello, useless," I said.

"It's those don't-got-a-job blues," said Jack, when I stopped by the garage later that day. I didn't much want to see him, feeling the way that I did, but I was tired of dragging myself around town. I felt the need to see someone, *anyone,* whom I did not mean to ask for a job.

"Maybe I should have stayed in the army," I said.

"Sure," said Jack. "And hoped for another war."

"I don't have any experience at anything," I said. "They all want experience."

"Naw," said Jack. "They just say that." He wiped his hands with a rag, and pulled some coins from his pocket. Dropping them into the Coke machine, he said, "You got to be confident. Forget all the other stuff—look them in the eye and say, 'Hire me!' "

"How do I do that?" I asked, accepting the bottle Jack handed me. An opaque wisp of steam drifted up from its mouth.

"Just say it."

"Say, 'Hire me'? Just like that? They'd throw me right out."

"Yeah, but it would be great to see their faces." He stoppered his smile with the Coke, lifting it high.

"Maybe I should deliver the *Chronicle,* " I said.

"And put Scottie Wilson out of a job? Nossir. This is what you do," he said, bending to place the bottle in the wooden crate of empties. "Try one of the new places, the big companies."

"The ones over on the bypass?" I said.

"Sure," he said, belching. "They're always looking for smartasses."

I found a place finally, at Devlin Company, the new commercial development firm located on a patch of land which had been pasture in my boyhood. It was a tolerable situation, but just that; as a paper-shuffler in the lowest ranks, I got to work in the basement of the huge low building, with a desk to myself and a half an hour for lunch. Imagine a roomful of desks under schoolroom lighting, identical sleek heads bent over files nine to twelve-thirty, and one to five. My job consisted of correlating the architect's plans with the builder's specifications, checking all cited measurements and stapling the mess together, to be passed along to a higher power. I suppose you would call what I did then glorified proofreading, but it was termed "entry-level management." It was uninspiring and undemanding, and the salary was small. But it was no worse than the army, and the house was paid for; we were comfortable.

We would have been all right even without Joan's contribution, and I urged her to quit.

But she loved her job. "It's great," she had said, at the end of the first week. "Nobody knows what I'm supposed to do, so they leave me alone. I can really talk to the kids."

"What do you talk about?" I had asked.

"Oh, anything," she said. "Why they hate school. What they're afraid of."

"Sounds like you're getting paid to talk," I said.

"Not talk," said Joan, "so much as listen."

Now, "It's only for a while," she said. "Until we get lucky."

Lucky meant pregnant. We both wanted children right away; Joan had already accumulated various baby things, soft plush animals and diapers and a second-hand crib, all of which she stored in the room down the hall from ours, which had been my boyhood bedroom, and which we now designated the nursery.

After some argument, I conceded, and Joan continued to go to work each morning, returning home at a little past two o'clock, after which she would do the housework and prepare supper. School began early, and she left the house before me every morning. Before, I had always been the one to leave her, and I discovered that I disliked being left. But I gritted my teeth and said nothing; it would be a moot issue soon enough.

* * *

Joan's position had been so recently created by the school board that the town hadn't the vocabulary yet to describe it. They referred to her as "that pretty new teacher over to the junior high," or as "that one G.I. married," and while she wasn't made a fuss of, she seemed to be accepted. But her dealings with the students began to filter back to their parents, and there were repercussions.

Earl Hawkins, who had worked with my father, approached me at the counter of the drugstore where I had stopped after work.

"Hey, Earl," I said, pocketing my change. "How's Rosalee?"

"She's fine," he said. "How's *your* wife?"

"She's just fine," I said.

"She from somewhere up north?" he asked. "Ohio?"

"Pennsylvania," I said, surprised.

"Look, G.I.," said Earl. "I'm not one to poke around in other people's affairs. But your wife is making that her business."

"What do you mean?" I said, taken aback.

"What does *she* mean, that's what I want to know," said Earl. "What does she mean, calling my Robby an undertaker?"

"I don't know," I said, honestly. ("I said *underachiever,*" said Joan later, when I told her.)

"He come home real upset," said Earl. "Saying she wants to talk to me."

"Well, that's her job, Earl. Taking," I said. "Care of the students."

"Raising Robby's up to Rosalee and me," said Earl. "I ain't heard no one say we're doing a bad job of it."

"I'm sure you're not," I said.

"You tell your wife that Robby's just fine. Lazy, that's all."

"Why don't you," I said. "Tell her yourself."

"She's got city ideas," said Earl, shaking his head. "You know what I mean. You talk to her, G.I., you tell her we're not stupid here." He slewed his eyes around, then back to me. "I've heard I don't know what-all, crazy things those doctors do to people. We won't stand for it here."

"Now, Earl—" I began, but got no further.

"You tell her what I said," said Earl. He put a hand on my shoulder. "Don't take offense," he said. "She's a nice woman.

She'll settle down once she's got herself a couple of kids to occupy her." He winked. "That's your department."

My department, indeed; but the time passed. Month after month we were disappointed.

"Maybe it's better this way, just now," Joan said, one night.

"What do you mean?" I asked.

"I got a promotion," she admitted, pleating the sheets with her fingers. "They want me to go full-time." She looked up at me. "I didn't say yes," she said, quickly. "I wanted to discuss it with you first. But there's no harm in accepting it, is there? For now," she amended. "It's more money."

"I thought this job was temporary," I said.

"Oh, it is," she said. "But why can't I do something I like to do while I'm waiting?" She looked down at her fingers. "I really like it, Gil," she confessed.

"What do you like so much about it?" I asked her. "Listening to kids talk all day."

"You make it sound boring," said Joan.

"It sounds boring to me," I said.

"Well, it isn't," she retorted. "It's—don't laugh," she said, severely. I shook my head. "It's exciting," she said. "So much responsibility."

"I'd think you'd hate that," I said, puzzled. "I think of you as kind of shy."

"I am," said Joan. "I always have been. I was even scared of *you* when we first met." She laughed, and I lifted my lips briefly.

"You hide from the paper boy when he comes to collect," I said. "That's shy."

"That's different," she said. "I don't feel like that at work. I'm not afraid there." She frowned at me. "Why are you looking like that?" she asked. "Are you afraid I won't keep your house and cook your meals? You're not that much trouble."

"It isn't that," I said.

"What is it, then?"

"I liked you before," I said, after a pause.

"I haven't changed *that* much," she said. "I just feel braver these days. In the house. In the office, most of all. There, I feel," and she hesitated, then breathed the word, "powerful."

Sheer practice made her more so. She began to work full-time, adding the role of college counselor to her list of duties.

She was certainly dedicated, taking unofficial visits at our home, ushering students into the downstairs study she had set up for herself, inviting them to supper. Through the imperfectly soundproofed door of her study, I caught parts of conversations.

". . . work harder," came Joan's most severe voice. "How do you expect to get anywhere?"

She tucked into the students' home problems and academic difficulties with an almost indecent zeal, using her solid tools of excavation: boundless sympathy, utter dispassion. Nothing shocked her. The students sensed this, and trusted her; they brought to her their wounds, their fears, their deepest secrets. They were undismayed by her stern lectures, recognizing them for what they were: the salt in her recipe for success. She exhorted them to greater efforts while they nodded, shamefaced, at the supper table, and they went off and tried harder for a few weeks. Then they were back, with new failing marks, related and unrelated problems: love affairs, family turbulence, bad dreams. Joan took them all in, listened to their litanies without expression, talked no-nonsense to them, and sent them away again, patched, healed for the moment.

At first, there was a clean division. When she entered our yellow house, she left her job behind. But soon she began to bring a new confidence home with her, a new brusqueness, carrying it into our house like a cloak of her profession, hanging it just inside the door. And sometime after that, she lost entirely the ability to strip it off; it had become a part of her. Her work had changed her: a hardness entered her philosophy. The new Joan believed in cutting one's losses, in facing facts; she liked informed decisions, and knowing what lay ahead. If the future was impossible to forecast, she wanted educated guesses, estimates, directions.

"Aim yourself," she told the career-boggled, the confused, the hopeless. "It doesn't much matter where. Correct your trajectory as you go."

In her new swift, assessing way, she diagnosed my shortcomings. "You're too sensitive," she told me. "You need to toughen up." And another time, absently, "You seem to have no ambition." But she remained devoted to me, so these remarks bore little sting; after saying them, she would rub her hands fondly across my shirtfront and kiss me. "I love you all the same," she would say. "I always will."

I could not justify the sense of loss I felt. Joan seemed to love me no less; but the form of her loving changed. And she changed. Her strengthening public image seemed to have its physical component; her whole skin was rosier, as though the work nourished her blood. Sometimes when I looked at her now, a vibrant woman with a trace of metal in her laugh, I found her utterly strange. Two years after our wedding, she was stronger, fuller, and I was still the same.

I had continued to work at Devlin Co., pushing papers across my desk for the office boys to collect and carry away. At least I'm not one of them, I thought, not at the *very* bottom.

Devlin himself stalked through the basement room on the average of once a week. His visits were unexpected; perhaps he meant to surprise us in something. He never did: whenever he arrived there was a little tumult at the door, and the men craned to see, and then the heads bent forward again in a silence restored, which lasted until he had passed through.

"Man's got a bug up his ass," said Rick Beller, one day after one of Devlin's appearances.

"I heard he started as a—" I said. "Farm boy."

"You only heard that once?" said Rick, rolling his eyes. "They must like you here. Shit, whenever you do something wrong, the office manager hauls you in and gives you the run-down, all that sob stuff about how Devlin made it to where he is without anything but his own grit. You never heard that speech?"

I shook my head.

"You *must* be doing okay," said Rick, and bent his head again, as Devlin passed by on his return. After the door shut behind him, Rick turned to me again. "There ain't no future in this bullshit," he said. "You got to have something on the side."

"Like what?" I asked.

"Stocks, bonds," said Rick, carelessly. "You got to make it big by yourself. Old Devlin ain't gonna do jack for you. I play the market," Rick said, proudly.

"You need money for that," I said.

"Yep," said Rick. "Takes it to make it, right? Sure as shit ain't making it here." He leaned a little closer to me, and lowered his voice. "So I'm taking it."

"What?"

"Got a friend in Billing," he whispered. "We work together. I work the figures, he handles the money. We split fifty-fifty."

"Aren't you afraid you'll," I said. "Get caught?"

"Shh," he said. "We're careful. Skim a little here, a little there. It all adds up, and no one the wiser. Every now and then we cut a deal with the contractors. That's big money."

"But—" I said.

"Got to take some chances in life," he said, and winked. "Sides, these folks don't know nothing about money. All they know is paper." He shook a sheaf at me. "I give them that, all right."

Since Joan had started working full-time, I had had the unpleasant experience of coming home to an empty house on a few occasions. So that she might get home before me, I had taken to dropping into Stokes' at the end of the day. The men there talked about all manner of things, from hunting to football to sex. They were mostly older than me, Jack's friends; and I frequently served as the butt of their jokes. But they suffered my company, and it was nice at times, sitting with the boys in the cool semidarkness, putting a word in now and again.

That night, I listened to them with new purpose. Was it part of the nature of men to steal, to cheat, to take the short way? I attended carefully, but there was nothing of dishonesty in any of their ramblings.

"Heard about some," I said. "Guy taking money from work."

"How'd he do that?" Ned inquired. "Yall don't have a till in the secretary pool."

"No," I said, above the laughter. "But we deal with figures and such. Easy to change some numbers," I said. "Make a penny."

"Losing a job ain't worth no penny," said Steve Grissom.

"Losin' a job ain't worth nothin'," said an old-timer.

"You thinking about telling?" asked Sam.

"Well," I said.

"That ain't your place," said Steve. "You don't know what kinda life this guy's got. Maybe family, maybe scraping to make ends meet."

"I could tell you about scraping," said the old-timer.

"I feel for the bastard," agreed Sam. "Working along in some shit job, watching the bosses make all the money, and at night he goes home to the wife and she says, 'The kid needs new shoes.' " He shook his head.

"Men don't stick together, we all go down," said Ned.

"Down and out," said the old-timer. "No way to be."

"Probly just a regular guy," said Andy. "Suffering along like the rest of us, wouldn't take nothing a-tall except it gets too much for him."

"He doesn't seem like that," I said, doubtfully. "He seems naturally crooked."

"Crooks, shit jobs, I seen it all," said the old-timer.

"This little extra he's taking, maybe it's all he's got to keep his family fed," said Steve. "You want to take it away from him?" He curled his lip at my treachery.

"I don't think he's struggling," I said.

"How can you tell?" said Steve, scornfully.

"I could tell you *terrible* things," said the old-timer, loudly. "Things you wouldn't believe. You had to seen 'em to believe."

"Here he goes again," said Andy, under his breath. He bent forward with the other men, listening.

"Joan," I said, that evening. "What does Freud say about good and evil?"

"That's Nietzsche," she said. "Basically he said we're all evil."

"Do you believe that?" I asked her.

"No," she said, slowly. "Of course not. I believe people do the best they can. There *are* the psychopaths, but then they're not really people."

"Not people?" I asked.

"I think to be a person, you have to have a morality structure."

"So someone who cheats someone else is not really a person?" I asked.

"No," she said, putting her book down. "Someone who cheats someone else is just an ordinary person, but weak. He knows he's wrong, but he convinces himself he's right. Moral structure, you see, but not a conventional one. He's putting his own needs above everyone else's."

"Uh huh," I said. "What about someone who knows about it?"

"You mean, knows and doesn't tell?" I nodded. "He's normal, too. Afraid of repercussions, afraid to hurt someone else. He's being overmoral, in fact, unless he just doesn't care or he's doing it for gain." She looked at me. "Why do you ask?"

"Just curious," I said. "Never mind." I moved closer to her on the sofa.

"Honey," she said.

"What?" I said, innocently.

"Not tonight."

"I'm not doing anything," I said.

"I know you," said Joan. "Look, it's not a good time."

"Oh," I said. "Why waste it, right?" I was a little hurt.

"Oh, Gil," she said. "I'm sorry. I'm just tense, is all. Give me a neck rub and see what happens."

The town got used to Joan quickly. Only three years of going to Purdy's Market every week had to pass before Maida Tolliver spoke to her. It was a quiet beginning, a consultation over the lamb chops, but it led to greater things. So accepted, Joan was now the province of gossip. The ladies all joined in, and decided many useful things—that perhaps Joan was a little too severe in her dress; that she was a good judge of honeydew; that she could stand a permanent wave. They could not agree on a reason why she might hold a job; after extensive speculation involving my salary, the liberal views on child-rearing in the Northern states, and our degree of marital bliss, they came separately to the same sympathetic conclusions. "Barren, poor dear," they whispered as she passed, smiling sweetly upon her, editing their conversations of references to infants and children.

Her role in their children's lives was not so incredible to them, by now.

"She can't be too bad," it was said. "Mickey Shaffer's Susie's going to be a nurse, and those Shaffers have been stupid since the Fall."

"She gets those kids to listen," others said. "Damned if I can do that. She'd be a good mother." Again, the sympathetic clucking.

Once they were softened, it was just a little while before they became enthusiastic as converts. What was good for the child was good for the parent; I was stopped in the street by people I hadn't spoken to in years.

"Tell your wife thanks," they said.

"Have you been giving out advice all over town?" I asked her later.

"We-ell," she said. "Just when they ask." Seeing my expression, she added quickly, "Well, why not, Gil? I like to be helpful. And it doesn't take hardly any time at all. It's not like they sit in my office for hours. It's no trouble."

But it became troublesome. I watched helplessly as Joan

became the town soothsayer. On our fourth anniversary we had dinner out. During the entree, a woman approached our table.

"My kid won't study," she said, without preamble. "He reads too many comic books. He sleeps a lot." She waited.

"I can't believe this," I said. Joan put a hand on my wrist.

"How old is he?" she asked.

"Ten."

"Take him to see the doctor," said Joan. "There might be something medically wrong with him. Don't worry about the comic books. Children need a fantasy life. At least he's reading something."

"If he doesn't start studying, he'll fail again," said the woman.

"Start giving him his allowance only *after* his homework is done. Kids respond well to systems of work and reward."

"Thank you," said the woman.

"Remember, take him to the doctor first," said Joan. "Let me know what happens."

When the woman had gone, Joan sighed.

"Sorry," she said.

"I didn't even know her," I fumed. "I'd never seen her before in my life."

"Neither had I," admitted Joan.

"It's out of control," I said.

"Sometimes," she conceded. "Let's not worry about it now."

"The nerve," I said.

"Forget her," said Joan, sweetly. "We're alone now."

But we weren't alone, except in the house. And there we were far too alone. The nursery remained empty, waiting.

"The way these people talk," said Joan one day, returning from Purdy's, closing the door behind her with her foot. I took the grocery bags from her and carried them into the kitchen. She threw her purse onto a chair with an exhausted little whinny, and followed me. I began putting up the groceries.

"I've been hearing about my uterus all over town," she said. "Everyone says, 'No offense, dear, but have you tried . . . ?' Some of the things they recommend are bizarre."

"Some of them might work," I said, shelving a box of macaroni.

"Like standing on my head right after?" she said. "No kidding, Gil, one woman told me that."

"Well, what does Dr. Greene say?"

"You know what he said," she replied. "Everything's normal, and we should be patient."

"I've been patient," I said. "We both have."

"All this talk," she said. "It makes me feel defective." She looked at me. "Do you think I'm defective?"

I shut the icebox, and held out my arms.

"Joan, Joan," I said into her hair. "Of course not."

We stayed like that for a minute, and then she began to shake. I held her tighter, thinking she was crying; but she pushed herself away and turned her face up to mine. It was red with mirth.

"What's so funny?" I asked.

"Just think, Gil," she gasped. "Fat Maida Tolliver, standing on her head."

The summer passed that way: watching Rick steal from Devlin, and wondering what, if anything, I should do about it; timing my sexual advances toward Joan to match the timetable she carried in her head; opening the door to her students and making half-witted tabletalk with them; rubbing Joan's neck at bedtime, often until she fell asleep; coping with the daily drifts of paperwork, vaguely musing about what might happen next.

And then, two things happened very suddenly: Joan got pregnant, and Beth Crawford started talking about divorce.

Chapter Twelve

At the Hospital

Goodness, I haven't thought about her in *years*. We used to be best girlfriends when we were about your age. Or a little younger. I went away to school after she was married, and we wrote a couple of letters, but that was all. I worked twenty years at a hospital in Charlottesville after that, before this job came through. I took it, though I knew the town had changed, and I couldn't be sure what I'd be coming back to. But the work was what I wanted, and for once the pay right. It's funny: Nurse is the first person you meet in the world, and she's often the one who sees you out, but while you're here you never think too much about her. If we got paid for the work we do, we'd be richer than the doctors. I hope none of them heard that. Well. We have to love the work; there isn't much else to draw us to it.

Oh, you don't have to worry, they won't bother you. They can't even get in here—this is a locked floor. Some say they trust you more if you don't lock them out, but I believe they might as well taste authority. I mean, there are locked doors in the *real* world, aren't there? You just can't see most of them. I wouldn't want these folks to get the idea they can ramble all over, without any kind of barriers. That's the problem with most of them, anyway, I think. They just don't know what's normal, and they can't remember when you tell them, so they don't know how to behave. They test you all the time, Lord, yes; just like children.

Used to be they all had the same disease, and all got the shock treatment, no matter what they come in for; but now things are more sophisticated. The doctors have split up that one disease about ten different ways, and invented some new ones besides. I don't bother to keep track of the labels they use. Doesn't help, anyway, they'll have new ones before the year is out. My job is more day-to-day, if you know what I mean. Keeping them comfortable, making this a home. Because it is their home; I mean, most of them never go anywhere else, even if they get some better here. Their families don't want 'em. This here's the end of the line.

What Beth would say if she could see me now. She never could abide sickness or smells. If you were sick she'd stay that far away from you, so she wouldn't catch it. She wasn't ever sick, never even had a cold, when I knew her. So I guess it worked.

We never talked much about what we were going to do when we got older. The time we lived in was fast, fast, all the boys going overseas and dying, and at home the football games still going on. Even football got colored by the war: the better an athlete you were, the better a soldier you'd be. That's what Beth's sweetheart told her; that wasd the kind of thing every-body said then. We weren't thinking about living, although we knew we would, being girls and all. We knew we'd live, but we didn't have the normal dreams girls had before us, home and babies. Who knew if there'd be any boys left to marry, or what kind of babies we'd have?

Everything had something to do with the war. You couldn't get away from it, and at first Beth and I talked about it a lot. We followed the news as closely as anyone; we were proud like we'd made up the whole thing ourselves. It seemed so faraway and dramatic: surely no one had ever lived through a war like ours. After the U.S. got in, I swear Beth and I would have gone to fight ourselves, if we'd been allowed.

But then after a while it stopped being so new, and there was more and more bad news, and it started looking like it would last forever, and we didn't talk about it at all. We spent a lot of our time on things that began and ended in a day, like combing our hair a certain way, or trying a new lipstick. It was a kind of hiding we were doing, in a silly, girlish way, and it didn't do much to take our minds off it. You couldn't help but feel the war all around you. It took the food out of your house, and the sugar out of your coffee, and the gasoline out of your car. In school, it was all they talked about, and even at the movies.

We did our part for the Effort, of course. Saturday morn-ings, Beth and I went with her ma to another lady's house, where we were all knitting for the soldiers or putting shirts together. Seems like I had a sore place on this finger for two years, from pushing the needle through that hard cloth. It was heavy, like canvas. We had to use big thick needles, and our stitches were all raggedy. Beth got mixed up once, and put an extra sleeve on. She had to spend a whole morning picking it out, cussing under her breath so her ma wouldn't hear. I don't know how anybody wore the things we made, but I guess it was all they had, and they were glad of them.

The ladies had a time of it, those Saturdays; they brought lunch and gossiped the hours away, but Beth and I were just young girls, and woman's talk held nothing of interest to us. We sewed like demons, sticking ourselves, bleeding into the stitches, and when lunch was over and Beth and I were free we'd run away—literally run away from the hill, where the house was, and down the street, all the way into town. Running like mad things. I never knew why we did it, but we always did. I guess it made us feel alive.

At the time, I thought it was a race we were having, and I treated it that way, laughing and sneaking glances at Beth running beside me. If I'd looked back on it from a dozen years, I might have said it was the war we were running from, and the gloomy old house with the piles of scratchy needlework, and the tedious chatter about sickness and weddings. But if you asked me now, I'd say different. For me it might have been just that, the war and the sewing, but not Beth. I remember the way she looked. I was clowning and puffing, but she was dead serious, running as though her life depended on it, not even looking at me. She was a pretty girl, but with her eyes squinched up and her face all red and the hair flying behind— not so pretty when she ran. She looked straight ahead, but not like she was seeing anything in front of her. She was only running. I thought we were racing each other, but Beth was racing something I couldn't see. She was daring it to hurt her, or trip her, daring it to do anything to her at all.

I've seen that same look since then, on the faces of some of the folks here. I'm older now, and I've seen some, and I guess I understand it now, what I didn't before. Crazy people are as various as the rest of us—some are mean, some are simple. A lot of them are afraid, even the mean ones. Like other mean people the world calls normal. They're afraid of something they can't see; they mumble to it, and the brave ones dare it to come closer, come closer so they can kill it. They know they can't kill it, but they don't know what else to do.

Beth told me once that she'd rather be dead than insane, and I agreed with her then. But I don't anymore. I've seen the way they are, and some of them are unhappy, but some of them aren't. You couldn't tell the two apart just looking; even their happiness is different from how we normally think of it. But there are some I wouldn't trade places with for anything—

the ones that are running even while they're standing still, running away from whatever pit of fire is in them that they don't understand, making it run, too, daring it to catch up. They're happy when they're running; it's when they stop and it catches up to them, they're sad.

"Listen to them out there. Most of them couldn't read a clock to save their lives, but they always know when my break's over, and start in like that. I guess they're trying to remind me to come back. They do it at the end of the day, too —invent problems right before I leave. Poor things, day after day I'm here, and they can't trust that they'll see me tomorrow. I better go out there again. You can go out that way; don't forget to hand in your visitor's tag, and pull the door shut behind you."

Chapter Thirteen

Solomon's Baby

I got everything here. Furniture, books, housewares, ladies' clothing, men's clothing, clothing for the kiddies. Even rare items, like antique medical tools and old firearms. Course, I can't sell those without you got a permit. The Smithsonian was here last year, bought up some old dentist's office I got hold of, didn't pay much for it neither. I hear from a cousin that those things are sitting in the museum now, people coming from all over just to look at 'em. It ain't junk I sell, nossir, it's art.

There ain't no such thing as Naples without Shade's Trades. I been here so long my own great-grandmother bought from me. I sell to young brides, everything they need for their happy homes. Furniture, household appliances, dishware. I got so many sets of dishware I can't display 'em all. There's crates just waiting in the back. Yessir, I got four floors of life's necessities, right here, at bargain prices.

I got wedding dresses. You ever seen anything pretty as this? Worn once, just like new. Why pay boutique prices when you can get it here for cheap? I got sweaters and overalls, good durable stuff, last forever. I got shoes. See these, button-up kind, you don't see those much anymore. Five dollars, and I'll even throw in the buttonhook. Here's bowling shoes, now, from that alley down the road that went out of business. Ladies' pumps. You ever seen a prettier shade of red? I called 'em Dorothy's slippers for a while, thinking they might move that way, but wouldn't nobody buy 'em. Folks don't want to know who's had the stuff before. So I took the tag off this morning. Watch 'em go now.

The bottom floor is furniture, cause it's the heaviest. I got some beauties down there, a stereo console like you'd see in a store for six hundred dollars new. I'm only asking two. Now, I won't lie to you. The console I got is used, and there's a few scratches on the top, and one ring where somebody put a cold drink, but you can't see that unless you look. You're saying to yourself I'm crazy, telling you all about them flaws up front, but I say what can I lose? You think four-hundred dollar scratches is a good deal, that's your business. And I don't make a sale that's gonna come right back in my door. Most of the televisions in Naples been through here at least once; some, I get to see three or four times. It's a hoot, what people try to sell me. One fellow brought in his old longjohns, wanted two dollars for 'em. 'They kept me warm for ten year,' he said. I had to say nossir to that deal, but I bought his sister's parasol. Her husband brought it back from the war, and looked like she'd never opened it. Made of paper, no good for the rain, but that very same day a woman from over in Nelson County bought it to keep the sun off her at her son's ball games. There's a use for everything.

I get most of my stuff from estates or busted businesses. Factory seconds too, and marked that way. I ain't out to cheat nobody. If I wasn't an honest businessman, I wouldn't still be in business. People learn when you cheat 'em, and they don't like it. It pays to be straight-arrow, then they come back. There's something of mine in every house in Naples.

It's a hard business, though, make no mistake about it. The worst part is the antique dealers. Just like vultures, some of 'em, the way they circle and swoop. It's not beneath 'em to hang around the hospital, seeing who's doing poorly, and then Johnny-on-the-spot with the family, soon as Granma's gone. They're in it for the money and they'll pay next to nothing for something that'll bring a pretty penny. I call that crooked. I don't mind a profit, but I don't sell blood. Dealers hate the smell of honesty, and they generally hate me.

But the worst time I ever had over any antique wasn't with a dealer. It was with a little girl who took care of an old lady out in the country—all the kin were dead or busy, and this girl had been hired to do for her. The lady was an old friend of my family, and I used to ride out to her place of a Sunday and take dinner with her. She was a real lady too, real polite, and she had the finest china you ever did see, in a china hutch her granpa had made, just a beautiful piece. The wood just glowed, like it knew it was pretty, and the doors slid back on their hinges smooth as silk. That piece would fetch a good bit of money and I knew it.

The girl knew it too; her name was Maggie, and she made it no secret how she hated me. She'd get our dinner with a frown that would scare Lucifer, and she'd slam down that plate in front of me like hammering a nail.

The old lady and me, we took our meal in the dining room,

with the girl standing by. She wouldn't never just *sit*. The old lady would talk about the old days, and I'd look at the china hutch while I ate, and I got to know it like it was mine and had been in my family for generations. That girl saw me admiring it, and smart as a whip thought of a way to bother me. She took to standing right in front of it, almost crowding the old lady into her soup, and blocking my view. All the time looking at me from between her braids as if to say, "Ha."

In the summer, the old lady took poorly, and looked like it might be the last trump for her soon. I went to visit on the Sunday, with some flowers and an old Victrola record that had come into my hands earlier in the week. I'd saved it out to play on the old lady's Victrola, that she kept in the parlor, all polished up and new looking, with the gilt detail on the trumpet like it was put there yesterday. A beautiful instrument, and I thought she might like to hear some old-timey music.

The girl, Maggie, greets me at the door and says her mistress isn't well, and shouldn't have visitors.

"Go away," was what she said. Behind her, I could hear the old lady calling my name. The girl hears it too, and steps aside glaring while I hang my hat and coat on the coat tree. Deacon's tree, I should say, and a lovely specimen, all thick dark wood, and not a knot anywhere. The pegs were rounded from the coats of a long family history, and there was a little trapdoor in the seat, below the mirror. It was a real nice piece of furniture.

The old lady was looking real bad. It just turned my heart over to see her so weak. But she was stubborn, and come into the parlor for my visit, and I played her the record.

"How nice to hear music from the Victrola again," she said, with her eyes closed.

"It's a beautiful machine," I told her.

"It's old. Everything I have is old. Older than me," she said, and laughed, a painful, sickly sound.

"Old is nice," I told her, while Maggie made faces at me from behind the settee, where the old lady was sitting. She was so spiteful to have me there that her hands shook with it, and she spilled a little tea on the settee, which was upholstered in old silk and didn't deserve such treatment. I pressed my handkerchief to the spot to soak it up, and the old lady laughed.

"Really, how you care about these old things of mine," she said.

"I do," I said. "I really do."

"Maggie loves them too, don't you Maggie?" said the old lady. "She goes on and on about the china hutch in the dining room."

"That's my particular favorite," I told the old lady, giving Maggie a mean look.

"Hers too," said the lady. "How funny. If Grandad had known how people would take to his "plate-keeper," as he called it."

"Your grandad was an artist," I told her.

"That's what Maggie says," said the old lady, and closed her eyes.

I thought it was the end, and I guess Maggie did too, because she went to the old lady at a run.

"I get so tired," said the old lady, opening her eyes.

We helped her back to her bedroom, set at the back of the house; when we got there I almost stopped right in my tracks, just to look. From the hall, I had just hardly been able to see the tall carved bedframe and the old bureau next to it with the brass drawer-pulls. That house was just crammed full of wonderful stuff, everywhere you looked.

I left Maggie to put the old lady to bed, and waited awhile in the hall, till she come out again. Then I sorta came to, and went to get my hat. Halfway there, she caught me.

"I know what you're after," she hissed, 'and you better just forget it.'

"You," I said. "You don't know anything at all."

"Ha! Don't I?" she said, and her eyes all sparkly like they'd spit at me if they could. "She's just a sick old lady, too nice to know what kind you are, lets you come around here and drool all over her stuff. I bet you got the price tags all made out already."

"That ain't so," I told her. I was hurt. "The old girl and me go way back. I can't help looking around, is all. Admiring."

"Admiring," said the girl, her cherry-red mouth twisting. "Coveting, more like."

Now I don't know much, but I know coveting's a sin. I puffed right up when she said that.

"You're the one to talk," I said. "Angling after that china hutch like you do."

"Me!" she said, pretending surprise. "Me!"

"I bet you whisper in that pore lady's ear while she's sleeping, all about how much you want her old plate-keeper."

"Get out," she said, really angry. Her hair come loose from

her braids some while we was talking, like it was angry too and wanted to whip at me. Little snakes of hair curled across her forehead, and her cheeks were all flushed. If she hadn't been so despicable, I'da thought she was pretty.

"I'll go," I said, "But only because she's tired, not cause you tell me to. And I'll be back tomorrow."

"See if the door opens to you," she shot back.

It opened all right, but only as wide as that Maggie's shoulders, which wasn't very wide. She stood guarding the way like a Gorgon.

"What do you want?" she said, like she'd never seen me before but hated me anyway.

"You don't like me much," I said.

"You got that right," she answered.

"And I don't like you," I said. "But that old girl, she likes my visits. Looking out for me maybe keeps her mind offa her troubles some, her daughter who never visits, and like that. It makes a change for her. She had many other visitors lately?" I asked.

Maggie's face turned color, and after a minute she opened the door a little wider, so I could squeeze through.

The old lady was worse that day; she didn't even get up from her bed, but she woke up when I was tiptoeing back out of the room. Even though it was a mighty hot day, she had a quilt pulled over her, an early American design I'd never seen.

"My granny made it," she told me.

"It's in beautiful condition," I said.

"It used to be snow white," she said, and then fell asleep so quickly that at first I thought she'd gone. I got up and stood over her till I seen she was breathing. The girl came in the room then, and made me jump.

"What you want, leaning over her like some old crow?" she asked.

"I thought—" I said. "She went off in the middle of a sentence."

The girl came over, worried, and leaned over the old lady too.

"She's awful pale," I said.

"It's the heat," said the girl. "Sometimes she can't figure out if she's warm or cold." She pulled at the quilt, then looked up at me. "You're awful pale yourself," she said. "Will you take a glass of lemonade?"

"Thank you," I said, surprised. These were the first civil words I'd heard out of the girl's head. So maybe her tongue wasn't all poison.

"Come on into the kitchen," said the girl.

We sat at the kitchen table for a while with our glasses of lemonade, not saying anything. I'd already used up some conversation saying how the lemonade was mighty good, and how it was mighty hot, and how there'd been a breeze yesterday but not today, and how it usually rained more than it was doing. To all of it she said nothing, just "Uh-huh," or "Oh," not even looking straight at me. I guess maybe she was embarrassed thinking of the awful things she'd said to me. It was like now we'd started being civil, we didn't know how to go on. Like we'd had a habit, and couldn't get out of it easily.

"She's a rare old thing," I told the girl. "Broke my grand-daddy's heart when he was a young man. She married somebody else, but he died young. My grand-daddy started courting her again, but she threw him over again, married a man thirty years older, who died almost right away. Grand-daddy trotted the horse-and-carriage around again, but after three months of Sunday rides she told him she was going to Raleigh to live with her sister."

"Uh huh," said the girl. She didn't seem overly interested, but I went on anyway.

"My grand-daddy gave up then, I guess, and married my grandma, and raised up a family. They were happy together, five sons and two daughters, and my grandma died at a good age, and left my grand-daddy alone for five years before the old lady come back into town."

"Uh-huh," said the girl.

"Well," I said. "At the age of eighty-five, he rode over to her place, *this* place, and asked her to marry him."

"Uh huh," said the girl.

"You know what she said?" I asked.

"Uh uh," said the girl.

She said, "No." He said, "You aren't going to tell me you're marrying somebody else?" and she said, "At my age, it isn't seemly." He said, "Why didn't you marry me before?" and she said, "Henry, you never asked me." And you know, he never had, not in sixty years of courting." I waited for the girl's response, but there wasn't any. "I guess he moved pretty slow," I said.

"Runs in the family, I guess," she said. I could see that we were back to the old way again, but for once I didn't say anything, just drank up my lemonade and left.

The next day the old lady was about the same. I sat by her bed for a while, and when I went to leave the girl offered me lemonade again.

"No thank you," I said. "It's awfully sour, the way you make it."

"I'm sorry about what I said," the girl told me. "I didn't mean to be unkind. I don't know, just sometimes these *words* come out of me. I'm sorry."

The strangest thing: those eyes that could be so mean could just as easy turn sweet. The girl looked at me that way and I just gave in, like that.

"All right," I said. "Thank you kindly."

We sat over our lemonade like before, but not so quiet this time. It was like the girl was trying to make it up with me— she did most of the talking, about her hometown in Tennessee, somewhere I'd never heard of.

"It's beautiful at night," she said. "When the river's high and there's a moon."

Talking that way, she was almost pretty. If I hadn'ta known, I'da said she was just a young homesick girl, and not a viper. But I knew better; I wasn't taken in.

"Will you go back there . . . after?" I asked her, trying to walk careful around the old lady's death. I coulda cut my own tongue out, the way the words sounded, nice as pie. I opened my mouth quick to add something sharp about taking all she could back to Tennessee with her, but the words stopped right there, and held, like I had no more breath to talk.

"I don't know,' she said. 'I haven't thought that far. Nothing much to go back to, my daddy's house is just run over already, what with my sister and her kids."

"This here ain't a bad town," I said. "Best town on earth."

"Not as good as home," she said. "I had friends there."

That girl could change. Now she was just a little lonely girl living way out in the country with an old woman, and never meeting anybody her own age that she could talk to. I almost felt sorry for her.

"You oughta get into town more," I said. "There's socials over to the church on Fridays."

"What church?" she said.

"Congregationalist," I said.

"We're Baptist," she said, looking shocked.

"Baptist is nice," I said.

"Couldn't get there anyway," she said, irritated again. "Who'd stay with the old lady if I was to go off?"

"That's true," I said. And the mention of the old lady brought us back to the same sad fact we'd been turning around without saying. "She's bad, ain't she?"

The girl nodded. Now I could see tears filling up her eyes. Crocodile, I told myself. Probly crying over the china hutch she won't get, cause the old lady'll die before she'd convinced her to sign it over.

"Her sister's girl will get everything," I said. "It's a pity." The girl looked up. "She'll haul it off to West Virginia or sell it to some dealer from the city," I said. "Hate to see good things go to those don't love 'em."

"Wouldn't you?" the girl said, snuffling. "Wouldn't you sell them too?"

"Some," I admitted. "But not all. That china hutch. I couldn't put a price on that. The old lady's granddaddy made it for his bride. That's love, that is. I couldn't sell that. *Give* it, maybe, to someone who appreciated it. But not sell."

"That's just exactly," the girl said, stammering. "Exactly how I feel about it."

"We agree on something, then," I said, embarrassed by my silly speech. "Thank you kindly for the lemonade," I said, and got up. She saw me to the door.

"You'll be back tomorrow?" she asked, without a bit of meanness to her. "She looks forward to your visits," she explained, jerking her head back toward the bedroom and turning red.

"I'll be back," I said.

"Well, the next day the old lady wasn't much better, but then she wasn't any worse, and to make a long story short, she recovered right out of her sickness like it had never happened. She lived another ten year and died peacefully in her sleep. Her kin had to get another girl to do for her, though, not too long after she got well, cause somehow Maggie and I wound up getting married. The china hutch was our wedding present from the old lady. We laughed and laughed when she gave it, and promised each other we'd never quarrel, because then we'd have to cut it in half like Solomon's baby.

Honeymoon talk, but we didn't do too badly. Maggie has her a sharp tongue and a fierce temper when she wants. They didn't surprise me none, being the first side of her I got acquainted with. Used to tell people I met a devil and married an angel, though I was stretching it. She weren't no angel, specially when she got after one of the kids for something. She's mellowed some over the years, though she'd deny it.

The china hutch is still in our house, still shining like it did in the old lady's dining room. I mean for our son and his wife to have it when I go. I know they'll take good care of it, and hand it on to their children, or someone else who'll appreciate it. One thing's for sure—it'll never pass through here.

Chapter Fourteen

The Midnight Round

The boy was a virgin. It stuck out all over him. No pun intended, thought Jack to himself with a smile. No doubt that's what made him so goddamn nervous all the time. He was a funny mix. Cowardly, like a dog that's been beaten; but bold too, like a sure-of-itself cat. Jack had been watching Buddy put himself forward for a week now. God only knew what he got up to during the day when Jack went to work.

"Half the shit I do ain't worth the doing," Jack said now. "Half the time if I knew what I was in for I wouldn't do any of it."

"Do you mean me?" asked Buddy, looking up.

How selfish he was. "Everything in the world doesn't have to do with you," said Jack.

"Because I really appreciate all your help," said Buddy. "I think some of those people wouldn't have talked to me, except for you."

"That may be so," allowed Jack, yawning. They were sitting on the porch in the chill dense evening, waiting for Rupe. "He'll be along soon," Jack told Buddy. "There's a guy you should meet." He wanted very badly for Rupe to come, to put things back into their places. More and more, the conversations with Buddy were bothering his senses, dulling some of them, heightening others, throwing everything out of order. The earnest sounds of the crickets were louder to him now than the smooth words of the boy folded up on the steps, two feet away.

"Will he talk to the camera?" Buddy asked. Jack winced. The inevitable question.

"No, he won't fucking talk to the camera," he snapped. "And don't go asking him. I don't want you bothering him with your nonsense."

"It isn't nonsense," said Buddy, looking wounded.

"Well, acourse it isn't," temporized Jack. "But Rupe'll sure as hell think so. You're gonna have it hard enough getting him past that accent of yours."

"Accent?" asked Buddy, faintly.

"You think it's normal," said Jack. "That's because you watch TV. You think anything on TV is the way it's supposed to be. But down here, you got an accent. Down here, *we* talk normal."

Why was he being so hard on the boy? He couldn't help the way he talked. It was the week, Jack told himself, the week of pimping behind him, and another one in front. Not that he'd have done things differently if he'd known how it would be. But maybe he wouldn't have been so quick to offer his extra bedroom. Then he could have gotten away from it some, left Buddy off at some motel, seen him in the morning. *Good night,* he thought to himself. *Sleep tight, see you tomorrow.* What a luxury. But he'd wanted to keep an eye on Buddy, to know what he knew, to keep him from the things he shouldn't. Heavy price.

The boy was still looking hurt, picking at his shoelaces, keeping his eyes down.

"Tell me again," said Jack. "You're making this movie about Naples."

"Right," said Buddy, muffled, to his shoes.

"And your mother."

"If she comes into it." Still curt, but bending and warming around the edges, like a dog that wants to forgive.

"She can't help but come into it, son," Jack said, patiently. There was just so much Buddy didn't understand. Beth and Naples were the same thing, almost. No matter that she left. No matter what had happened to her before she left, or since. The town was part of her, and she was part of it. "You can take the girl out of the country."

"Pardon?" asked Buddy.

"Never mind," said Jack. "Hope you know what you're looking for," he added. "I can point the way to people, but I can't tell if they're gonna say what you want."

"That's the whole thing about documentary," said Buddy, looking up now, smiling tentatively. "Nobody says what you want them to. They say what they want to say, and you film it. It's like real life."

"But it ain't real life," said Jack. "They act different in front of the camera, I seen em."

"That's true," said Buddy, eager now. "That's all part of it, too. Sometimes they forget the camera's there, but most of the time they don't. It's part of the concept, how the camera affects things."

"Huh," said Jack.

"They act different from the way they would if the camera weren't there," the boy went on. "But the camera sees the things they're trying to hide. They try to hide, and in doing so they reveal everything."

"To the camera," said Jack.

"That's right," said Buddy.

"How bout you?" asked Jack. "You somewhere behind that camera? Or aren't you part of the concept, too?"

"Well," said Buddy, uncomfortably. "I try not to be."

Crunch, from down the road.

"Here's Rupe," Jack said, with relief, as the pickup drove in.

Rupe spat out of the window before opening the door of the truck and climbing out. On the ground, he stood an inch or so taller than Jack, but was much heavier. Planting his feet, he grabbed his belt with both hands and pulled it up, resetting the waistline of his pants over the middle of his belly.

"Hey," he said, coming up to the porch. Buddy popped to his feet like a well-trained child and stuck his hand out.

"Buddy," said Jack, by way of introduction.

Rupe looked him over.

"Settle down, son," was all he said. He shook the pale hand gravely.

"Nice to meet you," said Buddy.

"You don't know that yet," said Rupe, sending Jack a glance. "Wait till you've gone out on the midnight round."

"What's that?" asked Buddy.

"You'll see," said Rupe. "When I don't like somebody, they know it."

"We got some hard drinking till then," said Jack, bringing up the bourbon bottle from the floor beside his chair.

"Say it again," said Rupe, and it seemed to be an old joke between them, because they smiled, while the boy looked on.

Glass on glass, the gurgle of pouring liquid, crickets. The only sounds for a few minutes.

"You're the moviemaker," said Rupe, turning to Buddy so suddenly that he jumped.

"Uh—yeah," said Buddy.

"You got nekkid girls in your movies?" Rupe inquired.

"Um, not so far," said Buddy, trying for a smile.

"Huh," said Rupe.

"You volunteering?" Jack said.

"Ha," said Rupe.

Silence fell again, over the sounds of men drinking. Buddy, unused to hard liquor, was struggling with the bourbon. He tried to take it the way the men did, into his mouth and straight down like water, but it burned, making him cough.

"Who's it this time?" asked Jack.

"Webb," answered Rupe. "He was fussin my dogs."

Jack nodded.

"Sonabitch won't know what hit him," said Rupe.

"Webb who?" asked Buddy.

"Dyke Webb," said Jack. "He's that kinda fat guy, wears a Cards cap."

"*Dyke?*" repeated Buddy. The men looked at him. "That's his *name?*" he asked. "Dyke?"

"Yup," said Jack. "What about it?"

"Well," said Buddy, feeling the bourbon loosening his mouth into a silly smile. "You know."

"No," said Jack. Rupe just looked, without changing his expression.

"Well," said Buddy, looking at them to see if they were joking. "Come on," he said. "You know what *dyke* means."

"Don't believe I do," said Jack.

"Whyncha tell us," said Rupe.

"I can't believe it's just a regional thing. I mean, well," and he stopped himself. *I'm babbling.* He took a breath, and his whisky-fogged head cleared for an instant. *I'm in too far now.* "Up north," he said, enunciating carefully, "the word *dyke* means, you know," he took in another breath, the eyes of the two men on him, "it means lesbian."

There was a pause.

"Well," said Jack, finally. "It don't mean that here."

Silence again, while Buddy contemplated his most recent humiliation. It seemed that these men could sit and drink without other entertainment, without even comment, for hours at a time.

"What time is it?" asked Rupe, after a while.

"There's time," said Jack, unhurriedly.

"What're you going to do?" asked Buddy, timidly.

Rupe considered the question.

"Could blow his head off," he said.

Buddy smiled, waiting for the punch line.

"Or I could blow his fucking head off," said Rupe.

"That's right," said Jack, pouring.

"You're kidding, right?" said Buddy, looking from one to the other.

"Never kid," said Rupe. "Do I?" to Jack.

"Nope," Jack said. "Never does."

"You have a gun?" asked Buddy.

Rupe didn't bother to answer this.

"Did you at least talk to this guy, what's his name, Webb?"

"Talk's no good," said Rupe, clearly tired of it. "Gun's the only language some people understand," he said.

"For bothering your *dogs?*" said Buddy, his voice scaling up.

"No one bothers Peg and Tillie without they get answered by me," said Rupe.

"Right," said Jack.

"But—" said Buddy, then stopped, a thought coming to him. He sat up straight and looked at Jack, whose face said *No, you can't film this.* Buddy's shoulders sagged again.

"Near time," said Rupe.

"Few more minutes," said Jack.

"Hell, it's close enough," said Rupe. "Who cares about a minute here or there?"

"Now, Rupe," said Jack with a kind of wounded air. For the first time, Buddy could see that he was drunk. "You know better."

"Well," said Rupe.

"It's got to do with *honor,*" said Jack. "Everyone knows it's midnight. You can't just go any old time, after all these years."

"They're expecting you?" asked Buddy. This was getting weirder and weirder.

"Hell yes," said Rupe.

"It's the midnight round," said Jack, significantly.

"Everybody knows about this?" Buddy asked.

"Only those who got reason to fear," said Rupe, holding his glass out to Jack. "Clean conscience, sleep like a baby. Guilty, toss and turn and one eye on the clock, waiting for midnight. Waiting for me."

"What if they shoot you first?" asked Buddy.

Rupe made a scornful noise, which turned out to be a laugh. It shook his arm, so that the bourbon Jack was pouring missed the glass and sloshed onto the wood of the porch.

"Rupe's best shot in the county," said Jack, steadying the

neck of the bottle on Rupe's quivering glass, letting it pour. He motioned to Buddy. "You're dry."

"No thanks," said Buddy.

"I didn't hear that," said Jack, thrusting the bottle at Buddy's glass.

Again, the silence while the three drank.

"Time," said Rupe.

"Not yet," said Jack.

"Shitfire," said Rupe. It's ten of. We gonna be late."

"Simmer down," said Jack. "I'll put the glasses inside."

"What're you nannying around in there for?" Rupe called through the screen door, swaying with drunken belligerence.

"All done," said Jack, coming back out. "Let's go."

From the back of the pickup, Buddy watched the moon bump over the trees. He'd made a motion to climb into the cab before they started off; but the other two would have none of it.

"Need room for the gun," said Rupe.

"And the bourbon," said Jack.

"You ride in the back," said Rupe, getting in the passenger side and slamming the door.

Buddy had gotten into the back obediently, figuring they were probably just used to riding alone in the cab together, and the prospect of a third person made them uncomfortable. Now, as the truck went over a dip, he took a firm grip on the side panel, shivering in the wind.

"This ain't the way," shouted Rupe, leaning out of the cab to look, his words tearing back to Buddy.

Jack was driving, and they'd already run up over two curbs on the way. Now they were on an unpaved, unlit road passing between dense banks of growth. Tree branches reached under Buddy's collar and pulled at his hair. Panicked, he pushed them away.

Finally, the truck stopped.

"Where are we?" asked Buddy, sitting up.

"Shh," said Jack. "We're here. Webb's place."

Rupe was already out of his seat. He carried the rifle loosely across his body, one hand under the muzzle, as though it were a pet.

"It's over there," whispered Jack.

They were at the edge of a heavily wooded area. Sighting

along Jack's arm, Buddy could just see it: a small dark shape emerging from the darker shapes of trees.

"It's just a shack," he said.

"Shack for a shithead," said Rupe, belching.

"Are you sure he's even home?" asked Buddy.

"He's there," said Rupe.

"There aren't any lights on or anything," said Buddy.

Jack just looked at him.

"No power lines either," he said.

"Oh," said Buddy.

Rupe's gait was unsteady as he came around the back of the truck. He hitched up his pants and set off toward the house. "Yall stay here," he said. "Won't take long."

"It's really dark," said Buddy, anxiously. "Can he see to hit anything?"

"Not likely," was the reply.

"Jesus Christ," said Buddy. "He might hit us by mistake."

"Yup," said Jack.

Buddy scrunched down in the back of the pickup, feeling the cold metal along his body through his clothes.

"That's the way," said Jack. "Keep your head down." He sounded amused.

They waited like that, five, fifteen, twenty minutes. All the time, Buddy expected to hear the shot, perhaps a cry of pain, Rupe crashing back through the bushes.

No sound.

"Jack," said Buddy, sitting up again, just as the sound of gunfire burst at them. "▮▮▮▮," he said, ducking down again, cowering, face against the truck bed.

It was difficult to count them, muddled as he was; the echoes and the fear mixed in together. There might have been three shots, and there might have been five. Then silence. Then another volley. Silence again; and then Jack was shaking him.

"Guess that'll do it," he said. "Let's go."

"What?" said Buddy. "Um," he said, unsure how to phrase his unwillingness. "They're shooting at each other over there."

"Come on," said Jack, and against his better judgment Buddy hauled himself out of the truck and dropped to the ground. His joints stiff with cold and waiting, he followed Jack into the brush, listening for every noise, feeling a vague absence in his midsection, as though his pelvis had melted away. They walked for a few minutes; the noise of crackling twigs was terrific.

"What if we run into him, um, Webb?" asked Buddy. "I mean, should we be creeping around like this? It's kind of dangerous, sneaking up between two armed men."

"True," said Jack, but he kept right on going.

They reached the house without mishap, and began to circle it slowly, clockwise, moving out in a spiral.

"Rupe," Buddy called softly, every now and then, his voice coming out feeble.

Jack said nothing. They kept a distance between them of about fifteen feet, circling, circling, with the trees passing between, taking them out of view of one another for minutes at a time. Buddy, now running a cold sweat, strained his eyes at the darkness, opening them wide. He listened for every noise— was it Jack, or Rupe, or Webb? Or just a woods animal, flushed out by the gunfire?

This must be what war was like, thought Buddy. Darkness; uncertainty; senses enhanced by terror. *I could die in this place.* How many young men must have formed that sentence in their minds on the murky battlefields of history? Formed it in English, German, French, Vietnamese? *I don't want to die here.* Another lonely midnight soldier thought. What had made him do this? Pride? Sheer recklessness? Stupidity.

Buddy tripped and went down. He landed on something soft; as he scrambled to his feet, it groaned and moved.

"Jack," he nearly shrieked. "Oh my God, Jack." He heard Jack coming, over the crackling brush. "It's Rupe, oh my God, they've shot him."

It was almost more frightening than being alone, to see the hasty dark shape blotting out the silent shapes behind, moving swiftly, an irregular patch of darkness, not obviously human or friendly. A few feet away, the shape became Jack, and knelt beside the body.

"He's not dead," said Buddy. "He's not dead yet, he made a noise. He's just lying there, oh," he babbled. "I fell right on him."

"Take a leg," said Jack, rising.

Buddy couldn't move for a moment, but then he had taken a leg and then the two of them were dragging Rupe, over the branches, through the dirt, all the way back to the truck. When they got there, Jack waited patiently while Buddy vomited in a clump of bushes.

"Help me get him in the back," Jack said, when Buddy had stopped heaving and was standing again, shaking.

Another superhuman effort; for a while, it seemed like they wouldn't succeed in transfering Rupe's huge bulk to the flat-bed of the truck. But then he was up there, with his trouser cuffs rucked up above his knees from the dragging, and mud and twigs in his beard.

Jack turned away from the truck, heading back toward the woods.

"Where are you going?" asked Buddy, the last word high and cracked.

"Get the rifle," said Jack.

"Fuck the rifle," said Buddy, wildly. "Fuck the rifle. He's been shot, he might die, fuck the rifle."

"Nossir," said Jack. "He'd never forgive me for leaving his gun out all night."

"~~Jesus fucking Christ,~~" said Buddy, but Jack was gone. Buddy stood rigid by the pickup, unable to look at Rupe again, afraid to see the damage, the blood, remembering another gunshot wound, another death. A few minutes later, Jack came out of the trees again, carrying the rifle.

"Let's *go*," said Buddy, but Jack climbed into the back of the truck, and knelt by Rupe. Buddy could hear the sound of cloth on cloth.

"What are you doing?" he asked, nearly hysterical.

"He'd want to die with his gun," said Jack, solemnly. "It ain't his best, but it's his favorite."

"This is *insane*," said Buddy, his teeth chattering, the tears starting. "We've got to get him to a *hospital*."

Jack leaned close to Rupe, turning his head as though listening for something.

"Oh, God," said Buddy, trembling, not able to look, his face wet now, with frustration and fear. "How bad is it?" he whispered.

"Bad," said Jack.

"Where . . ." said Buddy, but couldn't finish. He heard a wheezing noise. Was Jack crying?

"Well," said Jack, getting down from the truckbed, shutting the gate. "He'll be hungover as hell tomorrow." He turned, and Buddy saw that he was laughing. *Laughing.* "He ain't dying, son," said Jack. "Jes drunk." He laid a hand on Buddy's shoulder. "Don't get into a fuss."

"I don't understand," said Buddy.

"Get in," said Jack, going to the driver's side. Automatically, Buddy obeyed, climbing into the cab, fastening his seat

[handwritten margin note: your language is disgusting]

belt while Jack started up the engine. "The only shot old Rupe had tonight," said Jack, turning on the headlights, "was bourbon."

"How'd you know?" asked Buddy, finally. "There were so many gunshots," he said.

"Happens about once a month," said Jack, backing up. "Rupe gets to thinking somebody's messed with Tillie or Peg. He loves those dogs."

"Has he ever shot anybody?"

"Naw," said Rupe. "Came close once." He smiled. "Before I learned to keep him drinking till midnight. He's big but he can't handle his liquor." He reached down to the floorboards, searching, and brought up the bourbon bottle. "Usually he doesn't even get a shot off," he said, untwisting the cap with one hand, taking a drink. "Most of the time he passes out on the way, or in the fields somewhere, and I load him back into the truck, drive him home, walk from there. It ain't far. He never remembers it."

They were on the road now.

"Tell you though, this time had me worried," said Jack. "He took a long time to drop."

There was a silence, while Buddy absorbed the reality of the situation: nobody was shot, nobody was dying. It was all part of some weird routine, a drunk backwoods vigilante, wandering at midnight through a tolerant populace.

"I guess you think it's pretty funny," said Buddy, finally. "How scared I was."

"You'd guess wrong," said Jack, pleasantly. "I didn't bring you to laugh at." He swung the truck easily along the curves of the road—had he been drunk at all? wondered Buddy. "Every year puts another ten pounds on old Rupe," said Jack. "Used to could throw him right over my shoulder. Now I'm older, he's bigger. An extra hand is welcome on the midnight round." The road ahead warmed a little, warning of an approaching car; he tapped his foot on the high-beam pedal just as the car heaved up into view. In the light from the oncoming headlamps, Buddy could see the thin unsmiling set of Jack's lips.

"It ain't no joke, son," he said. "It's hard work."

Chapter Fifteen

Twins

Buddy was looking grey on Tuesday, in Stokes's. Jack was looking pleased with himself.

"Boy's been raising a little hell," he told Wallace, darting a glance at me.

Buddy didn't have the air of one who'd been out all night, and proud of it. He looked vaguely ashamed, and estranged, and sat in a corner of the bar, holding his beer bottle in a lax grip. I went over to him.

"Where's your," I gestured, "camera?"

He raised dull eyes to me.

"Left it at Jack's," he said. "I think it makes people uncomfortable."

"You figured that out," I said.

"Stupid," said Buddy. "I should be carrying it everywhere. That way I don't miss anything. But I seem to miss everything anyway."

"Go easy on yourself," I told him. "Everyone needs a vacation. And you haven't," I hesitated, "missed so much. I hear you," I took a swallow of beer. "Been talking to the whole town."

"The town's been talking to me," said Buddy.

"That's what you want, isn't it?"

"I guess so," he said.

"Cheer up," I said. "Even old," I paused. "Pennebaker puts the damn camera down sometimes."

He looked startled. "How—" he began, and then subsided. "Oh, forget it. Everybody knows everything around here. Except me."

"Now, now," I said. "We don't know everything. Just a hell of a lot," I smiled, "more than you think."

Long after the honeymoon, Joan and I were self-absorbed: we spent a good bit of time merely being married, and seemed to have little attention for much else. We socialized minimally: Jack and Marie came to supper once a week, and sometimes we went to another couple's house. But mostly we concentrated on each other, and for a while, I hardly noticed Beth's relative absence in our life. I saw her from afar, and heard the occasional talk. I guessed that she was still running with that same crowd from the Trough; I recalled the party she'd given, and how she'd changed. When I thought of her, it was with a mental shrug: I didn't imagine we'd have much to say to one another now. Thinking it over, I wondered if there ever really had been anything much between Beth and me, apart from some wartime summer walks. At one time I had thought there was; some kind of alliance, whatever kind of alliance might have been possible between an awkward boy and a slightly older, smarter girl. I felt then as though we understood each other, Beth and I, and that I knew her better than Jack.

But I accepted her diminishing presence in my life. It was too bad, how life had a way of separating people; but marriage, after all, sets you up for the small kingdom of family. Outside friendships drain off, like smaller tributaries to a great river during a drought. The weak shall perish.

It was unusual, therefore, for Beth to telephone. She did exactly that, three years into our marriage, after a long silence.

"What did she want?" I asked Joan, when she rejoined me in the living room.

"Lunch on Saturday," she said, curling into the arm I held out to her.

"That's nice," I said. "Here or there?"

"Neither," she said, smiling that smile that women use when they are amused by male stupidity. "Girls only this time. Shopping and lunch downtown."

"Oh," I said.

"I hope you don't mind."

"Not at all," I said.

"I won't go if you don't want me to," she said, taking my palm in both of her hands.

"No, no," I said. "It's all right with me." After a pause, I added, "Tell her hello."

The two women managed to see one another fairly often after that, meeting once a week in the afternoon, and at intervals repeating their shopping Saturdays. I was a little curious about their friendship; they had been friends before me, I knew, but to my mind they were unlikely companions.

"What do you all do together?" I asked Joan, one Saturday. "Look at you; you're exhausted."

"We shop," she said. "And talk. Mostly talk," she said, and laughed.

"What in the world can you all find to talk about for—" I looked at my watch "—four hours?"

"This and that," said Joan. She looked at me. "Jealous?"

"I'm just trying to understand," I said.

"Well, what do you talk about at Stokes's? Between beers, I mean." A gentle poke at my drinking.

"Nothing much," I said. "Baseball."

"Think of it as our baseball," she said.

But that couldn't be it. I knew what Joan didn't: that men's talk was aimless and filler, that it provided a semblance of companionship, but left one deeply hollow. It was more the being together than the talking, and I never felt comfortable with other men. So maybe it was just me who left Stokes's with a hungriness and confusion.

"We tell each other things," said Joan, seeing that I was unsatisfied. "Things we don't share with anyone else."

"Do you talk about me?" I asked.

"Now that would be telling," said my wife.

Rick Beller, having let me in on his secret, now assumed great friendship between us.

"You want in?" he asked one day.

"No, thanks," I said.

"I wouldn't ask just anybody."

"I know," I said. "I" and I stopped. "Guess I'll make my money the hard way."

"Chicken, eh?" he asked, with understanding. "Listen. Don't tell him I told, but Cafferty's in. He's a smart guy, wouldn't do anything risky."

I inspected Cafferty from across the room. Unaware of my attention, he was absorbed in his paperwork. He has a pleasantly honest face and open manner; I was surprised to hear of his involvement in Beller's shady dealings.

"If your feet warm up, let me know," said Rick, casually.

When I ran into Beth downtown, I hadn't seen her in nearly four months. She had changed again; I was startled by the heaviness in her face, the deep circles under her eyes.

"Say hey, G.I.," she said, smiling up at me.

"How've you been?" I asked.

"Nothing happening," she said, but then there seemed to be

too much to tell about, and so we went to get a cup of coffee. When it was served, we seemed to have run out of things to say, and there was an embarrassed little silence.

"How's Bill?" I asked, at the same time Beth said, "How's Jack?"

"He's fine," I told her.

"Of course," she said, making a face.

"And how's Bill?" I repeated.

"Great," she said. "I'm thinking of divorcing him." Seeing my face, she said, "Now why do I *do* that. Always telling you everything straight out and shocking you."

"I'm not shocked," I said, though I was.

"Well, hell," said Beth. "Fooey on this stuff," she said, pushing away the coffee. "I need a beer for this."

I beckoned the waiter over and ordered one, and when the bottle arrived Beth picked it up, ignoring the glass, and took a drink.

"I don't know what was in my head that weekend," she said. "Honestly. To think I could be happy with Billy Crawford."

"You're not happy?" I said.

"I can't stand him," she said. "To be fair, he can't stand me either. I don't know what he thought I was, but he seems awful disappointed now."

"Then he's crazy," I said.

She smiled.

"I think he wanted another mama; or maybe a tame little wifey, to sit at home and knit. Shit," she said, and drank. "Hell, I wanted something, too."

"The wildebeest," I said.

"You remember," she said, quietly. "Well, *that* didn't happen. Jesus Christ. Things are really a mess now."

I thought, not for the first time, that it was the moneyed, privileged girls who tended to curse and drink, while the poorer, churchgoing ones kept pure. I thought of Joan, who was probably getting home from work right now.

"Do you have to be somewhere?" asked Beth, reading my thoughts.

"No," I said. "We can talk."

"Well, Billy's gone all vindictive these days, and he won't let me have a divorce. Meanwhile, his parents are willing to pay me to stay with him."

"They offered you money?" I said, aghast.

"Not in so many words. The wealthy are good at folding their money around things," said Beth. "I don't understand why Billy doesn't want out," she added. "He's as unhappy as I am. But he's convinced that he'd be releasing me to my lover."

"Lover?" I repeated.

"I think he's afraid of divorce because then so-and-so can start to pester him about marriage."

"So-and-so?" I asked.

"He doesn't know I know about her. I'd have to be an idiot not to." She drank again, and then let out a gust of laughter, clapping her hand to her mouth. "Did I tell you?" she said. "That's what they call him."

"Who?"

"Those people," she said, waving her hand, somehow conjuring up that brittle painted crowd she'd been so much with in the last few years. "They call him 'The Village Idiot.' Is it *perfect?* Anyway," she said, with an abrupt return to seriousness, "I think I can get him on grounds of adultery. If I wanted to, I could cite a dozen times. What a day in court," she said, and then added thoughtfully, "Though it would kill old Lucy."

"Are you sure—" I began, and blushed.

"Oh, yes," she said. "How he finds so many willing I'm sure I don't know. Maybe he pays them."

"Don't you care?" I asked.

"Stupid," said Beth. She tapped her empty bottle on the table, and the waiter came over with another: it was that kind of bar. "Of course I cared, once," she said, when the waiter had gone. "But that kind of caring stops. It gets killed. I don't care anymore. If you want to know the truth, I'm glad. If he's getting it from them, then he isn't bothering me."

"Same old Beth," I said. "Flippant as always."

"Not quite the same," she returned, tipping up her bottle. "This one's pregnant."

"Wonderful!" I said. "Joan is, too."

"I know," said Beth. "She told me."

"Oh," I said. "Well, congratulations."

"Oh, please," she said, with a sour look. "I can't have it, of course."

"What else can you do?"

"Well, I can't have it. It would be the worst thing. Bill would never let me go then. I'd be trapped."

"But—" I began.

"Listen," said Beth. "Do you have any idea what it's like, knowing that it's *in* you, that you can't get it out, that it's just going to grow and grow and grow—"

"You make it sound like a monster," I said. "It's a baby."

"It's a ball and chain," said Beth. "And it's—goddamn it—inside me." She tapped the table again; this time, the waiter brought two bottles, and took our empties away. "But I'm afraid of abortion," said Beth.

Abortion. The word scared me, with its implications of blood and infection, of heedless slaughter. Under the table, I crossed my fingers, so that even hearing the word should not affect the child that Joan was carrying.

"Shocked you again," said Beth. "Damn," and she leaned her forehead on her hand.

"It's illegal," I whispered.

"Don't be stupid, G.I.," she said, without looking up. "You don't think Tillie Coombs really went out to Iowa last year to help her aunt. She came home pregnant, and her pa was so mad he threw her out. She went over to Tall Creek, where there's a lady does them for fifty dollars. She got septic, and died." Beth was a little pale at the end of this story. "I don't want that to happen to me."

"It won't," I said.

"Of course," she said, brightening, "there's always the possibility of miscarriage."

I blanched.

"Oh, God," she said. "I'm sorry. I shouldn't be talking about these things." She drank, slowly; there was silence for a minute. "Look," she said then. "I'm really happy for you and Joan. It's wonderful about the baby. I mean it."

"Thank you," I said.

"My situation's different," said Beth. "You all love each other; you have a happy home. Can you understand? I need you to understand," she said. Her eyes were wide and honest, whole separate worlds inside her head. I realized how completely I did not know her.

"Yes," I said, the single syllable sent across to her like a key. *Unlock your door,* I was saying, *let me in.*

"I thought you would," said Beth, and for a moment we held the gaze. Then she looked down, breaking it. "Good old G.I.," she said. She patted the crackling bags arranged on the seat beside her. "I've bought consolation gifts for myself." She smiled. "I won't be able to wear them for long."

"Beth," I said.

"Don't you worry," she said. "That worryface you get. I don't know how Joan stands it." She smiled and ran her fingers under her eyes in a fatigued manner. "I have to get home and slip poison into Billy's supper," she said. "Just kidding."

I helped her with the packages, but on the sidewalk she insisted on taking them from me.

"Go on, now," she said. "Go on."

I turned once to look back at her, a dozen yards away, but she had already turned the corner, and was out of sight.

Joan's pregnancy galvanized our marriage. By then, we had almost given up hope; time and routine had settled us into a comfortable pattern of work and childlessness. When Joan missed a period, one after four years, we scarcely dared to hope. She went off to Dr. Greene casually, alone, as though she wanted treatment for a cough. "It's probably nothing," she said. "I'll be home in about an hour." I watched her drive away, her face neutral and calm, wearing nothing of the hope that must have been leaping inside her.

When she came home, several hours later, she was utterly different.

"Hello, Dad," she said, and started laughing. I laughed, too, and then suddenly we were both crying, sunk to our knees in the entrance hall, faces damply in one another's shoulders.

We ran out immediately, to do shopping that needn't have been done for months yet. We bore our prizes home—heaps of tiny white undershirts, miniature ruffled socks, terrycloth bibs with bunny rabbits and ducks floating across them—and laid them reverently on the altar of our faith, the now-dusty nursery.

Joan gave notice at the school.

"They said they didn't know what they'd do without me," she told me. "They said they'd hold my position until I felt ready to return." She looked up at me, and smiled. "They'll be waiting a long time," she said. "I'm not missing a minute of this baby."

"And this is just the beginning," I said. "We'll have dozens."

"Let's get through this one first," said Joan practically, putting her head on my shoulder.

* * *

Joan found out soon enough about Beth's pregnancy; when she reported the news to me, I reacted as though I hadn't already known.

"How does she feel about it?" I asked.

"What a question," said Joan. "She's thrilled, of course. She says it's perfect timing; we can bitch to each other for nine months, and the children can be playmates. Like having twins, but without the bother."

It sounded like something Beth would say, although the optimism of it surprised me.

"I wish she wouldn't drink so much, though," said Joan.

"She always did drink," I said.

"But not so much," said Joan. "It's those people she's been running with. The way she tells it, they're never sober."

I remembered the three beers Beth had downed in less than an hour, the last time I'd seen her. The first no doubt had been need, and the second pleasure. The third, I was sure, was habit. And when she'd stood up, there had been no unsteadiness about her: a bad sign.

"Maybe the baby will settle her down," I said.

"It's settled me," said Joan, with a wry smile. "Everything but my stomach."

The first months were rough for her; she did not look obviously pregnant for a long time, but suddenly she ballooned, and in her fifth month she was enormous. The nausea persisted throughout, alternating with fits of voracious hunger. By the last few weeks, she was in a sort of daze.

"I'm sick of not seeing my feet," she complained. "Hurry up," she told her belly.

"It doesn't work," said Beth, patting her own abdomen. "I've tried it."

The two women were spending a lot of time together now. Beth seemed resigned to her pregnancy, and had never referred, by glance or statement, to our conversation of that afternoon, in the downtown bar. We heard nothing from her about Bill, who was conspicuously absent.

Early on, we had invited the two of them to a dinner party. They arrived together, but divided immediately after stepping across the threshhold, staying at opposite ends of the living room until dinner, when they took chairs as far apart as possible. Down the long length of the table, I could see the relief on Joan's face: despite the obvious schism, it seemed there would be no overt nastiness.

One of the couples bred hunting dogs, and had a new litter; table conversation for a while centered on the naming of the pups.

"I know I should follow the book," said Vi. "But I get these terrific urges just to name one of them Daffodil, or something like that. Something simple."

"No one would buy a hound named Daffodil," said June Nuckols, seriously.

"Well, Spot, then, or Rover. The pedigree names are so long."

Bill had been largely silent all evening, drinking whisky, carrying his glass with him to the dinner table, and topping it up all through the meal. Now he looked up.

"We should call ours Spot," he said, loudly. "It's a good mutt name. Or maybe Rover, after the mother."

There was an embarrassed silence, which Joan filled quickly, turning to her dinner partner and starting a new topic of conversation. Beth excused herself from the table, hurrying off in the direction of the downstairs bathroom. Bill continued his remarks, not seeming to notice that their target had left the company. I felt that I must do something. I stood up, not a little nervous. I had never been involved in anything like this; Bill was clearly out of control. I had never been so close to the threat of physical violence.

"Come on," I said, going over to Bill, taking his arm.

"Whaddya want?" he said, pulling his arm away, peering up at me. "It's you," he said.

"You're drunk," I said. "You're disturbing the party. It's time for you to go."

"Shaddup, you," he said, jerking away.

"Let's not make a big deal out of this," I said, desperately. All the guests were watching the two of us; even Joan had given up her pretense at conversation, and was looking our way.

"Bill," she said, clearly. He turned his head in her direction. "Go home," said Joan.

"Huh," he said, and slumped.

"Go home," said Joan. She jerked her chin at me, and I left off tugging at him who outweighed me by thirty pounds, and backed away. "Go home," said Joan, again, exactly as though she were speaking to a dog. Just then, Beth reentered the room, and watched with the rest of us as Bill shambled blindly to his feet, and toward the front door.

"Night," he said, vaguely, pulling it open, and passing through.

"Well," said Vi. "That was amazing."

"Do you want to go with him?" I asked Beth, quietly.

"No," she said. "He'll find his own way home." Seeing the other guests' careful attempts not to look at her, she raised her voice a little, and addressed them.

"A pedigree doesn't always guarantee breeding," she said, lightly and charmingly, and there was a wave of polite and forgiving laughter.

"I'm glad that's over," Joan said, when the guests had left. "What a *horrible* man."

"What do you think he meant?" I asked her.

"I didn't hear," she said, evasively. "He was slurring pretty badly."

"He was angry about something," I said.

"He was drunk," she said. "He didn't know what he was saying."

"Beth handled it well," I said.

"I guess she's used to it," said Joan, sadly. "Here's hoping we don't have to have him here again."

And we didn't; he seemed perfectly happy not to be included in our jaunts. For several months we made a bizarre threesome, two swollen women and one skinny man. On weekends we went to movies, and on weekday evenings we played card games, consuming enormous quantities of popcorn, one of the few foods Joan could tolerate. If that weren't enough, the two women spent weekdays together while I was at work. They did desultory shopping, waddling from store to store, buying almost nothing, coming back to our house, exhausted.

"What have you all been doing all afternoon?" I asked Joan. "Never mind, I know what you're going to say. You talk."

"That's right," said Joan, putting her feet into my lap.

"What about?" I asked, taking her left foot into my hands, beginning to rub it.

"Nothing, really," she said. "How fat we are."

"It worries me," I said. "You're so tired all the time."

"You'd be tired, too, cowboy," said Joan, with a sardonic look. "Hauling this blubber around."

"That's no blubber, that's our baby," I said, drawing a finger up her insole.

"That tickles," she said, squeezing up her face. "Uncle."

"We still haven't picked out names," I said.

"Blubber Corbin," said Joan. "Ow, stop. All right—after you if it's a boy, Margaret Emily if it's a girl."

"Margaret, yuck," I said. "People will call her Margie."

"Or Maggie. Or Meg. Or Peggy."

"Too confusing," I said. "Maybe we should think of something else. What are Beth and Bill considering?"

"They aren't, as far as I know. Beth calls it the Tumor. I think Bill is still trying to figure out where babies come from."

"That sounds like something Beth would say," I remarked.

"It was, actually," admitted Joan. "She can be awfully funny. I just laugh and laugh. Some of the stories she tells, about that crowd she used to run with—you wouldn't believe what they get up to."

"Try me," I said.

"Beth tells them better," said Joan. She looked at me. "You're always so interested in what we talk about."

"I'm curious," I said.

"It's not all that exciting," she said. "I mean, we hardly ever say anything serious anymore. We joke, mostly."

"Sounds more like gossip," I said.

"That, too," said Joan. "But not really nasty, just funny. It's almost like she wants to distract me, keep me laughing. In case I get too close."

"Too close to what?" I asked.

"To whatever." she said. "Beth's very private," she told me. I felt a little stab of resentment: *I know.*

"She seems more so lately," Joan went on. "I think if I asked her what her favorite *color* was, she'd make a joke. To throw me off. I don't know what it is she's protecting, but she does a darn good job."

I remember quite well the day of Amanda Crawford's birth. It was also the day that Joan gave birth to Emily. The two women went into labor almost simultaneously, while I was in the kitchen making supper.

"Ooh," I heard from the living room.

"Joan?" I called.

"Agh."

"Beth?"

"It's time," the two women said together, as I walked toward the couch. Then they both doubled over with laughter, clutching each other's hands. "Let's go," said Beth.

I picked up the phone and asked for Dr. Greene.

"Is it time?" said Bedelia, the night operator. "Oh, my, I'm so excited."

"It's time," I said. "Please put the call through. Oh, hello, Doctor. Uh, Gilbert Corbin. I—yes. Okay, thank you." I hung up. "I'll call Bill, too," I told Beth.

"Call from the hospital, G.I.," she said, panting. "Tumor won't wait."

I drove them to the hospital, feeling oddly like a harem keeper, my two wives hissing in the car with me.

Dr. Greene met us, and raised his eyebrows when he saw both women.

"Well," he said. "Looks like a long night."

They took Joan away, and a nurse showed me to the waiting room.

"I need to make a phone call," I said. She pointed to the pay phone in the corner of the room.

I tried the house on the hill first; no answer. At a loss, I asked Bedelia to put me through to the Trough.

"For heaven's sake," she said.

"I'm looking for Bill Crawford," I told her.

"You don't mean—?"

"Yes," I said.

"Well, isn't that amazing," she said. "But you won't find him at the Trough anymore. He goes to the Broken Weasel, these days. I'll connect you."

"I need to talk to Bill Crawford," I shouted, when the other end was picked up.

"Who needs him?" asked the man who'd answered the phone.

"He's having a."

"Having a what?" said the man impatiently.

"Baby," I managed. "His wife's in the hospital now."

Bill showed up an hour later.

"Am I late?" he asked.

"The doctor was just here," I said. "Could be a couple hours."

"Oh," he said. "How bout a hand, then?" and he pulled a deck of cards out of his pocket. "Just to pass the time."

It passed the time admirably. I was down twelve dollars when Dr. Greene came in to tell me about Emily.

"How bout mine?" asked Bill.

"Be a while yet," said the doctor. "You have time for a hand or two."

"When can I see her?" I asked.

"The baby or Joan?" he teased.

"Both," I said, then, "Joan first."

"Wise choice," said the doctor, winking. "The baby doesn't look like much yet."

"Did you see her?" asked Joan. She looked slightly ill, and her hair lay across her forehead in damp streaks.

"Not yet," I said.

"You'll never believe it," she said. "She's got dark hair. Almost black. And the tiniest fingernails, like sequins."

Emily Margaret was beautiful, an apparently healthy baby; her hair was darker than Joan's or mine, and her skin was a surprisingly Mediterranean olive, where the two of us were rather fair. We carried her home and laid her gingerly into the crib. In a few days, her eyes opened and turned from that cloudy newborn blue into a rich brown.

Beth also had a girl; born two hours after Emily, her name was Amanda Joan. She was small, and the two of them had to stay in the hospital a few extra days.

"They scolded me about the drinking," Beth told us, when she had finally been released. "I told Dr. Greene to try getting through a pregnancy sober, and then come tell me about it."

We were sitting, all four of us, in the living room on Worth Street, fussing over the babies.

"How'd she get so damn blonde?" asked Bill, poking at Amanda.

"Stupid, from me," said Beth.

"You ain't *that* blonde," said Bill. "Some of that comes out of a bottle."

"You shut up," said Beth. "I used to have hair that color when I was a baby. It'll darken on her, too."

"Yours looks overripe," said Bill agreeably, to me.

"She was certainly brewing long enough," said Joan.

I have a photograph somewhere, taken that day, of the six of us. Amanda was asleep, a small white bundle in Beth's arms, but Emily had turned her berry eyes toward the lens. Joan's parents came to visit the next week, bringing their camera; after they left, a small package arrived from Pittsburgh, containing dozens of the glossy expensive squares. Emily in bath. Emily asleep. Emily squinting at the flashbulb. We spent hours choosing one to put into the silver frame which matched the one holding our wedding picture.

So many photographs; I could not put my hand on any of them now. I hid them, during the first miserable days of mourning, hid them so well that I never came across them again. I would like to see them now; they are our only physical proof of Emily, our glorious Emily, who mysteriously stopped breathing twenty-one days into her life, while Joan and I were sleeping down the hall.

It was worse for Joan; she blamed herself. At the funeral, she was poised and solemn, and in the days right afterward she wrote a dozen thank you notes. Gently, then, quietly, she lost her grip on herself, and began to slip away from me. My reassurances did little to puncture the thick gloom of grief which had settled over her. I tried to pick up the old routine, going off to work in the morning, kissing her good-bye. She got into bed and stayed there, and I took up the slack, grocery shopping and cooking and even making a try at housecleaning, all the time hoping that Joan would magically rouse herself. Instead, she sank deeper into her twilight state, eating little, hardly speaking, not even dressing herself. When I came in at night, I found her exactly as she'd been when I left her; I had the uncomfortable impression that she hadn't moved all day.

The news spread ahead of me, so that upon leaving the house in the morning I was forced to run the gauntlet of opinion. People were voluble on the subject, pursuing me through Purdy's with their comments on my misfortune. Some were not above catching me on the fly, so to speak, tapping on my car window where I idled at a stoplight. I ignored them, leaving the glass rolled up; still I could hear them: *Sorry. So sorry.* I nodded to everyone, saying nothing, averting my eyes. *It's not like he was the mother,* I heard one of the ladies say, behind me. *Sensitive,* agreed her companion.

I stopped going to Stokes's. I went in there once about a week after the funeral; the men, some of whom had been there at the gravesite, seemed not to know me. Their eyes slid toward me, and away, and they stood me drink after drink in a confused fashion, until at one point I had two drinks before me on the bar.

"You only got one mouth," said Jack, coming up behind me, and appropriating one of them.

When I spoke, all other conversation stopped, respectfully. It was ludicrous, as though no one had ever died in Naples before. Thinking longingly of the Irish wakes of my ancestors, I drank up and left, the brittle silence dissolving, normalcy restoring itself, behind me.

Beth telephoned the second week.

"How are you, G.I.?" came her warm voice through the receiver.

"Oh, God, Beth," I said.

"You didn't give her rutabagas, did you?" came a third voice. "Rutabagas what did my sister's baby in."

"Shut up, 'Delia," said Beth. There was a gasp, and a click.

"Beth, you shouldn't," I said, smiling weakly. "Now she won't put your calls through for a year."

"I know it," she said. "It's worth it, for a little privacy. How are you, Gil, really? How's Joan?"

"Um," I said.

"Stupid question," she said. "I want to see her. Am I welcome?"

"Of course you are," I said.

But when she arrived, Joan refused to see her.

"No," she said.

"It's Beth," I said.

"Leave me alone," said Joan.

"Joanie, look at me," I pleaded.

"Go away," she said, stonily.

Outside the door, I cried, a noisy weep; I collected myself, and went downstairs again.

"It's okay," said Beth, when she saw me. "She doesn't have to."

"But you're her friend," I said. "I don't think she really likes anyone else."

"Except you," said Beth.

"Not even me right now," I said, shaky.

"Oh, G.I.," said Beth, putting her hand out to me. I went to sit beside her on the sofa. "We have to be strong for Joan," she said, holding my hand hard, "but there's nothing says we can't have a little cry all our own."

The news preceded me to work. There, I was greeted with subdued, skittish hellos, and the office manager, Benson, took me into his office.

"You take it easy," he said. "You need a coupla days off?"

"No," I told him.

"I understand," he said. "Work takes your mind off. When my wife passed, I put in eighty-hour weeks." He looked blank for a few moments, rocking back and forth in his chair, and then his eyes came back to me. "But that's no good," he said shortly. "You take it easy. Any extra comes in, I'll slide it over to Eddie. Don't push yourself."

Back at my desk, I fingered the stack of meaningless paper. Rick Beller leaned over to me.

"Hey, too bad," he said. "Rough break." Getting no response, he poked a stiff finger into my shoulder. "You gotta think positive," he said. "When our old dog got run over, Sally said she'd never have another one in the house. But I just went ahead and brought home Juniper, and she's never looked back."

I looked at him.

"Have another quick," he said. "That one musta been defective anyway, or it wouldnta died so young. Next one'll be stronger."

"You asshole," I said, quietly.

He was taken aback.

"What you want to go and say that for?" he complained. "You got no call to say something like that."

I got up from my desk, and left the room. I knocked on Benson's office door.

"I have reason to," I told him. "Believe that Rick Beller is stealing from the company."

Benson regarded me sorrowfully as I explained. When I finished, he turned his back to me for a moment, then turned back around sharply. "I know you're under a lot of stress," he said. "But this isn't worthy of you."

"What?" I said, surprised. "I'm not," I protested, "making this up."

"I'm sure you're not," he said. "But you've known about this a long time, haven't you, before coming in here."

"I didn't know," I said, "what to do."

"That's hard for me to believe," said Benson. He shook his head. "What hurts the company, hurts us all. I don't mean to be harsh," he said. "But I'm disappointed in you."

"I'm sorry," I said.

"I thought you were a company man."

"I was," I said. "Confused."

"Well," said Benson, holding my eyes gravely. "Better late than never, eh?" His expression relaxed a little. "We'll follow this up," he said. "We'll keep your name out of it."

As I left the office, he patted my arm.

"We all make mistakes," he said.

I spent the rest of the day in a kind of fog. There were, it seemed, two codes between men. The men in Stokes's had preached solidarity; Benson had rebuked my hazy morals and lack of company spirit. By the end of the day, I had figured it out. There was only one maxim, after all: Us against Them. A man, it appeared, had to choose his home team, his Us, and then pull hard and unstoppably for glory. But what, I thought, if no team was home?

Joan continued to refuse visitors. Beth called every evening at nine; I put the telephone on the hook just before, and took it off again after we'd finished our conversation. I was getting used to the funereal hush that pervaded the house on Worth Street, and was just beginning to worry that it might never change, when suddenly it lifted. Three weeks after Emily's death, Joan's catatonia resolved itself. As I came through the front door one evening, I smelled cooking vapors. Joan sang out a greeting from the kitchen, and then appeared briefly, fully dressed, to kiss me before whisking back into the kitchen.

"Gil," she called. "Where are those pictures of Emily?"

"I don't know," I said, bewildered.

"Well, think," she said, coming into the room again. "I need them."

"I don't remember where I put them," I said. "Maybe in the attic."

"I've been all through the attic," said Joan. "They're not there."

"Why do you want them?" I said, going to her, taking her hands.

"It's a surprise," she said, kissing me. There was something slightly off-center about her expression, but I didn't notice it then. How could I have known?

Two days later, Beth called me at work.

"Come get your wife," she said, and her voice was unrecognizable, taut.

"What's wrong?" I said. "Is she okay?"

"Just come," said Beth, again. "Right away."

It was a strange tableau that greeted me. Beth was seated on the sofa, looking grim, and Joan was in the chair across from her, holding Amanda and smiling widely.

"Honey, look," she said, when she saw me. "I've found her."

"Found who?" I asked.

"Emily," said Joan. "It was all a mistake. But I've fixed it now. It's going to be all right now."

I looked at Beth, who shrugged her shoulders.

"That's great, honey," I said. "Let me talk to Beth for a minute."

"You explain it to her," she said.

In the kitchen, Beth told me what had happened. Joan had come over about an hour before, with a story about how the babies had been switched in the hospital, and how Beth and Billy had gotten Emily by mistake.

"My God," I said.

"I would've called you earlier, but that damn 'Delia wouldn't put me through," said Beth. "I've been trying to call Dr. Greene, but same thing. I tried to calm her down by letting her hold Amanda, but she can't take her."

"Of course not," I said. "Oh, Beth."

"It's terrible," said Beth, her eyes filling. "I'm so sorry about what happened, G.I. But I want to kill her when she talks about taking my baby."

"I'll talk to her," I said.

"That won't help," said Beth. "I've talked myself blue. Call the doctor."

Dr. Greene came within the hour. He persuaded Joan to let him lift Amanda out of her arms.

"Just a checkup," he said.

"Gil, you take her," said Joan, anxiously.

I took the soft warm weight, and held it while Dr. Greene examined Joan. I closed my eyes, and could almost understand Joan's unreason. It was the only cure for what ailed us—a baby bundle, the smell of talc, the hummingbird pulse. Dr. Greene touched me on the arm, startling me. He motioned me into the kitchen.

"She'll have to go into the hospital," he said. "It's been a nasty shock. She needs professional care."

"Um," I said, confused. "Will she get better?" Shifting Amanda to my other arm.

"Should be right as rain in a few days," he said, reassuringly. He patted my shoulder. "Don't worry."

I gave Amanda back to Beth.

"I'm sorry," I told her. "I had no idea this would happen."

"I'm sure she'll be all right soon," said Beth, friendlier now that she had her baby safe again.

* * *

Joan was in the hospital two weeks, and when she came home she was a little thinner but otherwise normal. We didn't mention Emily. Though I watched Joan carefully, I couldn't see any lingering traces of the brief madness.

After a while, she started talking about going back to work. "It'll take my mind off," she said, "things."

Life returned to the way it had been before Joan's pregnancy. We still didn't talk about Emily. In a way, we healed around that one sadness, walling it off. Despite all of the shock and grief, she might have been a closed episode, a dark comma in an otherwise happy marriage, had we not had the ever-present reminder of Amanda, her spiritual twin, growing up in the house on the hill. Turning two, and then four. Joan and I were pressed into service as godparents, and went to the birthday parties with a kind of false cheer.

The doctor had assured us that the odds of another crib-death were very small. He examined Joan, and declared her perfectly fit. We listened to his words together, but didn't discuss them at home. It was months before Joan and I were able to make love again. The yearning seemed to have passed from us. It returned to me before it returned to Joan, and I tried to remain patient with her mourning, her long granny night-gowns, her sisterly bedtime kisses on the cheek.

The night of November sixth, when Emily would have been six months old, I was lying wakeful while Joan slept next to me. Or didn't sleep; suddenly she raised herself on an elbow, shaking the mattress slightly.

"Come here," she whispered.

I went to her; she pressed tightly against me, and wound her fingers in my hair, pulling hard, so that I gave a little cry of pain.

"Shh," she said.

She unbuttoned her nightgown slowly, and I lifted it over her head. Gently then, quietly as though someone were listening, we rediscovered one another.

Afterward, we lay on our sides, turned toward each other. By the light of a streetlamp, I could see the tear tracks on her cheeks. She patted my hand, and I watched her fall asleep.

But even after that, when we might have begun another child, Joan did not conceive. Or could not: it was impossible to tell what havoc grief might have wrought upon her internal organs. I envisioned my own heart as smaller, somehow, shrunken like a winter apple, since Emily's death.

And all the time Amanda was growing bigger, crawling toddling then walking, stumbling across our front yard on weekends, while the two women sat together in the glider. Joan spent a lot of time with the child, who spoke Joan's name before anything else, pronouncing *Mama* as a sort of afterthought.

"She's taken up with that crowd again," Joan reported, disapprovingly. "She's gone all the time, leaving her with that nanny, who never even finished eighth grade, did you know that?"

"What's that matter?" I asked, unwisely.

"Well, it doesn't matter, that's all," said Joan, really angry now. "It doesn't matter at all that a woman who calls herself a mother is out every single night, drinking and carrying on. It doesn't matter that the father's even worse, and that the nanny is a simpering fool who wouldn't know what to do if something really serious happened. None of it matters a bit, I suppose."

"All right, all right," I said, giving in.

It was remarkable, really, how often people took Amanda for Joan's child. She had a lot of Corbin about her; in photographs it was particularly striking, the three of us in a row pale as sunlight (Joan and I had nary a freckle between us), and she had blue grey eyes exactly the color of mine, gleaming out beneath her yellow hair. Looking at her, I glimpsed again the seed of Joan's earlier delusion: apart from her hair, Amanda might have been a changeling, slipped into the Crawford home under cover of night.

By the time she was four, we had all adjusted to the situation. All, that is, except Bill, whom Beth was divorcing. She had come home one night to find Amanda sticky with ice cream and asleep on the living room rug, and Bill sticky and asleep upstairs with Mary Sue Cudahy.

"In our bed," she told us grimly, the next day. "It was just too much."

She threw him out that night, and started divorce proceedings. He was belligerent at first, but after he got over his drunk he tried to court her again.

"Can you believe it?" she said. "He's sending me roses. Paid for on account. The florist called me to ask if he should deliver em." She laughed. "I told him not to waste his time."

"What are you going to do?" asked Joan.

"Don't pretend," said Beth. "You never liked him. Hell, *I* never liked him. It'll just be easier with him gone. Lucy's having seven different kinds of fits, though," she said. "Seems any kind of husband's better than dee-vorce." Something seemed to occur to her. "Also, I think she heard about Jack and Marie having trouble, and she's thinking the worst. Old Lucy's got a devious mind, all right. Oh, and listen to this," she said. "My in-laws are trying to bribe me. Old Joe sent over a present yesterday, rolled it right up to the house. Four wheels and a big old bow on the side." She giggled. "Guess what."

"A new stroller," said Joan, unimaginatively.

"Nope," she said. "A brand-new Mustang convertible, redder 'n red."

"You can't *accept* it," said Joan, shocked.

"I always wanted one of them," said Beth, carelessly.

"Are you going to go back with him, then?" I asked.

"Hell, no," she said, grinning. "I think of it as a divorce present."

Things in general were looking up: Joan was back at her old job, and I was still at mine, having gotten a raise in salary; Rick Beller had been fired, and the fellow who worked next to me now was jolly and hardworking. Joan and I were passionate again, and I believed we might soon be talking about having another child. Progress. It had taken a while, but it seemed we had weathered the storm.

Chapter Sixteen

The Nanny

Of course you want to know about Amanda. Why else come to me—I'm not pretty enough for movies, never was, even when I was young. 'Pretty is as pretty does,' my mother used to tell me, but sometimes I wished I *did* less and *was* more. Listen to me going on—I guess I'm a little nervous. That's normal, isn't it? I mean, everybody you've talked to's been a little nervous at first, haven't they?

I looked after Amanda from the time she was very small. I hadn't ever had the care of children before, but I had some brothers and sisters, so my mother put my name forward when Mrs. Crawford was looking for someone to help. She wasn't much older than me, Mrs. Crawford, and just as young looking as if she was still in high school. I was real nervous at the interview—must have dropped my gloves three times—but in the end she said I'd do. I was surprised, as I'd hardly said two words, but Mrs. Crawford said she liked quiet.

Quiet for the baby, I guess; *she* wasn't all that quiet. Not that she was a bad woman, oh no; you could tell just by looking that she was bred right. But she and Mr. Crawford got into some awful fights. They'd go at it hammer and tongs in the living room, while I'd be upstairs with Amanda. I guess I was hiding; there weren't many raised voices in my house when I was growing up, and I thought someone would get killed, from the way they shouted at each other.

But they always quieted down after a while. Mr. Crawford would go out, and there'd be a rattle at the cupboard meaning Mrs. Crawford was making herself a drink, and then she'd call upstairs to me, to bring the baby down. Sometimes I didn't want to; I could tell that Amanda was upset by all the noise, even if she was so young. I think babies can tell things, don't you?

I'd bring her down, and Mrs. Crawford would fuss over her for a while, and ask me questions about her diapers and her feeding and such. It kind of surprised me, how little she knew about babies. Even I knew about gassy foods, and things like that. But Mrs. Crawford would give her anything she wanted, even if it wasn't good for her, and it just got worse as the child grew.

Not that she was a bad mother; oh, no. But she just didn't spend as much time with Amanda as I did, and she didn't know what kind of foods made her ill. Babies have their habits, same as older folks. Some babies take to vegetables like they were candy, while other ones won't have anything to do with green. It's kind of an art to get a baby to eat what it needs, and sometimes Mrs. Crawford's spoiling went a ways to ruin my careful work. I was glad when she'd give Amanda back to me and let me put her down for the night. Most times I left then, to go back home, but sometimes I stayed late, so Mrs. Crawford could go out. She went out a lot, mostly with girlfriends, women who didn't look or act like her, the kind that laughed loud all the time and had no children. Except for just one of her girlfriends, they were all like that.

I don't like to say, but I think she drank more than was good for her. Sometimes she'd come home late, with all of her girlfriends honking and calling from the car, and I'd have to help her to bed. I could smell the gin on her, strong enough to curl your hair. It didn't seem to hurt her none, though: the next morning when I came she'd complain of headache, but she'd be as cheery as ever. I didn't hold with the gossip that said Mrs. Crawford was a drunk. She wasn't ever falling-down, just tipsy, and who would blame her, with that husband.

It was a scandal, of course, the way she threw him out in the middle of the night, in the rain. I wasn't there, but I heard about it. And then the divorce. People didn't divorce then the way they do now. There was something kind of fast about divorcées and no one wanted to be one. There were probably just as many bad marriages then as there are now, but I guess people just tended to stick it out more, and try to make the best of it. I know of one woman who's been divorced two times, and both times I believe she and her husband could have managed, if they hadn't been so quick to get offended, and so deaf to each other.

I'll say this for Mr. Crawford—he was sad about leaving Amanda, even if he and his wife didn't like each other much. He never had paid the child a whole lot of attention, but you could see he was fond of her. He was a little afraid of her, I think, afraid to hold her, like she might break. No wonder,

with his wife snapping at him all the time. 'Don't drop her,'
she'd say. Well, to my mind that's the surest way to get the
thing accomplished. Someone says don't drop, the first thing
they do is drop. But he kept on trying—to hold her, to talk to
her—for a while at least. So it was hard for me to hate him,
even if he was a terrible kind of husband, and not much of a
father.

His going settled things down a bit. Amanda was very
grown-up about it; she only asked once about where her daddy
was, and after it was explained to her she kept quiet. It was
Mrs. Crawford took things hard, and you'dve thought she'd be
nothing but glad to be rid of him, the way he treated her. But
she mooned around like her best friend had died. She acted
real mixed-up; one day she'd get up late and laze around in her
bathrobe, and the next she'd be up early and dressed like she
was going to a party, even if she had no place in mind to go.
She was mixed-up about the child, too. She'd say she wanted
to spend more time with her, and she'd hug her close all day,
and then the next day she'd push her off onto me and ask me
to keep her quiet. It was a real confusion, and I was glad to be
there so the little girl had someone she could count on, besides
that one friend of Mrs. Crawford's.

The friend was over most every day, and she knew how to
handle babies, it was clear, although she didn't have any of her
own. I heard she had something wrong with her inside. Isn't
that just the way—the ones who want them most can't have
them, and the ones who don't want them are in the clinic every
year. I felt sorry for her, and used to let her give Amanda her
bath, even though that was my job usually. She just lit up, and
bathed her real gentle, without getting the littlest speck of soap
in her eyes. As I say, you can tell a natural-born mother.

I was happy working for Mrs. Crawford. I'd clerked before,
but had never liked the job much. Selling ribbons in the five-
and-ten with a bunch of giggly girls trading gossip behind the
counter and ignoring me. They thought I was low, because I
had no education, and it was likely I'd be at work all my life,
and never marry. I guess they figured it right; and now it's no
disgrace to be a working woman, but then I felt the shame of
it. I used to try all kinds of new things with my hair and face,
hoping to look in the mirror and find somebody new and glamorous. It was always me looking back, same old peanut-face
under the rouge and curls. "Why bother, Elsie?" Mrs. Crawford asked me. "Anybody can't see your heart isn't worth

having." I thought about that, and I can't say I gave up my primping right away, but it did seem a little less important what I looked like after that. Babies love you no matter what.

And Amanda loved me. Everybody loved her, but she loved me best of all. She told me all the things she thought up by herself and she'd say, 'Don't tell.' A baby's secrets. I kept them safe. She was a golden child, always sunny; all that spoiling she got didn't hurt her a bit. She never threw one tantrum, not one; and there's not many children I can say that about. I would have loved her if she'd thrown a million fits, I've loved children since who hadn't her good temper, but Amanda was my first, and I loved her best.

Mrs. Crawford took to going out in the middle of the day; she took up with her old friends after Mr. Crawford left, and she'd go shopping with them over in the next town. Or they'd see a movie. They'd drive as far as Charlottesville to see a new movie. When she got back, if she wasn't too tired, she'd tell me all about it, so it was like I'd seen it myself. And then when it came to Naples I'd go see it; it helped to know about it already, because then I could pay more attention to the people, and not so much to what was happening.

She'd be gone all day, sometimes. I'd go get Amanda from school (they went until noon) and bring her home to dinner. Then we'd color or play dolls, something quiet; I seen the way they let them run around at that school. A little girl needs quiet, and so Amanda had her afternoons, and when her mother got home she saw her little girl all tidy and smiling, pretty as a picture.

If the day was nice, we'd go for walks, just the little girl and me, looking at wildflowers, telling each other stories. That child had an *imagination.* I'd get so caught up in her tales that I'd forget where I was, or who. Instead of Naples, it was like we were walking through a fancy-land filled with palaces and kings and fairies. I half expected something magic to happen to us right there while Amanda told me her stories.

That was how I met Winslow. He wasn't a terribly handsome fellow, or a terribly rich one either. He worked at the organ-building factory downtown, and was kind of plain-looking. But he smiled a lot, and he had big strong hands. Just looking at them made me think of the organ music coming out of those pipes he made.

He spoke to us first. Not to me, really, but to Amanda. She was in the middle of a fairy tale, when he sort of popped out of the bushes, and said hello. She was a well-bred child (I'd seen to that), but she knew better than to talk to strangers, so she just nodded, cool as you please, and we passed on.

He kept after us though, meeting us every day at the same place, and raising his hat like he knew us.

"Who's that man?" asked Amanda.

"Nobody," I said.

"Nobody's *nobody,*" she said. "He's probably a prince in disguise."

Amanda had a quarter, given to her by her grandpa. It was more money than she'd owned at one time, and she kept in her hand from the moment he tucked it there. She'd take it out of her pocket to look at fifty times in fifty paces even though I told her to be careful. "You'll lose it," I said, "and then you'll be sorry." But she wouldn't put it up in her piggy bank; it was her first quarter, and she wouldn't let it go, no matter how I coaxed.

Well, of course she dropped it. Not just on the sidewalk, so that it rolled away, but near a little grating. It disappeared; and she bit her lip and said nothing, holding back her tears. Even though I'd warned her it might happen, and she oughtn't to have been so careless, I felt sorry for her, standing looking down into the grate so hopelessly.

At that moment, Winslow appeared. I didn't know his name then, nor anything about him, and I wouldn't answer him when he asked what was making the little girl cry.

"I lost my quarter," Amanda told him, pointing down.

"Well now," he said. "We'll see what we can do about that."

Quick as a wink he had his sleeves rolled up, and was on his knees by the grating, pulling some shiny kind of tool from his pocket, and his hat was somehow in my hand. Not ten minutes later he was handing the quarter back to Amanda.

"It's covered with germs," I said. "Give it to me; I'll wash it when we get home."

"Excuse me, ma'am," said the man. "But we could as easy wash it in the fountain, and it would make the little girl happy."

Of course then she would have nothing else; so we walked with the man to the fountain, where Amanda washed her quarter, and the man washed his arm, which was all dirty from messing about in the grating. He began to talk then, and that was when I found out his name and where he worked. For a factory man, he was very polite. He offered to walk us home, but I wasn't that taken with him that I didn't know what was proper.

"He didn't talk like a roughneck up to no good," said Amanda, on the way home.

"I think maybe I was mistaken, dear," I told her.

The next fine day, we saw him; and all through that summer. And when Amanda started school again in the fall, our little walks had to stop, as she was going for a full day now, and it got dark soon after she got out.

The winter came, and dragged on. Amanda was learning to read, and we spent the afternoons sounding out words together. By February she was reading almost as well as me, and the first time she brought me a word I didn't know, I felt afraid.

"Why so blue?" asked Mrs. Crawford one day, noticing my mood.

"Guess I'm just longing for spring," I said, and it was true. I was looking forward to the warm, when Amanda and I could walk outside again, and stop all this fussing with books. And I had a hope too, without even knowing it, that we might see Winslow again.

The first warm day came early, and Amanda and I took our walk. She was bigger now, and ran ahead of me. I went slowly, telling her that a lady didn't run, but all the time I was looking for Winslow, thinking he might come looking for us.

We didn't meet him that day, or the next time, or the next. I began to despair; what if he had moved on, left the factory for some other job, gone back to his home in the Tidewater? I had no way of knowing what had happened to him, and after awhile I tried just to forget him. Amanda and I took shorter and fewer walks; she wanted to read, or to play with her schoolfriends in the afternoons. Our walks shrank down to just the distance between school and her house, one way in the morning, home again at two.

I always left the house at a twenty to, so I'd be in good time to meet her. In early May it could still get chilly, and one day I took along an extra sweater for her, so she wouldn't be cold, coming back.

I had just rounded the corner when Winslow popped out of the bushes, the way he had that first time.

"Hello," he said, just like before, but this time I didn't snub him. There was a whole winter past full of things to say. We'd been there fifteen minutes before I thought of the time. It was ten past two!

"I have to hurry," I said. "I'm late getting Amanda."

"I'll walk with you," said he.

So we walked fast, nearly running. Seven blocks have never seemed so long. And all the time we didn't talk; I think Winslow guessed I was upset. I was seeing poor Amanda, standing outside the school and waiting, not seeing me, maybe even starting off for home by herself, crossing the street . . .

When we got to the school, she wasn't there.

"She always meets me right here," I said.

"Maybe she went inside to wait," said Winslow. "It's nippy."

But she wasn't inside; her teacher hadn't seen her since the bell rang; none of the children could tell me if they'd seen her on the playground, or even if she'd been at school at all that day. One of the little girls finally said that she'd seen her, but she wouldn't say anything more.

"Where did she go?" I asked.

The child put her finger in her mouth and looked at me.

"Which *way?*" I cried, startling the little girl so that her mouth opened in an O.

"Mama," she said, and went off toward a figure at the edge of the playground.

We looked and looked, and finally Winslow suggested that we walk back toward the house, the way she might have gone. We did, but didn't see her; and when we reached the house again I burst inside, hoping against hope she'd be there.

But she wasn't. No little coat tossed on the floor, no impatient little voice scolding, 'Where *were* you?' She was gone, that was all, just gone. She had disappeared into thin air.

Winslow was outside on the steps. I hadn't let him in the house, knowing what was proper. After a while, he knocked at the door.

"We'll find her," he said.

"Like you found the quarter?" I cried. "She's a little *girl.*"

He put his arms around me, and then I got angry. It was his fault, wasn't it, that I'd been late to get her. I'd never been late before. He had caused all of this, with his sweet talk and his charm.

"Go away," I said, pushing him.

"Elsie," he said.

"What if she's been run over? You're a murderer, the same

as if you'd done it yourself," I said. "Go away." I was pushing him with one hand, and in the other was the little sweater, and I started to cry again, and gave him a shove so that he fell right down, and then I slammed the door.

I never saw him again. Oh, he came around from time to time, and knocked on the Crawfords' door, but I wouldn't answer. If Amanda had come back, I suppose I would have forgiven him. The whole thing would have been lost, gone the way of all bad days. But it wasn't just a bad day; it never ended; and Winslow was all tied up with it in my mind. I remembered how happy I was that day to see him, how we were flirting and laughing at the very same time that Amanda was waiting for me. . . . I hated myself, and I hated him, and I couldn't put any of it aside.

Mrs. Crawford was very kind to me; she said it wasn't my fault, and even when she'd been crying all day she tried to look on the bright side.

"You stay on, Elsie," she said. "She'll want you here when she comes back."

But finally I had to leave the household. No use for a nanny in a childless house. Mrs. Crawford wrote me a nice letter, and I found a good position with another family, new in town, who had two boys and a baby girl. I had my hands full with them, and didn't see much of Mrs. Crawford after that. I stopped by sometimes on my day off, just to see how she was getting along, but it was plain that my visits disturbed her. She had a friend looking after her, so I wasn't needed.

Winslow gave up looking for me, I suppose. Maybe he didn't know where to find me, or maybe he stopped caring, found himself another girl, or moved away. I know I didn't want to see him. The thought of him bothered me the way the sight of me bothered Mrs. Crawford, and I did my best to put him right out of my mind.

I work for a different family now, over on the hill, very near where the Crawfords used to live. And on fine days I take the children for walks, almost the very same steps I used to take with Amanda. It's been twenty years and more, but still every time we pass that clump of bushes where Winslow first said hello, I stop and walk a little slower, looking around. I don't guess I hope to see him. But wounds heal, and time takes some of the pain away. I can see that I was just a young girl then, and I've tried to be a good Christian. I figure the good Lord has forgiven; maybe Winslow too.

Chapter Seventeen

Strangerland

During the early years, he was afraid of the dark. When the lights went off, he lay rigid with terror, aware that the room had changed, and that the secret underworld was heaving up through the invisible seam that bound it to the everyday. He called to his mother, never telling her why; and she came and listened to his excuses about thirst and sleeplessness.

"You're afraid," she said.

He nodded.

"You're not always afraid."

"The room looks different," he whispered.

"I guess you've seen it, then," said his mother, letting the rocking chair fall back with her weight.

"Seen what?"

"Why, Strangerland, of course." She sat forward again. "You've never heard of Strangerland?"

He hadn't; and so she explained it to him. Strangerland was a place where everything was double, where every house, person, and animal had two natures. Superficial inspection didn't reveal the duality; you wouldn't find it by looking. It was only at unexpected moments, in glimpses out of the corner of the eye, that things might suddenly shift and lay bare their otherness—their Strangerland quality.

"You've seen it tonight," said his mother. "In the dark. Of course you're afraid, because everything is strange. But Strangerland can be wonderful, too." Her voice was low, story-telling, calm. "The first snowfall is Strangerland," she said. "You get up in the morning, and without knowing how you know, you know something is different. You look out the window, and there it is—a new place, unfamiliar. All the things you know so well buried in white. It's all of a sudden a place you've never seen before." He poked a hand out of the bedclothes and found her warm dry hand, the nails smooth and polished. The second snowfall doesn't count; only the first heavy one, the one that comes in the night. It catches you unaware, and lets you see it—Strangerland."

She told him adventure stories: about a different little boy, a Strangerland alter ego, fearless and very strong. That other boy saved villages, swam oceans, rode on the backs of eagles. It wasn't until many years later that he realized his mother had simply condensed all of the common fairy tales into one endless interweaving story, with one perpetual hero.

When he was afraid, he called for her, and she spun him another tale or two, until his eyelids dropped. She stayed with him afterward, so that he awoke in the middle of the night sometimes to see her, sitting patient by his bed, completely idle, not even rocking.

They were alone then, mother and son, moving from thin-walled house to thin-walled house, across three states and back. His mother wore a strong perfume then, and went out to work in the daytime; he stayed at home and kept quiet, or went to another lady's house and played with her rough children. That part of his childhood concentrated later into just a stretch of colorless, raucous hours, one ear cocked for the sound of his mother's footstep on the stairs. At four years old, he had learned to cook hot-plate spaghetti, and had it ready for her sometimes when she came home. His world was complicated then, nipped and pincered by rules—NO COOKING IN THE ROOMS—NO CHILDREN UNDER FIVE—and he danced it daily, fanning the fumes of illegal supper out of the boarding-house window, wincing when the lady's children hit, but not hitting back. He was past five when William Gates came along to fall in love with Beth. After the adoption, Buddy let his father preserve the fiction that he had always been there. But Buddy knew better, although he didn't say so. There had been a time before, a time when it was just the two of them, and no Bill Gates bringing presents.

Strangerland disappeared after they moved into Bill's Connecticut house; every room was well lit there, and the little boy was growing, and no longer afraid of the dark. Now his mother told him stories about Robinson Crusoe, and Sherlock Holmes; and sometimes Bill read to him from colorful books. Strangerland was something they had clung to, the son and mother, when they were alone and sometimes hungry; they had needed that possibility of magic, of things being more than they seemed. After the move, his mother seemed content with the single-edged world, and those bedtime stories dissolved into memory. He would have even believed she had forgotten all about it, were it not for that one day when he was thirteen, and came home after school, to find her drunken on the sofa.

"Mom, you drink too much," he'd said, removing the glass from her hand.

(Had he really said this? He'd known more than he credited himself with knowing; such a clue, to have been so easily and totally misplaced in subsequent years.)

"Only sometimes," said his mother. She reached up and touched his face. "You're so much like your father."

"I don't think so," said Buddy, but he was pleased. Skinny, he admired William Gates's masculine physique and air of imperturbability.

"It's true," his mother had told him. "Where's Bill?"

"You know he's out of town," said Buddy. "Or you wouldn't have drunk so much. He'd worry if he knew."

"Let me tell you something," she said. "You never expect what happens to you. All those books people write, saying how they planned it all, they're lies. Things just happen, good and bad. They just happen to you." She reached for the glass Buddy was holding; he pulled it away from her. "Don't play games with me, young man," she said. He shrugged and gave the glass to her; she took it and held it without drinking. "It all keeps coming back," she said.

"What does?" Buddy asked, embarrassed to see his mother like this, confidential in her bathrobe, stinking of liquor.

"Strangerland."

So she did remember. It had given him an odd feeling of displacement listening to his mother reel out the old bedtime story, a different version, out of context and askew.

"When you least expect it," said his mother. "There it is. Everybody suddenly a stranger. People you know—you don't know. Everything's frightening, everything's dangerous. It *looks* the same," she said. "And yet it isn't."

As she spoke, the world seemed to waver around Buddy; he felt drunk himself, and scared, listening. He clenched his fists and buried them in his lap.

"*Mom,*" he'd said at last, breaking into her monologue. The single syllable seemed to recall her.

"Oh, honey," she'd said. "I'm sorry. I didn't mean to frighten you. Come on, I'll get up now, I'm okay. See, I'm okay."

She was standing now, bending over him where he had sunk down onto a chair.

"I'm sorry, baby. You're right, I shouldn't drink whisky. It makes me so maudlin."

"What's that mean?" Buddy had asked; even so disturbed, he was curious.

"Creepy," said Beth, after a little interval. "I just get creepy, is all. No more of that." Her voice became brisk. "Up with you, now. Put on something nice. We'll go out for dinner."

"I'm not hungry," he had said, hating himself, but wanting to punish her.

"I'll let you back the car out," Beth had said, ignoring his refusal, going away to dress.

He had seen Strangerland again the day of her death. Wrapped in a blanket one of the officers had put around him, still blank in the chair long after they had left, waiting for his aunt to come. Everything changed character then, slipping suddenly from familiar to alien, from benevolent to sinister. Even the furniture had been menacing; and he had ignored the whining of the dog at the door, afraid of any swift treachery, believing in some small, frightened part of him that his old friendly hound might spring at him with jaws gaping. The scary side of Strangerland; he'd met it, and recognized it, then. And buried it again, until now.

He hadn't been prepared for the Strangerland in Naples. But he'd found it, the other night.

Nothing more frightening than the seemingly benign turned evil. Stumbling after Jack in the dark the other night, Buddy had met again the old fear, and understood how imperfectly he'd conquered it. The woods by Webb's house had been filled with terror and with cruelty. Jack's laughter had wounded his pride, and more: it had frightened him deeply, had brought out in a moment all the worries he'd kept locked away since he was small. For a while among the trees that night he'd been alone again, and threatened, and this time no Mama to sit by his bed and watch over him.

The doctor had warned this might happen. *There might be a delayed reaction,* he'd said, and had suggested counseling, had even recommended a therapist, but Buddy had taken the piece of paper and shoved it into his pocket, later taking it out and screwing it up into a tiny ball and tossing it onto his desk, and then later taking it up again and unfolding and refolding it, spending minutes at a time smoothing and then crumpling, until the name was illegible, just a trail of ink across the broken fibers.

"It won't make her come back," he'd told his father finally, cruelly, and the subject of therapy was closed.

Now he wondered how wise it had been, to come to Naples with this time bomb ticking away inside him. But where else might he have gone? Christmas in California had been miserable; his father had even had a girlfriend. *Nothing serious,* he'd assured Buddy, but his clumsy attempts to hide the evidence of her in the house had indicated otherwise. She'd come to dinner, a gentle young thing in an old-fashioned velvet dress, and she'd paid so much attention to Buddy that he'd been overwhelmed with resentment and retreated into rudeness. Afterward, his father had taken him to task.

"Was it necessary to be so hostile to Debbie?" he'd asked. "She was just interested in you."

"Too interested," Buddy had said, knowing he was in the wrong, and yet unable to stop himself.

"Son, I know it's hard for you," his father had said, capitulating. "But we have to move on. It's been almost two years."

"You act like you've forgotten her," Buddy had shouted, startling both of them.

"I haven't forgotten her," Bill Gates had said, after a pause. "How can you say that? I wanted to spend my life with her. It's just," and he'd taken a breath and turned his face slightly away, "she's gone now. There's nothing I can do about that." He'd brought his face back, and Buddy saw the tears there. "There's nothing *we* can do. We have to accept that."

That was Christmas. When Buddy had decided at the last minute to spend spring break in Naples, his father had seemed relieved.

"Sorry you can't make it this time," he'd said. "Drive carefully."

There was no refuge in California. None in New York either, the dorms taunting him with their emptiness, reminding him of the hordes of normal students who had places they were wanted, expected, places they called Home. Something they took for granted, it was peppered throughout their conversations; and backing away from them, he had brought himself here, to this alien village. Patting the camera, telling himself that together they'd find something, learn something, that the project would lay some ghosts to rest, and help him to move on.

He hadn't expected what he'd found here—the sense of familiarity coupled with eerie imbalance, as though he were Rip van Winkle coming down from the Catskills, looking for home. Knowing that some nugget of the town he sought still lived on, unsure how to find it.

He'd learned something from that nanny, but it hadn't been the right story. Not the right version. The version he wanted was hidden in Strangerland, and he'd have to make up his mind to go in after it. Or to turn away, and leave it behind forever.

Chapter Eighteen

Men and Women

O n Thursday, Joan and I had a dinner engagement. It was a rare thing for us to commit to an outside invitation, and I thought we might cancel it, but Joan insisted on going.

"We always go to the Bruckners," she said. "I promised Polly I'd help serve. It wouldn't look right if we didn't go. Too many things . . ."

So we went, dressing nervously beforehand, ready half an hour early, sitting like patient children in the living room, hands folded, watching the clock.

"She won't need me earlier than six-thirty," said Joan, rearranging the brooch on her blouse for the tenth time in as many minutes. "Oh, I *can't* get this thing right. Will you do it?"

I crossed to where she sat and took up the cameo which had been my mother's. Ellen had given it to Joan a few Christmases ago, it seeming likely that she would never herself have any daughters. I slipped the pin into the sheer fabric of Joan's blouse, and clasped it.

"This okay?" I asked. She looked down and nodded. "Let's go," I said. "We can drive slowly."

We were still a little early, but Joan relaxed once we were inside the Bruckner's house. We had been there often enough to disarm her; she was as familiar with their kitchen as she was with our own.

I wandered into the living room and made small talk with a few of the early guests. All faces I knew, apart from one Bruckner cousin who had travelled from afar and in whose honor the party was being given.

"You can't believe what it's like in Boston nowadays," the cousin said to me. "I left my car in Cambridge for one minute —no more than five—and when I came back the radio was gone." She paused for commentary.

"That's terrible," I said.

"It's drugs, of course. The revenge and consolation of the underprivileged." The hyperthyroid wife of a well-known magazine publisher, she was a silly woman, infused with a languid arrogance, as though she had long ago divined all of the modern causes of misery, and found them disappointing. "I love visiting Harry," she said now, turning her salamander eyes on me. "This town is so precious. It never seems to change, does it? Like a treasure, preserved in amber."

"Isn't it usually," I said, "bugs get preserved in amber?" Out of the corner of my eye, I saw them enter, Jack and his latest girlfriend. "There's my," I said to the Bruckner cousin, "brother. Excuse me for a moment."

I went toward Jack and just as I drew near saw the shape of Buddy behind him, lingering in the entrance hall.

"I have a little shadow," I said, in a voice ruthless and low. It was the first we had spoken directly in twenty years.

"Nice to see you, too," he said. "You remember Caroline."

I exchanged tight smiles with the blonde, and then Buddy was among us. He was no longer wearing the despairing look I had seen him sporting last. Now he looked wary, as though he had strayed into an enemy camp unwittingly; and crafty, as though he intended to bluff it out.

"Nice place," he said.

"Tell Harry," I advised him, indicating our host standing by the drinks table. "He and Polly worked very hard on it." Speaking, seeming casual, I turned my head to see: Joan was still in the kitchen. I moved with Buddy now, blocking the living room with my body, not seeming to, leading him. "Where's your camera?"

"Taking a vacation," said Buddy. "Like you said." He shot a glance around the room, and lowered his voice. "I don't think these people would have minded too much, though."

Surprised at his insight, I nodded. "These people" were the fashionable few of Naples, the new money, the chic, and of anybody in town they would have welcomed the camera, indeed expected it. Their arrival roughly ten years ago had struck a jarring chord in a town where prestige had always been dictated by family lineage and street address. These new aristocrats had brought their own rules. They set themselves up separately from the old guard, without even a token courtship; they had come to Naples for leisure, but they were by nature busy folk. As though by habit, they prospered, buying up rundown houses and renovating them into palaces, dabbling in various business ventures. They summed us up accurately, and soon their craftwork and bait stores were doing a booming business, and there was not one Goldfish Emporium, but three; and they were again complaining of exhaustion. They pulled out again, most of them, after seeing their specialists in the city. With rueful smiles, they extricated themselves from the money-making machines, and turned their attention back to their homes. What had been pleasing now had to be ideal; and diligently they built their dwellings into splendor, sending to Atlanta for upholstery fabric, scouring the countryside for suitable *kitsch*. They kept company, quite casually, with figures of mild celebrity, and frequently imported them to town on long weekends, in the old English country-house style. They were slightly decadent, highly frivolous, and on the whole very nice.

They brought us a touch of fame—the magazine layouts, the occasional mention in gossip columns—but true to its sturdy ways, Naples was unaffected. In fact, in the core community, where daylight savings was still a heated topic, people like the Bruckners were simply ignored. Joan and I had become friendly with them through complicated circumstances, and had long been accustomed to receiving invitations to their lesser gatherings. I supposed that in their constant sweeps for interesting party guests, they'd seized upon Buddy. And of course, where Buddy went, so did Jack.

"So you're the Spielberg we've all been hearing about," said Harry, clapping a hand against Buddy's back.

"I hope not, sir," said Buddy, suddenly self-effacing, with a kind of orphanage politeness.

"Not in it for the money, then?" asked Harry.

"You have good instincts," commented a woman from across the room. "I always said there was a movie or two in Naples."

"Film I hope, not videotape," someone drawled.

"Is there a lot of sex in it?"

"Are you going Art or Hollywood?"

Buddy, now the center of attention, blushed.

"Um," he said. "It's sort of a documentary."

"Erroll Morris–type stuff?" asked Harry. "Well, you can't be wanting for material. This town is crammed with colorful characters."

"What exactly is it about?" inquired Midge Plum, the diminutive movie actress who had been staying with the Bruckners for two weeks, hiding from the tabloids after her divorce.

"I'm not sure," said Buddy, honestly. "I mean, I thought it was going to be about one thing, but now—"

"You finding the locals hard to talk to?" asked Sweeney Phillips. His wife gouged him with her elbow, nodding toward Jack.

"Have you talked to Diana Busby?" asked Polly, coming out of the kitchen, having caught the last sentence, smoothly covering it over. Joan was following closely; her face went pale when she saw Buddy, but she hid her agitation well, setting down the tray of hors d'oeuvres she was carrying and fussing a while with the napkins.

"Um, no," said Buddy.

"You've read her, of course," said the Bruckner cousin, not waiting for an answer. *"Watusi* was so raw and primitive, and just *riddled* with imagery."

"Sounds painful," said Jack.

La Bruckner summed him up in a glance as having no true interruptive power.

"She's simply marvelous. You must talk to her," she told Buddy.

"She's as eccentric as they come," said Polly. "A whole movie in herself."

They all pitched in to elaborate on the many attractive yet odd features of Diana Busby.

"But she never gives interviews," said Marcus Stone.

"Reclusive," agreed the Bruckner cousin. "Naples' own Salinger."

"I can give you a letter of introduction, if you like," said Harry, carelessly.

While they talked, I moved over to Joan.

"I've checked the seating for dinner," I said. "He's very far away from you."

"Thanks," she muttered, picking up the tray again.

"Let me take that," I said.

"I can handle it," she said, a stubborn crease between her eyebrows. "You just handle *him.*" She moved away, and I watched her go, helplessly. Her anger tonight was no doubt a product of her surprise; she would get over it. At any rate, I would see to it that Buddy would not get near her.

By the fall, we had stopped looking for Amanda, although the tattered posters were still everywhere, nailed onto telephone poles, pleading in hand-printed letters: MISSING. Each with a plastic-protected snapshot of the girl, blurred so that all you could really recognize was her big light eyes. The photo had been taken at her sixth birthday party; Joan was in the foreground, but cropping had reduced her to an unidentifiable lighter blob of forearm. The posters had been the work of an afternoon, Joan's idea for something useful the women could do while they waited. Meanwhile, the men of the town had searched the town and surrounding area, wandering over farms and through building sites long after dark, swinging flashlights and calling out her name.

Joan was privy to all the facts of the tragedy since that windy May Monday when Amanda didn't come home. She'd vanished right out of the school yard, Joan told me, though I'd already heard that part on the radio. She was wearing a red sweater, and should have been easy to spot in Naples, where after the first news bulletin everyone was on the lookout for a fair-haired child in a scarlet cardigan, and would have been quick to pounce on the strange man holding her by the hand. For it was certain to be a stranger; no one from the town would have done *that,* no one was that deranged, and even those citizens who were a little off wouldn't have done it to Beth, not so soon after the divorce. It just wasn't that kind of town.

But we didn't find her, not a trace, not after three months, despite the community vigilance and the early publicity, Beth pleading tearfully on television, Joan holding her hand and looking grimly into the camera. Bring my baby back, said Beth, just bring her back, and I won't ask any questions or press charges. When she returned from the Crawford house that night, Joan reported that the police had been unhappy with Beth; they had told her she shouldn't have said that part about not pressing charges. I thought, privately, that any kidnapper seeing that television spot wouldn't have believed it anyway, not with the way Joan looked, sitting rigidly beside Beth on the sofa, her face frozen and grey against the white collar of her blouse. While Beth spoke of amnesty, Joan embodied retribution. Her expression promised murder, disembowelment, hot pokers. My wife could be a severe woman, when the situation warranted it.

After a month or so, the initial horror and dismay subsided a little, and a new feeling crept into the town. It was confusion of a sort, sympathy and the clean love of gossip pulling people two different ways.

The scandal of the Crawford divorce had sustained the townsfolk for months. It was common knowledge that Beth had asked for the divorce, although Billy was a good fellow, an occasional churchgoer, hardly drank at all anymore. He sobbed out the story in bars all over town; the citizens absorbed the details, and carefully weighed the evidence. Everyone had always gotten along with the Crawfords; they'd been pillars of the town since its settlement. Beth, on the other hand, was Miller stock, always stirring up trouble. Most people still remembered the story about her great-grandfather; and of course, Lucy Miller was pointed to, with great effect. In this rational, evenhanded way the town reached its verdict: Beth Crawford was a shrew. Some even called her a gold digger, although Bill had never gotten his hands on much of the family money, and she was asking only modest child-support. There was the shocking red Mustang, which Beth drove around town shamelessly, the top down, the wind pushing back her hair. Tongues clucked at that. Some of the women believed that Beth might be a feminist, though she'd never given any previous indications of such leanings. And the real root of the mess was the adultery at the bottom of it. No one had forgotten the elopement; the matter was brought out again, and reexamined, and hindsight put a whole new light on things. It was clear to just about everyone now that Beth and Jack had never fallen out of love. The romance-novel readers put it best: evidently the two of them had been *longing* for one another the whole time, and were engaged right now in a *torrid affair*. There was proof: *she*'d been seen getting out of a foreign-looking car late at night, and walking unsteadily up the flagstone path to her house; she was hanging around with the fast crowd again, no way for a mother to behave, and who knew about their morals? *He*'d been taking days off work, and of course Marie had up and left him less than a year ago. Count was kept of the number of times *she* went out of town "to the movies," leaving Amanda in the charge of that half-witted girl. Movies, indeed! The whispers went ahead of Beth as she walked down Beverley; they rippled through Purdy's of a crowded Saturday morning; after a while, Beth stopped going to PTA meetings, and she quit the bridge club. It was too uncomfortable, she told us, to have those mean eyes all over her.

A few months after the divorce was final, Bill moved away. He had run up debts all over town; and right before he left he started flashing money around, talking big about some job he'd found out west. After he was gone, it was rumored that Joe Crawford had offered his son a deal, in effect that he had paid him to go away. A few sensationalist types murmured Mafia, wiggling their eyebrows suggestively, but nobody believed them. The town knew why Billy had gone. Driven, they said, by his grasping wife. Long after he left, the talk continued, no less harsh than before.

Then Amanda disappeared, and Beth Crawford, who had been so satisfactory a villainess, was now perceived as a victim. Mothers and fathers regarded their own children playing, healthy and safe, and repented some of their remarks of the past. No one could blame them for having indulged themselves in a little speculation; but maybe they needn't have been so *thorough.* The damage had been too extensive for easy reparation; besides, stubbornness makes repentance difficult. The matter was debated, in the social groups and in the bars. It took up a whole meeting of the PTA. The solution was formulated simultaneously by several different groups, who met in the middle and fought about whose idea it was. Apart from that small dispute, there was general agreement: they needed a go-between.

Joan was the natural choice. As Beth's best friend, she had stood by her through the ordeal of the divorce. It might have been expected that a portion of the criticism would shift onto Joan in the process, but it didn't; it seemed her reputation was tarnish proof. It was said of her that she was a *good friend, couldn't have a better one;* and *she'll stick by you, thick and thin.* It was only proper, then, that a few months later she should be the one to carry the town's apology to Beth. She was hinted to, in Purdy's and at church teas. She was bemused at first, and then furious.

"Those old biddies," she said. "After all the *things* they said."

"They feel bad," I said.

"Now they feel bad," she said. "What about before? Now they're feeling all guilty, and they want me to get in the middle."

"I wouldn't think you'd mind," I said.

"What do you mean?" asked Joan, stiffly.

"You've done a lot of good works, is all," I said. "Isn't that your job, getting in the middle?"

"I wouldn't put it that way, exactly," she said, but she was softening.

"People naturally turn to you," I said.

"They turned against me at first," she said. "Just like they did to her."

"Took them a while to get to know you," I said.

"They don't know me," said Joan.

"They trust you," I said.

"Huh," she said. "I wish someone had stood up for *me* then," she added, following her own train of thought.

"I stood up for you," I said, hurt.

"I guess you did," she said, absently. "In your own way." With a little shake of her head, she brought herself back to the matter at hand. "I just despise their cowardice," she said. But her anger was gone; she'd seen a way in which she could be useful, and she was bound to take it.

Cautiously, then, through Joan, the women of the town extended their hands to Beth. Joan passed on invitations to lunch, and to wedding (never baby) showers.

"Hey ho," said Beth, as we helped her sort through her mail. (She had been getting some nasty letters, evidence of a horrid spirit still lingering in the town.) "Here's another one about that club membership. All of a sudden, I'm the most popular gal in town."

"You always were," I said warmly. She looked at me, but said nothing.

"They're trying to comfort you," said Joan. "In the only way they know how." She had found an unsavory note and slipped it adroitly into her purse as she talked, to pass on later to the police.

"Screw em," said Beth. "I liked being a pariah better. It's sure as hell *quieter,*" she said, wincing as the phone rang.

Beth's refusals were met with understanding.

"Of *course,*" they said. "Poor thing. Under the *circumstances.*"

"It's a good thing she's got Joan," people said.

"Can't have a better friend than Joan," it was agreed.

The matter was settled, and the town's conscience salved. It went about its business: the investigation was left to the police, and the comforting was left to Joan.

* * *

Amanda's abduction had been a shock, but a quick one. By four-thirty that afternoon, the situation, although horrifying, was clear. Now followed the much more painful, longer process of waiting.

"We can't leave Beth there alone," I said to Joan.

"She has that nanny person," said Joan.

"Elsie," I said. "That's no help."

"She hasn't even cried all that much," said Joan. "It's strange."

"She's in shock," I said. "She should come stay with us."

But though we urged her, Beth refused. Amanda knew her own address and phone number, but although she'd done much of her growing up there, it was never imagined that she might need to know the particulars about the house on Worth Street.

"What if she tries to call," said Beth, "and I'm not here?"

We couldn't argue with that. So Joan and I took turns sitting with her; we arranged our schedule around her, and one weekend evening Lucy Miller, smaller and less brassy now, sat by Beth's telephone while the three of us made a stiff, sad procession to the movie theater. It was a horrible parody of our jolly trips of the past, and I am sure not one of us paid any attention to the screen. Beth cried silently all through. I could feel her shuddering in the seat next to me, but when I put my hand out to her she didn't respond. The lights came up to reveal her damp but collected; something in her expression warned us off, and we accompanied her wordlessly home.

Meanwhile, the investigation proceeded, slowly. It had started with a dozen of us beating the bushes and shouting ourselves hoarse. Now it went to the next level: paperwork. Because Amanda might have been taken across state lines, the FBI got involved. They considered Billy a prime suspect, and threw some telephone calls west after him. He had quit his job and moved a couple of times, but they located him pretty quickly, living in Texas with a sixteen-year-old girl. He was booked for that, but close questioning indicated his innocence in the disappearance of his daughter.

"I hoped," said Beth, when they told her. "Better Billy, you know . . ." and her voice trailed away.

There were other false leads, and the disappointment after they had been tracked to their vaporous ends; and there was the ghastly occasion when the police from two counties over summoned Beth to identify a body.

"All the way there, she was talking," Joan reported later. "Babbling. First one way, then the other. She seemed unhappy that it *wasn't* Amanda."

"You can't blame her," I remarked. "Maybe at this point she just needs to know."

"Sure," said Joan, looking at me strangely. "But there's no point in giving up."

Amanda's disappearance was taking its toll on Joan. All day, she ministered to the needs of her students, and at night she tended to Beth. The stress was beginning to tell on her. She fell prey to attacks of self-doubt, the dispassion in which she usually reveled now making her occasionally fragile. She would need comforting, and would curl her legs beneath her on the sofa, clutching a brandy snifter, whispering into its wide mouth.

"They *listen* to me, Gil," she said, while I stroked her hair. "It scares me sometimes. What if I say the wrong thing? *Why* do they listen to me?"

They listened because Joan seemed to know. The students listened, and the school board listened, and all of the sisters and cousins and parents of the town. They listened because they had never seen her like this, with her feet tucked under her thighs for warmth, terrified by her own power, shaky. They saw only seamless Joan, confident and certain, and they begged for her directives, and they carried her wisdom away. Words from the mountain. I yearned to snatch her from her guru perch and hide her away.

"You can't take everyone else's sorrows onto yourself," I said. "It doesn't help them, in the end. People have to learn to be strong by themselves."

"I'm a fraud," said Joan. She added in a very small voice, "I'm a liar."

"What do you mean?" I said. I had never heard her speak this way before.

She flicked her glance toward me, then away.

"Tell me," I said.

We looked at one another for a long moment, miserably uncertain. She opened her mouth to speak.

The phone rang.

"Don't answer it," I said.

"But—it might be Chlorinda," she said, slowly uncoiling herself. "She took her driver's test today." And she took the call, while I watched her transformation. Her arm thin and helpless, going toward the receiver, and her hand wrapping around it, cold and unsure. Her movements steadier, as she lifted it to her ear, her limbs thickening where she stood next to the telephone table, until she was solid again, and strong.

"Slow down," she said into the mouthpiece. "Take a deep breath. In and out. Now tell me again."

Murmuring, she carried the phone away, into her downstairs study, pulling the cord behind her, shutting the door with her foot. Calm again, definite, Joan.

The first time I spoke to Jordan Devlin was at an office party in the middle of April. I had come home that day to the usual situation of late: an empty house and a note from Joan saying that she was staying the evening with Beth. Office parties did not normally attract me, but it promised a buffet-style meal, and I was tiring of my own dispirited efforts at feeding myself. Moreover, I was wishing for some lightness of heart. I brushed the dust off of my good suit jacket, shaved carefully and reknotted my tie, and attended alone.

I was surprised to see Devlin there; I had thought he stayed away from the swell of underlings. Apart from his weekly tromps through the basement room where I worked, I had never seen him up close. A few minutes after I arrived at the party, I turned to see Devlin walking toward me, a crowd of admirers travelling with him. Standing, I was absorbed into the moving knot, and found myself face-to-face with him.

He cut an impressive figure, standing two inches taller than I, with hard-looking features and a full head of greying hair. He surprised me, stopping in mid-stride to grasp my hand, switching on a brief but dazzling smile.

"How are you getting along?" he said.

"Fine," I replied.

After that, there was little to say. The grovelers continued to buzz among themselves while Devlin and I indulged in a few seconds of that desultory sort of chat through which one labors at these affairs. Finally, each of us pretended to see someone else across the room, and jostled away from one another.

The whole incident puzzled me: I finally came to the conclusion that he had mistaken me for someone else; if he'd known my true identity, he would never have bothered to greet me at all. So it was quite a surprise two weeks later when, encountering him in my native environment—the long corridor running the length of the basement room—he stopped before my desk.

"I've had my eye on you," he said. "I like your style."

"Well," I said, flattered.

"You're an idea man," he said. "I can tell." He waved away the office manager, who was hovering nearby. "Not now, Benson." He leaned forward, addressing me in a lowered voice. "What do you say to a place upstairs on my personal team?"

"I don't know all that much about that," I said, considerably underplaying my ignorance, "part of the business."

He laughed, heartily, the kind of male whisky laugh that stops all conversation in a room, everyone pausing in wonder.

"Neither did I, when I started," he said. "We'll find something for you to do. I can always spot a good man."

"Well," I said, again.

"Take the weekend to think about it," he said, slipping a pasteboard card into the breast pocket of my jacket, tapping it down with a manicured forefinger. "Call me on Monday."

"The man's insane," Joan exclaimed, when I told her about it that night. "You don't know a thing about development." She was tired, or she never would have been so direct.

"I've been working there for years," I said. "I ought to know something about it."

"But what kind of job is it?" she asked. "What exactly did he say?"

"He liked my style," I replied, hurt. I was a little drunk, or I wouldn't have been so peevish. "Maybe I have all kinds of aptitudes you don't know about."

"Of course you do, darling," she said in a conciliatory tone, clearly regretting her bluntness of a moment before.

I maintained an injured silence; we didn't speak about it again that night, nor for most of the weekend.

Sunday was devoted to a marathon Scrabble session at Beth's. Usually an avid player, today I was distracted, fingering the smooth flat tiles, debating Devlin's offer.

"How come I always get all the *X*'s?" complained Beth, dipping a finger in her scotch and sucking at it absentmindedly. She pondered for a moment, and then laid down e-x-i-l-e. "Many, many points," she said, looking up at me.

"Good," I said automatically.

"Your turn," said Joan.

I laid down m-i-x.

"Boo," said Beth, and when she got no response, added, "Why so quiet, G.I.?"

"Devlin offered him a job upstairs," said Joan, knowingly.

"Doing what?" asked Beth.

"Who knows," said Joan.

"Are you going to take it, G.I.?" asked Beth.

"He doesn't know yet," said Joan.

"Please," I said. "I can talk, you know."

"Sorry," said Joan.

"Well?" asked Beth.

"I don't know yet," I told her. "Maybe he was drunk when he offered it to me. Maybe he thought I was someone else. I'll call him Monday and see what happens."

"Live dangerously," said Beth. It was a sentiment characteristic of her, something she might have said at any time in the past, but the words sounded odd, dense with strain. Her smile, too, was but a shadow of her old one, more of a wince than a grin.

I called Devlin's office the next morning.

"What d'you want him for?" asked Bedelia. "Shouldn't you be at work by now?" she added, suspiciously.

"Never mind," I said.

"Is it something about the little girl? You can tell me," she said.

"I don't have time now," I said. "I'll explain later." Saying it, I knew it wouldn't be necessary to explain later; when 'Delia was truly interested, she had no qualms about listening in.

"Devlin," grunted the man himself, frightening me so that I nearly hung up. I had expected a gentle Cerberus, in the form of a secretary.

"Um," I said.

"Who is it?" he roared.

"Gilbert," I said. "Corbin."

There was a silence, during which I had no thoughts at all.

"Call me back this afternoon," he said, and hung up.

I sweated the rest of the day out, and in the afternoon called again. A woman answered this time, and put me through.

"Well?" he asked, without preliminaries. "Coming upstairs?"

"I—" I said.

"What?" he said.

"Guess so," I said.

"Great!" he said, and seemed to loosen a little. By the end of the conversation, he was bellowing hearty promises through the phone line.

"We'll get you all set up," he cried. "Big desk, office, secretary, pencil sharpener—do you prefer manual, or electric?"

"Manual," I said, flustered.

"Good, wonderful. We'll get you one of those. Start tomorrow."

I went over before the end of the day, to extricate myself from the basement room.

"That's a hard one," said Benson. "You had a good spot," he said. "Nice and cool there."

"Yes," I said.

"Not too hot in summer," he said.

"No," I agreed.

"None of that cigar smoke from Wade gets over to you, either," he said.

"I haven't been bothered by it," I said.

"Some just can't tolerate it," he said. "Makes them sick." He looked down, considering. "Yep," he said. "It's a real choice spot."

"I'd like to take my things," I said.

"Well sure," said Benson, pulling open the office door, ambling into the large room. A dozen heads went up as we entered. "Maybe I'll move Eddie on over to your spot," said Benson, hissing sideways at me through his teeth.

"Eddie's a good fellow," I said.

"Shh," he said. He stood by the desk as I collected my few things from it—my picture of Joan, my leather-cornered blotter. "Upstairs," he said, wonderingly.

"Yes," I said.

"Kind of a sudden thing," he said. "What's Joan think about it?"

"She thinks it's wonderful," I said, through gritted teeth.

"That's all right, then," he said, heartily. "She's got a good head on her shoulders, that woman. We all set great store by Joan."

"I know," I said.

"All you had to do was tell me," said Joan. "Instead I get a call from the *Chronicle* and I have to pretend I know what he's talking about."

"The *Chronicle* called?" I asked, bewildered.

"About something else," she said. "Some kind of advice column they're thinking of running. John D. mentioned your promotion in passing. He assumed I knew. Which was a natural mistake," she said, picking up steam. "Everyone else in town seems to know about it."

"I'm sorry," I said.

"When he congratulated me, I nearly choked." She looked ready to choke now, remembering.

"I'm sorry," I repeated. "I had no idea you'd find out that way. But I've taken the job," I said. "You can't talk me out of it."

"Oh, Gil," said Joan, all of the rigidity going out of her. She sat down heavily, and put her hand over her eyes. "It's not the *job,*" she said. "It's you."

"What about me?"

She kept her head down, looking into the darkness of her hand. "You're so *afraid* of me," she said. "You act like a guilty little boy."

"I do not," I said, hurt.

"I'm not your enemy," said Joan, taking her hand away from her eyes and looking up. "I'm your *wife.*"

"I know," I said. "But sometimes you act like a tyrant."

"Me?" she said, surprised.

"You," I said. "It's hard for me," I said. "I'm not the same as you."

"I'll say," said Joan. "You're soft."

"I'd rather be soft than overbearing," I shot back, stung.

We stared at each other.

After a minute, I went over and sat on the sofa beside her.

"What is it?" I asked, quietly. She didn't say anything, and I dipped my head so that I could look into her face. "What's really bothering you?"

"Nothing," said Joan, putting the heel of her hand into her mouth and biting down.

"Come on," I said.

"Everything's gone mad," she said, into the cup of her palm.

"Not here," I said. "We're all right."

She shook her head.

"We are," I said.

"It's not just us," she said, taking her hand out of her mouth and putting it down. "It's us and all of them. I hate the way this town talks," she said, not looking at me. "It divides people."

I took her hand; I could see the marks of her two front teeth, one slightly crooked, slanting toward the other.

"We can leave," I said, boldly. "We can move away." Saying it, I felt lighter, and happy, and afraid.

"Gil," said Joan, laughing a little. "You don't mean that." She took her hand from mine, and wiped her eyes. "I'm sorry I fussed," she said. "I'm probably just hungry. Which reminds me," she added, standing up. "There's something incinerating in the oven right now."

At supper, I remembered something.

"What about that advice column John D. called about?" I asked Joan. "Are you going to do it?"

"Heavens, no," she said. "How can I make the time?"

"Well," I said. "You make time for all kinds of things."

"Important things," said Joan. "I have Beth to look after, and you, and—" She stopped.

"You don't have to look after me," I told her.

"Of course I do," she said, smiling. "And besides," she added, chewing, "I'm a Yankee. Naples hasn't forgotten that."

"That's silly," I said. "If it mattered about that, people would be asking *my* advice all the time."

"They might," she said, looking down into her plate, "if you were more aggressive." She caught my look. "I mean, you're so reluctant about putting yourself forward."

"I know," I said, irritated again. "Soft."

"I said I was sorry about that," she said with a little frown, and then went right back to making her point. "People believe what they want to believe," she instructed. "What they need to believe. That's all it takes," she said. "Confidence."

"Well, that's as may be," I said. "But I wasn't raised that way."

"Jack sure was," said Joan, freezing my next statement cold. She relented a little. "All I mean is, don't give me any of your Southern slop about gentlemanly behavior. Jack does exactly what he wants. He could talk the moon out of the sky, if he wanted to." She frowned a little, as if perplexed. "Of course, he doesn't seem to want to."

"I can't help what Jack is," I said, very slowly. "I don't want to be what Jack is."

"Don't take it that way," said Joan.

I ignored her. "Is that who you want me to be? Jack?" I examined her face coldly, as though I had never seen it before.

"That's silly," said Joan, finally. "Look, let's not fight," she said.

"I'm not fighting," I said.

"Yes, you are," she said, softly, sliding her chair over, leaning toward me, and placing her cheek against mine. "Love me," she said.

"I do," I said.

"You're still fighting," said Joan, her eyelashes tickling my skin.

"No, I'm not," I said, as gently as I could.

We remained like that for long moments, warmth against warmth, my heart cold inside me, twitching at the touch of a stranger.

"Are we friends again?" said Joan, leaning back, looking into my face.

"Yes," I lied, and stiffly picked up my fork, willing myself back to normalcy and Joan back to the girl I loved. "What about that column?" I said.

"Well," she answered, thoughtfully. "I guess I can handle a few letters."

It was no secret who Tell Tillie was. Letters addressed to her arrived at our house all the time. After the first few, Joan seemed to get the knack of the business, answering two or three a week, shutting herself away into her study to compose her responses, and then typing them out at the *Chronicle* offices downtown.

"I'm hardly here, anymore," she said one morning, poised by the front door, ready to leave. "Do you miss me?"

"Sure," I said. "But I'm glad you're having fun."

"Fun," said Joan. "Oh, the column," she said, as though she hadn't been thinking about it. "Funny about that," she said, with her hand on the doorknob. "All the letters are about the same thing. Or really, one of three things."

"Let me guess," I said. "Sex, loneliness, and money."

"Close," she said. "Sex, love, and money."

"Same thing," I told her.

"Right," she said. "Anyway, I'm already stretching for new ways to say the same thing. I'm running out of imaginative answers."

"Don't worry," I said. "You're a hit. Devlin's wife reads you all the time."

She said nothing, but kissed her palm to me, and left. I ruminated, drinking the last of my coffee, blinking in the early sunshine, so deceptively warming by the big window in the kitchen. I wondered if the fight we'd had a few weeks before was still rankling with Joan; she had a way of holding grudges. In that way we were well matched.

Joan had strong opinions about everything, and generally she shared her opinions with me; but she had avoided discussing the Devlins. We had had dinner with them a few times, and despite the charm Joan displayed on these occasions, it was clear to me that she didn't like him, and that she felt sorry for his wife, a meek overwashed-looking person. But she had said nothing about it to me. In fact, she'd kept mum entirely on the subject of my job, apart from occasional inquiries about how I liked the work and listening attentively to my glossed-over replies. She never herself expressed enthusiasm about it, but seemed sincere in her pleasure at mine. Joan was loyal, after all, and she had taken me on long ago. She never came close to saying "I told you so."

For of course she had been right in her predictions. For the first month, the job was formless and frustrating. Devlin trundled me around, handing me off to different department executives, each of whom explained his particular sector of the operation in exaggerated, childish terms. At the end of the month, Devlin called me into his office.

"The boys tell me you're shaping up just fine," he said. "They say you learn fast."

"Very—" I hesitated. "Kind of them."

"Kind, nothing," he boomed. "I don't pay them to be kind. I pay them for results. No room for deadweight in this outfit." I nodded. "Have a seat," he said. "I have a proposition for you."

He explained that he wanted to create a new position for me. The way he described it, I was to be installed as a kind of general troubleshooter, a liaison between what Devlin called "the creative side of the business" and the construction crews.

"This way," he said, lacing his hands together, "everyone does what they do best. The architect designs, the contractor constructs. You fill in the blank—you have some practical knowledge from working downstairs, and the arty stuff is no trick." He grew enthusiastic. "You'll be the link," he said, flexing his interlocked hands back and forth. "You'll help the two work together. I know I can trust you to keep things running smoothly while I do what *I* do best—brainstorming." He looked down, modestly.

"Sounds fine," I said.

"I've got something really big in the works now," he said. "The original plan was turned down, but I put my idea men to thinking on it." He grinned. "Now it should go through like prunes through my Aunt Mabel." I winced at the vulgar humor. "It'll give me a chance to see what you're made of," he said, and I smiled, weakly.

Late spring became midsummer, and then the heat began to wane. All the time, Joan was dividing her time between her various duties. I expected that when school let out I would see more of her, but then Beth's need grew more intense, taking up where the students had left off. I came home to the usual note several times a week; I was never invited to join them. Proud, I didn't ask but stayed alone, rattling around in the house on Worth Street, reading and fussing and missing my wife, wondering what the two of them were doing in the house on the hill, and why they didn't want me there.

"She's coming over tomorrow night," Joan reported, one morning. "She has to get out of that house."

After the meal, we sat around on the front porch, holding coffee cups and listening to the crickets, indulging in a light pattern of conversation.

"Last night I dreamed I found her," said Beth, surprising us. Until then, our remarks had been entirely superficial. "She wasn't glad to see me," she said. "She said she was happier now."

Her statement was followed by a brief silence. I glanced at Joan, but she put her coffee cup to her lips and said nothing, not looking at me.

"That's silly," I said, faltering.

"All dreams are silly," said Beth, sharply. "But they tell you something."

"What did this one tell you?" asked Joan quietly.

"I don't know," said Beth, after a short pause. "But I know that when I woke up, I was happy."

"But Beth," said Joan, her voice almost shockingly light-hearted. She launched into a series of incredible-but-true stories of children lost and found again, long after their abductions, safe and sound. Beth partially revived under the stream of solace, like speeded-up reverse footage of a plant wilting. Her features struggled painfully between despair and a kind of ravaged optimism. I was surprised: I had thought that Beth and I were the two people in Naples immune to Joan's persuasion. Embarrassed, I turned my face away and looked out over the darkened lawn.

Later, I drove Beth home. On the way, we said little; when we were about halfway there, she slid over toward me, and slipped under my arm.

"Cold?" I asked.

"No," she said, but she didn't move. We rode the rest of the way sitting close together like sweethearts, and when I walked her to her door she turned to me on the step and put her face into my shirt. I was confused, putting my arms around her gingerly, stroking her hair.

"I'm so sad, G.I.," she said, finally, into my shoulder.

"I know," I said.

"I feel like I'm in the middle of a big white room all alone," she said. "I dreamed that, too. A big white room like in a hospital, but nothing in it. Not even me in it, but I was there."

"Uh huh," I said.

"You Corbin boys," she said, pulling away suddenly. The three-quarters moon danced light off her eyes as she tossed her head back. "What big strong arms you have."

I realized how tightly I had been holding her; blushing, I released my grip and moved a little away.

"I'm worried about you," I said.

"Me, too," she said, going into the house, closing the door.

"How could you tell her all that stuff?" I asked Joan while we were getting ready for bed.

She shrugged, removing her earrings.

"Things look pretty bleak," she admitted. "But she mustn't give up." She slipped her blouse off her shoulders and unfastened her skirt. "And that dream," she said. "That was creepy."

"Maybe it's time she faced facts," I said. "She has to get on with her life."

"She's not strong enough for that yet," said Joan, getting into bed beside me. "She's still mourning Bill, remember."

"She's divorced, not widowed," I said, sharply.

"Loss is loss," said my wife.

* * *

In July, I found myself embroiled in a town hullabaloo. Devlin had sprung his big plan, which at first seemed flawless. Earlier in the year, he had acquired some property downtown, and wanted permission to build a minimall. The first time he had pitched the idea, the town had refused to approve the rezoning of more than a nominal percentage of the land, which was not enough for Devlin's purposes.

"We'll sweeten the deal," he told us, his henchmen, in June.

His new plan included a sop in the form of a new community center at Devlin's expense. It was to be built on part of the site, if the town would let him develop the area around it. Devlin was multifaceted: to the town council he talked jobs and taxes for the city; to the Historical Committee, he described the historical significance of an industrial building standing empty on the site, crying out for preservation. Devlin intended to renovate the abandoned structure—without, of course, altering its authenticity by one particle—and put it to use as the main building of the Community Center.

To the public, Devlin waxed eloquent about the wonderful design of the new center—it would have a main hall, perfect for dances and small theater productions, and could be hired out for private parties; the junior high school could hold their graduation there; how much more picturesque than the gymnasium.

Leaving the boardrooms and the town meetings, shutting the door behind the man from the *Chronicle,* Devlin was exhilarated.

"They vote on Friday," he said. "We start on Monday." He clapped me on the back. "I'm putting you in charge of the whole shebang," he told me. The other two "idea men," Warren Peavy and George Burke, looked at me jealously.

It was then Tuesday; public opinion was heavily in our favor; there seemed no reason to believe that the new center would not be approved.

But that portion of a town which always rises up against any kind of development sniffed out the real motivation behind Devlin's generous proposal. They launched their campaign in Wednesday morning's *Chronicle,* with an editorial titled "Devlin Our Midst."

Devlin summoned me and Warren and George into his office.

"This is killing us," he said, tapping the page. "Damned

antiprogress fools. Take away their laundromats and super-markets, where would they be? Progress gives them leisure time, and what do they do? Spend it screaming about progress. *Damn,*" he said, bringing his fist down onto the newspaper. "Didn't we contribute something to them last year?"

"A sizeable amount, sir, in December," said Burke.

"I thought so," said Devlin. "You'd think it would have bought a little goodwill." He looked at the three of us. "There's got to be a way," he said. "Some way to put this deal across."

We all furrowed our brows.

"What do they want?" asked Devlin, almost to himself. "They want luxury, of course."

"They're mostly women, aren't they?" asked Burke, nervously. "My wife says all women want a mink coat."

Devlin glared him into silence.

"Luxury," he repeated. "But luxury disguised to look like practicality. Safety. Luxury and safety."

"What about a swim," I said, and stopped.

"What's that?" cried Devlin.

"A swim," I said.

"A swimming pool," said Warren Piper, almost whispering.

"*What* did you say?" growled Devlin, rounding on him.

"Um," squeaked Warren.

"That's it!" cried Devlin. "A swimming pool. *Sheila,*" he roared into his intercom, mashing his thumb onto the button.

We listened, silent stooges, while he dictated the plan. "I can't believe it," Warren said to George. "It's perfect. And *I* thought of it."

Olympic-sized, heated, enclosed, the pool was to stand between the center and the minimall. No matter that there was a local quarry, to which all of the townspeople had always gone to swim during heat waves. No matter that the water there was pure, and the quarry deep and rockless. "Think of the danger," the *Chronicle* quoted Devlin in Thursday's edition. "If just one child hit his head diving from those high quarry banks—"

He had judged it right, of course. A new faction sprang up instantly, comprised mainly of anxious parents. Devlin had put the spark to their highly flammable fears. The antidevelopment clique clashed against the antiquarry clique, and in the stillness after the battle, Devlin rose triumphant.

"I thank the citizens for giving me the opportunity to give

something back to this fair town," he said, smiling humbly, waiting for Sam Dooley to catch the expression with his camera; Sam's flash didn't go off, though, and so Devlin had to hold the pose while he fiddled with it. Finally, the photograph had been taken; Devlin unfroze, and the reporters faded out of the room. "We'll make a bundle on the deal," he told me, after they'd left. "There's still a lot of square footage zoned for retail."

Devlin had done it again; and having gotten the thing going, he skipped away to another project, leaving me to supervise the construction of the center.

"Start on the renovation and the pool at the same time," he told me. "To show we're sincere. I don't want any more bad press."

I spent mornings on the site and afternoons near my desk which was, as Devlin had promised, big, although it was located in a communal and secretaryless office space. The pencil-sharpener was bolted to one corner of the oak surface; when I needed to sharpen a pencil, I had to get up from my chair, walk around the desk, and stand there cranking the handle, feeling foolish.

Together, the architects and I pored over site plans and elevations; they were articulate, capable men, easygoing types who seemed to accept me. I was much more out of place on the construction site, which seemed indisputably the province of the big-shouldered men with their rough voices and yellow helmets. They called to each other in hoarse syllables across the site, and spat streams of tobacco into the dust. They ignored me, but I seemed constantly to be in the way, and spent the first few days scurrying from one point to another, seeking a neutral patch of ground from which to oversee the project.

Within the first week, I understood that my discomfort was no accident. The men disliked me. They pretended not to know my name every morning when I walked onto the site; they answered my questions with monosyllables, rolling their eyes at my ignorance. To them, I was one of the enemy, a representative of the clean-linened, cravated ranks, a spy sent by the management to harass them. They had seen my kind before—tight-collared little efficiency experts, crisply jacketed, who minced around the site, placing their shoes carefully so as to avoid the mud. These busy men had appeared from time to time, and they were always trouble—poking their noses into everything, asking the same stupid questions I was asking now. Taking copious notes, nodding primly, returning later, with a sheaf of suggestions for improvements in procedure. Most of the crew had been working construction for ten years or more; they resented the little men, with their prissiness and their clipboards, their clean pomaded hair. And the posted suggestion lists, coming as they did from smooth-jawed physical cowards, weaklings who had never done a day's honest labor, inspired outrage. They were accidentally dropped in the mud, or set afire, or they simply vanished from the door of the site office.

I had heard all of the stories at one time or another in Stokes's, and I expected the crew to be set against me from the start. Still, I hoped to break through their resistance and win them over. I donned a yellow hat and hid my intimidation. I imagined them talking amongst themselves about me after I'd gone.

"He's all right," they'd say. "He's a regular guy."

But it was slow going. It didn't seem to matter that I removed my tie when I was on site. They knew me for what I was, a stoolie sent to pester and annoy them, a pencil pusher, someone whose masculinity was suspect. They made fun of my stutter, and eyed the clean leather of my shoes. I took to wearing beat-up work boots to the site, but then their glances drifted to my smooth hands.

"Sure *thing*, Mr. Corbin, sir," they said, when I spoke to them. "You *bet*, Mr. Corbin, sir."

Their hatred made me uneasy. I liked to watch them work, though, and so I continued to spend hours at the site, enduring their aggression and the grueling heat, breathing the soft red dust.

I was exhausted most nights, coming home, and so it took me a while to appreciate the relative absence of Joan. While I had been distracted, she had fallen into a routine: Monday evenings at the *Chronicle* (and sometimes Saturday mornings if something went wrong), Thursday night cooking (she made suppers ahead now, and lunches, and left them for me, neatly marked, in the refrigerator), and Tuesday and Friday with Beth. Often she went to see Beth on Sunday, too, or after she'd finished her weekly cooking; and sometimes she ran down to the *Chronicle* to discuss some last-minute changes with the editor or to look something up. After a month on the construction site, I rolled my head on my sleepless pillow, calculating that it had been three weeks since my wife and I had eaten a meal together. I felt guilty—I had encouraged her to do the column, after all; and, self-absorbed, I had been nothing so much as grateful for her attention to Beth. I had barely thought about anything but myself and my job for ages. Joan and I were moving apart. Was it my fault?

"All right if I come with you?" I asked her the following night, as she was preparing to go over to Beth's. The question was rhetorical; I was already slipping my shoes on.

"Well," said Joan. "It might be better if you didn't, this time."

"Why?" I asked.

"Girl stuff," she said.

"What, does Beth think I don't know she touches up her hair?"

"That's not it," said Joan.

"What is it, then?"

"It's just," she said, hesitantly. "Men—make her nervous, these days. Because of Amanda. Try to understand, honey," she said.

"She didn't mean *me,*" I said.

"I'm sure it's temporary."

"She can't have meant me," I repeated.

"You're a man, aren't you?" said Joan, impatiently.

Was I? On the construction site, I wasn't; here at home I evidently was. Like the fable of the bat, I thought, doomed to a life of ambiguity, neither bird nor beast.

I couldn't believe it of Beth. What about me could make her uncomfortable? I looked at my hands, patted them against my chest. So I'm male, I thought. That's how she sees me, in the end. I felt stripped and sickened, reduced from my complicated being to an obscene graffito. Back to the forest, I thought. Waiting for the Indians. With the dry mouth of eagerness, and of dread.

Chapter Nineteen

Flirtations

Dear Tillie,

I've been married six years and I love my husband but I've met a man who understands me. He's younger and he really listens. Me and him (I'll call him Carl) haven't done anything yet exactly, but I think we're going to. My husband would probably never find out. What do you think?

Confused.

Dear Confused:

Your problem isn't with Carl, it's with your marriage. Flirtations have the advantage of looking perfect without having to prove it. In other words, it's easy for Carl to appear understanding—after all, he only has to be understanding a few hours at a time, not all day the way your husband does. Temptation is natural, but when it threatens a lifelong commitment, it's time to take a good hard look at your priorities. Consider the consequences. You say your husband "probably" wouldn't find out. Would it be worth it if he did? I say, stay away from Carl for a while and try talking to your husband. Then decide if Carl is worth risking your marriage for.

Tillie.

Once, many years ago, Joan had had a sense of what it might be like to fall out of love with her husband. It was just a taste, a quick impression of unexplored possibility, and then it was gone.

It was at a faculty party, in the middle of the afternoon following a symposium. Gil was at work, like all of the other spouses, and the party had a restive air, a quality of unnatural freedom, simply owing to the one fact, that most of these people, ordinarily paired off, were at a social function alone. There was a heady recklessness to the way the chairs were dragged back against the wall, as though there might be dancing. And when the refreshments appeared, a faint cheer went up, for all the world as if the offerings were caviar and champagne, when they were really on the order of watery lemon punch and sugar cookies.

The pull-down projection screen, used that day for visual aids during the lectures, and at other times for educational films, was rolled back up against the ceiling with a flick and a snap; and an industrial-looking phonograph was liberated from one of the locked cabinets and its cord plugged into an outlet. A shelf in the same cabinet yielded a surprising cache of records. Ben Willow, who taught Geometry, set himself to monitor the music. It began to scratch out of the grey built-in speaker, and those who had been holding themselves back were released. This was, after all, a *party;* and they started to dance, on the flat brown carpet where in the corners still a few peanuts languished, from the last seventh grade tea dance.

The crowd was largely faculty, but the administration was sprinkled throughout the room, little nuggets of conservatism set afloat among the younger swell of teachers. Joan was a kind of bridge between the two groups; she was not faculty, nor was she purely administration; and she was of a median age, approachable to all. The teachers included her in their jokes, while the drabber ranks, the principal's secretary and the registrar, seemed to consider her safe harbor in the sea of irreverence, and sought her out.

In fact, the principal's secretary, Miss Pringle, quite attached herself to Joan. At first, it was endearing, the way she appealed to the younger woman for approval, but then it became somewhat irritating, the way she hung on and followed Joan about, clinging to the edges of whatever conversation she was engaged in. Whinnying her nervous little laugh, Miss Pringle was constantly at Joan's elbow, praying quite overtly for acceptance. Joan, moving freely through the throng, felt the older woman like a thorn in her side. Everywhere she turned, the sad little pony face was there at her shoulder, gazing at her with a kind of ingratiating despair.

"I'm going to the Ladies'," Miss Pringle murmured, after half an hour and three glasses of punch. "Do you need . . . ?" she invited, and then stood embarrassed by her own vulgarity.

Go away, thought Joan viciously, and was shocked at her own intolerance. With the sensitivity of the socially damned, Miss Pringle perceived Joan's animosity; her face went pink, and her eyes watered. Joan, repentant, made an effort at kindness.

"You go on," she said. "I'll wait for you over there." She pointed to a triad of empty chairs in one corner of the room.

"All right," smiled Miss Pringle, too easily forgiving.

She's just nervous, thought Joan, watching her push the heavy grey door open. I should be more patient; it's just a party. It will mean so much to her if I let her go around with me, and if she comes back and sees me waiting for her in one of those chairs, she'll be pleased.

But on her way across the room, she was entangled in a group of about half a dozen, playing audience to Alden Wood, the handsome English teacher, as he made some scandalous, some humorous, all disparaging remarks about different members of the gathering. He began, of course, in an under-tone, concerning himself with Principal Beckwith, and then worked his way up and down the ranks at random, until his caustic wit lighted on Miss Pringle, and there it found its home.

"Her face is constipated," he said, to the great amusement of the others. "All pinched together. She'd make a great advertisement for laxatives—

" 'Doctor, I eat prunes *three times a day,* ' " he warbled suddenly, in a fair imitation of Miss Pringle's quavery voice. "And that laugh," he went on. "I heard that she was kidnapped and brought up by a tribe of wild accordions." He laughed Miss Pringle's shuddering wheeze.

"Oh, oh," said Bella Long, who taught Health. "I'm going to pee my pants." She squeezed her false eyelashes together and opened her wet mouth wide in laughter. *Slut,* thought Joan, startling herself.

"What's wrong with our dear Mrs. Corbin?" asked Alden, suddenly.

"Nothing," she said, taken aback.

"But you're not laughing," he said. "You think I'm terrible, don't you?"

"No," she said, feeling uncomfortable, the eyes of the others on her, mouths parted, waiting to laugh again.

"No what?" teased Alden.

"No, I don't think you're terrible," she said.

"Yes, you do," he said, falling to his knees, screwing up his face in mock agony. She could smell the liquor on him now, pulsing from him in clean, aromatic waves, innocent as mouthwash. "I *am* terrible," he wailed, grasping her calves. "Forgive me."

"Let go," she said.

"Not until you forgive me," he insisted.

"What do you want?" she asked.

"Tell me I'm not terrible," he said, instantly, releasing her and leaning back on his knees, smiling up into her face.

She looked down at him, at where he knelt in his chalky trousers on the floor, at his hands clasped together under his chin.

"You're not terrible," she said, slowly. "You're merely thoughtless."

His face changed, and the circle around the two of them went poisonously calm. The whole room was watching them, now; even the dancers were still while Ben changed the record.

"You've never thought about what it might be like to be plain and unwanted," Joan went on, in a kind of robotic voice. "Or about anything except what's right in front of you. You've never thought about anything at all."

Alden's eyes were wide and serious, listening.

"A handsome face is nothing to be proud of," said Joan, severely. "If the head it's on is empty."

Just then, Miss Pringle reentered the room. She had evidently taken advantage of her trip to the restroom to groom herself. She had touched up her lipstick; now it shone wetly from her face like a cut strawberry set in a bowl of oatmeal. She had combed her hair; the dry wisps had been tucked back into place and trapped anew with bobby pins, and her temples gleamed. She crept into the room, imagining herself unnoticed, but as the door closed behind her she looked around, in the kind of deadly hush which could not fail to tell her she'd been discussed in her absence. Her face went slowly and painfully pink, and she looked beseechingly to the corner where Joan had intended to wait for her.

From the opposite corner, Joan watched Miss Pringle's face fall at the sight of the empty chairs. Miss Pringle turned her head then, searching the room, and saw her. Her little eyes took in everything: Joan's guilty posture, and the attractive man at her feet; the crowd around them, which was beginning to break into giggles again. Her gaze locked Joan's for a moment, and then slid away. Her pinkness went to pallor, and she stiffened her spine. Joan watched her march deliberately and alone through the stock-still dancers, past the single knot of staring secretaries, all the way to the punch bowl, where she helped herself to a cup of lemonade. She bore it alone to the empty chairs, subsided into one of them, and began to sip, holding her little finger out.

"Wait," said Alden, as Joan left the room.

In the women's room, she sat in one of the stalls for fully five minutes. Although she had no real need to urinate, she forced herself to do so, and afterward sat there with her hands on her knees, feeling the rush of air beneath her from the flushing mechanism. Sluggishly, she stood up and carefully adjusted her stockings and rearranged her skirt and blouse, smoothing them down.

As she stepped out to the row of sinks, the door opened, and Alden Wood slipped in, a finger at his lips.

"Don't scream," he said. "Anybody else in here?"

She shook her head.

"You're not supposed to be in here," she said, stupidly, as he closed the door behind him.

"I know," he said, with a wicked smile.

"Still playing the fool?" she said, angrily, moving to go past him.

"I wanted to talk to you," he said, touching her arm.

Although he had not grabbed her, or restrained her in any way, she stopped short, exactly as though he had.

"What is it?" she asked.

"I wanted to apologize," he said. "You were right in there. I do play the fool." He looked at her sadly. "I don't know any other way to be. I wish I did. I wish I had your courage." His eyes wavered away, and then back. "Sometimes I hate myself," he confessed.

If she'd been older, or more experienced, Joan might have laughed at him, at his heavy sentiments, delivered with such deliberate clumsiness. But there had been, really, only three men in her life—her father, a high school boyfriend, and her husband; her life had not brought her into contact with the rough welter of worldly men, and she knew almost nothing of their capacity for cleverness, and for hypocrisy. At twenty-seven, she was an innocent, and she was moved. She put out a hand, touched Alden's sleeve.

"I shouldn't have been so harsh," she said. "I have no right to judge you."

"Oh, you do," said Alden, coming closer. "Yes, you do. If I only had someone like you to help me, to be honest with me—" He moved even closer, and she felt a heat against her cheek, as though the door to a furnace had swung open before her. "Forgive me," he whispered.

She was confused; Alden Wood, seeking her forgiveness? Searching her eyes with his own, which were full of contrition? She saw that he was just a little boy, so like all of the boys she spoke to every day. Thinking those sympathetic thoughts, still she stepped back a pace involuntarily as he approached her.

"You despise me," he said, in a heartbroken voice.

"No," she said, willing herself to stay still as he came nearer.

For a moment, they looked at one another from very close range; Joan saw a change pass over him, like a curtain whisking away.

"You're so beautiful," he said, and kissed her.

A brief touch, lip to lip, and yet so much contained in it. It was the world of other possibility, what she might have known had she not married so young; there was the foreign breath, the exotica of beard and moustache. And, too, there was the familiar, the faint taste of whisky, something Gil drank, reminding her that Gil and this stranger were kin in a basic sense.

She surrendered to the kiss, but when he pulled away there was no feeling that they might go further; he saw something in her eyes, or face, which stopped him.

"You're drunk," she said gently, as though he were a child.

"So I am," he said.

She went out of the bathroom before him, and they walked back down the corridor together, unspeaking and not touching. When they entered the room, he went immediately to the punch bowl, and then rejoined his admirers. She watched him pull Bella Long onto the dance floor, clutching her tight for a slow number, but felt no sense of betrayal. She was more involved in the travel than in the conveyance which had carried her, fascinated by considering what border she had crossed, what new terrain she had sighted, through the kiss of a stranger.

He *was* a stranger; and she felt no possessiveness toward him, not then or later. Not even any curiosity; and the kiss had not gone any way toward forging a friendship between them. She never gave a thought to him again, save when he was directly in front of her, and then her thoughts were casual. *They* had not changed. But *she* had.

She had taken a journey, not with him, but because of him.

Because of him she had been transported, propelled out of herself and her same life for an instant. She had seen in herself a capacity for sexual response which was entirely random, and which had nothing at all to do with love. The discovery made her thoughtful, and when she went home to Gilbert in the evening, she looked at him and thought, for the very first time, *I could leave you.*

The knowledge made her tender, protective, as though it were someone else who menaced him, and not herself. That night, they made love for the first time in a long while. They didn't speak, during or after; and she heard herself, as if from a distance, giving a series of soft cries, really gasps.

Afterward, she lay on her side and looked at him gravely. She knew he was puzzled, and afraid to speak. She knew that he would watch her like this until she fell asleep. She closed her eyes.

I love you, she thought, and wasn't sure if she spoke aloud. *And what's more, I don't have to.*

Chapter Twenty

Regular Guy

"**S**orrel soup tonight," said Joan as I came through the door.

"Good," I said, but the word felt hollow. I sat in the big chair, and looked at my hands. "Jesus," I said. "No matter how I wash them."

"There's Lava soap in the bathroom," she said.

"My father had dirty hands," I told her, still gazing into my palms. "Jack, too. When I was growing up, my hands were always clean."

"Things change," she said.

"I never thought I'd have my father's hands."

"They're not his hands," she said, seriously. "They're yours."

I looked at her.

"It's your own dirt," she said.

"It's ours," I said, and went to the bathroom to wash.

By the second week in August, we had dug to ten feet. Glen Walker was down in the hole, compressing the earth; I stood watching him from the hill between the swimming pool site and the building renovation. He worked the enormous backhoe as if it were weightless, rocking back and forth on the bucket and the loader. The machine danced, knuckling back and gently forth, Walker twitching the controls delicately, pressing and patting with such economy of movement that I felt the hairs rising on my arms, standing out in a furry aureola along the muscles there.

Humans can do very remarkable things, and do them very remarkably well, if they practice long enough. When the Rubik's Cube craze was at its full, I saw a television program featuring a thirteen-year-old whiz. He manipulated the cube from chaos into order in a little under half a minute; smiling with big strong teeth, he handed it back to the emcee with an arrogant flourish. I envisioned him bent over the cube, at lunch hours, after school, during study hall, spinning the rows and columns of colors this way and that, the joints of the cube creaking. Mumbling instructions to himself: quarter turn, half, full, *twist*. Concentrating. Until he had it, and was eligible for his glorious half minute. He had earned the applause and the arrogance. At thirteen, he had a talent to be proud of the rest of his life. To that end he had consecrated sweat and discipline, and hours and hours of lonely practice. I admire his effort, and those of others like him, the baton twirlers and the billiard-hall sharpsters. I respect those people who have chosen, out of all of the possible talents in this world, one to which they will dedicate themselves, one to practice and believe in.

Walker's work benefited from long years of repetition, but there was also something else to it. Other crew members had as much experience or more. No, Walker had something separate: a kind of grace breathed into his body when he climbed into his seat and put his hands on the controls. The same divine breath which blows alongside Rampal's across the silver mouthpiece; the same which spreads warmly through the musculature of Olympic gymnasts, making their footing sure. Walker had such grace; it made the equipment he moved come alive for him; a mechanical ballet, it held me riveted, watching.

I had made the mistake of commending him, early on, walking from the hill after the lunch whistle, to meet him as he came out of the hole.

"Nice work," I had said.

He had hesitated, looking me up and down, then slid his eyes away. I could hear him thinking: *Goddamn faggot*. He wiped the sweat and dust from his forehead, nodded curtly, turned away.

I kept my praise to myself after that, arriving each morning and calling out a short greeting to the crew, striding to my observation point. I stayed there most of the morning, keeping my face impassive under my yellow hat, and watching Walker from the hill.

I was watching him when the news came; I was called to the phone shortly before noon, and a governmental voice informed me that work on the swimming pool would have to be halted.

"Water table's too high," said the copiously-titled Richmond official. "You're interfering with a stream bed. No, I don't know how you can fix it. No, I don't have any suggestions. Fixing it's your problem. All I know is you better stop your digging, and quick."

I put a phone call into Devlin immediately; he came roaring

to the site in his little roadster, a ridiculous car for a man his size. He heaved himself out of it and slammed the door.

"This won't do," he said, panting up the hill toward me. "Nossir, this won't do *at all.*"

"What can we do?" I asked.

"There has to be a way around this," said Devlin. *"I've got to have that pool."*

"I'll, um, investigate our options," I said.

"You do that," said Devlin darkly, glaring at the abandoned machinery, the empty hole. I had dismissed the crew half an hour before, when the stop order was confirmed.

We had run up against problems before, in the course of this project. The renovation had snagged several times: first, there was a dangerous interior staircase which would be difficult to remove and impossible to bring up to code; then it had been discovered that the roof would need to be completely retiled, at great cost. But those were the kinds of hitches one expected in projects like this one, easily solved by aesthetic or profit compromise. The government was formidable opposition. Of course, so was Devlin—he wanted that pool. While I watched, his face knotted and went dark red.

"Think of something," he said, finally, and stalked away from me.

I went back to the office, and found Warren Peavy.

"Tough one," he said, when I'd explained. "But probably not impossible."

"Do you have any suggestions?"

"Um," he said. "Well, now." He frowned. "I'm sure there's something. Have you tried George?"

"Yes," I said. "He said you'd know better than he would."

"Well, now," said Warren, obviously pleased by the flattery. "Let me think a while."

That day, I came home to find Joan in tears, curled up in the wingback chair in the living room.

"Honey," I said, putting my arms around her. It was unusual for her to cry.

"It's so sad," she said, finally, nasally.

"What is?" I asked.

"Amanda." The name provoked another cascade of emotion.

"I should have known this would happen," I said.

"What do you mean?" she asked, pulling away from me, looking into my face.

"You've been paying so much attention to other people you haven't allowed yourself to feel anything, all this time. I'm sorry," I said.

"Why?" she asked.

"I should have been paying more attention to you. I've been so busy with work, and we've hardly seen each other for months now." She nodded. "That's all going to change," I declared. "Starting now."

"All right," she said.

I promised myself that I wouldn't expend so much energy on the job; I could see that she needed me; I would dedicate myself to her well-being.

But work became more demanding, instead of less. I had expected that the situation with the Community Center project was temporary; but after a dozen consultations with Warren and George, I was no closer to a solution. None of the architects I spoke to did more than shrug. "We don't deal with that kind of stuff," one of them said.

So began a traumatic period. I woke from dreams in which I had devised a solution, and scribbled notes onto a pad of paper I kept by the bed. In the morning, the phrases I had written proved incoherent and absurd.

To make things worse, Devlin took to calling me into his office every day, haranguing me for variable lengths of time. Some days, he spent only a few minutes at it, going straight to the heart of the matter, slashing efficiently at my self-esteem. On other occasions, he devoted more than an hour to his outrage, expressing himself in exquisite, powerful detail. It seemed to depend on his schedule; there was no way I could predict, walking past his secretary, what I was in for on that particular occasion. One horrible day, he did not send for me at all; all day I waited, and at five o'clock I was weak with unrelieved dread. I began to have morning panic attacks, hyperventilating in the washroom, splashing cold water onto my face.

I gibbered to Joan about the problem; she nodded uncomprehendingly, and tipped vitamin tablets onto my breakfast plate.

"Jack says you should stand up to him," she said.

"Fuck Jack," I said, nastily.

"He's just trying to help," she said. "It's what he'd do. He doesn't understand how different you are."

*   *   *

The phone still rang at night. Most often, it was one of the students, adrift during summer vacation. Sometimes it was a Tell Tillie fan, too impatient to write a letter. Less and less often it was Beth. I was trying to be patient about the moratorium, and had not seen her in more than a month. From what I could gather, she was on the verge of independence, but Joan kept the lifeline stretched intact between them.

"She's talking about taking a job," said Joan one night, rubbing my back.

"That's healthy, isn't it?"

"I don't know why she wants to work," she said. "What with her parents and Joe Crawford, she doesn't need the money."

"Maybe she just likes the idea," I said. "You like your work."

"That's different," said Joan.

"I don't see how," I said.

"It's been too easy for her," she said. "I know you'll think I'm mean. But she seems to have forgotten all about—you know."

"You think she's forgotten?" I said.

"She never talks about her," said Joan.

"She talked about her all the time at first," I said.

"Not anymore," she said. "It's like it never happened."

"You can't believe that," I said.

Joan withdrew her hands for a moment; then they settled lightly again on my skin.

"People handle things differently," I said.

"I know Beth," said Joan. "She's not handling this at all."

"Joan," I said. "You've got to stop arranging people's lives. It doesn't leave you any energy for your own."

"What do you know about it?" she asked, sharply. I turned over and looked up at her. She was angry: little white lines stood out around her mouth.

"Nothing," I said, nonsensically. "But—"

"But nothing," she said. "Nothing and nothing and nothing. Most people are just like children. They never grow up. They're all looking for somebody to lean on, to fix things. That's me." She was calmer now. "I don't know why it's me, but it is. That's why we get along so well, you and I. You're not afraid to need me."

"And you like to be needed," I said.

She nodded. Her eyes were solemn and surprised by the

wisdom of her own words. *How do I know all of this?* she was asking herself. *How do I know so much, so well?* She was Joan, and that was all. She was Joan; no other credentials were required.

"Listen to this," Joan said over breakfast the next morning; she was holding a Tell Tillie letter.

" 'Dear Tillie,' " she read. " 'I told my son if he got good grades and did all his chores he could have a dog. My husband says no. He says we can't afford it, but we can. He's never been mean like this before. My son (he's eleven) cries at night. What do you think?' "

"Well," I said. "What do you think?"

"Dear," she looked at the letter, "Worried Mom. I think you should try to get your husband to talk about what's really bothering him. He's just using the dog as an excuse to fight. If he won't talk, take your son to the pound and rescue an animal. Maybe that'll provoke your husband into telling you what's really wrong. Good luck. Tillie." She picked up her coffee cup.

"Which category is this?" I asked. "Sex, love, money?"

"Mental abuse," she said. "Which goes under love."

"Very funny," I said.

"Speaking of mental abuse," she said. "How's Jordan Devlin?"

"As abusive as ever," I said, smiling a little. "The other day he accused me of reading the plans wrong and letting the crew dig up a sewer line. He said he could smell it from the street. He's always angrier on the days he drives by the site. I think it's seeing everything just sitting there, under tarps, losing money. You can't really blame him."

"I can blame him," she said. "I think he's an asshole."

"Joan," I said, surprised.

"Well, he is," she said.

I had to agree.

"Maybe Tell Tillie should write a column on vicious employers," she said.

"That isn't funny," I said. "He'd know right away who you were talking about."

"So?" she said.

"So I don't need you standing up to him for me."

"You think I want to?" she said. "I can't stand seeing what he's doing to you. He's just like a playground bully."

"That may be true," I said. "But it's my playground."

"Ha," she said. "It's Devlin's playground. He comes here from somewhere else and takes all kinds of advantage of this little trusting town."

"You don't know anything about this town," I said, angry.

"I know more than you think," she shot back. "Nice people thinking all they have to do is be nice and the world will be nice right back. That's not the way it works."

"How does it work, then?" I asked.

"You have to figure out what the other guy thinks he wants," she explained, carefully. "And then you give it to him, making sure that you get what you want in the process."

"You sound like Devlin," I told her.

"Actually, Jack said it," she admitted.

"I don't know if I like what you and Jack say to each other."

"We're only trying to help," she said.

"I don't need your help."

"Of course you do."

"No, I don't," I said.

"Gil," she said, making it two syllables, singsong.

"Don't do that," I said, furious. "Don't treat me like a baby and then harass me for not being enough of a man. I'm not your little boy," I said.

"I know that," she said.

"I thought you'd gotten better," I told her. "It seemed like the time we'd spent apart had changed you. But the minute we start talking, you're at me again. What do you want?" I asked. She looked at me blankly. "You're so fond of Jack," I said. "You want me to be like him?" She said nothing. "Well, all right," I said, standing up with exhausted dignity, collecting my jacket and briefcase. "Watch me now."

All the way to work, I fretted. *Watch me,* I had said. Ahead of me lay another day; folded within it, another acrimonious interlude with Devlin. I didn't really believe that I could change things, or that this day would be any different from the thirteen or so before it. Except that Joan and I had fought; and tonight, I would be slinking home to her, apologizing, agreeing with her. Giving in.

Anger gave way to guilt. What, I asked myself, about my vow to take better care of Joan? And she *was* only trying to help me. If only she hadn't held me up to Jack.

I no longer had the comfort of the open-air mornings. In the office, I learned that Devlin wasn't due in until after lunch. I slumped behind my desk all morning, making the same phone calls I had been making for two weeks now, trying to sort out the mess we were in, and at noon, escaped the building. I usually ate my lunch in, but not today—the cafeteria sold no alcohol, and I needed a drink. I marched down the street, feeling released. Turning the corner, I saw Devlin's little car; reflexively, heart hammering, I ducked into the nearest shop, a florist's.

"Hey, G.I.," said Beth, behind the counter. "What brings you in here?"

Prompted to confession by the cool, cloistered atmosphere, the panic that had sent me in here, the nearness of Beth, I blurted, "Oh, God, I'm hiding from my boss."

"What have you done?" she asked, smiling.

"Nothing," I said.

She nodded as though she understood. My heart began to slow down, and I took a good look at her. She looked better than when I'd last seen her—then, she'd had a yellow cast of strain to her skin, and dark circles under her eyes. Now, she looked just like the old Beth, as though the years had rolled away, and we were back in high school.

"Do you work here?" I asked. She nodded. "Joan told me you were working," I said. "She didn't tell me where."

"I wondered why you never came to see me. Seeing as your office is so close."

"I thought you didn't want to see me," I said. I wandered across the little shop, and drew a star on the clouded glass door of a case.

"That was true for a while," she said. "It's kind of hard to explain."

"Joan said men made you nervous," I said. She looked surprised.

"I don't think that's ever been true," she said, meaningfully. "Maybe she *thought* I was nervous, and was trying to protect me. She picks up things pretty well; maybe I was anxious about seeing men, and didn't even know it." She frowned, concentrating. "But I couldn't see you," she said. "I can't hide things from you."

"What were you hiding?"

"Oh, just," she said. "Stuff." She smiled, dismissing it. "It helps, working with growing things," she said. "Joan should try it."

"Joan," I said, remembering. "We had a fight this morning."

"Send her some flowers," said Beth. "I'm sorry if it's an obvious suggestion."

"I don't know what to send," I said.

"We have all kinds of arrangements," she said, mischievously, playing the salesgirl. "Here's a lovely one right here, only ten dollars."

"You decide," I said.

"Lilies," she said, promptly. "I'll do it right now." She moved around the shop, gathering flowers from the long chilled cases, snipping their stems.

"You're so good at this," I said, in wonder.

She smiled, poking the flowers into a vase.

"How's Joan these days?" she asked.

"Tired," I said. "You ought to know. You see her more than I do."

"No, I don't," she said. "We've talked on the phone some, but I haven't seen her for ages. Not since you all had me over for supper that time."

"But she's always—" I said. "Wait a minute."

"What?" said Beth, looking concerned.

"She's never at home," I said. "I ask her to slow down, but she says she has responsibilities. Looking after you, or going down to the *Chronicle* to type up her column. Or meeting a student."

"Well," said Beth. She'd been standing still, her hands on the lilies, looking at me with a puzzled expression. Now it vanished, and she snapped into motion again, busying herself with the flowers. "You know how she is about those kids. She can't say no."

"But mostly she says she's seeing *you,*" I said. "At least three or four times a week she says that. And you just said you hadn't seen her since—God, that dinner was in June."

"Maybe I've seen her once or twice," she said.

"She's always quoting Jack at me," I said, softly.

"Don't jump to conclusions, G.I.," said Beth, warningly.

"It seems so obvious now."

"No," said Beth. "Stop it," she said. "Don't think like that."

"*He* hates me," I said. "He's always tormented me."

"Now you're being ridiculous," she said.

"*She* says I'm too sensitive. She tells me how *he* would handle things. She thinks I'm not a man." I stopped. "But you were afraid of me."

"I never said that," said Beth.

"At work they treat me like a pansy," I said, unstoppable now in the release of my confusion, all that I had kept private and stoppered for so long. "They're right," I said. "I'm in here hiding from my boss, telling my troubles to a woman."

"Not just any woman," said Beth, feebly joking.

"I'm a failure at my job," I said, pacing. "My wife is having an affair."

Beth said nothing, busying herself with ribbon.

"I'm a man, I'm not a man, I'm not anything. Where do I fit?" I said, to a rigid spray of gladiolus.

"Maybe you don't," she said, in a hard, calm voice.

"What if I want to," I said.

"You choose," she said, briskly. "Don't ask me what or how. If you want to fit in badly enough, you'll figure it out." She smiled. "Or you could be like me, and run away."

"Where have you run to?" I asked, bending and putting my elbows on the glass countertop between us.

"Far away," she said. "Where nothing bad ever happens. Here you go," she said, giving a last tweak to the arrangement. "Want to put a message on the card?"

"Regards to Jack," I said, sourly.

"That's just stupid," said Beth, annoyed. "I promise you you're wrong about that. So quit being so obnoxious." She looked at the card. "I'll put 'Love' on it," she decided. "That's nice and ambiguous."

I spent the rest of the hour in a narrow bar two doors down from the florist's, lingering over a sandwich and a beer. I didn't notice the man detaching himself from his chums and coming over to me; suddenly he was standing at my table, holding his beer mug.

"Corbin," he said.

It was Henry Everett, from the construction crew I had dismissed. He had been one of the few on the site who hadn't hated me. Once, when I had found my hard hat filled with mud, he made one of the boys give up his own. Later, I had seen the culprit hosing down my hat, his face stiff with resentment. I liked Henry, and appreciated his support, but I guessed that some of his kindness derived from pity. Pity for the odd man out, the weak, the hopeless. If he hadn't pitied me, he'd have left me to handle the pranksters myself. Since the incident with the hard hat, seeing him had inspired a vague embarrassment in me, like the feeling in a small boy whose mother defends him against bullies.

"Henry," I said, with false welcome. "How's it going?"

"Not too bad," he said. "Working another site now. I hear you guys are still having problems with that pool job."

"Yes," I said, not wanting to talk about it. "Yes, we are."

"Strange," he said. "I mean, what is it besides the stream bed?"

"Nothing," I said. "I mean, that's it, the stream," I said, flushing. "Bed."

"There's gotta be something else."

"No," I said, finishing my beer. "Isn't that enough?"

"Huh," said Henry. "I worked a job a few years ago, over in the next county. They had the same problem, didn't have any trouble solving it."

"What?" I said.

"Just dug a few feet deeper to the bed, ran a culvert through. Filled in on top of it, and presto, no problem."

"That might work," I said.

"Surprised no one thought of it over there," he said. "Of course, the situation might be different in your case," he said, lifting his mug.

"Of course," I said, thoughtfully.

"I *knew* I could count on you, Gil," cried Devlin, getting up from behind his desk, all of his features pulling loose from their mask of anger and realigning in an expression of glee.

"It," I said modestly, "might work."

"Might! Damn, it's perfect. Come to think of it," he added, "I think I've heard something like it before."

"Hum," I said, helpfully.

"How'd you come up with it?" he said.

"Just thinking," I said. "Like you told me."

"Sure," said Devlin, pleased. "That's the way."

When I got home that evening, Joan was very quiet.

"Thanks for the flowers," she said, and then, "I'm sorry about this morning."

"Me, too," I said. My suspicions in the florist's seemed far away now.

"What's that on your breath?" she asked. "Beer?"

"Whisky," I said.

"Oh, Gil," she said, disapproving.

"Devlin took me out for a drink," I said. "I solved the Center problem."

"That's wonderful," she said, kissing me.

"Funny thing about it," I said. "Everyone else already knew how to do it, but they wouldn't tell me."

"Aren't you being a little paranoid?" she asked.

"Nope," I said. "I could tell from how they looked when Devlin told them. Disappointed. They were hoping I'd be fired. Rotten men," I said. "You never know them until they let you down."

"I think you should lie down," said Joan, taking my arm. Later, she awoke me, sitting on the side of the bed, smoothing my hair. "I'm going to run by Beth's," she said.

"Nnkay," I grunted.

She left the room, closing the door softly, and then I awoke. I swung my legs off the bed, and followed.

"Say hi for me," I said, from the entrance hall.

"Okay," she said, turning in surprise.

"Does she want to see me yet?" I asked.

"Not quite yet," she said, frowning, pulling on her gloves.

"I know you're not going over there," I said.

She stood very still.

"I know where you're going."

"What are you talking about?" she said, very white. I had shocked her.

"Do you sleep with him?" I asked.

"What?" she whispered.

"Does he make you come?" I hissed, taking two long strides toward her. "Is he better than I am?"

She was standing with her hand on the doorknob; her face had relaxed.

"You're disgusting," she said. "Listen to yourself. Everyone can hear you."

"Everyone who?"

She flung her arms at the door. "Everyone there," she said. "They're all out there, listening. Tomorrow, they'll be giving odds on our divorce."

"Is that what you want?" I said.

"I'm not going to talk about this now," she said. "Not while you're drunk."

"Come back here," I said.

"That won't work," she said, twisting her wrist out of my grasp. "Look what whisky does to you," she said. "Right back to the cave. You shout, and when that doesn't work, you try brutality."

"What are you complaining about?" I asked. "Sounds pretty manly to me. Isn't that what you want? Isn't that what you're going out of the door to find?"

"Brutality doesn't make you a man," said Joan.

She opened the front door; I could see her profile in the porch light. Her mouth was open; she breathed quickly from emotion; in the dimness, she looked younger, softer. My heart twisted at the thought that she was going to her lover.

"Joan," I said. But she was gone.

It took a little while for the state to be convinced of the feasibility of the plan; it was their water that was threatened, and they were cautious. We shifted our attention to other projects, waiting for the go-ahead on the center. It came in September, and we began digging down to the stream bed. I had my mornings again; I stood in the fine autumn weather with my collar open, watching the crew at work. The building renovation had been halted, too; now I stood on the hill between the two sites, and pretended to observe them both, when actually I saw only Walker, who was in the hole again, digging the extra six feet.

So I had my eye on him that early morning, when he stopped the backhoe and peered through the glass at the earth in front of him. I saw him climb down from the seat and go over to a spot and push at something with his foot. I saw him back away, and had already started down the slope to him before he called.

"Corbin!"

I jogged down to the lip of the hole and then around its perimeter, pushed by an urgency I couldn't have explained. Skidding down the sides of the hole, pushing my hand for balance into the soft dirt. Reaching Walker and slowing, walking to join him where he stood, pointing down.

"Look," he said, indicating an object half buried in the dirt. "I heard the crunch."

"Goddamn," I said.

I looked at the shapeless, the terrible thing, oddly humped, the red wool dark in places with mud. It was long past odor, but nonetheless a gigantic queasiness started somewhere in the bottom of my stomach. My legs tingled, and my head went light. Little lines and circles danced before my eyes.

"Aak," I said, involuntarily.

Walker stood squinting into the bright morning, watching me. I knew what he was thinking: *The fairy's gonna puke.* His face was twisted with scorn.

I made an enormous effort at control, forcing down my nausea, blinking my eyes several times, breathing hugely in and out. Finally, I trusted myself to speak.

"Shit," I said. "This'll set us back at least a week."

Walker looked surprised.

"We," I said. "Better call someone."

"Uh-huh," he said.

We set off up the slope.

"We gotta get the pouring done before it gets cold," he remarked on the way.

"I know," I said, angrily. "What a fucking pain in the ass."

Walker grunted, and spat into the dirt. "You said it," he said, and in his voice there was a note of approval, of comradeliness, that had never been there before in his tight *Morning*s and his *See you later*s.

The police came, and the coroner's boys, and then the flock of reporters and photographers. We were questioned at length, and then someone poked a microphone into my face. I turned to the camera, speaking easily, fluently.

"Anybody coulda put it there," I told them, truthfully. "Hole's been open like that, unguarded, for weeks."

"They could have slipped in and buried it any old time," agreed Walker.

We said the same words over and over, while behind us they were sliding the dusty lump into a zippered bag. A journalist turned his head away. Walker's gaze met mine, and he rolled his eyes, significantly.

There were forms to fill out, and phone calls to make. I left a message with Devlin's secretary. Walter Stirling, the police sergeant who'd taken my statement, tapped me on the shoulder.

"She's pretty beat-up about this," he said. "She could use a friend."

Beth greeted me meekly. At first she didn't say much, but when I put my arm around her she gave in, and wept into my cotton shirt, sitting close beside me. We stayed like that for a

while, Beth wailing against my chest, and then she took her
face out of my shirt and sniffed.

"I knew it," she said.

"How bout a drink?" I suggested.

She shrugged. I went to the liquor cabinet and took out the
bottle of scotch.

"Joan kept telling me and telling me, I shouldn't give up
hope," she said. "But I really knew."

"That was cruel of her," I said, handing her a glass, sitting
beside her again.

"She wasn't trying to be cruel," she said. "She just couldn't
face it."

"She couldn't face it?" I asked.

"It would be like losing her twice," she said, gently.

"Emily?" I asked, and my voice was rusty.

She nodded. "She used to call her Emily when she thought I
couldn't hear," she said. "It was so sad."

"That was so long ago," I said, but speaking, I felt a deep
twinge.

"It's never over," she said, and we were quiet for a while,
drinking.

"I felt so bad for giving up," Beth said, suddenly. "Like I
had abandoned her."

"Joan doesn't know when people stop needing her," I said.

"She doesn't have any practice at it," said Beth. "Children
teach you that." She began to cry again, softly, and talked
through her tears. "The funny thing is, I feel sorry for Joan,"
she said. "She's so unhappy. Don't look at me like that," she
said, blowing her nose. "She is."

"She's unhappy with me," I said, bitterly. "I think she's
happy with Jack. Although she's been home a lot more lately.
Maybe they had a fight."

"Are you still off on that?" asked Beth, scornfully, her an-
noyance interrupting her tears. "That's bullshit, G.I., and you
know it."

"I confronted her with it," I said. "She didn't deny it, and
she wouldn't talk about it later." I felt the tears pressing
against my eyelashes. "Oh, God, I'm supposed to be comforting you," I said.

"It's okay," said Beth.

"I want her to need me," I said.

"She does, G.I.," she said. "Or she did. I honestly don't
know anymore. She never talks about herself."

"That's true," I said, surprised.

"I think she needs us more than we need her," said Beth.

The front door suddenly opened, and Joan walked in. She stood silent in the doorway, her prepared look of sympathy dissolving into blankness. Behind her in the doorway, the reporters from Richmond and Charlottesville and Washington clamored; little bursts of flash went off, sounding like rain. She heard the ruckus belatedly, and closed the door behind her.

"Gil," she said, leaning back against the wood. "What are you doing here?"

"She needed a friend," I said, not moving.

But Beth lept up from the sofa, away from my side, and went to Joan. The two women clung together, a soft female mass of shoulders and shiny hair, and when they pulled away from one another, they were both crying.

I stood and watched them huddle, murmuring to one another so low that I couldn't distinguish any words. Although just a few feet away from them, I felt profoundly distant, and shut out, like a foreigner at a secret ritual, an intruder. Haggard, like a soldier at a celebration, and unimportant. I recalled my father looking on as my mother and sister surrounded me, comforted me, handed me from one to the other, my feet never touching the ground. Was it the lot of men forever to stand, rugged and yearning, at the edge of tender groups?

While I watched, they went upstairs together. At the landing Joan turned.

"I'll stay here tonight," she whispered, and I nodded.

Half an hour later, she came down again.

"She's asleep," she said.

We sat around the living room and looked at each other for a little while. She switched on the television, turned the volume off, and watched Walker and me talking, the camera swinging from our faces to the hole behind us. Joan's face was lit blue; when she turned to look at me, her expression was unreadable.

"You've changed," she said. "I hardly recognize you there." She gestured toward the screen.

"Everything changes," I said.

She nodded.

I stood up. She looked quickly up at me, flinching as though I had threatened her.

"I'm going out for a while," I said.

"Will you come back here?" she asked.

"I don't know," I said, and weakened. "Maybe."

Stokes's was crammed with people, all of them discussing the news; I pushed my way in among them and called for a beer, but no one heard me.

". . . blunt object," someone was saying.

"Whodja think done it?"

"Nobody from here," was the answer. "Some sicko."

"You mean from the hospital?"

"Look at him there, looks like he's gonna puke," said Sam, pointing to the television.

"Like you wouldn't," needled Ned.

"I saw worse things in combat."

"Not little girls," said Ned. "Not dead little girls."

"Whoever it was is long gone by now."

"He stayed around here long enough," said someone. "When'd he take her, April?"

"Where'd he keep her all this time?"

"In the hills, probly."

"It'd be easy to hide up there."

"Sicko."

Someone must have spotted me, because there was a sudden hush at the core of the crowd, travelling outward to where I stood on the fringes.

"Hey, G.I.," said someone.

"Hey," I said.

"Tell us about it," said a youngster, but he was shushed.

"Musta been awful," said Sam, wheedlingly.

"Well," I said.

They waited, an attentive circle around me. From them rose the familiar, the characteristic scent of men in quantity. To me, it had always been the liquor of warning, but now it invigorated me. My voice was husky, full in my throat, uninterrupted.

"Hell, what can I say? We found her," I said. "I need a beer."

Chapter Twenty-one

Conflicts and Allies

She had never been this close to him. Now, from the little, protective distance which her desk afforded her, she regarded him carefully, and had, surprisingly, a fierce sense of recognition.

"What can I do for you?" she asked.

"You knew my mother," he said, abruptly.

"Your mother," repeated Joan.

"Beth Crawford," he said, impatient. "Beth Miller, if you like. You knew her."

"Oh, yes," she said. "A long time ago." She wished that she could smile; a smile would be an excellent weapon; but she could do no more than keep her voice steady and her brow clear. She could not imagine how her face might change if she tried to smile.

"You've heard I'm making a film?" asked the boy. "Or trying to," he added.

She put her head on one side, carefully, and frowned a little.

"I heard something like that," she said. "I think you mentioned it at the Bruckners' the other night?"

"Right," said Buddy. "I'd like to interview you," he said. "With the camera."

She felt a sudden anger: how *could* he be so direct, so unabashed? He was worse than many of the teenage rebels she met in here.

"Why me?" she asked, and was pleased to hear in her own voice a perfect puzzled tone, a gentle bafflement, no more.

"I heard you were good friends with her," he said.

"Oh, well," she said. "We knew each other. But I don't know that you'd have called us close."

He looked surprised.

"I heard you were best friends," he said, but there was a hint of uncertainty now. She heard it, with relief.

"I don't know who said that," she told him, lightly. "I guess it might have looked that way, once. But your mother was born here; she lived up on the hill. I only came here for college. She had a lot of other friends. We ran into each other by chance, and I think she felt sorry for me—I was so much of an outsider. A kind of charity case, you might say."

"That isn't how I heard it," he said, dubiously.

"That isn't how I thought of it then," she said. "But that's how I've come to think of it."

"What was she like?" he asked. "Do you remember?"

"Of course," she said, a little irritated: he acted as though she were a thousand years old.

"What was she like?"

"Well," she considered. "She was pretty, of course. And popular. Intelligent, although she didn't care much for school."

"I've heard all that stuff from other people," said Buddy. "I want to know other stuff. What she was *like.*" There was a kind of desperation about him now.

"I never really knew her," said Joan, firmly.

He looked at her stonily; again she had the strange impression of intense familiarity.

"I feel like I'm in that stupid children's book," he said.

"Which one?" asked Joan. She was used to frequent changes in subject from the children she counseled, some of whose attention spans were unbelievably short.

"This one I used to have a long time ago," said the boy. "It was called *Are You My Mother.*"

"Sounds familiar," she said.

"It's about a duckling," said Buddy. "He's alone; I can't remember how he got that way. Anyway, he goes around to all the animals and asks them are they his mother. He asks a crocodile," he said, with a sour break in his voice. "He asks a hippo."

"I remember," she said.

"This whole town," said Buddy gratingly, "is a zoo."

They looked at one another in silence. Joan felt a strange sensation beginning deep within her, and with surprise she recognized it as laughter. She tried to squelch it, but it forced itself through. She put her hand over her mouth, the sounds spilling out.

Buddy stared, and his mouth twitched, and then he was laughing, too. She took her hand down, and for whole minutes they did nothing but laugh, simply and openly; and then their laughter died away and they sat silent, still looking at one another, but without malice.

"I'd still like you to be in my movie," said Buddy, while the echoes rang around them.

"I don't think so," said Joan. "It's not a good day for me."

"It doesn't have to be today," he said. "It doesn't have to interfere with your work, either. I'll be around for a few more days—we could set up at your house, if you'd be more comfortable."

"No," she said, gently. "I really have nothing to say."

Outside, he looked at his watch. Eleven in the morning, and the sun was already making itself felt through the wind. Up north, the weather would be uncompromising, cold with no hint of the brief forgiveness of the spring to come. He took the car to the river; parking and getting out, he took nothing with him but the tape recorder he took sound with during the interviews, and his box of cassette tapes.

He felt naked without the camera. Going barefaced into the ranks of townspeople was a very different proposition, that comfortable heavy bulk gone now from his right shoulder. It had protected him, its great glassy eye recording everything, remembering what he might not; and people had spoken to *it*, not to him. There had been nothing of him during those interviews; he'd liked it that way. Why, then, had he taken the camera down?

It had stopped protecting him, that was why. That afternoon with the nanny it had seemed to melt away, another traitor, crouching conspiratorially on his shoulder one minute, vanished the next. For the first time, he'd heard a voice above the machine's hum; what he'd heard had alarmed him. Taunted him, even: *Are you ready for this?*

He settled himself on the grass at the water's very edge, regarding the scenery without surprise. *I'm already getting used to it here.* Twelve days ago, he'd been amazed by such beauty, flowing unheralded and quiet through this modest patch of civilization. He'd known only cities or suburbs in his lifetime. Nothing like this.

He knew you couldn't swim in the river—or at least that you weren't supposed to. There was a dangerous undertow in the narrows, and soft deep mud in the widest places. His mother had talked about the river a lot: about the courting couples who lay by its banks in her youth, the murmuring of the water, the answering murmurs of love.

"You all think we were so chaste back then," she'd said. "Ha."

"What did you want?" Buddy asked now, aloud. "What was it?"

So newly sprung from adolescence, he found it hard to credit an older person, a *mother,* with the passions and ferocities he himself felt; but he knew that she must have wanted something. Something that she'd died from not having. Love? But she'd had that in Connecticut. A career? She could have had that if she'd wanted: she'd been intelligent enough, and had never lacked motivation. He couldn't imagine her languishing at the foot of a hill, fearing the climb. She was much more likely to have toiled to the top, and then been disgusted with the view.

Peace. The word came to him as though it had been spoken by the waving treetops. Peace. But hadn't she had that here? The place seemed peaceful enough, even drowsy. But there was a dangerous element cutting underneath the sleepiness; even Buddy had caught on to it, during his short visit. He did not know enough to give it its name.

She hadn't told him everything, not by a long chalk. That was obvious, from what he'd been told. What *had* he been told? The film was locked into the cans now, along with its secrets. He reached lazily toward the box of tapes and chose one at random, slipping it into the tape recorder clipped to his belt. He fitted the earphones on his head, rewound the tape some, and let it play.

"Not that she was a bad mother."

He thought of the nanny, her squinting eyes and rough skin, her innocent witnessing, telling him things he'd never imagined.

Now he began a game with himself, pulling tapes from the box, putting them into the machine and fast-forwarding. Stopping, letting them play for a few seconds; stopping again and ejecting, changing the tape without looking, hearing only snatches.

"I guess it made us feel alive."

His mother, terribly young, running down a long hill; the canny nurse-to-be, probably plump even then, behind her.

"There's a use for everything."

The flea-market man, pulling himself up out of his cheap plaid suit, trying to look tall for the camera.

"Sadder, and deep, like a bell tolling."

Tess, the old woman, wrinkled, her left arm crooked across her body, her voice fading in and out.

"It was the only thing you could do."

He was hearing his mother, in the country voice of a man past sixty, made lyrical with the power of memory.

"You pick the strangest damn times to pay attention."

He smiled. That was certainly true.

"She was dead serious."

He opened his eyes.

"Dead," he repeated. He ejected the tape, and inserted a blank one. "Testing," he said, and then played it back. "Um, March thirtieth," he said, hating the raw sound of his own voice. "So far, I've learned three things. She had a child in nineteen fifty-six. The child was kidnapped a few years later, around sixty-two." He shut off the machine for a moment, and then started it again. "The child never came back."

It seemed too bare, a skeletal summation of a tragedy. He looked at the water, which said nothing, moving serenely on in the way it must have done for centuries, impervious to the battles which had raged now and again on its shores. Men taking up arms against men; men taking women into their arms. Conflicts he knew nothing about, not really, despite all he'd heard of war, and notwithstanding his father's prepared speech when he was twelve. Love and battle, glory and death. Loss.

Was it enough?

Taking up a short twig, he dug it into the hard packed mud of the balding riverbank. What had he really come for? He'd told Szilardi some nonsense about doing a portrait of a small town. He'd told the people here different versions of the same thing, whatever he'd judged would convince them to talk to the camera.

But then they'd stopped talking to the camera, and started talking to him. He'd been frightened by that; frightened, too, by that night in the woods with nothing but himself and the darkness and all that he'd never guessed could frighten him, waiting somewhere between the trees.

If he'd come looking for Beth, he hadn't found her. She wasn't in the woods that night, or in her old house that Jack had pointed out to him, or anywhere he had yet been. Perhaps his father was right: she wasn't anywhere anymore; she was just gone. Then what *was* here, making the mention of her so poisonous and sweet to this small town he had invaded for two weeks? What was it, that flitted just out of frame, dancing beyond him every time he lifted the camera, creeping up behind him every time he put it down?

Whatever it was, it held secrets; and that's what he'd come for. Stalking them, wasn't he, snapping on the sound, focusing the image? Protecting himself, keeping the reassuring heft and buzz of the camera always with him, a barrier against the sudden viciousness of cornered prey. And then quite suddenly he'd run it to ground; he'd trapped it so it couldn't escape. He'd had it there before him. He'd had it; and he'd put the camera down.

She cancelled a student conference that afternoon, and set off for home. She meant to go straight there, but instead found herself taking a different route. She pulled into the garage with a kind of surprise.

"Hey," said Jack, seeing her. He came over to the car and squatted by the driver's side, his head level with hers.

"Just passing by," she said, shyly.

"I was afraid there was something wrong with the Toyota," he said.

"It's fine," said Joan.

"Well, good," he said. He squinted off into the sun for a moment, and then looked back at her.

"I was feeling restless," she confessed.

"Must be going around," he said. "I'm about ready to crawl out of my skin these days."

"Hey," called Rupe from inside the garage.

"I'm sorry," said Joan. "Are you very busy?"

"Naw," said Jack. "He only does that to cramp my style. He gets jealous when pretty girls come to talk to me. He only dreams about that."

Rupe, coming across the asphalt toward them, caught the last part of the statement.

"Har de har har," he said.

"We're gonna grab a cold drink somewhere," said Jack. "Can you handle it alone?"

"Do it all the time, don't I?" Rupe grumbled.

"Tough life," said Jack, going around to the passenger's side of the car. "See you after while."

They drove in silence to Susie's. The lunch crowd had cleared out by now; the place was nearly empty. Joan felt a prickle of amazement, sliding into the booth across from Jack.

She had hardly been alone with a man, except for Gil, in many years. Jack had used to come around to their house for supper fairly regularly, with Marie while they were married, and then alone in the twilight period of separation. She'd encouraged his visits, feeling tender toward him, sensing the confusion behind the careful defenses, the sadness packed tight into every quip. After the divorce was final, she'd made it clear that his girlfriends were welcome, too; but he never brought any, looming up at the door alone, always alone, for Sunday supper. They'd been a tight family for a while, she and Gil and Jack, but many things had happened since. Something dark had risen up between the brothers, and Jack had become a stranger to their house. He and Gil had even stopped speaking to one another, their silence sudden but not astonishing, merely a formal acknowledgment of some long-lurking private enmity. Now, sitting openly with her brother-in-law, resting her elbows on the shiny-topped table, she felt almost disloyal.

"It's hard to believe you're brothers," she said.

"We're more alike than looks," he said. "He takes after our ma."

"He doesn't talk about her much," she said. "I don't think he remembers her."

"He wasn't *that* young," said Jack, raising his eyebrows briefly.

They ordered from the slow, friendly waitress. When she had gone away, taking the menus, Joan spoke again.

"Tell me about her," she said.

He didn't pretend not to understand.

"Well," he said. "She had a real soft voice, and hands like iron."

He told first simple things, hazy childhood memories, sensation more than sense; then things a fifteen-year-old boy might remember, followed by more adult observations. Their milk shakes arrived, and she poked a straw into hers while Jack talked on, his comments passing now into speculation.

"She was a strong woman," he said. "Not mean; more like determined. Gil, he idolized her. After she passed on, he made her out in his mind as kind of an angel. She wasn't that." He paused, and sucked up a little of his milk shake. "She'd a been softer, maybe, with a harder man. But the way things were, she had to train all of the softness out of herself. Dad was just an old rag doll. Like Gil." He smiled. "I got Dad's outsides, and Mom's insides. Gil, he got it the other way." He lit a cigarette. "I remind him of the way she really was. Part of why he hates me." He spread out his fingers, and flexed them.

"He doesn't hate you," said Joan.

"Well," said Jack, taking another pull on the cigarette, and letting out the smoke in a series of graceful rings, finishing by shooting one quickly through another. He laughed, destroying the lacy smokework. "I think that's why I keep on smoking," he said. "Get cancer, but impress the ladies." He stubbed out the cigarette, and met her eyes. "You're like her some," he said, serious again. "Not so much in the way you look. She wasn't all that pretty." He considered for a moment, lifting his straw out of the melted ice cream, letting it fall again. "But something tough about her, something hard and smart." He took a mouthful of the milk shake and swallowed. "Gil's smart that way now," he said. "But he wasn't always."

She nodded.

"He didn't get it from her," he said. "He got it his own self, later."

"I know," said Joan, very low, almost a whisper.

"Now and then," he said, shaking his head. "It's like night to day." He looked at her. "You've had a hard time of it," he said.

"So've you," she replied.

"Well, better not think about it anymore," he said. "It's over now."

"Is it?" she asked, trusting, like a child. He didn't say anything. "Your friend came to see me today," she said, at last.

"Uh-huh," he said.

She meant to say more, but her attention wandered to a couple sitting at a table in the window. They were young, cleanly attractive, plainly in love; the boy was clowning for the girl, who pretended to smack at him with her open palm. All the greasy light in the room collected and clarified around them. They were sweethearts, uncomplicated and hopeful, oblivious of the world around them, immune to its age and complexity.

"Look at them," she said, with wonder.

Jack flicked a glance at the pair.

"They're just starting out," he said.

"That's right," said Joan. "Poor things."

The library turned out to be one of the row of impressive white-stoned buildings all in a line along the same street as the

Historic Committee. He'd crisscrossed the town for the interviews, and yet hadn't been back this way much since the morning he'd interviewed Tess. He'd almost forgotten that this section of Naples existed. Quiet and groomed, tucked into the shadow of the hill, it was a genteel reproof to the barbarians living, as Jack did, near the railroad tracks.

He had tried the high school library first, but they had sent him here.

"We don't keep them that far back," the lady explained. "We don't have the room."

He entered the building and marveled at the brittle-paper smell, same the world over.

"Excuse me," said a voice. It was another of those antique ladies Naples seemed to be filled with. Or maybe it was just this part of town. "May I help you find something?"

He sighed. He'd hoped that he might be able to slip into the appropriate room and do his research unaccosted. He was getting tired of talking to these people. It was amazing how many niceties had to go into everything here; a simple conversation was exhausting.

"I'm looking for high school yearbooks," he said now. "Back to the fifties."

"Which fifties?" she asked.

"Excuse me? The nineteen fifties."

"Well, of course," said the lady. "I mean, *before* nineteen fifty-three, or after? More than thirty years back, we keep off the shelves. No room," she said.

"Oh. Before," said Buddy. "Maybe junior high school, too. From the um, forties."

"Are you looking for anything in particular?" she asked. "I might be able to help you narrow it down."

"My mother," said Buddy, wearily.

"Of course," said the woman. "She graduated in, let's see, nineteen forty-nine? No, forty-eight."

"That's right," he said, astounded.

"She was Tobacco Queen," said the lady. "My goodness. It's hard to forget a thing like that."

She led him through the big reference room and down a little corridor, stopping in front of a plain grey door.

"We don't usually let people into the back rooms," she said, looking over her shoulder at him mischievously, working her key in the lock. "You wouldn't believe what they get up to.

Well, maybe you would," she corrected herself. She pushed open the door. "Here you are," she said.

The room was square, about fifteen feet on a side, lined with bookshelves tightly filled with books, their goldstamped spines glinting out at him. There was a long table fitted in between the shelves somehow, two intact chairs and a broken one, and a reading lamp. Also, Buddy noticed, a crumpled paper bag.

"My lunch," said the woman. "I usually eat in here. So cool and private." She smiled. "The yearbooks are over on that wall. Left to right by year. Bound school newspapers, too," she said, and then suddenly looked worried. "We don't have the academy," she said. "They keep their own. We just have the public schools."

"That's what I'm looking for," said Buddy. He smiled for the first time, and the lady's own smile broadened in response.

"You're making a movie, aren't you?" she asked, curiously. He nodded. "Some said it was about your mother, some said about the town," she went on. He nodded again. "Well," she said, brightly. "Which is it?"

"I'm not really sure," he said, shortly.

"They must get kind of mixed up," she said, surprising him with easy understanding. "It must be so interesting," she said, smiling. "I could just talk to you all day." She paused, apparently taken with this idea. "But then you'd never see your yearbooks, would you?" and she adopted a brisk attitude. "All right, then. If you need anything, come find me." And she closed the door.

"You went out with her," accused Buddy.

"Never said I didn't," said Jack.

"The high school newspaper said you were steadies. The yearbook called you Couple of the Year."

"Silliness," said Jack.

"You never told me," said Buddy.

"High school sweethearts," Jack said. "What's to tell?"

"They made it sound serious, like you were going to get married."

"Seventeen years old," said Jack. "What the hell does seventeen years old know?"

"Seventeen isn't that young," said Buddy.

"Not to nineteen," said Jack. "Sulking's for girls," he added, after a pause.

"Fuck you," said Buddy.

"Ho," said Jack, and sat back for a while. In the silence, Buddy sneaked a look at him, and then tightened his own jaw. It was a short siege; Buddy broke first.

"I thought you were helping me," he complained.

"Let me get this straight," said Jack, finally. "You're mad because I didn't tell you that I used to date your mother."

"You went steady," said Buddy.

"More than thirty years ago," said Jack.

Buddy, about to speak, stopped himself, awed temporarily by the concept of looking back on anything from thirty years.

"It doesn't matter how long ago it was," he said, at last. "Why not just tell me? What's the big deal?"

"All right," said Jack. "I used to go steady with your mother. What else do you want?"

"Tell me about her," said Buddy, instantly. "Tell the camera."

"Nossir," said Jack. "The world ain't no place for what high school confessions I got." He looked at Buddy. "Your mom and I, we went to dances, she wore my sweater and jumped up and down at the football games. That's what happened."

"There has to be more," said Buddy.

"Nope," said Jack.

"But there's so much I don't know. I hear bits and pieces, never the whole story. I can't get at it."

"Maybe there ain't a story to hear," said Jack.

"There is," insisted Buddy. "I know there is. But—"

"But what?" said Jack.

"I don't know if I want to hear it," he admitted, scraping his left thumbnail along the rubber of his tennis shoe. "It kind of scares me." He blushed, keeping his head down.

"Some things, once you know 'em, you can't un-know," said Jack. "It's an unfortunate thing about this world."

"I'm thinking about just giving up on the movie," whispered Buddy, and then forced loudness into his voice. "I mean, I'm not getting anywhere."

"What the hell," said Jack. "I been hauling you around town so you can just throw all that film away? What about Dr. Max, and that writer lady? You gonna cancel her?"

"It seems stupid to cancel," said Buddy, reluctantly. "I might just go ahead and film some more, edit it together, see what I get."

"That writer lady never knew your ma," said Jack.

"What else is new?" said Buddy, wryly. "Half the film I've

shot isn't about her." He thought for a moment. "But it's interesting stuff," he conceded. "Even if it isn't what I came here for."

"Seems to me," said Jack, "you don't know what you came here for."

There was a silence, into which a bobwhite called its sadness. Buddy felt all of a sudden very tense, as though he might run or explode or combust. His heart beat in his ears; he held himself still, terrified.

"Sometimes," said Jack, very quietly, "people think they got to do something exactly the way they set out to. They even think they made a promise to somebody, that they'd do a certain thing a certain way."

The words reached Buddy where he crouched within his panic; their calmness began to work a magic on him, soothing him, driving the fear away.

"They make themselves miserable," Jack went on, just as slow and quiet. "And you know what? There weren't no promise in the first place. They never promised anybody anything, except maybe themselves, and welching on yourself ain't welching."

"What is it, then?" asked Buddy, shakily.

"It's called *tailoring your expectations,*" said Jack.

Buddy considered this for a moment.

"Sounds reasonable," he said. He caught Jack's eye then, and burst out laughing. A minute ago I would never have dreamed I'd be laughing now, he thought. A minute ago, I thought I was going to die.

"Why'd you break up with her?" he asked, after another pause.

"It wasn't like that," said Jack, not smiling anymore. "Not breaking up, noisy, like folks do nowadays. We just kinda didn't feel the same about each other anymore. We changed."

"The war," said Buddy. "Was that it?"

"The war changed more than high school sweethearts," said Jack.

"So," prompted Buddy.

"So, I'm not saying you're wrong." He stood up. "Not saying you're right, either." He looked at the boy. "Some things ain't your business," he said. "Some things ain't for discussion. And no amount of poking and camera toting and wishful thinking will make it different. I'm going to bed," he said, opening the screen door. "Good night."

"Night," said Buddy, and "Damn," to the flapping screen door. He crossed his arms over his chest and scowled, for an instant looking very much like Jack.

He felt uneasy, as though he'd made some decision unwittingly. He was committed now, to the interview with the writer; and he knew Jack had lined up one or two more besides. I'll have to abandon the other idea, he thought; and he waited for the misery to come up in him like a sap of sadness filling places left empty after sorrow. But it didn't come. *I failed,* he said to himself—but felt nothing. He was unstoppable, like a tongue poking after a loose tooth. "I wasn't enough," he said aloud. And the sadness indeed came, but it was of a different nature, sympathetic rather than self-directed. "Mom," he whispered, and winced instantly, expecting the crippling blow of grief immeasurable. But instead of the usual tide rushing at him, this time the sensation was within, a single knock with expanding reverberations, as though someone had struck a gong.

The wind started up then, in the fat warm currents that mean rain; and the boy on the porch rested his chin on his arms, thinking nothing, watching the storm blowing down into the countryside, watching it moving the world around.

Chapter Twenty-two

House Call

I suppose it's time I stopped using that little disclaimer, which for a while became automatic—"I'm not a native." When I came here, it was true enough, although I didn't come from so very far away. I came straight out of school to work with Dr. Greene, meaning to get some good solid clinical experience. It was to be just a stepping-stone, of course. I had great things in mind for the future—a big practice in the city, brilliant diagnoses, my name in the textbooks, maybe even a disease named for me.

Dr. Greene wasn't even my first choice, if you want to know. I'd wanted to go right into an urban practice. And I don't think I was his first choice, either. But I hadn't the capital to set myself up right away or the academic standing to talk my way into a partnership in the city, and he hadn't any other applicants; so we lucked into one another.

I showed up with a set of slick tools in a black leather bag stamped with my initials, and impatience all through my body. Two years at the outside, and then on to greater things, I promised myself, stepping down from the train. I quite expected to change the face of medicine in this part of the country during my short stay. After all, I knew all about the newest treatments, and I guessed that old Greene, with his pokey house visits, hadn't kept in touch as he should have done. I planned to dazzle him, and dazzle Naples, and move on.

He came to get me at the station; to me, he looked like any old country dweller, and I couldn't have picked him out from a crowd. But I suppose I was unmistakable, an Earnest Young Doc. He strode up to where I was standing on the platform, and put out his hand.

"I'm Greene," he said.

"Maxwell," I told him.

"Come on then," he said. "We have a patient."

I was surprised: apparently I wasn't to have a chance to get my bearings before being rushed off to someone's bedside. I followed the old man to his car, thinking hard.

I had heard that Greene was a soft old fellow, nice to underlings; clearly I'd been misled. From all evidence, he was turning out to be a 'grinder,' a member of the gruff old school. One of those country docs who carried a chip on his shoulder and who enjoyed tormenting their ambitious juniors. There were dreadful stories passed around about these men: how they whisked you from the train to the hardest cases imaginable, the ones who hadn't much time left, and made it look like you had killed them with your incompetence.

I looked sideways at Greene, taking in the beetling brows, the grim expression. They linked up nicely with my mental image of the tyrants of country practice. I quailed: many a new doctor had broken down and wept in the hands of a grinder. Then I rallied: it would not happen to me.

We drove a ways up into the hills. It was many years ago, but that first house call is vivid in my memory. I could lead you there now, if you wanted. We passed house after house without slowing, and then we hit an uninhabited stretch of road. More like a rutted cow path than a road, actually. Only cows wouldn't be up so high.

"Have we come too far?" I ventured.

Greene raised his eyebrows, and shook his head.

I had heard how to handle grinders. Haggard survivors of their mistreatment had come back from the dead and instructed us all. The worst thing, they said, was to speak overmuch. 'Whatever you do,' I had been told by one escapee, who broke into perspiration at the mere memory of his travails, *'don't volunteer.'* So I kept quiet now, and we bumped along even further, until it was clear we had missed our destination. He must stop soon and admit his mistake, I thought with satisfaction. I confess my spirits rose at the prospect of so early a victory for me.

But then we came upon a house. A hut, to be precise. Twelve by twelve feet, and two windows set opposite one another, so that one looked right through the one large room and out at the mountainside. There were two men outside as we drew up, one fortyish and one twenty, and across their laps they held rifles.

Greene didn't hesitate, but opened the gate which stood in front of the house. There was no fence, just the gate, and he could easily have walked around it, which was what I began to do. But he caught my sleeve and pulled me with him through the freestanding hip-high doorway. The men didn't move as we went by. I nodded to them, but they didn't so much as twitch. It was as if they hadn't even seen us.

It was gathering dusk outside by now, but inside the house it was like midnight. A low fire burned in the grate, giving little light. At first I could see nothing at all. Greene must have known his way around, because he bustled right in while I stood in the doorway, and within a minute or two had lit a kerosene lamp and was adjusting the flame.

God! how to explain my first sight of that place, my first patient visit. In medical school, it had been hinted that some rural dwellings might be unsanitary; the subject had been dismissed again with blithe references to boiling water, and keeping a clean examining space. There was no clean space that I could see; and from the looks of things, no hot water to be had. I stood still, literally afraid to touch anything; the thought of defiling my lovely shiny medical instruments by bringing them out made me shudder.

Greene went right over to one of the beds below the far window, and bent over the figure lying there. I moved closer, and saw what I took to be an elderly man.

"Same thing again, Mrs. Price," said Greene.

The patient made a muffled reply.

"We'll take a look first," said Greene, putting his bag down on the bedside chair. "We'll have to roll her over," he told me.

I couldn't imagine touching those filthy blankets or that foul-smelling creature, but I nodded and began to roll my sleeves up.

"I'll just wash," I said.

"No use," said Greene, with a smile. "You'd have to go out to the pump, and we don't have time for that."

Now I knew he was a grinder. He had brought me up here to humiliate me and watch me squirm. I could see that it was hardly an emergency case; yet he had insisted on dragging me up here straight from the station, as though someone were dying.

"This is Mrs. Price," he told me. "Mrs. Price, this is my new assistant. Dr. Maxwell."

"We'll teach him a thing or two," came out of the creature's mouth, followed by a series of crackling noises which I belatedly understood to be laughter.

"That we will," said Greene. "Maybe Maxwell would like to ask you a few questions before we take a look."

"Nice to meet you, Mrs. Price," I said, smoothly. I was at

least comfortable with this part of medicine—taking histories. "What's the trouble?"

"Same thing," she said.

"Same thing," I repeated. "And what's that?"

"Can't get up," she said, and went off into that creaking laughter again.

"Mrs. Price had an accident—was it five years ago?"

"Five year, three month, two day," said Mrs. Price promptly, surprising me. "It were Betsy," she said to me. "Never trusted her, not from the moment we got 'er. Too wick for the price, what I told Clem. But he didn't listen." Bemused by her accent, which was ritish Isles swallowed in hill dialect, I let her go on. Too late, I realized my mistake. She digressed freely while I hung on, saying "Uh huh, uh huh," waiting for her to draw breath. Finally she did, and I slipped in my next question.

"How did the accident happen?" I asked. "Betsy kicked you, is that right?"

She looked confused, and then impatient.

"Betsy never kicked," she said.

"Then—how?" I fumbled.

"Ran off," she said. "And I lost my feet."

"Lost your feet," I repeated.

"Betsy ran away," explained Greene. "And Mrs. Price went after her, isn't that right, Mrs. Price?"

"Lost my feet like a ninny," said the old woman. "Like I hadn't lived here all my life."

"You mean you fell?" I asked.

The woman nodded, emphatically.

"I'd never a believed it, it hadn't happened," she said. "I lost my feet in the dark."

"She fell down the side of the mountain," said Dr. Greene, into my ear. "Snapped the spine at L2."

"Didn't she go to the hospital?" I asked, turning away from the patient.

"Hospitals are for dying," spat Mrs. Price, recalling my attention.

"But you went there for a little while, didn't you?" asked Greene. "And then they let you out, and you came back home."

She nodded.

"And have you had any other troubles since I saw you last?" asked Greene, smoothly taking up the questioning. My face burned; obviously, I'd failed at my very first task. I had done what all the textbooks cautioned against, and Let the Patient Take Control of the History. If Greene had left things to me, I'd have been there all day, saying 'Uh huh,' while the old woman talked.

"Just the same," she said.

"Good, good," he told her. "Well, let's take a look."

He lifted aside the bedclothes, and I saw an astonishing thing. Mrs. Price, whose wasted head lay on the pillow, and whose shrunken feet stuck out the other end, had an enormous swollen belly between, big enough for twins.

"Ascites," murmured Dr. Greene.

He did a thorough but effortless-looking examination, squinting at Mrs. Price's fingernails, feeling her calves gently.

"What am I looking for here?" he asked.

"Thromboses," I said, disdainfully. It was an easy question.

He stood up. "Time for you know what," he said cheerily.

"I hate this," said Mrs. Price, and squinted up her face.

"We'll need warm water and soap," said Greene.

The patient opened her mouth and roared, "Harry!" The younger of the two sentinels came to the doorway. "I told you get the water going," she said. Harry stepped across to the fireplace.

"It's nearly hot," he said.

"Nearly's not good enough," she said. The boy poked up the fire, scowling, and went out again. "What am I to do?" she said, turning to me. "Look what's happened to my house with them two running wild in it." Her chin quivered. "The door-step used to be white as milk," she said. "And you coulda eaten off anywhere on that floor."

I was embarrassed at the woman's tears, and didn't know where to look or what to say. Dr. Greene reached over and took her hand. "Your boys are a handful," he said.

"That they are," she sniffed, brightening a little. "Bigger than their pa, and twice as wild." She smiled. "He wasn't any too tidy himself," she said.

Finally, the water was hot enough.

"We'll just clean the area today," said Greene. "And then put on a new dressing. Mrs. Price is used to this, aren't you?"

"Get it over with," said she.

"Help me here," said Greene, to me. "We have to roll her onto her side."

We pushed and pulled very gently until Mrs. Price lay facing the window, with her back to us. Her gigantic belly rested on the bed, and she laid her arm across it, as though it were a pillow.

"You're not using that nasty stuff this time?" she said, over her shoulder.

"Not this time," said Greene.

"Hurry up," she said.

"We'll be as quick as we can," he said, and pointed to the dressings, which had started out some time ago as sterile white bandages, but which were now quite black with dirt. "Those need to be peeled away," he said. "That's about the worst part for her, so go gently."

I began to remove the dressings. What with the poor light and the general filth, it was hard to find the edges of the tape, except by feel, and there was quite a bit of resistance when I pulled them away from the skin, as though they'd become part of it. Mrs. Price gave a little cry as the last one came away. I gasped as the sores emerged: deep and wide, revealing a glimpse of bone.

"Now, a little wash," said Greene, taking my place at the bedside. I stood and watched him laving the wounds, bizarrely jealous. "Looking better this week," he said to Mrs. Price. "Are you doing what I said, and letting them shift you?"

"It's so much better on my back," she said, evasively.

"I know," he said. "But you really must try."

He rubbed on salve, and then moved aside, handing me the clean white bandages. I felt a rush of gratitude, taping them into place.

"The larger the better," he said. "Keeps out the germs."

"You done yet?" fussed Mrs. Price.

"All done," said Greene. "But you should probably stay there like that for a while. Saves them having to shift you later."

"All right," she grumbled.

"We'll see you next week," said Dr. Greene, leaning over her so she could see his face.

"Bye," she said to him. "Bye, Doctor Max," she added, a little louder.

"How do you like that?" said Greene, smiling. "A name for you already."

We left, again passing the silent men, going through the disembodied gate, shutting it carefully behind us. In the car, Greene smiled.

"Soon's we're gone," he said, "she'll have Harry in there, rolling her onto her back again."

"Shouldn't she be in the hospital?" I asked. "She needs regular care. Those sores."

"She won't have the hospital," he said. "And the sores have gotten a little better. They're just the things we treat, anyway."

"I've never seen ascites like that," I said, remembering.

He nodded. "She's pretty orange, too," he remarked. "Hard to tell in that light. Advanced hepatitis."

"Infectious?" I asked with horror.

"Alcoholic," he said, with a smile. "If you percussed out her liver it'd probably be smaller than a melon. Did you look under the bed?"

"No," I said.

"Dozens of mason jars," he said. "Good homemade stuff. She's got a lifetime supply right on hand. Her lifetime, anyway," he said, his brow wrinkling.

"In the hospital—" I began.

"In the hospital," he said, "we'd do a batch of procedures on her, and each one would leave her a little weaker than before. She'd last maybe two weeks of it. Up here, she'll live much longer."

"She can't be comfortable," I protested.

"She's more comfortable with what she knows," he said, firmly. "You heard her. Hospitals are for dying." His mimicry was excellent, completely without condescension.

"That belly should be drained," I argued.

"We do that when she lets us," he said. "She hates it, so I've got it down to every other week. I know it's hard for you," he said. "You've just learned about all these miracles that doctors and hospitals can do. You're eager to avail yourself of all that beautiful equipment." He was reading my thoughts, exactly. "Maxwell, welcome to the rest of your education. Here, you'll learn what we can't do." I was silent. "It's not so bad," he said. "In *can't,* there's always *can.*"

I didn't understand what he meant; we didn't speak any more, all the way back to the practice, which was open for evening hours. There was one woman in the waiting room; she'd been there twenty minutes, the nurse reported.

"Be with you in a minute," he said, popping his head into the waiting room. He washed up, and I after him, and then the patient was shown into the consulting room.

She was as different to Mrs. Price as anyone could be while still belonging to the same sex. About twenty, very beautiful, clearly well-off.

Dr. Greene introduced me, and the woman nodded politely. "I wanted to talk to you alone," she said. "I don't mean to be rude," she said, to me.

"Dr. Maxwell is a fully qualified physician," he said. "I will no doubt discuss this case with him. But if it will make you feel better . . ."

She nodded, not looking at me, and I tactfully withdrew.

Half an hour later, Greene came through to the dispensary, where I was chatting with the nurse.

"You'll be wanting your supper," he said to me.

I took the remark as implying weakness on my part.

"I'm fine," I lied. "I can last out the rest of the patients."

He raised his eyebrows.

"I'm starving, myself," he said, gently, and I felt ashamed of my defensiveness.

"I'd like to stay and help," I said.

"Thank you," he said gravely. "But there shouldn't be anyone else tonight. You can go on home, Miss Miles," he said to the nurse. When she was gone, he spoke again. "That last patient," he said. "Maybe I'm getting old?"

"The unmarried pregnancy?" I asked.

"Close," he said, surprised. "But a little wide of the mark. She's married."

"But pregnant," I said.

"Quite," said he.

"What did she want?"

"These girls get married so quickly," he said, irrelevantly. "Without even a moment's thought."

"She wanted to see you alone," I said.

"Exactly," said the old man, heavily. "I told her it was illegal. That I shouldn't even be listening to her." He sighed. "It's not the first time I've had to say that."

"It's a terrible thing," I said, wanting to comfort him.

"I used to think so," he said. "But," and he looked at me. "I've seen so many lives ruined. Bright young girls, with a chance of getting out from under the terrible burden of poverty. I see them when they're babies, all pink and fat and promising; and not much more than a dozen years later they're in the clinic, for their first. They've still got fire and

hope then, but after the baby comes they've changed a little.
And each one takes a little more out of them. By twenty-five,
they're old and used-up. They don't even remember the things
they used to dream of."

I stared, not sure what to say.

"The first time, maybe the second, they come to me and
ask," he went on. "I have to say no. Some of them give up
then, but others, the desperate ones, the ones with a little fire
left, they go off and get it done anyway. They end up my
patients again, bleeding to death or hideously infected. I don't
know what's right anymore."

In school, we had been taught that even therapeutic abortion was at best shakily justifiable. I had heard ugly rumors, of
doctors who flouted the law and lost their licenses.

"If it were legal," I said. "You'd do it?"

"I have four children myself," said the old man. He looked
at me. "Three of them girls, and my wife and I have tried to
bring them up sensibly. They have fine futures." He sighed. "I
don't know, Maxwell," he said. "But I ask you this. Why am I
the one to choose? That was a full-grown woman in there; I've
known her since she was a child, and know her to be highly
intelligent and reasonable. She's twenty-six years old; she
knows her mind, and her life. But she cringed before me like a
beggar. Why? I'm not God." He looked fierce as any god,
saying it. "I know," he went on, in a kinder voice, seeing my
confusion. "You think I'm not playing my part right. I'm supposed to be the wise old doctor, who knows right from wrong,
who can solve everything. When I was your age, I thought
that's what I'd be someday. If only," he patted my arm. "If
only it were that easy."

I worked for him for six years, until he retired. And then I
stayed on. Somewhere in that time, my dreams of a city practice dwindled and disappeared. I don't miss them. I hardly
remember what it was like to have them. Not that the life I
have chosen is perfect. If I had it to do over—I'd do the same
again. The thing is to choose knowingly, right or wrong, to
look things in the face. Then you *can't* regret; you can say, 'I
chose the best I knew at the time,' and let it lie.

There's always doubt, young man. Greene was right about
that. It doesn't go away. But if you make a choice, and stick to
it, and take the good with the bad—you've done all that you
can do. Otherwise, you are nothing, and your life counts for

little. Every life is a statement, right or wrong; conviction won't make your life smooth, but it will make it meaningful. That's all the wisdom I can offer you, as a wise old country doc.

Chapter Twenty-three

Good and Evil

S aturday afternoon, Joan and I took a drive.

"Where to?" I asked, when we'd strapped ourselves in, with the picnic basket behind us.

"Anywhere but here," she said, and her hand fluttered up toward mine where it rested on the wheel.

I drove north and west, picking up the Skyline Drive near its southern end. Suddenly we were on a trail through wilderness, following the path where it climbed the belly of the valley, the mountains watching us on either side like parents.

"Beautiful," said Joan.

It was; a man-made beautiful thing. People had died here, during the War, and some sixty years later, during my infancy, the path had been cut for cars, hundreds of hungry men working again. Hoover had started it, Roosevelt finished it, giving it over to the CCC. Government funds had flooded out over the impoverished land. Money spent on luxury during hard times: apparently incongruous, it had had a rejuvenating effect on the sagging spirit of a country.

I pulled off the road, bumping along to a campsite.

"Where are we going?" asked Joan.

"Surprise," I said, and we pulled into the campsite. Stone outdoor grills were scattered at intervals; two tents were set up, but there was no evidence of their occupants.

When I popped the trunk and brought out the tent, Joan's eyes widened.

"Well," she said.

"Just like we were kids," I said, grinning. "We missed all that hippie stuff."

"Gil," she said, laughing. "I've never slept in a tent."

"It's like a house," I told her, punching the canvas, "only uncomfortable."

She watched me struggling with it; a few minutes later, a man appeared from the direction of the other tents.

"I'm Bob Howard," he said. "Need a hand?"

"Mine don't seem to be doing me," I said. "Much good."

The man turned and shouted back toward the place he'd come from.

"My son," he said proudly, as a stocky boy appeared. "Bobby."

"Easy to remember," I said, and the three of us set up the tent.

"We come here every year," said Bob, when we were finished. "We belong to the birder's club."

"I bet you get to see some here," said Joan.

"Yes, ma'am," said Bobby. "It's a good place to come."

We thanked them for their help, and I invited them to share our picnic basket.

"I didn't pack much," whispered Joan. "And what about breakfast?"

"Don't look in the big cooler in the trunk," I told her.

"Aren't you the magician today," she said, squeezing my arm happily. Competence always pleased her.

A little while later, we were joined by a couple from the other tent, a boy and girl, not long out of high school. They'd been hiking, they told us, flopping down. The girl had short shorts on, and long red scratches on her legs.

"I'm not much of a hiker," she said. "Cal's the outdoor nut."

"Women," said Cal, looking to me for sympathy. I gave him a level look, which might have been taken as agreement. He was so young yet; he didn't know the character of the battles to be fought. Unless he wised up early, he'd come to at fifty to realize that he'd misidentified his enemy, and that it wasn't this girl beside him, nor any of the other girls he'd bring up here.

Without planning it, we all joined for supper, and afterward we sat around looking into the Howards' efficient campfire.

"Thank God it's too early for mosquitoes," said Joan.

"We need a guitar," said Cal's girl, Sandy, "to make this really perfect."

"Well," said Bob. "It so happens."

"Dad," said Bobby.

"Go on, son, get it," said his father. "Make this lady's night perfect."

The boy fetched his guitar, and played us a couple of songs. Sandy took the instrument after a while; she was much more accomplished, and the two of them worked up harmonies while the rest of us listened.

"He came to see me yesterday," Joan whispered.

"Why didn't you tell me?" I asked. "Are you all right?"

She nodded. "I think he's leaving soon," she said. Her eyes glistened in the firelight. "I think he hasn't gotten what he came for."

Bobby and Sandy were singing "Barbara Allen." Joan's statement, coming as it did against a poignant patch of music, threaded with the rising and falling of the two young voices, seemed final and sad.

"I've been so afraid," I said.

"I know," said Joan.

Bobby hit a wrong note, and the singing broke off suddenly.

"What brings you two up here?" asked Cal idly, during the interval.

"We ran away," I said, looking at Joan. "No one knows we're here."

"Hey, us, too," said Cal, smiling. "Our parents would freak."

"Hell, boy," I said. "There's better things than parents to run from."

Construction on the Center had to be stopped for a while, of course, but within two weeks we were back at work. To make up time, we worked at full speed, six days a week, and with Devlin's approval, I hired myself an assistant. At the end of the day I was exhausted but happy: everything had changed. The men had discarded their animosity as easily as taking off a hat: they looked at me now when they spoke; they called hello to me when I came on site; they told me obscene and complicated jokes. Somehow, I had gained their respect. I liked my work; liked being a boss, liked being accepted by the other men. We were all putting in overtime, but for me the days were easier.

I was spending a lot of time at Stokes's. Since that one sensational day, I had enjoyed a kind of celebrity in the bar, as though I had committed some heroic deed by happening upon Amanda Crawford's dead body. Here, too, I was accorded greater respect than before. I was no longer on the fringes; the regulars moved their chairs so that I might join them; my opinions were solicited, and scoffed at; I was right in the thick of things now.

I was sitting at my regular table near the counter the day Sam and Ned came in. They were arguing about something, as usual; involved, they didn't see me as they went up to Wallace. I caught shreds of their conversation as they went by.

"I tell you that's what he said," said Ned.

"Well, I don't believe it," said Sam. "Willie Kyle was never right about anything in his life."

". . . about this," said Ned.

". . . turn on a buddy . . ." said Sam.

"Not my buddy . . ." said Ned.

They stopped when they saw me.

"Shh," said Ned, unnecessarily. "Hey," he said to me.

"Hey," I said. "What's the fight about?"

"Nothing," said Ned, quickly.

"You all are raising a ruckus about something," I said, smiling.

"Nothing worth talking about," said Sam.

I soon found out that what Sam and Ned had been so heatedly discussing was being passed around the whole town; everyone was debating the same matter, everywhere I went. And everywhere I went, a chorus of *shhh* went before me; and at my back, the buzzing started up again. I withstood it as long as I could, hoping to hear enough to explain; but it was no use. Something about a hair ribbon was all I understood, and that was because Effie Sweet was deaf, and didn't hear the shushing in time.

"What the hell are you all whispering about?" I demanded finally one day in front of Purdy's.

"Tell him," said Lester Wilson. "Go on, somebody."

"All right," said Harry Page.

"What is it?" I asked Harry.

"Ask your brother," said Lana Wilson, shrilly.

"Shush," growled Harry. "It's hard to believe," he said. "We none of us believed it when it was only Willie saying it. But then some others, they seen it, too."

"What?" I asked. "What did they see?"

"Your brother, Jack," said Harry. "Well—"

"He's the one stole the little girl," cried Lana.

"What?" I said.

"Lester, hush your wife," said Harry. He turned to me, apologetically. "Willie saw Jack with a whole bunch of baby things late at night. A long time ago, he didn't think nothing of it but warnt it strange, until the little girl was found, and then he got to thinking."

"Willie never did any thinking," I said.

"Well, now, you're right about that," said Harry, agreeably. "I guess it was the rest of us did the thinking. But we only started thinking at all after it come out that Sarah Jane Turkel saw it, too."

"What did Sarah Jane see?" I asked.

"Well now, this was a few days later. Jack gave her a ride home; and she saw a pink hair ribbon on the floor of the truck."

"So what?" I said. A hair ribbon, to hang a man.

"Well, no one's accusing anyone of anything, exactly," said Harry. "We know there's penalties for that. But it just makes us uncomfortable, like, not knowing."

"I have a little girl myself," said a woman.

"You're his brother," said Harry. "We want to do the right thing. What do you think?"

I stood there for a moment.

"Why would he do it?" I asked.

"We thought about that," said Harry. "And about how he and Beth used to go together, and how they both got divorced around the same time. Acourse it could jes be coincidence, but—"

"Coincidence, shoo," said Elva Wilson, behind Harry.

"Hush, now," said Harry. "Well, now, I'll get to the point. It seemed likely to us that maybe Beth made Jack divorce Marie while she divorced Billy, and then she, I mean Beth, changed her mind and wouldn't marry him, I mean Jack. That'll make a man mad." The crowd nodded. Harry went on, apologetically. "He's a good fellow, is Jack, and I wouldn't say nothing agin him," and he looked at me. "But he's strange. You know what I mean," and I nodded. "Kinda unpredictable."

That was true; considering, I could just barely believe that Jack might want to take revenge on Beth, after all these years. But in this way—? I couldn't believe it of him. And then I was swamped by memory, the cold dank barrel of my childhood, the cold blood of my brother, leaving me to die. The child is father to the man.

"What do you think?" repeated Harry.

"I . . . don't know," I answered, finally.

"We've known Jack Corbin all our lives," said Sam Lucas, pushing through the crowd to me. "Harry, you been hunting with him a dozen times. LuAnn, he fixed your car for free when you was hard up. And you," he said, turning to me. "You oughta be ashamed."

The crowd murmured, and there was a lot of scuffing of feet, while people decided whether they were going to stay or go. Then suddenly the cluster broke apart, like a seeding dandelion in a tornado, and I was alone on the street with Sam. He spat in the gutter and walked away.

Beth herself didn't believe it.

"They're saying the most terrible things," she told me, when I dropped into the florist's one afternoon.

"I know," I said.

"Oh, G.I.," she said instantly, disappointed. "You don't believe them, do you?"

"Well," I said.

"Shame on you," she said. "You should know better."

"They're always gossiping about somebody," I said. "It'll blow over."

"Ha," she said. "Not the way this town talks. I'll die before it will." She brought her attention back to the matter of my treachery. "I don't *believe* you," she said.

"Honestly, Beth, I don't know."

"Well, I *do*," she said. "My opinion ought to count for something."

But it didn't. It was the character of town talk that no one person's opinion stood alone. No one person ever said anything, except Sam Lucas, who made his stance clear early on. The tale was told in whispers, gathering form with its passage in the way a snowball grows rolling down a hill. There was no recourse, no way to refute the accusations, because they were never actually made. It was innuendo and suspicion; and quickly Jack was an object of hatred.

He took it well; he had never much cared what people said about him, but I was surprised how well he stood up under the constant whirl of rumor. I couldn't confront him, of course; how would it do to ask one's brother if he had kidnaped and killed a little girl? And of course he didn't volunteer any information. I didn't understand him: in his place I would have been eager to defend myself. As they whispered, the people watched him, waiting to be released from their suspicions. One word from him could have stopped the rumors, but he did nothing. I watched him as he came alone to Stokes's, taking the table near the window and drinking his regular quotient, neither hurrying through nor lingering there. I had the feeling that he hardly noticed that the men he usually sat with had moved, and were now surrounding me. I realized that his life was less changed than ours by the flurry of gossip. He was indifferent to us. Irritated, I began to hearken to the tales I was hearing, and gave them more credibility than before.

The long hours at work were telling on me; one Friday about a month after Amanda had been found, I left work early, putting my assistant in charge.

"Corbin, you lazy sonovabitch," cried Walker as I left, and I waved a cheery good-bye.

It was her half day, but Joan wasn't in the house. I wandered into the kitchen, looking for a note. I got myself a glass of water from the tap and drank it leaning against the closed porch door. Through the glass and screen, I thought I saw a movement. I put my face close to the door to see.

It was Joan, striding away from me, away from the house, toward the bottom of the garden. I pushed the door open and called to her, but she didn't hesitate. I went after her, still sipping from the glass, stepping carefully on my mother's paving stones. Once they had been white, and the grass around them trimmed. Now they were overgrown and heavily mossed.

Where was Joan going? That way lay only the roses and the little birdbath, and far beyond those the old workshop. It had fallen into disuse since Jack had moved everything out; we stored old gardening tools there now, and things we no longer wanted but couldn't bring ourselves to throw away. I hadn't been out there in more than a year.

"Joanie," I called, but there was no answer, just a glimpse of white blouse flashing through the trees. "Damn," I said, brushing away a spider that had dropped engagingly onto the back of my hand. I quickened my pace.

I caught up to her at the rose border; she was sitting on one of the small stone benches flanking the birdbath, absorbed in examining something in her lap. Something red; I couldn't see it.

"Hide-and-seek?" I asked, a little breathlessly, from five feet away.

She looked up, and her face changed. She dropped the item she'd been holding; I bent to pick it up. At first it didn't mean anything to me: a red shoe, a little sneaker, the laces dirty, with a mashed blob of chewing gum on the sole. Then I realized.

"Oh, Joan," I said.

She looked at me blankly.

"I didn't hit her, they're wrong about that," she said. "She fell."

"Oh, God." I sat down on the bench beside her, a heavy thump, the glass I was still holding sloshing water into the weeds. I set it down, idiotically precise about it.

"She loved me," said Joan. "She was happy with me."

"Oh, my God," I said.

"She was all by herself on the street. I found her all by herself, Gil." Her voice was persuasive. "That's when I knew."

"Knew?" I repeated, my voice cracking.

"She wasn't being taken care of," said Joan. "Can you believe, out on the street by herself? Just a baby."

"How," I began. "Where?"

"She had trouble sleeping at first," she said, not listening to me, looking down at the shoe I was holding. "She had nightmares. So I gave her some of my tablets crushed up in water. I knew better than to give them to her dry," she told me, looking into my face now with wide, mad eyes.

"All that time," I said.

"We had fun together," she said, in a light, happy voice, remembering. "We played games. *I* never let her wander around alone. She was happy." Her face hardened. "She never asked for Beth once."

Without thinking, without even being aware that I was moving, I was on my feet, shouting.

"How could you?" I cried. "How could you do such a thing?" I took hold of her shoulders, and shook her back and forth, her hair spilling across her features, brushing like silk against my hands.

"She needed me," she said, when I let her go. "She needed someone to look after her." Her face was red and her eyes wet, but her voice was even. "Her own mother didn't want her."

"How can you say that?" I said.

"She didn't," she said. "Not from the first."

"You saw what Beth was going through. And you . . . consoling her. It's demented, Joan, it's—evil." I was whispering now, my own words terrifying me.

"Beth never wanted her," said Joan stubbornly. "I wanted her."

"You can't just take what you want," I said, but the anger had gone out of me. I was numb, dead in places. I thought of sitting down again, but my knees wouldn't bend.

"She was happy with me," said Joan. "I fixed up the shed like a little house. I brought her all the books she wanted." Her face lit up. "How she could read, Gil. So much like you. She was reading fifth grade books."

"That's wonderful," I said, dully. "And now she's dead." Joan flinched, as though I'd hit her. "You gave her too many tablets."

"She fell," said Joan.

"You kept her in a *shed,*" I said. "She must have been afraid out there. She tried to get up, to escape, to go back home—"

"She was *happy,*" said Joan, in a panicky voice. "She didn't want to go back."

"—all those dangerous things in there," I said.

"I was careful," said Joan.

"—and maybe she lay there for a little while. Before she died." I looked at my wife; she was crying. "You killed her," I said.

"It was an accident," she whimpered. "I found her—oh God—lying so still. Like a little doll, all the life gone."

She could hardly speak through her tears. I felt ashamed. "Joan," I said.

"I *had* to leave her alone sometimes," she whispered, fiercely. "I couldn't help it."

"*Joan,*" I said; she looked at me. "Is that where you went . . . all those times?"

She nodded, tightly.

"You weren't—" I said, then stopped myself. So many clues; why hadn't I seen them?

"It's kind of a habit, now," she said, smiling a little. "I come here just to sit."

"I thought," I said. She nodded.

"I almost told you," she said. "That day."

I remembered her tiny voice, the telephone ringing.

"You could have told me," I said.

She shook her head. "You were so worried," she said. "So worried, about so many things."

I thought of something.

"Does anybody else know?" I asked.

She looked away.

"Who?" I urged.

"He cleaned it all up for me," she said, still hiding her face from me. "He said he'd take care of everything."

"Jack?" I said. "Jack knows?"

"I didn't know he'd put her *there,*" she said, turning back to me. "I don't know what made him do that."

"You went to *Jack?*" I couldn't believe it.

"He's not so—moral—about things," she said distantly. "He just *does.*" She reached out, touched the shoe with a finger. "He forgot this," she said.

"Listen to me," I said. "Joan. Jack is not your husband. Look at me." She did. "What happens to you, happens to me. Do you understand?"

She hesitated, then nodded.

I put out my hand; after a moment, she laid hers into it, unspeaking. Abruptly, I was filled with a new power, filling up my arms and legs, making me bigger than I was, more confident.

"I'll take care of this," I said. She nodded. I led her back to the house, and sat her down.

"Jack won't tell," I said. "I'll kill him first."

I left her there and walked swiftly back to the rose border and then past it, plunging into the denseness beyond. I moved faster and faster, until I was jogging, the creeper pulling at my hair and dangling into my face, the branches slapping at my chest, the vines whipping up to trip me. I reached the workshop, and stood before it, breathing hard; then I pulled the door open.

One quadrant of the big room, it was easy to see, had been rigged up as a kind of living quarters; the floor there was cleaner and the shelves nearby empty, with sharp dusty shapes on them, as though they'd recently been used to hold books or piles of clothing. I found a little footprint, and winced; then scrubbed it away with my foot. I tumbled through the crowded far shelves until I found a small box; I stuffed the sneaker into it.

Carrying it, I went back to the house.

"I'm going to do a little gardening," I told Joan, who was sitting in the rocking chair by the cold fireplace. "Before it gets dark. A little gardening," I repeated.

"All right," she said, tonelessly.

I made a good job of it, choosing a patch about twenty feet into my father's land, chopping and hacking until I had a clear patch of earth. I dug straight down, turning the soil over with the spade, ripping open a seed packet I had taken from the neglected shed. I dug the shoe in, burying it deep. *Dust to dust.* I scattered the seeds, willing the chives to grow tall in this mild autumn, to blend with the other foliage. I finished the job and put the tools away, locking the shed.

Back in the house, I told Joan, "I've put in chives."

"Chives," she said.

"It's a little late, but I never was much of a gardener. Tomorrow I'll clean out the shed. It needs it, after all this time."

"It needs it," she said, obediently.

I put my arms around her. Everything I had ever known of ambivalence had fallen away in the last two hours. There was only me and her and my fierce need to protect her. At any cost. She'd done wrong, but it didn't matter to me; I wanted to wallow into that wrong, join into it with her. I wanted us together in it; I could not leave her alone with what she'd done.

It didn't even matter that she'd gone to Jack first for help. Nothing mattered now except the two of us, undivided. Her presumed infidelity had weighted me more than I knew; now relieved of that burden, I was giddy. *She hadn't slept with Jack.* It made a rhythm with the digging. In a crisis, she'd hesitated to trust me. But I had been weak then; I was weak no longer; she would trust me now. I took her sins onto myself, unquestioning. And my heart sang. *Forgive me, Beth.* I closed my eyes tight and sent up a prayer to the woman whose daughter had been sacrificed on the altar of my marriage. Joan and I were going to be whole again now, and strong.

That was how I learned it, after all. Beth had said *choose,* and I had chosen, but it hadn't meant anything until now. All of my life I had struggled with the shadows, avoided them, made fitful attempts to join them. And the shadow had been within me all along; it had lain there dormant, waiting. Waiting to show me what a man was for.

This was what he was for: to protect, to guard, to build his strong house, and keep it strong. In an afternoon, all of my doubt had changed to passion, a man's dark passion for his home, his way of life.

My forefathers had carried that passion onto the battlefields with them, a century before; my father and brother had been wounded defending their country. Seeking combat, I had found myself behind a desk; warless, I had spent my life casting about for something to defend, something to belong to. Something worth fighting for, dying for. Now I had found it, my war and my country. Joan. Joan. There was nothing else.

* * *

No one came nosing around my patch of stunted seedlings. The shoe rotted away in quiet; we were safe. But Joan had changed that day, and forever after. Twenty years later, she would still be battling a memory she couldn't even name. We never spoke about it; I wasn't sure she understood what she had done, what I had done. I knew, though, and the knowledge made me powerful. In the house I was her guardian, and she took the strength I gave her and went out into the world with it. No one noticed any change in her. It was done. It was over. We had changed, but we were safe.

The silence between Jack and me had its beginnings in that afternoon. Rightly, I should say it started thirty years before, in a dark moldy barrel in my father's cellar. I had feared and worshipped my brother these long years; and he had all the time been like me. Not my usurper, not my devil; just a man. Knowing this about him ought to have brought us closer; it ought to have trampled down the barricades between us. Instead it built them up, higher and thicker and absolute. Jack knew too much; he held our secret. Logically I ought to have befriended him, to ensure his complicity. But I was outraged, coldly punitive—he had taken it upon himself to defend my territory, my house and garden; he had appropriated sin which was none of his; I hated him. I was glad for the outbreak of war; it had been too long in the coming. I hoped for the day when we should be pitted against one another, and I should win.

Joan went off to visit her parents for two weeks in November; I was left alone in the house on Worth Street, cooking for myself again. I had taken to eating my suppers on the porch, looking over the land my great-great-grandfather had marked out for himself when he'd brought his bride to Virginia. The Ridge glowered in the distance, anchoring the horizon. I drank my coffee and wondered what it might be like to grow up in an unmountainous place.

A footstep on gravel. I looked, and it was Beth, walking up the road toward me. She came into the yard and stood there smiling, the same summer smile, and without a word, I put down my cup and followed her. We walked into the fields which had been fenced off now, and chopped up, and developed. Farming didn't pay; the pastures of our youth were transformed into subdivisions and rental properties. More buildings, less land. The geography of Naples was changing.

We walked without speaking, winding our way toward the river. When we got there, I spread my jacket on a flat piece of ground; she dropped onto it, and I sat a little way away, hugging my shirt-sleeved arms in the breeze.

"Winter soon," her first words.

"Yep," I said. "And then spring."

"I wonder if winter's the same other places," she said.

"In Florida it stays warm all year."

"I know. I mean up north."

I was silent.

"I've figured things out," she said. "I used to think it was just me. But it's not—it's Naples, it's the life I've had here. Somewhere I went wrong, and I can't go back."

"Wrong?" I said.

"I think they're right, you know; I really do take after old Lucy." She smiled. "Never satisfied." She tossed her hair off her shoulders.

"You're leaving?" I said.

"Not running away," she said. "Running to." Then, not looking at me, biting her lip, "G.I., did you ever have something that you wanted, something you wanted *so bad?* Something impossible?"

For a moment, I saw her again as she'd been at sixteen—her skirt tucked under her legs, her knees drawn up. The darkness softened the signs that daylight picked out to tell you she was past thirty. The sweater thrown across her shoulders participated in the illusion. Even the air smelled different, the breath of a long-ago wartime summer. She had loved Jack then, I knew, but she had trusted me more. She had made of me a confidant; awkward as I had been, it was the first beautiful thing that had happened to me. I had had fantasies about her —the usual thing, rescuing her from disaster, sweeping in where no one else dared and saving her. Very chaste daydreams they were, involving great danger and bravery and very little sex. After the rescue, she'd turn to me and cry, "I've been so blind," or some such nonsense. And I would give a sad little smile, as if to say, I've been here all along. And we'd kiss.

The fantasies ended there, not from any lack of ingenuity on my part, but because the kiss stretched the boundaries of even my fertile imagination. The notion of Beth Miller placing her lips on my downy, unmoustached own, of her clasping my slight frame to her bosom, were frankly ridiculous, and I prudently stopped my dreaming there, aware that to carry it too far would be to threaten it, to force it to disintegrate into folly.

"Beth," I said, at exactly the moment she said "G.I."

"You first," I said, after we'd laughed a little.

"Well," she said, looking across the water. "I've felt something for a long time—wanted something. For a while I thought it was Jack. I guess I never really believed it was Billy." She hunched her shoulders, thinking. "I guess I was using him, all right. Trying to get the hell out of here."

"But why?" I asked. The world to me seemed just a multitude of strangers.

"Oh, I don't know," she said. "The wildebeest. I feel like *I* have a wild beast inside me, and I have to find something to feed it, to calm it down." She thrust her hand into the pocket of her skirt, bringing out a silver flask. She uncapped it and drank with a practiced fluidity. "It likes bourbon," she said, laughing, offering the flask to me. I took a mouthful, and passed it back.

"So you're going away to scavenge for the beast," I said.

"It sounds crazy," she agreed. "But I'm afraid that no matter where I go the beast will still be with me. I have to *know,*" she said. "I have to *know* if there's food out there somewhere. I'm afraid I won't find out," she looked into the mouth of the flask, "before I die."

I shivered. She capped the flask and laid it down.

"You're cold," she said.

"A little," I said. She moved closer to me, and for one long moment we saw each other very close, and I smelled her hair. And then we were together on the ground, moving gently like we were in water.

"That's right," she said once, and then was silent.

Afterward, I was never sure how it happened; it was so easy, like another fantasy, only this one adult and complete. So dreamlike, so fluid, everything accomplished gracefully, and without hesitation.

"Well," she said, when we were finished. Her breathing was loud in my ear.

She sat up after a while, and I pulled myself up on an elbow.

"I'll miss the mountains," she said softly, the implication of her words putting an ache into me, and a fear.

We didn't go back right away; we watched the night drape itself over the mountains and the river, sitting close together. I put my arm around her, that delicate possessive gesture so hard won, so important.

She stayed that night, sleeping with me in the bed I'd had as a child; the mattress barely held us. We curled and lay quiet, her knees bent, holding mine. Sleeping, dreaming nothing.

In the morning I made breakfast. A kind of jubilation feast —pancakes and eggs and grits. She awoke while I was cooking, and appeared in the doorway in my bathrobe. She wrinkled her nose.

"What is all that?" she said.

"Thanksgiving," I said happily, filling her plate.

We ate for a while in silence, concentrating on the tastes and smells and the magical process of chewing, the counterpoint swallow of coffee following syrup. There was nothing else for a time, and then Beth reached her hand across to me.

"Beautiful day," I said.

"Uh-huh," she agreed, gathering up my fingers, leading me from the table.

I built a fire in the living room fireplace, and we lolled before it, the bathrobe dropping off her shoulders, her white skin revealing itself for my greedy touch. We spent the day there, putting new logs into the grate, laughing over the old photograph albums I pulled down from the bookshelf.

"And who's this?" asked Beth, pointing to a pudgy toddler.

"Jack," I said. "No, maybe me. No," peering closer, "it's Jack."

"You all looked a lot alike back then," she remarked.

"All children do," I said.

"No," she said. "You and Jack changed later. You went different ways, like a path forking." She forked with her fingers, to show me.

"We're very different," I said.

"Who should know better than me?" said Beth, putting her head on one side, her hand mischievous on my belly. The innuendo awoke my desire, and for a while the books of yellowed snapshots went ignored. Beth sat up suddenly after, much as she had done the night before on the riverbank. I looked up at her, apprehensive.

"Food," she said. "Food, or I'll die right here."

I laughed, and we helped each other up, and fairly ran to the kitchen.

It was food and love and laughter for three days; and through them all, my senses were glutted; I felt new.

"No," she said, on the third morning.

"No what?" I said.

"No, it couldn't have happened before," she said. "That was what you were going to ask."

Beth, my goddess and my prize. Through some happy chance, I had won her; I was filled up.

On the evening of the last day, we sat on the porch after supper, swollen with food.

"Things might have been different," said Beth, "without the beast."

I understood.

"Where will you go?" I asked.

"North," she said. "I want to see if it's really as horrible as everyone says." She smiled. "I have a cousin in New Jersey."

"What will you do?" I asked. She shrugged.

"I have some sympathy money left," she said. "Lucy and Joe won't want to help me. I think I'm the most interesting thing that ever happened to them; they want to keep me around to weep on. I'll miss Daddy though," she said. "I figure I'll careen around, see the world a little."

"New Jersey," I said.

"Oh, I won't stay there," she said. "I don't think I'll ever stay anywhere again. You know I wouldn't have stayed here this long—" and she stopped.

"Except for Amanda," I supplied.

The evening seemed to settle around the word, and it seemed to me that the world suddenly became a little harsher, more rock, less grass. The wind swept across the porch: winter was indeed on its way.

"I resented her from the beginning," she said. She bounced her fist against a knee. "I have *hated* myself for feeling that way." She looked at me. "Is that horrible?" she asked. "Are you disgusted?"

"No," I said. "Of course not."

"Joan is," she said. "She could tell, right away. The way she *looked* at me sometimes."

"I thought you all were friends," I said, surprised.

"Of course," said Beth. "That doesn't mean we can't hate each other a little." She frowned. "Don't get mad, okay?" she asked. "I mean, I hate to talk against your wife."

"It's okay," I told her, and oddly it was. It seemed as though the world itself was different, temporary, all rules broken. Beth and I were lovers; here the bond between us was the oldest and most primitive possible.

"I had the feeling she was glad about Amanda," she said. "Now see how terrible I am."

"What do you mean?" I asked.

"Well, like she thought it served me right. I don't know," said Beth, turning away. "It's crazy."

"She has changed," I said, carefully.

"We all have," said Beth. "She's colder, but weaker. Or maybe she's only like that with me. Sometimes it's almost like she's afraid of me," she said. "I remind her." She added in a low voice, "She reminds me."

"That's only natural, I guess," I said, the sweat crawling down my back, but my voice firm and even.

"It's terrible to say," she said. "But I think I can get over Amanda." She looked thoughtful. "There was a time I couldn't speak her name."

"I know," I said.

"You know how it is," she said. "Losing a child. It breaks your heart in two. Before, and after."

"Yes," I said.

"How can one life hold so much sadness? I used to wonder how I'd survive it. I can't imagine what it must have been like for Joan. I lost one child. She lost two."

"Yes," I said.

"For her it was like losing Emily all over again. For me," she said, and paused. "It was like a chapter closing."

"Which chapter?" I asked.

"The Jack chapter," she said, raising her eyes to mine slowly.

"Jack," I said.

"You really don't know," she said. "Jack told me that you didn't, but I couldn't believe it."

"Didn't know what?" but I was beginning to suspect, seven years late.

"Amanda was Jack's child," she said, simply. "Couldn't you really tell?"

"Of course," I said. "Of course." In the silence that followed, I put it all together: Jack's reluctance to bring his girl-friends around, Beth's absence during the time I had suspected Joan of being unfaithful. No wonder she had been so convinced I was mistaken. It had been a lengthy love affair, then, not just the schoolboy romance I had thought.

"It's not that I didn't want to be a mother," she said. "Maybe later on. But I didn't want her to die either," she said.

"Of course not," I said.

"I feel guilty anyway," she said. "Maybe that's part of what I'm leaving."

She pulled a cigarette from the pocket of my robe, and I lit it for her, shielding the match flame from the breeze.

"How do you men *do* that?" she asked, laughing, drawing on the filter. "It's funny, all the men I know can do that, even if they don't smoke."

"We learn it at our mothers' knees," I said, and then was serious. "Actually, I learned it from Jack."

"See, he's not so bad," said Beth. "I never have understood the two of you."

"How different we are?" I asked.

"How much the same."

"Why are you leaving him?" I asked.

"Because he won't leave with me," she said, and then, "No, I haven't asked him to. I just know he won't. Just like you," she said, teasing now. "And yet you all carry on this ridiculous fight, each waiting for the other to give in. But you're on the same side."

"No, we're not," I said.

"Of course you are," she said. "It's like a whaddyacallit—a siege. Both of you digging in. It's stupid."

"I don't see it that way," I said.

"I know," she told me. "But it's true all the same."

"I hate him," I said, telling her in these last minutes what I hadn't voiced before, making it a pact.

"Maybe a little," she said. "And maybe he hates you a little, too." She smiled. "That's not so bad. It keeps things hopping."

We were silent for a minute, and then she spoke again.

"So much has happened," she said. "So much, and so little." She lit another cigarette. "I don't understand how it can be like this. It's like the ocean, making all kinds of fuss, all that crashing and pounding and foam everywhere. But underneath nothing changes. Of course," she said, with a little laugh, "how would I know? I've only seen it in movies." She tapped her fingers against the porch railing. "I feel like the ocean inside out. The crash and the foam all inside me, and the little fishies swimming around outside like nothing's happened at all." She drew on her cigarette. "And in the end," she said, "nothing has happened. Nothing at all."

"Nothing?" I asked, hurt. She heard it, and looked at me.

"It's been lovely," she said. "It's been perfect."

"I love you," I said, twenty years of adolescent yearning in my voice.

"I love you, too," she said. "You know that."

And then I did know: she did love me, in the way that she could love. I saw that love changed nothing for her; it killed nothing about the beast she struggled with. I was abruptly very sad.

"I wish," I said.

"Oh, yes," said Beth. "Me, too." She put her cigarette out, and flicked ash from her fingertips. "Dear G.I.," she said, and kissed me lightly, completely without passion, as though we had not been entangled on the living room sofa not so many minutes before. "Tell Joan good-bye for me," she said. "Tell Jack, too."

She stood up, and went away to dress. She had brought nothing with her, and would take nothing away. Fifteen minutes later, we stood in the doorway, facing one another.

"Well," I said.

"Don't make me say it," she said, her voice straining a little behind the smile. "Don't make me say it to you."

And she was gone.

Joan came back two days later. She was looking rested and healthy; the haunted look was gone.

"I missed you," she said, hugging me.

"I missed you, too," I told her, and it was true.

Having her back settled things; the house seemed to sigh and assume its proper order around her, as though her absence had caused a temporary disturbance in the gravitational force. I noticed with relief the reduction of my own sensory perceptions: the porch light seemed normally dim again, the furniture solid and real. When Beth had moved among them, these things had risen up, floating in her wake. At Joan's touch they rooted again, so that the whole house sat vast and solid on its land; home again. Food went back to being food, no longer ambrosia; and I found it nourished me better than the nectar past.

My guilt I tucked away into a corner of my mind; and when at last I dared to bring it out again, I saw that it was not truly guilt at all. Just a secret, without any implications. Something with no power to hurt; something pure and complete; a resolution. Something I would remember, and cherish, and never, ever tell.

Chapter Twenty-four

Fireman's Daughter

Of course, I don't live here all year *round*. When the first breath of summer comes, I fly just as far and as fast as I can. It's hell in August here, you know. It's hell in August everywhere, unless you're on an island with a good stiff breeze. Or in Australia, I suppose. In Ireland, it rains all through August. Fifteen times a day. That's the price they pay for all those shades of green. I spent two weeks in western Ireland once, at the height of the rainy season; some misguided travel agent had assured me of the advantages of travelling off-season. It was beautiful, anyway; even through a curtain of rain, the magic of Connemara cannot be denied. Joyce Country. When I was twenty I wanted nothing more than to write like he did. Now I'm—well, older—and I write what I like, and I don't give a damn. I will confess that sometimes I take out old *Dubliners* and shed a tear or two, for what I will never have.

I grew up in a town just like this one. As like as two peas, as they say here. If someone slipped out in the middle of the night and changed the street signs and transported all of the inhabitants in a fair exchange, no one would ever know the difference. Whenever I go into town I deliberately leave off my glasses, and that extra bit of fuzziness makes everyone look familiar. We had the same grocers, I swear it; and the same florist and sheriff and firemen. My daddy was a fireman. It sounds so glamorous, but it wasn't; we hadn't many fires, and so all they did was sit around and play poker. And drink. In a fire, they'd have been in real trouble; all those men were highly flammable. My daddy actually died sliding down the fire pole. It was an extraordinary night. My sister was born, and Daddy broke his neck. They had to sponge him off the floor, he was so pickled.

I was thirteen when he died. A miserable age; they ought to ban it completely. Just skip from happy twelve to settled fourteen. I was all over freckles and elbows. My knees were bigger than my feet. My mother didn't know what to do with me; I wouldn't listen in class, and I wasn't old enough to work.

Finally, she left me alone, and a good thing, too; if I'd listened in class, I'd be something deadly now, a wife, or maybe a postmistress. Those schools squashed all the *vim* out of people. I saw it everywhere I looked. We learned everything from workbooks written a thousand years ago, by some person who'd never gone out of his house. Dick and Jane, stuff like that. No room at all for adventure. If I'd attended to my teacher—I don't even want to *think* about it.

I was a lonely little girl. Imagine being ugly *and* stupid. And poor. I look back on that sad little fledgling and shudder. If I hadn't been so stupid I might have given up on myself; but I didn't know enough to know that I was hopeless and without future, and so I set myself for glory. Maybe I was rebelling against the Dick and Jane books, or maybe I was seeking to create a more palatable world for myself, an alternative version, but anyway I decided I wanted to write stories. To tell a deeper truth was what I told myself, only I went the other way around, and overcomplicated things. Life's much simpler than we want to believe.

After I left school, I went to work in a bakery. It was a real old-fashioned kind, where we baked all night and opened early in the morning. Closed up shop at three, and came in again at midnight. The place smelled like heaven, and the night hours were so peaceful, just the other girl and me making buns and shaping loaves. The old woman Mrs. Mince, who did the fancy stuff, didn't talk much, and didn't like us talking. But she sang while she worked. Sad songs when she was blue, old spirituals and the more sentimental hymns. When she was angry, it was the bloodier hymns: 'By the light of burning martyrs/Jesus' bleeding feet I track,' that kind of thing. She was never really happy, but in her times of lighter gloom she'd bless us with Easter offerings, all that gladness and Festival Day stuff. My family wasn't very religious; most of what I knew about God came from the old baker woman, and so my impression of Him was bizarre indeed.

I might have worked there forever, and missed my destiny entirely, if it hadn't been for Mr. Walpole, Mrs. Mince's nephew, who came along about two years after I'd started working there. He'd failed out of some college or other, and his father, exasperated with him, had sent him to our town to teach him some good old-fashioned values. He didn't seem to have learned any, in the time that I knew him. He'd come into the shop and speak to us girls, who minded the place in the daytime; while he was standing there, he'd pinch all of the candied cherries out of the hot cross buns, leaving just the green pieces, and little gouges from his poking fingers. No one would buy them then, the way they looked.

The other girl and I disliked him, and we tried to keep out of his way when he came into the shop, but it was difficult. He'd come behind the counter, and follow us around, saying "Whoops!" when we turned around not knowing he was there, and bumped into him. He didn't try anything with me; I guess I was too young and plain looking for his tastes. But the other girl, Patsy, was a couple of years older, and plump, with dimples in her cheeks and on the backs of her hands. She was very pretty, and I envied her her laugh, which sounded like sleigh bells. I used to copy it myself at home, until my mother pressed cough mixture on me. She thought I had the croup.

"Patsy had a young man to whom she was engaged; but I noticed after a while that he wasn't coming round the shop so much anymore. And it had been a while since I'd heard the sleigh bells.

"What's happened to Ted?" I asked her. "Have you had a fight?"

"Oh, Deenie," she said. (That's what I was called then.) "I don't think I can talk about it."

But I wormed it out of her. It seemed Ted had come to meet her at the shop one afternoon when she wasn't expecting him, and he'd looked in the window and seen Mr. Walpole and Patsy, kissing.

"Ugh," I said.

"That's not all," wailed Patsy into the gingermen. "He's broken off with me, and I think—I think—"

What she thought would be obvious to any reader of dime romances. She thought she was pregnant.

"Oh, Patsy," I said. I was more upset by the image of Mr. Walpole's long white fingers poking into Patsy than I was by her condition.

"Gin and hot baths," I told her, briskly. My knowledge was gleaned from overheard scraps of conversation between my mother and aunt. "Try jumping down a flight of stairs."

"I've jumped from just about everything in this town except the bell tower," she said. "I'll try the gin."

The gin made her sick, she reported the next day. The hot baths left her scalded, but no less pregnant.

"We'll go see my Aunt Maisie," I said.

Maisie lived in the middle of town, a block away from my mother and sister and me. Her respectable-looking house sheltered a secret apothecary. Patsy and I went up the steps together, and knocked on the door.

"Aha," said Maisie, through the screen. "Come in."

She hadn't expected our call, but she took one look at Patsy and hustled her into a chair. "Wait here," she said, and went off into the kitchen.

"It's okay," I said, patting Patsy's hand absentmindedly, peering after Maisie.

She returned in a few minutes with a bottle, sealed with a cork, dripped around with wax.

"This'll do it," she said. Giving the bottle to me, she instructed, "Once in the morning, once at night."

"It's Patsy who needs it," I said, confused.

"Ah, but you'll give it to her," said Maisie. "And you'll set by her. She'll need someone with her."

We waited until the weekend, when Patsy's mother went to visit her own mother, and I gave Patsy the first dose on Saturday morning.

"I don't feel anything," she said.

"I think it takes a while," I told her, self-important, Maisie's deputy.

We played card games all day, and then at dusk I gave her the second dose. "I hope this works," said Patsy, drinking the brown stuff down, and making a face.

She started to cramp up around eight o'clock; the rest of the night passed in a wretched blur of fear for both of us. She was delirious, and I could not make her lie down in one place. She kept getting up and walking, all hunched over, and then she'd sit down suddenly and start to moan again. I mopped her forehead, and talked to her, unsure what else to do. In the course of the night, she told me everything—how dearly she loved Ted, and why she'd gone with Walpole.

"He was different," she babbled. "He doesn't come from here. My mama married a man from here, and my sister, and my aunt. They've never been anywhere else, seen anything else. I knew I'd marry Ted, and start having babies. And they'd grow up here, too, and never leave."

I soothed her, and freshened the cloth for her forehead, and followed her about when she started her wandering again.

Around two in the morning, the blood came. I hadn't expected so much of it. I used all of the towels I could find, and most of the dishcloths from the kitchen, before it stopped coming.

In the morning, Patsy was asleep. I tucked her into bed, and cleaned up the kitchen floor; I washed out the towels as best I could. When I held my arms up before me, they were crusted with blood to the elbows; I'd used up all the water I'd boiled, and so I scrubbed myself with cold, using my fingernails. Then I dragged myself home; my mother thought I'd been at the bakery, and she let me sleep.

The next month, Patsy married Ted, and I went to New York. I told myself I'd always meant to go, but really it was on account of Patsy, whose terrific yearning for something unfamiliar had led her into such misery. I vowed I'd never try to get out *that* way; I took my savings and bought a one-way bus ticket.

I starved away in a cold-water fifth-floor walkup, taking in typing, and at night writing my idiotic little stories. I didn't know that I was uncomfortable; in fact, I felt sanctified by the whole experience. I was *so* dumb. I thought I was unique. I had no idea that there were millions like me, or that I was just another Young Thing with a Typewriter and a Dream.

Dreams. I had a few, and all of them involved *New Yorker* typeface. I pined after print, and read everything that was being published, all the greats of that time. What must it be like for a young writer now? No Thurber, no Salinger. Everything reading 'he goes, she goes,' and no rich descriptions. No one takes any *time* anymore. Today's short stories are like sound bites. Pith without context. If I were a young writer today, I'd think seriously of becoming a scuba diver. Or a public school teacher. Something dangerous, and challenging.

So I wrote and I wrote and I wrote. And I mailed my little stories off with notes which might as well have said Please Sir. And my little stories winged their ways back to me, with other little notes attached, printed anonymous squares which might as well have begun Forget It. We kept up a healthy correspondence, the Editors and I, and I tried not to let it wound me. I'd met some other writers by then, and I'd heard all about the fickleness of editors—how the reception you got depended on their mood, which depended on the quality of their lunch, or how their income tax returns were going, or whether or not their wives were sleeping with them. I believed in my heart that I'd hit a Happy Editor, that the sturdy envelope I'd so carefully sealed up, filled with all of my youthful hopes, would come into his office and find him In the Mood.

Well, it never happened. I got little square after little square. One kind man wrote a single indecipherable sentence to me in blue ink; I never knew what it said, but it was personal, and I was thrilled. My hopes went sky-high, and I shot off another story to him at once. It came back three months later, looking as though it hadn't even been read. Can you believe it didn't even daunt me? I just kept on, typing out my prose in smeary ribbon onto middling bond, messages cast onto the water in bottles of manila, praying for the Happy Editor.

All the time, something had been creeping up on me. Every writer dreams of her First Novel, and I was no exception. Every now and then I'd get an idea, and I'd chase it down, only to find myself at the end of a trail of words, having lost the scent entirely. I had drawers full of First Novels, some no longer than a chapter, some as long as sixty pages, all of them worthless. So I became stubborn; and when the next Idea came to me, I ignored it, and went on pecking at my short stories, reading Katherine Mansfield and Dorothy Parker, yearning after the first one's sensibilities, and the other one's wit. Thank God I burnt all of those efforts, years ago. How embarrassing they were, how motley.

The Idea wouldn't go away; it crept around and bothered me at night, until in a kind of a fit, I sat down and wrote at it, to teach it a lesson. Surprisingly, this time it didn't peter out; I got up from my desk with a little more than twenty pages of copy, and more ringing in my head, waiting to be attended to.

I'm making it sound so easy. It was months and months of hard work before the thing began to take shape. But when it did, it did with a vengeance, and I lived at my typewriter, skimping on meals to pay for ribbons, resenting the time my clients' offerings took from my own work. There's nothing worse than typing someone else's fiction, when you write your own. And when yours is unsuccessful, the insult goes even deeper. I'd find myself in the wee hours, pounding out some-one else's hashed-up sentence structure, just as it was, not even correcting spelling, crying 'Ha!' every time I found a comma splice, and gleefully leaving it in.

When the Thing was finished, I couldn't believe it. I held the chapters in both hands, incredulous at its sheer weight. It felt like an infant, and I certainly treated it that way—swaddling it in brown paper and string, marking the name of a publishing house on the outside, and pushing it into the box with my fingers crossed.

It came back, a heavier boomerang than any of my stories. Halfheartedly, I unswaddled my child, and rewrapped it in new paper, sending it on its way again. Then I got involved in someone else's deadline, and forgot about the Thing I had birthed.

The little envelope was a surprise; I hardly ever got letters, and certainly never ones with typewritten addresses. I assumed that the alien which had passed through the letter slot was a notice about library fines. I had a dreadful habit, and still do, of holding on to library books for months past their due dates. I hadn't any money to pay my fines, and I cursed myself as I slit the letter open.

Of course it was a check. For an amount that would make any modern author cry with laughter, but which sent me dancing giddily around the room. I was an Author. I sent half the money to my mother right away, and then paid off the library and bought a good dinner and a new typewriter ribbon.

I sold two novels before my first short story was accepted by a magazine. Not even a very good magazine, at that. Certainly not the *New Yorker*. But it was enough for me; I'd gotten an agent by then, and I was crafty; I was making enough money to be able to give up the typing almost completely; and while the second went to press, I worked on novel number three.

Those were wonderful years. Yet frightening ones, too. *What if?* filled my ears like a promise. *What if I'm no good after all?* was the loudest. And *What if I can't think of anything else to say?* That one was potent, kept me awake until the early hours of the morning. Especially after a bad day. Or I should say, a day of bad writing. I had enough of those to make me wild, although people never believe it when I say so. I get letters, asking me for encouragement; people send me their manuscripts, their own tender children, and beg me to tell them if I think they have any talent. I always write back and tell them it shouldn't matter what I say. You'll stop writing if you're no good. Nobody should write if she doesn't *have* to.

I put my little sister through college, and saw her married to a man from Ohio, who took her away with him, back to his farm. I went to her wedding, but I didn't go home again, not until my mother's funeral, and then I was only there for three days.

Eventually I realized the great truth about New York. You go there in order to earn the right to leave. I had earned my passage, and now I had to choose where I should live. At first, I thought of the south of France, and then of Ireland. Picturesque places. But I don't speak French, and the prospect of Irish winters didn't appeal. I didn't know about the rainfall then. I never considered either of them really seriously; at heart, I expect I always knew where I would go—back home.

I went there for a visit, touching down in an airplane on the tiny runway miles from my mother's old house, riding into town in a hired car, feeling like a conquering hero. I'd heard of a house for sale, and I meant to inspect it the next day, but first I wanted to look over my breeding place.

Do you remember *The Odyssey*? The part when Odysseus comes back to Ithaka, and doesn't know it? 'What is this land and realm, who are the people?' he asks Pallas Athena. When she tells him he is home, he cries, 'I cannot believe that I have come to Ithaka./It is some other land.' Well, that's how I felt, exactly. The town I had grown up in looked mighty small, and strange, and even the people I recognized were strangers. And they received me as one; all they knew about me was that I'd gone away for a while. None of them had read my books. They'd heard about them, though, and made remarks along the lines of 'You use a lot of dirty words, in them stories.'

I went by Patsy's old house, which had been ramshackle, on the very edge of town; now it was a smart little dwelling in the middle of a clean residential area. I thought about the bloodstains that were no doubt still clinging to the baseboards in that dingy kitchen, and then realized that that old floor would have been taken up, and the walls stripped, and modern recessed lighting put into the ceiling.

I went by the old bakery, which wasn't there any longer. A hairdressing salon stood in its place; I could not even tell by looking if the building was the same one.

Patsy and Ted lived in an apartment above his stationer's shop, and to my delight, she remembered me. She showed me around the shop, proudly.

"We even have a rack for books," she said, tapping a fingernail against the bright jacket of a paperback romance. "I kept hoping you'd write one, and we could sell it."

"But I have," I said. "I've written six."

"Maybe they're not the kind we sell," she said, dubiously.

"Probably not," I agreed. "Do you remember Mrs. Mince?"
I asked. "How she sang at night, while we did the baking?"

"I remember her," said Patsy. "But I can't say as I recall
any singing."

So I came away. I didn't even look at the house I had
thought of buying. I went far from that little town, and instead
found another just like it. They treat me here a little like
Garbo, have you noticed? When I come out, they peer at me,
and they tell visitors about me with pride, and point out this
house. I am a kind of national possession to them, whereas at
home I was nothing more than Lou the fireman's daughter,
who went off and wrote herself some dirty books. Jesus was a
carpenter's son when *he* was at home.

I'm happy in Naples. I'm here half the year, and add a little
glamour to the town. In return, I am made to feel as though I
have really come home. Home, I've decided, is never where
you seek it. The old familiar places change, and leave no place
for you. You've got to scrabble your home out of hard rock,
carve Ithaka wherever you find it, and settle in. Otherwise, you
might wander all your life, looking."

Chapter Twenty-five

Treaties

I awakened stiff and claustrophobic in my sleeping bag. Beside me, Joan rolled over and groaned.

"Ugh," she said. "I feel like I've been sleeping in a tree."

Bob and Bobby had set out on a last birding expedition, I suspected; they'd left us the embers of their breakfast fire. I poked it up and brewed some coffee; and Joan and I sat in the thin early sunshine and drank it, speaking little.

The magic of the night before had gone; the other tents were zippered and silent. The campsite was empty, the morning cold; even the coffee, though hot and pleasant, did little to raise my spirits. It had been a good idea to come here; but now it was time to go home.

I took the tent down while Joan packed the car. Half an hour later we were on the road to Naples. The day before, the drive had been happy, full of daring. Playing runaway, we had almost convinced ourselves; the narrow world had expanded before us, and there had seemed no end to the possibilities for escape. For a while last night by the camp fire it had seemed we need never go back. But the morning light chased away delusion; the music and the darkness were past, and with them whatever harmony had entered into us. Joan sighed beside me, plucking at her skirt, gathering pine needles which had lodged in the weave of the fabric, dropping them into her cupped hand. I settled both my hands on the wheel, driving cautiously, automatically west; toward home, toward whatever lay there, awaiting us.

Beth's departure shrank the world smaller; I experienced something new to me, a fitful restlessness, a wanderlust. I saw Naples with new eyes. When the leaves fell, I saw them swirling in slow motion, like the clumsy plastic flakes in a tourist's toy. I envisioned Beth in New York, a city I had never seen; for want of proper images I put her in Washington, D.C., its wide parkways charged with traffic, rushing past where she stood on the corner, arm crooked before her eyes, watching the stoplight. The streets of Naples seemed smaller and its inhabitants more primitive than ever by comparison with the domain of my fancy. I waited impatiently to hear from her.

Ironically, as my dissatisfaction with Naples grew, I found a greater welcome there. The center was finished, and received great praise from the mayor; I moved the same crew on to build the adjoining minimall. Devlin gave me a raise in salary, and I bought myself a new car. On the site the men chaffed me about it in their new, friendly way. I listened to their constant profanity with equanimity now, having learned, unwittingly, the great truth: that the conversation of men is largely bluff, falsely and forever contentious. "Fuck you," I understood, was an all-purpose phrase, like *Aloha.* Hello, good-bye, thanks a lot; it was all in there, in those two words; and when Walker yelled them down at me above the noise of the machinery, I smiled and waved.

All the time I waited to hear from Beth. I wanted to know what she'd found, whether she was happy, what the world she'd lunged out into was like. I awakened one morning near Christmas with a deep sense of disorientation. I had lost something, I thought frantically, and, sleep muddled, began searching the bedclothes for whatever it was.

"You're dreaming, honey," said Joan, and I came awake fully then, with my hands bunched up in the covers and my breath coming fast.

Later in the day I recalled the dream, its creeping sense of unease, faded now. And I understood abruptly what it was that I had lost. The sense of apartness which I had carried everywhere with me since childhood was gone, misplaced like a despised sweater. Sometime in the last few months I had found my place in the world, or at least in my little part of it. In a cascade of revelations, I understood much more: the pattern of my life before, how I had brought much of my suffering upon myself. I was an easy target; any casual remark had found its way unerringly to my private core of shame. I had sown the fertile earth of my uncertainty with the careless speeches and glances of others, and had reaped for myself a gigantic loneliness. I had cherished my apartness, held it close. Now, with the winter wind brushing my face and driving away the last shreds of the morning's dream, I relinquished my martyrdom. It had been nearly accomplished already, I realized; the dream had come at the end of the process. Without meaning to, I had relaxed into the small, familiar place where I had spent all of my life, even as I was scanning the newspaper for tidings of greater cities and foreign lands. Wanting to leave, I had come suddenly home.

I heard from Beth at the New Year. I didn't recognize her handwriting right away; the thin, creased envelope in my mailbox seemed almost intolerably alien. She wrote: *Not so different here but different enough, I guess. Staying with my cousin though I think I might leave soon, she hints all the time. I may have a job in the city in the spring. How's tricks in the construction biz? You wouldn't believe how tall some of the buildings are here.*

It was a sparse missive, one that told me nothing of her daily life. The disjointed sentences held no breath of Beth, nothing of her grace and wit. The postmark was New Jersey; there was no return address. That, at least, was like Beth: to cast a message out, allowing no possibility for reply.

I showed the letter to Joan, who commented merely, "How odd." From her tight mouth, the quickening of her pallor, I presumed that news of Beth was not welcome to her. It stirred, perhaps, some ugly memory. A shoe, shouting, a child's limp body? I didn't ask, but folded the letter away. We didn't speak of it again.

In superficial ways, Joan had changed very little. As always, she was heavily involved in the lives of her students, although she had stopped inviting them to the house. She continued to write her column; and if there was any difference in Tell Tillie, any new hesitancy or qualm, I never detected it. I read Tillie faithfully, as did the rest of the town; and in 1968, at its annual dinner, the *Chronicle* presented Joan with the coveted Golden Quill. "In appreciation for many years of wise words," the editor had said, handing it over. The applause was wild. Joan had become something of a celebrity.

That year, Dale Miller died. I was frantic—how to get word to Beth? Then I realized that this was exactly the reason she'd given no return address. She was afraid of news like this, bait at the end of a long cast, pulling her back to Naples. Her good-byes had been permanent ones, I thought sadly; I would surely never see her again.

I heard from her a few months later, for the second to last time. *I'm getting married,* she wrote. *Maybe.* And that was all. From the comfort of my home, cradled in the broad arms of the Blue Ridge, I sent out a telepathic message: *Be happy,*

Beth. I could be generous; for the first time in my life, I had happiness to spare.

As we reached the outskirts of town, a gentle rain began. I switched on the wipers, glancing quickly over at Joan, who had fallen asleep. I admired her ability to drop into sleep the way she did, suddenly and with complete dignity. Her eyes were closed; her hair made soft dark wings over her ears; there was a faint tracing of blue at one corner of her mouth. Looking at her, I felt the same intense protectiveness which I had carried before me like a shield these twenty years.

I turned from one familiar road onto another. Of course I had heard the cliche about knowing a place "like the back of my hand," but never until now had I attached a deeper meaning to the words. This morning, I saw Joan and myself, moving in our car over the same worn avenues, following the same curves, idiosyncratic as the lines on a palm. My own life line, love line, heart line, here in the map of this town.

How had I ever feared Buddy? I wondered. He was lost in Naples, a naive scout without a decoder ring. The town had deflected his probing without effort. He was powerless, even pathetic. He was also a potent and uncomfortable reminder, gawky the way I had been, the butt of all humor at Stokes's, of an evening. Jack's plaything. The similarities went deep. But I was not like that now, no longer afraid and wandering. I felt a spark of sympathy for him. Like him, I had spent years unknowing.

I thought of Jack, who had kept himself apart in Naples these long years, segregating himself the way I'd felt segregated before. True to form, the town had tried and sentenced Jack a dozen times over, without any one citizen ever bringing a formal accusation. They muttered about him, and looked askance when he passed. Work slowed down at the garage for a while, but strangers, not privy to the secrets of the town, kept on bringing their cars to him, and he got by. The only other mechanic anybody went to was Reed Darcy, who did shoddy work and overcharged besides. Gradually, work shifted back over to Jack. The vicious talk calmed down, but never quite went away. Beth was right: it had outlived her.

Jack had set himself apart all those years ago, on purpose; and he had stepped back into the ring as deliberately, two weeks ago. Why? To play with Buddy? For a change of pace?

No, I thought. None of these.

He'd stepped in to protect me. Suddenly, as though a lens had dropped in front of my eyes, it all came into focus—Jack took his responsibilities seriously, and I was one of them. As I had always been my mother's baby, I would always be Jack's younger brother, and like it or not, he had to take care of me.

Half a century after its inception, I released myself from my bondage of suspicion. Jack at nine was not Jack now; and what boy at nine did not want to dispose of his younger brother? The barrel had meant nothing; perhaps it had not even happened at all.

An enormous relief welled up in me, and I laughed aloud, waking Joan.

"What is it?" she murmured.

"Nothing," I said. "We're home."

After dinner that night, I went into my study, pleading paperwork. I shut the door and went to the bookcase, where I pulled down a tattered volume. It fell open naturally, where I had slipped something thick between the pages, damaging the spine.

Her very last communication had come three years ago, a bulky envelope. I had brought it in here to open in private while Joan was busy elsewhere. Ripping open the top and shaking had disgorged the same heavy paper-wrapped square that slid out of the book now. I picked it up, now as I had then, and unfolded the paper. Within was a small piece of carpet. I turned it over in my hands, then examined the paper. *Ha ha,* it said. *I finally got it.*

I forced back the page, yellow now, and read the passage I had marked.

> . . . *The answer was obvious. Life had no meaning.* . . .
> *Man, no more significant than other forms of life, had come not as the climax of creation but as a physical reaction to the environment.* . . . *There was no meaning in life, and man by living served no end. It was immaterial whether he was born or not born, whether he lived or ceased to live. Life was insignificant and death without consequence.* . . . *Happiness mattered as little as pain.*

I closed the book and replaced it on the shelf.

* * *

The next morning, I found myself driving in the opposite direction from work. I drew up to the yawning entrance of the garage and tapped the horn lightly. A minute or so later, Jack appeared. He hesitated fractionally, and started toward me.

For the first time, I appreciated his age. Nearly sixty now, with grey all through his hair. Only I, and only with effort, could see the springy boy he had been, once upon a time. His loneliness, I mused, was greater than mine—he lived alone most of the time, the stream of casual girlfriends having slowed to a trickle in the past few years. His wife had left him, taking their infant son, more than thirty years ago. Somewhere, he had a child. Did that knowledge prey on him? He had lost everything, or had never had it. As he made his way across the asphalt, I looked upon him with a kind of pity, the last of my hatred going cold and sinking away. My brother. I knew too much, and too little, about him.

"Car's making noises," I said, when he approached.

"Pings?" Jack said, delivering the syllable casually, as though it were an appropriate sound to end twenty years of silence.

"Uh-huh."

"Or knocks?"

"Those, too."

"Pings *and* knocks," said Jack. "Now, that's trouble." I popped the hood and he propped it up, bending over the engine. I went to stand next to him.

"Where's Buddy?" I asked.

"Wandering," said Jack. He grunted at some mysterious anomaly he'd found. "Walking off his disappointment."

"He didn't get what he wanted?"

"He doesn't think so."

We stared into the black insides of the car for a minute.

"See that?" he asked, pointing to an evil-looking hose. "That's your trouble. Good thing you brought it in when you did."

"Yes," I said, appreciating the charade. There was nothing wrong with my car, and Jack knew it.

"You might not a seen it, you looked yourself," he said. "Takes a trained eye."

"I'm glad I brought it to you," I said, playing along.

He grunted, and wiped his hands, going back into the garage. He came out with a piece of tubing. Squinting down the length of it, he said, "This'll do."

I watched my brother work, his large sure hands manipulating the rubber, removing the old hose, installing the new.

"It's all tore up here," said Jack, indicating a place on the rubber which looked perfectly sound to me. "It don't show unless you bend it," he said, without doing so.

"Uh-huh," I said.

"Things just wear out quietly like that," he said. "You got to know where to look." He stuck the old hose into a pocket and pulled out a rag, wiping his hands on it over and over, unconsciously. "How's Joan?"

"Fine," I said.

"Good woman, like a good car," he said. "Both have their peculiarities, but nothing you can't live with."

"Uh-huh," I said.

"Both of 'em, you have to love and look after," he said.

"I do," I said.

"Well," he said, severely. "You better love that woman twice as hard." His eyes crinkled up. "Because your car's a piece of shit." He cut off the smile which had never left his eyes, and turned back to the Ford, unhooking the hood brace. He stood there for a few seconds, holding the hood up with the deltas of one hand. "Looks real complicated in there, don't it," he said, gesturing at the engine. "But just as simple as can be." He let the hood slam shut. "Too bad life ain't as easy as engines."

We looked at one another directly. Dark and stocky, thin and fair, regarding one another like foreigners, past enemies, meeting at a carnival in peacetime. Facing off, uncertain.

"Dollar for the hose," said Jack.

Always the last laugh, I thought, fishing it out. "Thanks," I said, passing it to him, our fingertips touching for an instant.

"Some things just ain't worth talking about," he said, and stood back, watching me get into the car. As I closed the door, he darted forward suddenly, and put his head in the open window.

"Bring her back," he said.

"What?" I said.

"She needs new shocks," he said. "Shocks and struts. I can tell by the way she rides."

"Oh," I said. "Sure. Thanks."

"See you later," he said, his words nearly swallowed by the roar as the ignition caught. I nodded, and he gave a little salute before turning away.

"By the way," I called.

"What?" he said, half turning.

"I wanted to tell you—Beth—"

"What?" he repeated, walking back a little way toward the car.

"Beth told me to say good-bye to you."

Jack digested this information, a kind of storm sweeping over his normally impassive face. Curiosity and jealousy and grieving struggled there for a minute before he squared his shoulders, bringing up a hand to tease the hair of his forelock.

"She told me before she left," I said, as though making an offering. Saying it, I felt contrite, and lightened, a long-over-due bargain kept.

"She never needed to," Jack said, finally. "Good-bye was always in her, from the first." And he turned his back on me again, and moved slowly away.

Chapter Twenty-six

Farewell

He found the boy on a hillside, filming the setting sun.

"Pretty," he said, shutting the car door.

"I needed some scenery shots," said the boy.

"Some say they can't tell the difference between sunrise and sunset from a photograph," he said. "I just don't believe it."

"What's the difference?" said Buddy, still filming.

"One says, Get on up. The other says, Take a seat, you've earned it. Rising sun makes me want to go places. Setting sun makes me glad of where I am, no need to go anywhere else."

"I've never felt that way," confessed the boy.

I know.

"It's been a strange two weeks," said Buddy.

"You get your movie made?"

"I still have to synch it, and edit it. I'm not sure what angle I want to take."

"I thought it was just people talking."

"It is, but different editing makes a different movie. They might end up sounding like they're agreeing with each other, or disagreeing. Or like they have a message."

"Do they?"

"I don't know," he said, shortly.

They were silent for a minute, just the hum of the camera between them.

"I think my professor will like it, though," he said. "There's a lot of good stuff in it."

"How can you tell good from bad? I thought you were after pretty specific stuff."

"I was," admitted Buddy. "But it didn't turn out that way."

"Are you glad you came?" asked the other.

"It's not what I thought it would be," said Buddy. "Hearing about it my whole life."

"Hearing and living are different," he said.

"I guess," said Buddy. "No one wanted to talk about my mother," he said. "Like there was something secret about her."

"Maybe they just don't remember all that well," said the other. "It was a long time ago."

"That doesn't matter," said Buddy, scornfully. "I've learned that much. I could live here my whole life, starting now, and die a stranger. And I could have been born here, and moved away for thirty years, and come back and be home."

"You figured that out."

"You know she had a kid before me?" asked Buddy. "A little girl, who died?"

"Sad story," said the other, nodding.

They looked off together toward the horizon, one squinting through the black eye of the camera, the other barefaced. It was the last of the pageant, a marvelous and various glow of pinks and oranges, the shirred clouds stained and spreading toward where they stood on the hill. A bird called. They watched for minutes, the dusk falling around them like snow.

"Put down the camera, son," urged the older man. "Sun's gone now."

The boy lowered the camera, slowly, and turned to face the other.

"My name's not Buddy," he said.

"Oh?" said the other, politely.

"My mother named me after my father," he said. "I never met him. I think he was just somebody she met up north. Not that she was loose or anything," he added quickly. "I think she was in love with him."

"I thought your father was called Gates."

"That's my stepfather," said Buddy. "They married when I was four." He was thoughtful. "She must have cared about my real father a lot," he said, "to have named me for him."

"That how you think of him?" asked the other. "Your real father?"

"No, not really," said the boy, surprised by his own words. "Dad's the only father I've known." He thought a little. "He's all right."

The other nodded.

"I'm really Grahame," said the boy. "With an *e.*"

"How bout that," said the other.

They were silent again. The dark was truly upon them now, and the moon was beginning to shine.

"She killed herself," said Grahame, a small boy's voice squeaking out of him.

Ah, Beth.

"You came here looking to find out why she done it?"

"I guess so," said the boy. "But I failed."

"You were bound to fail, son," said the man. "Bound to. Hacking your way in here, like going after a cancer with a chain saw. People are subtler than that; their darknesses and sorrows are their own. You can't always understand them."

"I miss her so much," said the boy, in a rush of misery. "I thought she loved me."

"She did, son," said the man. "It was the hardest thing in the world to leave you. She was just the leaving kind."

"You loved her, too," said the boy, sensing something.

"Once," he admitted.

"How can I live?" cried the boy suddenly, a man's voice now, strong and clear. Taking his lament up to the sky, where the birds wheeled and settled. To the ears of what might be listening, or might not. The same cry so many had sent up before him, the pure essence of a torment contained. Filled with pain and disbelief, it went up into the clouds and spread there, until it was thin and forgotten, only the echo remaining behind, in the ears of the man and the boy who stood together on the hill.

"You got to," said the man, after a respectful silence. "There ain't nothing else to do."

"I guess not," said the boy, crumpled now by release.

"And you can't go on blaming yourself," he continued. "Some people are sad, for no reason you can ever see. And some fight their friends, make enemies of them. Some roam all over the world, looking for a home they never had. Some spend their whole lives at home, and never know it." He paused. "Whole lives get taken up with foolishness."

"Huh," said the boy, not really listening anymore. "Hey," he said, seeming to realize something. "You're talking all right."

Gil smiled.

"Comes and goes," he said. "Like everything."